"*Tar and Feathers* is a great choice for those wanting ... ...
with an element of mystery, a look at the environmental issues of energy development set against the day to day background of a northern community.

In Tar and Feathers, **Jim Tanner** engages the reader on a variety of levels; a good tale set within a current topical context – the presence of "Big Oil" in the everyday lives of an aboriginal community, and the element of an unsolved mystery. Tanner draws one into the lives of the people of a small northern community as they contend with the realities of a changing world. Their environment is shifting and they struggle to find a balance between potential benefits of energy development and potential risks; is anyone actually sure of all the potential risks? As he moves through the action, Tanner weaves in background and legends of aboriginal peoples of the region and their customs. He explores how traditional values are challenged and impacted by outside influences, not just of energy exploration but also of non-traditional big city aboriginal points of view.

What sets Tar and Feathers apart is that the elements are interwoven on a level which clearly indicates the author's working knowledge of the cultural challenges and intricacies of the relationships between the First Peoples and oil resource development. Tanner's fist-hand experience is evident."

– Anne Green, Founding Director, WordFest

"Tar and Feathers is not just an engaging mystery story, but an accurate and compassionate depiction of the challenges facing the Aboriginal peoples of the developing oil sands region of northern Alberta, as they struggle to balance the loss of their culture and the realities of survival in modern day Canada. This is a must-read for anyone trying to understand the conflicts and challenges experienced by two diverse cultures in a changing world."

– Nikki Phillips, Arts Editor, Carteret County News-times

Tar & Feathers

Tragedy in the Oil Sands

Love
Dad.

James N. Tanner

Tar & Feathers : Tragedy in the Oil Sands
ISBN 978-0-9696693-4-0

Published by :
Nicomachian Press,

246 Chaparral Ravine View
Calgary, AB, T2X 0A6

148 Munden Farm Road
Newport, NC, 28570.

Acknowledgements:
Cover Painting by Michele Zarb
Sketches of Katie, Mary and Miriam by Michele Zarb
Sketches of fisherman, hunter, muskrat, beaver, party by Trevor Michael
Layout and design by Francomedia

Acknowledgements

I could not have completed this book without the gracious assistance of so many people. At the very beginning, over 3 years ago, Jeannie agreed to read my early musings and politely suggested that I focus on this topic. Then Nick spent hours helping me climb out of the pit of novel despair. I appreciate the continuous support of Cathi which cannot be underestimated and the encouragement and patience of John and Alice without whom this book would not have been written. I owe so much to the people of Fort Chipewyan who allowed me to work with them for so many years and provided the experience that led to this story. I must thank Bertha, posthumously, for it was Bertha who taught me my first lessons in Aboriginal culture. I would like to thank Willie, Alice, Reggie and Margaret as well as all of the Elders that I interviewed about subsistence living in northern Canada. I would like to thank Bernadette and David for very important spiritual insights and stories. I would like to thank Caroline and April for their support and all of the other people who have contributed to making this book possible. I would like to thank Anne and Nikki for their edits and encouragement and the people at Francomedia for their expertise.

Cover Artist – Michele Zarb

Michele's love for the rich aboriginal culture and heritage is evident in her ability to capture the mystery, symbols, color and tradition of the First Nations people in her paintings. On the cover page and some of the portrait sketches Michele provides us with an understanding of the main characters in this book.

Michele's work has been accepted in international competitions in Canada and the United States. She was the only artist in Canada accepted to the Cowboy Artists of America Workshop in Bozeman, Montana. Michele was also selected to design the 2004 Stampede Western Art Show collector pin. In 2007, Zarb had the distinction and honor of being named the Feature Artist for the Calgary Stampede and Exhibition.

Michele's work can be found in private and corporate collections throughout the United States, Canada, Switzerland, Germany, the Middle East and Japan. Some of Michele's collectors include Hyatt Hotels Calgary; ABC News, Washington, D.C.; Nova Corporation; Virgin Records, NY, NY; and Lenny Kravitz, Musician. (michele@michelezarb.com)

Sketch Artist - Trevor Michael

Trevor is a member of the Athabasca Chipewyan First Nation. His artwork is featured on the cover of "Footprints on the Land; Tracing the Path of the Athabasca Chipewyan First Nation" and several of his sketches are printed in that book. He is well known in the northern Alberta region for his depictions of the emotion and culture of his people in his art.

Legend of the Warriors of the Rainbow

There are many versions of this legend. The version presented in this book reflects several versions of this legend but relies significantly on the story told by Dr. Lelanie Fuller Anderson, "The Cherokee Lady". Apparently she was told this legend when she was a young girl by her Grandmother.

The basis of other legends and stories presented in this book have been provided to the author through discussions with Elders and First Nation members, however, all legends and stories presented in this novel are not intended to be recordings of traditional knowledge and are not accurate reflections of traditional stories or legends but are a fictional parts of the novel.

Preface

The characters and the events in this novel are fictional but based on events and situations in the oil sands region of northern Alberta. This book wanted to be written. I had no choice; experiences demanded it. At first, rather than write fiction, I was tempted to write policy recommendations on how to solve problems in Aboriginal communities in Canada. Then I realized that it had already been done and published as a Royal Commission, which is read primarily by researchers or lawyers.

I had intended to write an assortment of stories about the day-to-day lives of the people exposed to the intense development of the oil sands in northern Alberta. It was only when the book was more or less complete that I realized it was primarily about women, including the theme story of *Than-ad-el-thur* and the stories of the two main characters. The role of women in this struggle is important. Dr. Amartya Sen, Nobel Prize winner for Economics, showed that women's education and participation in democratic and powerful institutions is the key to successful development. I think this fact is supported by the stories retold in this book.

When I was writing this novel I sent this note to my family after a morning run on the Calgary river bank:

A sunny but crisp Calgary morning greets me as I stretch my legs preparing for a much needed run. This fall the leaves are almost gone off the poplar trees and they cover the ground, crunching as I run down the slightly wet path. I draw in the cool fresh air, passing by other Calgarians, each making the best of one of the last gorgeous fall days before the winter pushes them into their exercise cubes. Calgary is clean and affluent, as are so many Canadian cities. All types of cars and trucks pass, including several shiny high-end sports cars speeding towards Banff, and diesel trucks and campers escaping to a campsite or ranch for the day. A family with a young Caucasian dad and Asian mother are taking their infant son and daughter for a walk through the park in their fancy tandem baby buggy. Life in Canada is good, even in the middle of the 'great recession.'

I run up the steep river bank to the Tim Horton's Restaurant across from the hospital. As usual, the customer line stretches almost out of the shop, but I stop for a tea and breakfast sandwich anyway. I sit with my tea, looking casually through a real estate advertisement as a native man enters. His white sweatshirt has large stains; he is unshaven and looking a little disoriented. One eye is bloodshot and he seems to have trouble walking between my table and the next. As he sits down, he shyly acknowledges me. He doesn't get in line as everyone else does, and I wonder if he has any money.

I speak to him instead of giving him an uncomfortable brush-off. Few Calgarians have avoided being accosted for spare change from a native down on his luck. Many of us have developed a city shell a hardened response so that we can get on with our day without the inconvenience of dealing with this native problem.

I ask him where he is from.

"Morley." he replies, pushing out his lips and pointing them towards the mountains. He tells me he has just been to the hospital and the doctor has told him he has permanently lost the sight in one eye. He says, "I don't think it's true; he's not God. God may give me my sight back; what does he know?" Then he says something in his native language. He says something about sleeping outside.

I look around the Tim Horton's. There is a group of young students speaking Farsi, an older couple with a walker, a father with his two clearly ambitious sons and a couple of young women out for a quick breakfast. I can sense the native guy has no money, and since he appears to be a bit disoriented I asked the fellow getting up beside me if he has a buck to buy this guy a coffee. Uneasily, he says he doesn't but gets in line to purchase something else.

The native guy tells me that when he was younger, his grandmother told him about how his people would lose their language and culture and how they would end up stealing each other's wives and falling into chaos. He says when she told him that, he just thought she was old and senile. Now he sees it happening just like she predicted.

I want to at least buy him a coffee but I have no more money, so I look to a nicely dressed thirty-something fellow walking into the shop. I ask him if he will buy the native man a coffee. He just ignores me the way you might ignore someone begging for money on the street.

The native guy smiles. "Don't worry about it." he says. "I'm okay. Thanks anyway; it's just nice to meet someone to talk to." He stands and waves goodbye.

Some people think there is little or no poverty in Canada, even when they see it and live with it every day. I used to think like that too, before I had the experiences that led to this book.

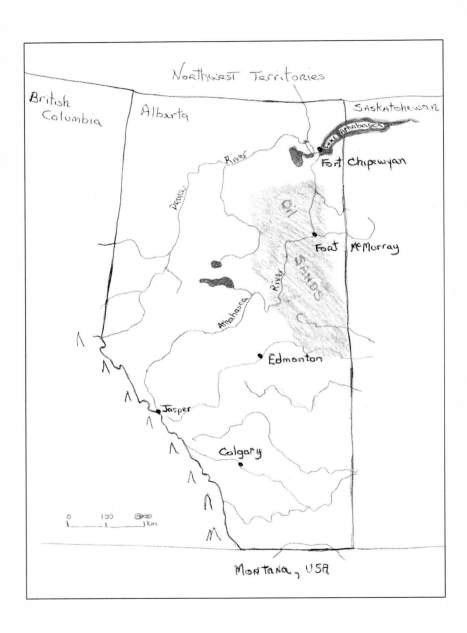

Prologue

The Legend of the Rainbow Warriors

There was an old lady from the Cree tribe named Eyes of Fire, who prophesied that one day there would come a time when the fish would die in the streams, the birds would fall from the air, the waters would be blackened and the trees would no longer be. Mankind as we know it would all but cease to exist.

There would come a time when the keepers of the legend, stories, and the ancient tribal customs would be needed to restore us to health. They would be mankind's key to survival; they will be the Warriors of the Rainbow. There would come a day of awakening when all the peoples of all the tribes would form a new world of justice, peace, freedom, and recognition of the Great Spirit.

The Warriors of the Rainbow would spread these messages and teach all peoples of the earth. They would teach them how to live the "Way of the Great Spirit". They would tell them of how the world today has turned away from the Great Spirit and that is why our earth is sick.

The Warriors of the Rainbow would show the peoples that this Ancient Being, the Great Spirit, is full of love and understanding, and teach them how to make the earth beautiful again. These warriors would give the people principles or rules to follow to make their path right with the world. *These principles would be those of the ancient tribes. The Warriors of the Rainbow would teach the people of the ancient practices of unity, love, and understanding. They would teach of harmony among people in all four corners of the earth.*

Like the ancient tribes, they would teach the peoples how to pray to the Great Spirit with love that flows like the beautiful mountain stream and flows along the path to the ocean of life. They would once again fill their minds, hearts, souls, and deeds with the purest of thoughts. They would seek the beauty of the Master of Life — the Great Spirit! They would find strength and beauty in prayer and the solitudes of life.

Free from the fears of toxins and destruction wrought by the Yo-ne-gi and his practices of greed, the rivers would again run clear, the forests be abundant and beautiful, the animals and birds would be replenished. The powers of the plants and animals would again be respected and conservation of all that is beautiful would become a way of life.

The tasks of these Warriors of the Rainbow are many and great. There will be terrifying mountains of ignorance to conquer and they shall find prejudice and hatred. They must be dedicated, unwavering in their strength and strong of heart. They will find willing hearts and minds that will follow them on this road of returning Mother Earth to beauty and plenty once more.

The day will come; it is not far away. The day that we shall see how we owe our very existence to the people of all tribes that have maintained their culture and heritage and kept the rituals, stories, legends, and myths alive. It will be with this knowledge, the knowl-

edge that they have preserved, that we shall once again return to harmony with nature, Mother Earth, and mankind. It will be with this knowledge that we shall find our key to our survival.

The Legend of the Whi-ti-koh

There are many legends about a mysterious creature of the northern forest that has a voracious appetite for human flesh. Many forest dwellers who have disappeared over the years are said to be victims of this cannibalistic monster. Different tribes of the region name it different names like the Wendigo or Witego. Both translate to mean "the evil spirit that devours".

They say the Whi-ti-koh is over fifteen feet tall and had once been a hunter who was starving in the woods. Unable to find any other game, he killed and ate another man. This horrendous act transformed him into a monster with glowing eyes, long yellowed fangs, yellowish skin and a long devilish tongue. He continues to be driven by a voracious hunger for human flesh.

Historically the early white settlers took the Whi-ti-koh stories seriously and each time one was seen it was taken as an omen of a death in the community. After each sighting an unexpected death would follow. There are still many stories told of Whi-ti-kohs that have been seen in the north, spotted by traders, trackers and trappers. Whether it seeks human flesh, or acts as a portent of coming doom, is anyone's guess.

Vancouver

Chapter 1

The door closed, shutting out the bar noise as Janet helped me down the rain-soaked front step. She steadied me as I leaned against the wall to keep from falling. "I'm beautiful, that's what he said."

"Yeah, beautiful Shauna, you could be an actress." Janet said. "But we need t' get outta here, now."

"He said I was beautiful—like an actress."

"Did he take money from your purse?" Janet swung her arm around my waist and pulled me onto the sidewalk.

"I don't think so," I said without looking.

"He'll only be in the men's room for a minute," she said. "We gotta go."

The smell of cedar and wet pine needles penetrated my skin. Thank God I didn't have to wear that bulky coat or mitts here in Vancouver. I took a deep breath of the cool moist air. So sweet.

Janet pulled me down the street. "There's a cab. Taxi!" she shouted. The yellow cab pulled over at the corner. Janet jerked the back door open and guided me into the soft leather back seat.

"Broadway in Kitsilano," she told the cabbie.

The cab was warm. "This place is wonderful; I wanna stay here forever!" I raised up my arms. "Don't you love it here in Lotus Land? You said you loved it."

"Shauna, have you forgotten what happened here, what he did?"

"Oh. He's okay. He got some extra dope for it. It's just once, one favour an' he said now I can go to Whistler with him."

"Shauna, he sold your body for crack!" She turned my shoulders, looking directly into my eyes and said, "He prostituted you so he could get some more dope!"

"Yeah" I looked out the window as we crossed a bridge. There were lights on sail boats and I could still see the midnight beach at False Creek. It was hard to believe it was winter in this heaven. The warm humidity opened my pores and my spirit.

"It is so bloody cold in McMurray," I said.

"Earth to Shauna—we're getting out of here. I found that ride to Edmonton," Janet said. "The driver's gonna meet us at the 24-hour café on Broadway. He's goin' back to Alberta for Christmas. D'ya have any money left?" she asked me quietly.

I opened my empty wallet. "Oh crap, he did take it."

"Okay, okay." Janet glanced down at her purse. "I think I have enough change for the cab but ..."

"That Fernando," I lamented.

"Fernando?" she gasped. "What do you think he would do to you in Whistler?"

"Yeah." I was relieved that Janet had come to Van to get me. Deep down I knew I was going down but I couldn't help it. It was like I was on a circus ride.

We pulled up to the café. Janet emptied her change purse into the hand of the driver and we jumped out and rushed towards the entrance.

"Hey, it's eleven fifty!" the cabbie shouted as we closed the door to the café. I could hear him shout "Indian whores!" as he pulled away.

"Our ride is Cree from Athabasca," Janet told me as we looked down the line of café booths filled with the regular late night customers drinking their precious coffee. "He said he would be here around midnight, sitting alone. We can leave tonight and he wants us to share the driving. "

"Ha! I'm not drivin'," I told her.

As we weaved down the row of booths an old crack-head leered at me. "Come here, honey," he beckoned. Janet dragged me into a booth several rows down. "Do your jacket up!" she said.

"Do ya think the guy we got the candy from is around here? I could really use an eye opener."

"Shauna! Stop! You're gonna kill yourself. Try some strong coffee. It'll pick you up." Janet looked exasperated.

As we were being served a tall native looking guy pushed through the front door. Janet was sure he was the driver and started to stand up, but suddenly she stopped and opened her eyes wide. I turned around to see what it was. Coming in behind the native guy was Fernando!

"How did he know?" Janet asked.

"They're together?" I asked.

"No. Thank God," Janet whispered as she sank behind the seat.

Fernando was looking out the front door as if his car was double parked.

"Quick, get to the ladies' room, now!" We ducked into the ladies room hallway as our driver took a seat next to the front door. He was cute.

Janet pushed the ladies' room door shut and leaned back against it. "Shauna, ya see, he thinks he owns you an' he looks mad."

"He's ugly when he's mad," I said.

"How come Fernando is here?" Janet looked at me accusingly.

"But he didn't see us," I said.

"What did you tell him?"

"Just that you wanted me to go back to McMurray with you."

"You're nuts!" She swore.

"Ya know he'll hurt me," she complained. "Ya gotta realize Shauna, ya can't trust him. *We* can't trust him. Who knows what he'll do t' me an' he'll take you back to be his bag bride."

"Well, what're we gonna do?" I asked.

"I hope our ride doesn't leave while we're stuck here in the can. How're we gonna tell him we're here without Fernando seein' us? Maybe I could ..." At that moment a young woman pushed against the door shoving Janet towards the sink. "What's going on?" the woman asked.

"Nothing," I blurted out.

"No. Something," Janet corrected me. "Um ... would you help us?" she asked the woman still standing beside the door and now quite curious about us hiding in the ladies room. She had red hair and a blue sequin dress. I figured she had just come from a club.

"Help you with what?" she asked suspiciously.

Janet explained that we were being followed by a guy and needed a ride with another and would she inform the ride guy, without alerting the other. She described them.

"Maybe our ride guy could meet us at the back door of the café with his car in say, ten minutes," Janet suggested. "An' if that's okay would you come back and tell us?"

"Okay, I'll help you. But don't get me involved in anything else," she stated nervously.

"We won't, we promise." I said.

After our sequined woman finished in the ladies room she told us she would be back one way or the other. We thanked her and waited. It seemed like such a long time but she did return. "Your student friend seemed real nice," she said with a twinkle. "He will meet you at the back door in 10 minutes. Good luck, you two." She smiled and left.

I peeked out the door. "How are we gonna get to that back door?" I asked. "We'll have to go back into the kitchen."

"Let me see," Janet said. She carefully peeked around the hallway wall. "Fernando's sitting facing the door. He must be waiting for us to come through the front door. We'll go quickly one at a time. Wait until we are sure our ride is there."

Then Janet said, "Okay—go. I'll come right after ya."

I left the hallway. I could see the back of Fernando's head. He was sipping his coffee. I pushed against the kitchen door but it didn't open! Oh God, he'll see me. I pushed again. Was it locked? Just then it opened towards me and I realized there were two – one coming out and one going in on the other side.

The waitress coming out said, "Can I help you, Miss?"

"No, err ..." I pushed the in-door open into the kitchen hoping Fernando had not turned. By then Janet was right behind me.

"What are you two doing? You aren't allowed back here."

"Where's the back door?" asked Janet.

"There," pointed the cook.

We bolted out the door and our Cree savior was standing there in front of his Jeep Cherokee.

"Hello, Sir," Janet said uncomfortably. "Ya goin' to Edmonton?"

"Hello," he said. "Yes."

"Hello," I said. "Can we get outta here?"

"Let's go," he said as he opened the passenger door. "All aboard for Edmonton."

As we left the alley I looked back and saw Fernando lunge out the backdoor with the cook and a waitress following.

"What a relief," Janet sighed. The coffee had taken its effect.

"I'm sorry, my name is Shauna and this is Janet."

"Archie."

"Hi Archie."

"Ya, hi Archie, it's really nice to meet you!"

"It's so nice for a couple of Dene girls to be rescued by a Cree boy."

"What?"

"You're Cree, right?"

"Yeah."

"We're Dene, mostly."

"Archie? Can we take a route where Fernando won't be able to find us?"

"I suppose so."

"What's this all about anyway? Why is this guy chasing you? Do you have something of his or is he an unwanted boyfriend?"

"No. Not really."

"He thinks he owns Shauna," Janet said as she quickly put her hand up to her mouth.

"Not funny," I said.

"He's possessive?" Archie asked.

"You might say that," Janet said.

"You don't want to be his girlfriend."

"That's right."

"Well I'll drive for a while but someone needs to get some sleep 'cause I can't drive all night."

We fell asleep easily. After a couple of hours, we woke to Archie cussing. "Shit, that bastard."

"What?"

"Is that him, your boyfriend? He tried to pass me on that curve. He's waving a baggie. He's trying to offer us a baggie. It's drugs!"

"Fuck," I swore.

"Ya," Janet said. It's crack cocaine."

"Shit. I thought the native center told you, no drugs! I'm letting you out. You can go with your druggie boyfriend."

"No. Please. It's not what you think. He's a pimp! He's trying to suck Shauna back into his harem," Janet pleaded. "I came to Vancouver to bring her home. She's trapped. Please help us get away from him."

"What?"

"He's not a boyfriend, he's a criminal," Janet said. "Please help us."

"Hey, my purse is ringing. It's a cell phone." I said.

"You don't have a phone!"

"Hello?"

"Hey baby! You want a buzz? I got it right here. Come on back with me. Whistler is waiting for us." It was Fernando!

"Shit." I closed the phone.

"Let me see that phone," Janet said. She opened it up and looked at the screen after typing a few keys. "Navigate, oh yeah, he's been following us with the GPS on this phone. It is married to his!"

"Great." said Archie. "So you don't have any drugs?"

"No."

"Well, okay, I'll stop at the next town and you go into the ladies' washroom. I'll try and speed up and leave him a little ways behind. Leave the phone in the washroom. Come out and we'll take a different route. He may feel confident and not try and keep up to us because he may think he still has the GPS."

We did it. Archie was right. Fernando was far enough behind for us to get to the gas station, drop off the phone and leave before he got there.

After about a half an hour Archie said, "I think we really lost him this time."

Janet fell asleep but I couldn't.

"I guess the deep freeze really hit Alberta this week."

"Yeah, 30 to 40 below."

"Cold."

"Really cold."

"You like BC?" I asked Archie.

"Yeah, but I'm just studying there. I'm gonna go back and work for my band at Home Lake. The oil development is taking over our lands and we need help. It's not like McMurray. It's just starting to

get bad. So I'm studying aboriginal law, governance and account-
ing. It's okay. I'm gonna do something for my band."

"Wow!" I said. "You're at UBC?"

"Yup."

"How did you get in?"

"My marks were okay," he replied.

"From Grade 12?"

"Yeah."

"I couldn't finish." I admitted.

"Oh, why not?"

"Got kicked out."

"Oh?"

"Yeah, first my Mom's boyfriend tried to do me—and when I
told Mom she didn't believe me. She needs him. She can't afford to
create a problem or we'd have no money. So I moved over to Janet's
house in Fort Chip and then I forgot some grass in my locker at
school. It's a long story. I ended up in Vancouver just to get away
from it all."

"You can fix it. It doesn't sound too bad. You can get your diploma even if you have to do it in McMurray or Edmonton. There
are people who will help. I can get you in touch with them." Archie was so sweet and cute too. "You could go back and help your
people," he suggested. Then after a while he told me about some of
his drug experiences at school. Somehow it never got him down.
His mom was a band councilor and his dad was still a hunter and
trapper. Not many of them left. We had time to talk.

"I'd really like t'finish school but ..."

"But what?" He asked.

"But I don't want to go back and help my band."

"No?"

"No. Let them help themselves. Let em fight through it without me. I wanna live a happy life without them dragging me down, pulling me down trying to climb on me to get out of the pit."

"But if you finish school you'll be out an' ya could help someone else," he said.

"It's not that I don't want to help. I just want a normal life, ya know? Normal."

"What's normal?" he smiled.

Eventually Janet woke up and helped with the driving. When it started to get light we entered Alberta. That afternoon he drove us up north to Athabasca. It was close enough, so we called Janet's brother to pick us up from there. Her brother said we could stay at his place in McMurray.

Before we got out of his car, Archie gave me the number of native resource people in McMurray. "Don't wait. Do it on Monday," he said. I smiled at that cute guy. "I will." I said.

Janet's brother was nice; I hadn't seen him since school days in Fort Chip. Now he had a good job driving in one of the pits, making tons of money. He said that even though it was really easy to get drugs in McMurray, he had to be clean for a month before he went back to work so he couldn't touch anything more than beer.

That Saturday night he had some friends over and we drank some beer and danced to some good music. But I really couldn't get into it; something was missing. I started watching one of his buddies closely and I could see he was high by the way he was always laughing. I wanted to be there too. I followed him into the kitchen and watched him pull out his "bubble gum." He held it up, offering it to me. I couldn't refuse; I needed to get up again. These guys were so generous and rich and it felt so good—such a rush. But after half an hour I was down again and he said he used the last of it so we tried some whisky. It took the edge off.

Janet went with the other guy into the bedroom and her brother and Mr. Bubble Supplier passed out on the couch. I gazed out the frosted window at the frozen Christmas lights on the walk up apartment building across the street. It was a quiet neighbourhood. Ice coated the window handle and frost circled the window panes like a Christmas card picture. I needed a smoke so bad and there was a drug store right on the corner. I could run over there and back in no time.

I'm out the door on the sidewalk. It's so cold. I should'a put a coat on. It's not too far. I thought it was on this corner; I had seen the smokes behind the counter. Lots a' snow an' ice on the sidewalk. Where's that store? Slippery. I feel the wet snow in my shoe, bend over. Stand up … too fast! Ooooh ….

The street lights were still on but there was a glow from the hills in the east as the sun was hinting at morning. A police car was parked beside the curb.

"Frozen. Passed out in the snowdrift. Over. "

"Any identification? Over. "

"No. A ten dollar bill in her pocket. That's all."

"Call the coroner."

This Land Owns Me

Chapter 2

I figured if I told him some of our legends it would help explain
why it was important to preserve our lands.

"They jumped into the fire at Cree Burn Lake, committing suicide." I repeated for the second time.

"Oh … yeah … fire." He didn't look up.

"You're not listening!"

"Yes I was. It's called Cree Burn Lake."

"No you weren't. You were reading the paper. You don't understand. The fur trade undermined our way of life." It was *his* job as the Royal Oil community liaison officer to respond to our concerns but he seemed deaf and indifferent to our plight.

Instead of taking notes he was relaxing in my comfortable overstuffed chair staring at the newspaper. There was a photo of a giant oil sands truck on the front page.

"They paid 200 million for it," he grumbled. "And to think I could be running that company!"

"You ... running it?" I snipped impatiently.

"Yeah, I was skipped over for promotion. A young engineer got the big salary."

"That's too bad," I said sarcastically. I couldn't imagine John Jesperson running an oil company. He wasn't even doing his current job properly.

"I've worked for the company longer than him, an' that little bastard is so conceited. I would have got that land for cheaper-two hundred million dollars!" He complained.

"They paid so much," I said mockingly, "so they can dig up our-forest?"

Jesperson glanced up. "It's not much when you consider that the-cost of an oil sands project is eight billion, that's *billion* with a 'B'."

"Eight billion?" I repeated in feigned surprise.

"They paid the *government* two hundred million dollars for my land," I said, thinking of all the problems oil development was bringing to our lives.

"It's not *your* land," Jesperson sneered.

"Yes, it is. We were here before any of your people."

He looked up from the paper, this time with a supercilious smile. "That doesn't make it *your* land. Anyway sweetheart, we're talking about big government and even bigger business. Royal paid two hundred million dollars for it, so it is their land. It's the golden rule; he who's got the gold makes the rules."

"Well they didn't pay *me* anything, and I won't sell it." I shot back.

Jersperson's mocking expression made me want to lash out more but for some reason I remained civil and repeated what Mary said about our rights. "Anyway, my cousin the lawyer told me that our food comes first before oil or mining or anything; she told me that the Supreme Court defended our rights to at least eat. We have to have some land protected. The government is supposed to consult us about our hunting rights. They can't sell something they don't have the rights to."

"Well, they just did!" He rolled his eyes, finally stood up from the chair and took a step towards the window. "They bought it and they're gonna mine it. Seriously, do you think that they'd let some *Indians* hunt a few moose instead of supplying millions of barrels of crude to the US? Not a chance!"

"Indians?" I said. "You mean from India?" I scowled.

"Yeah, yeah, okay—natives, Aboriginal People. Look, you want to drive a nice truck and live in a nice house like everybody else, don't ya? And with this mine, there'll be plenty of jobs for your relatives too."

I wanted to fight back. I wanted to change his attitude and convince him how important it was to preserve our lands but I felt tongue-tied. After weeks of exposing our innermost sensitivities I now realized that he wasn't interested in anything but his own career. What am I supposed to do when the guy who is to take our concerns back to the company doesn't bother to listen? In desperation I tried to bait him. "What are you gonna do when the Americans stop buying your dirty oil, if they turn down that new pipeline?" I asked.

"It's not dirty oil! The synthetic oil produced by the crackers is as clean as any oil. Cleaner!" he pouted. "Have you been listening to the Eco Peace nonsense? They won't stop the pipeline, they are addicted to oil."

"What about the 500 ducks that died in the tailings pond?" I countered. "The whole world heard about them." But I realized there was no point in continuing. I had failed to get through to him. He had no respect for my people. Up until today he was just pretending so they could get a check mark for extended consultations. I've let my nation down by thinking that the company would hear our concerns. I should have hired a lawyer to defend us from the beginning. I guess Elder Willie was right. It is democracy for the rich, anarchy for the poor. Now what can we take to the environmental hearing? I suppose we will have a few weeks to prepare.

Then as if we were the best of friends, he stood up and walked towards me, smiling.

"Listen, Katie!" he said abruptly, changing from sarcasm to honesty. "*We* have a chance, just you and me, to escape all this mess." He pointed out the window. "All these lands will be dug up, gone. Don't ya see? There's gonna be nothing left here—just a big dirty pit, big steel trucks, and toxic tailings ponds."

I said nothing. He continued. "What I'm talking about is a way out. It's a pretty big bonus they're offering me if you sign the trappers agreement. It can be ours, yours and mine together."

"What do you mean *ours*?" I was confused. *He* was going to get a bonus for me signing the trapper's agreement? And why would he offer me part? The trap line was big, covering about half the area, and Dad said it had been a good trap line, but why does *he* get a bonus? Why weren't they offering our family more?

"Well, together, with my savings and that $250,000 bonus we could buy a nice house in Victoria." He stood directly in front of me with a lecherous look in his eyes. He held out his arms as if he wanted to hug.

"Together? With you?" I said incredulously.

"Yeah, you and me, escaping to Lotus Land. How does that sound?" He put his hand on my shoulder and gazed into my eyes as if he were looking for some affirmation or signal. I was repulsed by his advance and I raised my arm, knocking his hand off my shoulder.

"Are you nuts?" I looked him straight in the eyes. "I'm not goin' anywhere with you, mister. What have you been smoking to think that anyway? And why are they offering *you* a bonus for *me* to sign the agreement?"

"Because you are the last one to sign."

"Well, I'm not gonna sign it. There has to be some part of our land left intact." He said nothing; just frowned and took another drag on his cigarette. Then he clumsily leaned back, supporting himself against the wall of the cabin trying to look nonchalant. The sleeve of his wrinkled blue blazer brushed against the gum oozing from a knot in the pine log. When he felt the gum tug on his jacket, he jerked away and tried to brush it off.

"You shouldn't have to live in these run down cabins," he said, looking disparagingly at the wall. He angrily craned his neck to look at his sleeve and his long cigarette ash fell onto my clean pine floor. He looked like a fly struggling in an invisible spider's web. He started to grunt like a cornered animal. Then he shook his head. I leaned over to clean up the ash and as I looked up I caught him leering at my breasts, ogling my body. I looked at him with disgust. So that's why he was now so attentive.

He moved so close I could smell his cigarette breath. "The company knows how you feel so I thought I might be able to get you to sign if I shared the money with you. If we bought a place on the coast together, we would have a nice place to go."

He tried to put his arm around me and I felt his big belly press against my side. I abruptly thrust my elbow into his chest and pushed him away. "Jesperson, you can't expect me to move to Victoria with you!" I was a bit frightened, not knowing how he would take rejection. "I don't feel that way about you."

"Well, I ..." He looked down.

He was so strange and pathetic. I would have gone easier on him, but he wasn't just a lovesick fool, he was an agent of the companies trying to get rid of a problem—me.

"Ya can't fight progress, Katie." He leaned forward and lowered his voice to a whisper. "*We* really can escape all this, just you and me. Just sign this agreement." He held out the agreement and took the last drag on his cigarette. My anger and frustration turned to disgust. All this letch saw was an opportunity to take advantage of a woman in distress. The scary part was he didn't realize how obviously pathetic his effort was. He continued. "Your band member, Leonard Berube, has made millions off mining the Royal Oil project and now *he* has a mansion on the water in Victoria. He's set for life. Don't you see, now it's *our* chance?" Now Jesperson's phony smile and his crooked yellow teeth made me want to vomit.

"Don't you know Leonard's son has cancer? Probably from the tar sands exposure from that mine. Anyway, I don't take bribes and I'm not goin' with you. You think I'd sleep with you in Victoria, don't you? Forget it, it's not happening, Jesperson. Never! An' you can stuff that agreement!" I looked angry but inside I nervously looked for a reaction.

Angrily he buttoned his blazer over his protruding belly and mashed his cigarette butt into my new white ceramic sink. "Indians," he mumbled.

"What?"

"Nothing. You know, if you keep this up, there's no way you'll ever get another job around here," he warned.

Jesperson jammed his fist into his blazer pocket. "Oh! By the way, here are the free pain killers you need. I got the last ones at the drug store on my way out here. Maybe you wouldn't have to take 'em if ya lived in Victoria." He threw the box on my kitchen counter.

"Thanks, but maybe I wouldn't need them if I didn't have to put up with you." Now I was angry. I couldn't wait for him to get out.

"Why don't ya just pay us for our lands instead of this bribery?" I asked, managing not to raise my voice.

"Giving you a share is my idea, not the company's," he admitted.

"So it's you who is bribing."

"Katie, come on now, I'm only trying to help. You can't tell anyone, anyway I will deny it. I'll say *you* propositioned *me*."

"Ha! You think your boss'd believe that *I* wanted to go with *you*?" I pointed to the driveway. "Get out!"

"Katie, no, I would never …"

He stopped, paused for a moment, looked down, and as if he was trying to justify his failure, he said, "I just thought you might like the coast." He slowly turned and shuffled to the door of his truck, mumbling again. He jerked his door handle and it slipped out of his hand without opening. He suddenly switched from hurt to anger, "Katie, ya better not make trouble for me."

He grabbed the handle again and angrily yanked the door open so fast it slammed into him, knocking him back. He only avoided falling by holding on for balance. His comb-over flopped over his face and he quickly reached up to flip it back. Consumed with embarrassment, he pulled off his gum-stained, dust-covered blazer and threw it indignantly onto the seat of his truck. His yellow shirt tail was flapping, revealing his bloated belly.

"*Uway gul*! Leave!" I shouted again, and pointed down the driveway.

After his truck disappeared over the hill, I stood still, numb, and battling a bit of fear. Who knew what this creep might do? The dust from his tires was thick over the driveway.

I sighed as a breeze waved the branches and rustled the leaves of the poplar trees. "Good riddance," the trees seemed to say as the dust settled on the long grass. It took me some time to calm down, but the cabin and the land had given me strength to stand up to more than just Jesperson. I realized what my cousin Mary meant. This is how the government protects our lands—setting me up for prostitution? I am a proud Dené woman—warrior defending our nation's culture. I've got children and a grandchild and I'm not selling myself or my people. Guys like Jesperson are why the Cree say *mooneow* for white man. It means 'ignorant person.'

I opened the box of the anti-inflammatories and took two. Maybe it's because I don't know how to get them to listen. My father explained it better than anyone. He said, "In the white man's world, land is a thing to own. But we don't think that way. Instead, I tell you the land does not belong to me, I belong to the land. We Dené People are a part of this land."

But now I would ask Father: "What do we do when the land that owns you is taken?" We are getting sick with diabetes and cancers. Cousin Mary was right. Why isn't Queen-Mother-the-Crown protecting us? I need help-help from my elders and my spiritual grandfathers, help from the Creator and someone with some sense, some feelings. Not a lustful company monster.

The Whi-ti-koh
Chapter 3

Later that day, an old grey pickup chugged up my driveway. The slim and agile elder named Willie Grandlegs, whom I had known since childhood, sauntered up the path to my cabin. As he opened the thick wooden door I caught a whiff of his newly tanned moosehide moccasins. The strong smoky odor reminded me of my youth. He nodded to me as he entered and sat down at the kitchen table without saying a word. Pulling some tobacco out of a plastic pouch, and cradling a small paper between his long brown fingers, he began to roll a cigarette.

Willie was a true Dené elder who had taught the wisdom of our culture through his stories. A native elder is more than just an old person. True elders feel the spirit of the Creator.

He seemed to sense something was troubling me. "Katie, how are you doin'?"

"Okay" I replied.

He leaned back in the chair, looked at the warm wood stove and asked me. "Did I tell ya my father killed a *Whi-ti-koh?*"

I had heard this story before. I wondered what he was up to, but you don't stop elders from repeating a story.

"He was alone out on his trap line, lookin' down inta his campfire. He didn't get any game that day and he was worried. Then everything around became too quiet ... as if even the bugs were hidin'.

He sensed somethin' evil and he knew he was goin' ta be attacked. Suddenly, a monster twice the size of a man, and powerful like a wild animal, jumped out ta strike him. But greed for human flesh made the monster callous. Father's knife quickly found its mark. He made a fire and burned it where it fell. He had a ceremony ta rid himself of the bad spirits. Those are the bad spirits that brought the monster and the poor hunting, and that's what ya must do. Go to a ceremony, a Cree ceremony, get rid of those bad spirits."

He paused and then looked into my eyes. "Yeah, a *Whi-ti-koh's* been here, I sense the greed."

"Willie, it wasn't a *Whi-ti-koh,* only Jesperson from the oil company."

"He's a *Whi-ti-koh*. Watch out," he warned.

"Don't say that word!" I said.

"Ya need to be careful, Katie. I'll give ya an eagle feather and ya go to a Cree ceremony. Rid yourself of his spirit."

I knew I must take his advice.

"Katie, I worry about ya. You're the only one left here who's willin' ta fight. Ya gotta take care of yourself. We need ya. Everyone else is takin' the money and if they can they're leavin. It's not good."

Then, he started talking about the sludge dykes he helped build when he was working on the first tar sands mines years ago. "It seems like everyone is gettin' sick with somethin'. Maybe even more people will get cancer," he said. "It's because they buried oil in them dykes. We live too close. They'll get a rash from the chemicals, like me."

He was ashamed he'd had to quit because of the rashes on his body that made him no longer able to work or hunt, and I thought he was going to cry when he told me that he now realized the dykes he helped build were leaking.

"I pray that the Creator will help us." His voice cracked. Then he panicked again.

"Everybody needs ta move. It ain't safe."

He told me about when he tried to get some evidence to expose the company's practices. And because he couldn't read, he took his son with him to the old office where he used to pick up his paycheck. They couldn't get into any file rooms and even if they had, they didn't know what to look for, that is if any 'evidence' was there to find.

"All they want is money," he said. "And they'll kill us ta get it."

I knew what he was feeling. I came back to help my people preserve our culture and language but so many of our people have challenges. "You know, we can fight them somehow," I tried to reassure him. "We have rights. Even if the government is not listening, the courts have said we have rights."

My cell phone rang. It was Mary, from Fort Chipewyan.

"Katie, I met Jamie at the Northern Store and I am usin' his phone."

"Oh Mary, I was just thinking of you. You were right about Jesperson."

"Yeah, you can tell me later. But, I just got hold of that development report we were talkin' about."

"Oh, go on," I said.

"They want all the lands by the river including your trapline."

"By the river?"

"Yeah. Do you know how much meat the band still gets from there?" she asked.

"Well, we haven't really counted," I said. "But most of it."

"Well, you're gonna be lucky if you can get any after this."

I remembered Jesperson's description of the pits and my stomach churned.

Elder Grandlegs heard Mary and he shook his head.

"What we gonna do, Mary?" Willie asked. "We're gonna lose everything and if ya ain't strong, you'll die."

Mary agreed. "Hello Willie. Yeah. We gotta do sompthin'." She respected her elders.

I figured that the key to stopping them was keeping the rights to our lands but that was Mary's expertise. I spoke into the cell. "We can't let them take the rest of this land from us. They will kill the whole damn society, including themselves. We're gonna have to fight them."

"I know," Mary said. "I'm so glad you're here, Katie. It's been so hard to get people to stand up against them."

"Well, they're not gonna get my signature on that trapper's agreement, that's for sure."

"Good, Katie. But you've also got to prove you use the land. Ya gotta prove that their mine will cause you irreparable harm or they can literally bulldoze right over ya," Mary warned. She frightened me because I knew she knew the law.

"How do we prove that?" It sounded almost impossible to prove, especially since my family did not trap anymore.

My Cabin on the Deh Cho

Chapter 4

If there was one place that would help save our way of life it was the family trapline. As soon as I regained my treaty status, I offered our cabin and trapline to the band for youth training and cultural retention. I wrote:

> "Healthy lands not only allow the continuation of our language and culture, but are the foundation of our self-esteem, our confidence, and pride. That's why one of my goals has been to maintain my family cabin."

Everyone at the band office agreed and they were excited about using it. I truly love the cabin made of the straight pine logs from our sacred forest and perched on the bank of the great Deh Cho. But it seems much smaller now, not only because I've grown bigger, but because I live in a changed nation. In older days, a wood stove cooked our foods and gave us heat. A half-wall partition allowed the air to circulate and separated the rough-hewn bunks from our metal-legged chairs and vinyl covered table. During winter trapping seasons, the cabin would be full of stretched furs hanging to dry from every nook. Now it contains magical memories of those wonderful days.

The location was perfect. It was built right by the river, but high enough on the riverbank to avoid ice jams. A winter cabin is used for trapping fine, long-haired furs like martins, fox, lynx, and ermine, but we also used it in the summer when we weren't fishing at the lake.

After Father passed, we all moved away. I got married right out of school, Brian got a good job in Edmonton and Mother didn't like to go to the cabin alone. Then Chief Charles, my second cousin, reminded us, "You can't keep the trap line and cabin if you don't trap and report pelts every year."

But my brother Brian replied, "I can't afford to trap anymore! There aren't enough furbearers left. Clear cutting and tar sands pits scared them all away."

It was Brian who knew more about trapping than anyone, but after the tar sands started he moved to the city. Now that I have come back, it is solely up to me to do what I can to keep it. In the end, it was Mother who came up with the idea that picking berries should qualify to maintain a trap line. And I'm comfortable picking berries and herbs.

The cabin is now my refuge and a symbol of our culture and traditional livelihood. When I stand on the porch and look between an old dark green spruce and a spindly lodge pole pine, I can see the swirling currents of the swollen Athabasca. This spring, our sacred pathway had become a cold soup of silt, debris, and the occasional old tree trunk that carved the soft clay banks and pushed the last bit of winter downstream, north towards the granite of the Canadian Shield. We call the granite "the barren lands," where the legendary giant fell, his body becoming the mountains extending right up to the Arctic Ocean.

Spring breakup was spectacular on our wild northern rivers, but this year there was no violent scouring of the banks, no mountains of ice crushing rocks and snapping trees. No, it wasn't the same as it was in Father's time, when ice jam floods clogged the breadth of the river and enormous slabs of ice, each more than ten feet thick and longer than big semi-trucks, would grind together, pile on top of one another and dam the flushing spring flow. No one knew when frigid water might rush over the riverbank. One moment the ice pack was quietly but ominously moving downstream; the next it was violently piling up, uprooting trees and forcing the water to escape into river flats and over high banks. The river groaned as the ice sealed the channel and an awesome volume of water covered the entire delta.

Father said we had to be respectful of the river's strength, for not only were the ice and frigid water dangerous, but the flooding regularly refreshed and renewed the small lakes and ponds, providing homes for the animals and plants. Some floods refreshed hundreds of square kilometers.

Before the hydroelectric dams and tar sands changed the river flows, they say that the Peace Athabasca Delta produced the best muskrat pelts in the world. That's one of the reasons why Fort Chipewyan was one of the most important fur trade centers in the west and the oldest permanent settlement in Alberta.

Father explained that when a flood refreshed the perched basins above the normal level of the river, the muskrats thrived for at least two years. The basins were a perfect habitat and the explosion of muskrat populations not only provided furs and food for our ancestors, but they attracted other fur-bearing predators.

The muskrat harvest came in the early spring, followed by the waterfowl hunt—every type of duck and goose you could imagine. In the summer, we fished at lake camps and hunted across country. In the fall we hunted moose, gathered berries and herbs, and prepared for the winter fine fur trap. We followed the cycles of the seasons, harvested the fruits of the land that the creator provided and we were grateful.

But ice jam flooding doesn't happen anymore. The dams and tar sands changed that.

When I travel down the river I see the old cabins of my relatives, my father's friends, and others. These cabins line the river, our highway, the main artery of our culture and our way of life. My grandmother said that "the Deh Cho pours life into our world."

Each fall, Father left the village, taking his dogs and supplies across the river in a small canoe. He took several trips and he needed to go early enough before freeze-up.

When I was very young, before I was sent away to residential school, he took me, my brother and mother to the cabin for freeze-up to help. It was beautiful. In the fall, the bright yellow and red leaves covered the stones and mud of the river bank as we loaded the canoe. I remember kneeling in the bow of that fine birch bark canoe, crossing the river and poking my fingers through the smooth surface of the cool clear water. Father told me not to get my sleeve wet. He told me that a big jackfish might bite a sweet girl's finger. I wasn't sure whether he was serious or joking, but I took my fingers out just in case.

Some people think that living in the bush is difficult, with no running water and no electricity. But Mother and Father said Mother Earth would always provide, as long as we continued to thank her. During those early years, I was able to feel the love my father and mother had for bush life.

The first time my kids were at our cabin they asked, "What was it like living here?"

I told them, "Back then, when we got to the cabin we carried all the supplies up the riverbank. The sled dogs carried a load on their backs in small leather packs. First, Father repaired the cabin by replacing moss in the holes between the logs. I remember the sounds of him chopping wood for the fire and the smell of the hides when he was making sled and dog harnesses, and the gleam in his eyes when he was cleaning his rifle and sharpening his knives. Mother made the wilderness home. Using bear fat, she cooked the pike and walleye that Father netted from the river each day. I remember how good the fish tasted and how it almost melted in my mouth. Nothing went to waste; Father used the rest of the fish he netted to feed the dogs and he would carve moose bones into fleshing tools.

"We had delicious juicy steaks as Mother prepared fresh moose meat from a bull Father had shot and butchered beside the cabin. She showed me how to dry the rest of the meat on wooden poles over a slow burning fire surrounded by a tarp. I still love the stringy texture and smoky taste of the fresh dried moose meat. We all picked sweet blueberries, saskatoons, tangy cranberries, greens

and fresh mint. Father even got some fat geese in the late fall. The land produced so many different foods and medicines. Mother gave us rat root for sore throats and Labrador tea for everything else.

"The land not only provided foods. Mother made the finest, most beautiful gloves and moccasins. There was no end to the different clothes she made. We all worked to tan the hide and Mother made the moosehide wrap for the sled. She showed me how to combine furs with fabrics she bought from the Hudson's Bay Store. She showed me how to sew the hide, bead the gloves, and line the moccasins with rabbit, marten, and mink. She showed me which fur to use for the inside and for the hood's trim—"so it didn't freeze with your breath."

My girl asked me, "Didn't you have other kids to play with?"

"Yeah, I played with my brother and sometimes cousins," I said. "We were never bored."

I told her how I helped stoke and feed the fire during the tanning and how I learned which types of wood to use for heat and which for smoke, for fast burning and slow. And how, in the evenings around the fire, Father told stories of his old friend who went out on the land alone with a hatchet, a knife, and rifle loaded with only three bullets. He stayed in the bush all winter and returned in the spring, smiling at all the ladies, floating down the swollen river, his little one-man canoe stacked with furs.

"Bush life was magical," I told her. "The waxwings came and ate crumbs right out of my hand, and before the first frost there was a constant buzz of mosquitoes and flies, reminding us that summer was still here. At night, Father told stories about all the sounds the owls, moose, bats and frogs made and he would tell stories of the olden days, of giant beavers and the history of the Deh Cho flowing forever under our ancestors, the northern lights."

"Giant beavers? Yeah, right – Do you believe in giant beavers, Mom?" My daughter looked at me.

"My Girl, your people have lived here for thousands of years. Have you ever seen pictures of saber tooth tigers and wooly mammoths?"

"Yeah."

"Well in those days, thousands of years ago there were large sloths, giant beavers and small horses. They have found their bones."

"Where did they go?"

"They went extinct. Father told me a story about when our people journeyed through the land of many lakes to come here. He told about two giants who were so tall their heads scraped the sky. The two giants were fighting, and a Dené man who was tiny compared to the giants helped the good giant by slashing the bad giant's heel. It was just enough help to bring victory. When the bad giant fell, his head landed around Lake Athabasca and his backbone formed the mountains that stretched all the way down the Big River to the northern ocean. The giant's body became the lands of the Dené People. Today you can trace the settlements of the Dené all the way to the Arctic Ocean, where the fight took place."

It was around the campfire that I received my Dené education. Everything was alive and real and everything had a spirit—a purpose; and the best thing was we were a part of it.

"What about wars? Did he tell you about native wars?" my son asked.

"Yes. My father told the story of his Cree grandfather who fought at the side of Louis Riel in the Métis war. His grandfather, my great grandfather, and your great-great grandfather, was the son of the honorable Cree Chief Big Bear. He escaped with his band from the battlefield of the great rebellion of 1885. The Canadian scouts chased the Cree families for weeks, but they moved into the deep bush. They moved north to our *Athapaskow* country, so far that the tenderfoot scouts grew weary of the chase. He told me how these so-called scouts knew nothing of the land and how Big Bear's people easily avoided them. They could never catch Big Bear, but it was hard for him to keep everyone fed and on the run.

"Eventually he had to turn himself in to stop his people from starving, as they could not survive through the winter. Fortunately, Big Bear's son stayed up north with us. His Dené friend, who he fought beside in the war, was the great warrior, Wandering Spirit. He had taught him some of the Dené language, so it was easier for him to make friends with us."

"Dené is hard," my son complained.

"But because he knew some of the language, the Denesuline People let him camp with them and become a member of the band. It must have been a challenge for him, but sitting listening to your elders around the fire is the way you can learn our history. The bush gave me the values and the understanding of what it means to be Dené."

I learned my language in the bush and I tried to give some of the same gifts to my children. Today, standing in front of the cabin, I am older than my mother was the first time she brought me here, but my children rarely come out. What will become of our language and culture if the children are not taught?

Eden No Longer
Chapter 5

From the porch, I can see far down the misty grey-green ribbon of water. This spring, the ice just seemed to disappear—no ice jams, no floods. But the river is still wide with eddies swirling around the broken spruce boughs sifting the muddy debris. The river banks are still lined with lush aspen, pine, and spruce with the occasional birch; but the beauty is deceiving. Water is being sucked out by huge pumps and is heated to separate the oil from the sand. The elders say that their favorite berries and herb patches are covered with dust from the mines and the air smells like rotten gasoline.

The river is too low; there are too many sand bars and there's no more work as a ship's pilot on the river barges during the summer months. South of the village, huge pits of sand and oily water have replaced the beautiful forest. It is so different now from the wonderland of my youth, or as Willie would say, my grocery store and pharmacy have been destroyed.

A few years ago, while I was away on the farm, an oil spill from one of the tar sands plants made the fish taste so bad, nobody could eat them. Instead of silently floating downstream in a canoe surprising a moose, the Tucker family has a jet boat they pull out on weekends that makes an awful noise and destroys the tranquility.

Mom didn't like the Tuckers even back then. She would whisper that they were *Enna*—enemies. She would say, "You know those

Cree," and shake her head. Father said he was related to the Tuckers, he was part Cree and she didn't think of him as an enemy, at least not yet. He joked that Mother liked the part of him that was Cree. He said it excited her. She would lower her eyes and giggle.

I began thinking about Jesperson and Elder Grandleg's worries about the land. What would become of our people if we all had to move away? I needed the faith of my mother, who managed to combine traditional spiritualism and Christianity, and even though I hadn't figured it all out, I knew there was truth in them both. I hoped that God and the Grandfathers would help me with the decisions I had to make.

Suddenly my cell phone rang.

"Hello?"

"Katie?" It was Eleanor, another cousin, this time from the village.

"Yup."

"Are you at the cabin?"

"Yup."

Eleanor wasted no time explaining why she called.

"We went out to church this morning and when we came back, Grandma Mable was gone! We've looked all over town and can't find her. We're goin' to start another search and we need your help."

"I'm on my way," I assured her.

My mother's sister, Auntie Mable, and her husband had the trap line south of town. It was now just a desolate pit. Since her husband passed on, Auntie Mable was living in the village with her daughter, Eleanor. The last time I visited her, it seemed like she was forgetting things.

In the past, each community had leaders. Mable's husband was a successful hunter, and Mable lived all of her life on the land. As a result, she never had to learn much English, just enough to know what kind of a deal the Hudson's Bay man was giving. However, she spoke Dené, Cree, and French fluently. She was always there for her family as a midwife or doctor, always giving advice and food to those less able to support themselves. She was close to Mother and together they taught me to sew. She always had an ample loving lap for me. Whenever I had something private I needed to talk about, I went to Auntie Mable.

How did she get lost? Auntie Mable knew every path and twig in the area. And now that she was forgetful, Eleanor's family had someone with her all the time. I wondered where she possibly could have gone. If she went into the bush, we might not be able to find her quickly, but if she went back towards her trap line? Well, it doesn't exist anymore. Her trap line was razed; literally raised by the first oil sands mine, and now is a big empty sand pit with dirty sludge ponds and pitiful grass planted at the very far end. Auntie claimed that the *Whi-ti-koh* giants had devoured her trap line. I understood what she was saying, because it was if some creature had taken a huge bite out of the earth.

As I crossed the bridge into the village, I looked to see if she was walking out this way. Where would she go this spring? What had she been thinking? Or had she just became disoriented and wandered off?

When I got to Eleanor's house, the muddy yard was packed with pickup trucks and three men were in front of the house on their phones. Chief Charles was one of them. She was his favorite auntie, too.

As I ran into the house Eleanor greeted me, "Oh, Katie, I'm so glad you're here. We're dividin' into groups-search teams."

Chief Charles came in, holding out his arms to give me a hug. "We have to find her before nightfall." He looked worried.

I added, "I don't have any good ideas about where she may have gone. She didn't shoot ducks this spring, did she?"

"No, Dad always did that," Eleanor answered. "She sure could prepare them, though."

"Have you looked in the pit?" I asked. Eleanor looked at me with a foreboding stare. She knew it was likely she had gone down into the pit.

"Well, that's about two miles away, so I think she might be some-where in the bush between here and there," my other cousin, Ned, added quickly.

The first search group immediately started to march through the woods towards the pit. My job was to go to the pit directly. Three of us got in Cousin's truck and drove the two miles over to the wire-fenced mine entrance.

The flagman at the gate recognized we were from the WaPaSu village. What did they want now? Joy riding in the pit? A demon-stration? A road block? He came out to see what we wanted.

"Where ya think yer goin'?" he said to Ned.

"We're not sure, but our elderly mother may have wandered into the pit area from her house two miles away. She's been missing for three hours and she's not anywhere in town. We thought we should look over here. Can you help us look for her?"

Meanwhile Ronny, Ned's younger brother, had gotten out of the truck and was trying to look over the gate into the pit.

The flagman nervously glanced over at Ronny. "Ya can't enter into these pits, not with no authorization. It's dangerous down there, and ya don't want ta hurt no one."

It was my turn to talk. "But what if our Auntie is down there? She may be disoriented." I tried to get him to understand. "We think that she has wandered into the pit, maybe through the holes in the fence."

The flagman looked over at Ronny again.

"I'm gonna call the super," he said after he realized that Ronny was not trying to climb the fence. "Pull 'er up here, 'side the office." He motioned us through the gate and towards the parking area beside a small shack.

As we drove through the gate, we saw the enormous pit. None of us had ever seen a pit quite this big. It must have stretched for five miles in all directions. We looked down a cliff to the bottom, about four hundred feet down. She could be anywhere down there. To the left, there was a dam around a pool of suspicious liquid. It was a murky, muddy mess. About two hundred meters out, the liquid stopped at the dyke they built when they were mining. The road was rocky and uneven and divided the liquid from a section of dirty sand. No wonder they didn't want us driving down there.

I could barely see the rim of trees lining the top of the cliff on the other side of the pit. She couldn't have gone that far. She couldn't even have made it halfway through this pit.

The flagman came out of the office. "The Super wants ta talk to ya," he said to Ned. Ned took the phone.

"Yes?"

"... Three hours"

"... No, not for sure, but this used to be her trap line"

"... She's forgetful"

"... It's a pretty good chance she went down there."

"... A helicopter from McMurray... Okay ."

Ned gave the phone back to the flagman. He said, "Better safe than sorry."

The flagman motioned for us to come over closer to the edge of the cliff.

"While you're waitin'," he said, "I've got binoculars. We can take a look." We searched what looked like the surface of the moon. It was a flat sand and clay bottom without a plant or tree in sight. It had an occasional mining road running through it and miles of denuded sand with pools of oil soaked water scattered over what looked like twenty-five square miles.

After about half an hour of searching, we saw another pickup truck coming up the road and stopping at the gate. It was Eleanor's Cree neighbour, David.

David got out of the truck, "There's no sign of her in the woods between her house and the pit, but there are lots of places she could have gotten through. We think she's in the pit."

Our hearts sank.

Just as he finished, we heard the sound of the helicopter in the distance. We all looked to the horizon and soon we were able to see a red copter flying towards us. It was almost below us. They were down searching the pit even while they flew towards the office.

They landed in the clearing on the other side of the hut. A man wearing an orange and yellow jumpsuit came running towards us.

"We need to take one of the old woman's relatives up with us." he shouted over the roar of the engine. "We need someone she will recognize, someone who can talk to her."

Ned volunteered me, "Take Katie! Auntie always liked her best."

The pilot grabbed my hand, told me to keep my head down and we raced towards the noisy machine. He dropped me into the seat, gave me a headset with a microphone and helped me fasten the belt over my shoulder. We could see directly below through the bubble window. The fellow sitting behind motioned to the earphones and mic. Over the noise of the engine I could hear him say, "Welcome aboard." through the headset. As I looked up, I saw the handsome pilot grinning at me. I smiled back.

As we took off, he asked me what I knew of her whereabouts. I didn't know where she would go, but I thought she wouldn't go too far into the pit. The copter jerked and I was pushed against the pilot's strong shoulders. I noticed his tanned, strong and sinewy forearms. We swooped towards the stone walls so close to the trees at the top of the cliff. I thought we would hit them. My stomach felt like it was in my throat, and I tried to swallow without the pilot noticing.

Then, as I started to feel dizzy, I imagined Auntie covered in tar, lying face down drowned in a pool of oil. I looked around the edge of the tailings pond for signs of dear Auntie. We circled around the area and flew around a corner in the pit to the west of town. Flying low into the pit as we approached the steep wall, the pilot pulled the chopper up until we rose above the cliff to the forest-covered plateau. On the grassy ledge overlooking the chasm, I saw a lonely figure sitting on a fallen log right next to the cliff.

"There she is!" I shouted so loud into the microphone the pilot lifted his hand to his headphone. He turned the copter towards the pit and spoke into his mic.

"We found her," he radioed the gate office. "And she appears to be fine."

"She looks a little dazed," I said. "And she won't trust the helicopter. It might be better to get the ground team to pick her up."

What a relief to see Auntie Mable quietly sitting, gazing out over her vanished trap line. She was safe and the whole village would rejoice.

As the pilot, who was about my age, took me back to the village, he asked me over the headphones, "You live in the village?"

When I told him McMurray, he asked me if I wanted a ride back home in the helicopter. Then he said, "Or maybe your husband could pick you up at the airport."

I said, "I'm not married … anymore … anyways."

He looked relieved, but I had a sinking feeling. He asked me if I knew of any really good fishing lakes to the north. He said that he heard that I knew the country really well, and he had a group of fishers who were looking for a good guide.

I started to say that I really wasn't interested, but I could use the money and he was so handsome. *I will give him my number,* I thought. His eyes met mine.

"Maybe I could call you and we could talk about it," he asked.

"Yes. Call me." I pushed the words out.

He said, "My name is Daniel."

"Katie," I smiled again.

"I know," he said and grinned.

I asked the pilot to drop me off in the village so I could see my Auntie.

When I got to Eleanor's house the rest of the family was leaving, but Auntie was in a flap.

"How could you think I was lost?" she said in Dené as I entered the living room.

"You two!" She glared at me. *"You both have a lot to learn. You need to understand what is really important. Do you know the changes that I have experienced in my lifetime? You should be thinking about what you're gonna do, not worry so much about me."*

"Well Auntie, you were gone for hours."

"There was a time I was gone for days or even months and you didn't worry."

"Mother, that was a long time ago!" Eleanor said as if Auntie was being unreasonable.

"Yes a long time ago and things are changing. Sitzu, have you finished making that tea or not? I need to sit and relax after that frightening machine interrupted my afternoon. You girls come here and sit, too; I want to tell you something. You know this has been my home for a long time."

"Yes, Auntie,"

"Yes, Mother," we both replied dutifully.

"I can remember when I was a tiny girl, about the age of your granddaughter; yeah, just about Jenny's age; about six or seven? It was the summer that my father and grandfather took the family on the annual round—on the same route they took before they built our permanent winter cabins at WaPaSu. Our cabins were there before there were any roads, before they built the railway line. That is how long this has been my home."

"It must have been a wonderful place then," I sighed.

"It was the summer after the great flu of 1919, which wasn't so wonderful! I remember that winter so many people were sick and my uncle coughing blood and sweating and always in bed, my mother crying and the neighbours carrying their dead grandmother out of the cabin wrapped in a Hudson's Bay blanket. They laid her out behind the woodpile and covered her body with heavy logs and stones so the animals could not get to her. They let the body freeze because it was too hard to bury during the winter.

We lost my auntie and an uncle in that epidemic and then in the springtime we heard stories about the devastation at Lake Claire. The whole town was wiped out; the few survivors moved away. There was no one left to bury the dead. Was it wonderful? Was it wonderful just before I was born when we signed the treaty? My parents were starving because of over-trapping; too many new people competing for the same game. You know that's why we signed the treaty, don't you? It wasn't because we were happy. The beaver, moose and bison abandoned us. So take a look around you girls. Life has never been as good as it is right now. You have trucks and cell phones and plenty of food. You have gone to school and can get good jobs. Be grateful for what you have."

"But Auntie, our lands are being destroyed! And you were just looking at what used to be your trapline."

"And they haven't lived up to the treaty we signed and we're just trying to recover from the residential schools," added Eleanor.

Auntie nodded her head. *"There will always be challenges in life. That is what makes it worth living. Yes, it is worth protecting the lands from pollution. Look at Willie's rash and the people with diabetes and cancer."*

"And we are losing our culture and language. What can we do about that?" I asked rhetorically.

"Here is your tea, Mother, it's hot," interjected Eleanor.

"Good, now let me tell you a story about how we adapted to changes."

"As I was saying, when I was very young we were leaving in the spring and we would be gone on the round until the beginning of winter. It seemed like forever until winter, and the idea of leaving our cabin and going on a boat frightened me, especially after such a horrid winter. Mother told me we would travel in the canoe-boat and birch bark canoe and we would have to portage for days. It would be hard work and I had to be a good girl.

I was the youngest child at seven years old and I was just learning about the local river and lakes, about rabbit snares and the fresh streams in the spring. I helped Mother pick berries and herbs and tended the camp fires. But when Grandpa announced we were going on the river, I didn't want to go. Why couldn't we stay home?"

We could imagine Auntie as a little child as she recounted this story.

"Before we left the men took the winter furs into the post to get supplies. In those days there were only two trading posts in the area-one here and one at Fort Chipewyan. They came back with ammunition, flour for bannock and blankets and cloth for making clothes. They brought back salt, sugar and a very special treat-candy! That was the first time I had candy. It was magical. Oh, so good! It was sweeter than the sweetest blueberry and the sweet taste lasted so long.

I asked Father for another but he told me, 'One piece is all you get. I don't have any more and it's not good for you to eat too much.' He said it was made by the Cree or Ojibwa traders who came to the post. 'It's made from maple sap and they called it "Sinzibuckwud," drawn from trees.' He said we could make it from our birch sap too but it must be done in the very early spring. Did you know that making maple and birch syrup is one of our Aboriginal traditions? It was one of our gifts to the French explorers when they first arrived in our lands.

When I was young we had very few luxuries but maple sugar was one of them. So many times when we finally got something we over-indulged, probably from being deprived for so long. It is hard to go from near starvation to feasts every night. I think that is why we have so much diabetes and alcoholism. We survived without support for so many years and now we are killed by kindness-too much food, alcohol and welfare. Are you listening to me?"

"*Yes, every word,*" we answered in unison.

"I know why you were worried about me. Because you think I'm

getting senile, right?"

"But Mother, you have been forgetting things, you know."

"Oh, I know. But do I sound senile to you? Do you think I've lost my mind, Katie?"

"No, Auntie. I don't."

"Listen. It was the late spring, just when the weather started to warm up when we left on the round. We packed our boats and started down the deep green river floating with the strong current. I was petrified because the water had been so cold and I never did learn to swim properly. What if the canoe should turn over? I know some people dream of the good old days but I was sure glad to see motors when they came out. In those early days we had to paddle and walk everywhere and we used the dogs as pack animals."

"All of you went in two boats? How many people went?" I asked

"Well, there was Mother and Father, Grandpa and Grandma, my uncle and three of us kids. We sat four in each boat. They were pretty big and not that easy to paddle. Oh, and we took one dog with us too.

The first camp we made on the river was not too far down where there were globs of tar seeping out of the riverbank. We unloaded our gear and turned the boats over to waterproof them. It really didn't take too long for Father to rub it onto the bottoms of the boats. It stopped up any leaks and made them float better. That was our way of using the tar sands.

The next day we just drifted down the river while Father watched for game. He and Grandpa floated well ahead of us scanning the riverbank. We were told not to make any loud noises, even though we were well behind them. Sure enough, that afternoon we saw two

moose swimming across the river. They were caught by the river current, unable to run from us as we floated up closer. Father skillfully
steered his canoe towards the bank and Grandpa prepared his rifle.
They waited patiently until the bigger one was out of the water and
BANG! It collapsed with a thud right at the edge. I had never seen
anyone shoot a moose before and I was frightened by the gunshot.
As the big ugly animal fell, the other one crashed through the brush,
madly escaping to safety.

My parents and grandparents were smiling. "Good shot," crowed
my father. We headed for the kill and prepared to butcher and dry
the meat. Grandpa made a short ceremony to give thanks for the
moose and we camped there, right at the kill site. Mother said if we

shot a moose far out in the bush in winter we would have set up a cache that we could come back to later. But this time of year it was easier to stay and dry the meat so we could carry it with us. Now our canoes would really be loaded!

I helped gather wood for the fire and tended the meat drying process. There were two ways to dry the meat. We set up a rack which we made by stripping tree branches, placing them between posts. We then covered them with thin strips of meat so they could dry in the warm sun. My uncle made a smoker which was really just a stand sheltered from the wind, close to a smoldering fire. He liked smoked meat better, he said. Meanwhile we prepared the best cuts for the feast we would have that night.

We were only one day's paddle from the delta and two days away from Fort Chipewyan. Mother wanted us to share some of the meat with her relatives on the delta and Father would trade the rest at the fort. We camped there for two nights, just long enough to do a good job.

After a short trip down the river we arrived at Jackfish, a little village on the eastern edge of the delta. There were three families staying there that spring, hunting and trapping muskrats and shooting waterfowl. This was Mother's home. She grew up at Jackfish.

When she showed her family the dry meat they smiled and told us they were sick of muskrats and geese. It was there I first saw a handsome little boy over by the other camp fire. He was about 10 years old at the time and he was curious about me too. I did not imagine that we would marry 11 years later.

The next morning we paddled out of the delta onto the lake. What a monster of a lake! It was breezy and the waves were so big it made it difficult to paddle, but we crossed to the north shore at Fort Chipewyan to trade some meat. I was cold, wet and tired by the end of that experience. I dreaded having to get back in the boat the next day. At the fort Father and Grandpa traded meat and some furs.

That evening we tented with some other families from across Lake Claire, which was a Dené settlement just one day's paddle away from the Chipewyan Post. This is the first time I saw hand games which we played around the camp fire all evening. It was my family against the others. There were four people to a team and one team had to guess in which hand you held a stone. Each time a team guessed right they got one of the sticks. Once you got all the sticks you won the prize. The prize that evening was beautiful moose hide slippers. It was a lot of fun." Auntie grinned and her eyes narrowed.

"The next morning we paddled close to the south shore to cut down the wave action. And a day or so later we stopped to camp at huge mountains of sand which were right along the lake shore. Have you ever been there? You both go and see these magnificent dunes. It was an incredible sight for a seven-year-old girl, huge hills of sand, right on the shore. My brother and sister and I rolled, slid and played in the sand for what seemed like hours while our family prepared the camp and got a meal going.

Our land is filled with wonderful places. The lake and delta are so big. No wonder our leaders agreed to share this land with the white man. Not too long after the sand dunes we entered a different river, except this time we had to paddle up the current. Fortunately it was not a swift river, but it was hard work just the same. We all had to paddle, even me. That night Father explained that we will travel up this river until we hit bottom and then we would portage to a beautiful lake where we'd spend much of the summer. He also told me that we'd portage again to other beautiful lakes and then to the Clearwater River, which would take us back to the cabin in the fall. He knew I was a bit homesick.

When we saw the first lake it was so clear I saw right to the bottom. There were lots of walleye and whitefish and plenty of game in the surrounding bush. My brother and sister and I spent our days exploring, helping to fish and tanning the hides of the game the men brought in. We followed the animal trails almost all the way around the lake. At night Grandfather told stories and we practiced hand

games. The clear lake got warmer as summer progressed, and my brother showed me how to swim. It felt like paradise.

So you see girls, I know this land and I'm not about to get lost in my back yard."

"No ma'am," we said in unison.

Professor Thomas
Chapter 6

As the morning sun cast tree trunk shadows on the cabin wall, I heard a car's engine—an early visitor. It was Leonard and a white-haired man.

Leonard and I were sweethearts in residential school. I think he still carried a flame, but after he made some money in the oil sands mines, he married a girl from Vancouver. She was much younger and pretty. I think she was Métis. Despite his transformation into a successful businessman, he still loved the bush culture. He wanted to support my efforts in maintaining our world, even if he only hunted on weekends. He was worried about what the mines were doing to our health because his son, who grew up here, was now sick from cancer. With all of his contacts, he'd find someone who'd help me.

"Hello Leonard," I said as I came out to greet them.

He was leaning on his SUV, trying to look casual in his clean pressed denim and beaded buckskin vest. "Hi Katie. Quite a bit of excitement yesterday?"

Leonard did not appear to be comfortable. I sensed guilt. Maybe because he got rich from the mine that destroyed Auntie's trap line.

"But everything is okay now?" he quickly asked. "Katie, this is Dr. Franklin Thomas."

"Pleased to meet you, Dr. Thomas."

"Call me Franklin, please; pleased to meet you as well, Ms. Cardinal."

"Please call me Katie," I said. "It looks like a fine morning."

It appeared that Leonard had followed through on his promise. He told me a lawyer couldn't help until we got a land use study done.

"Ya need someone who will help prove how ya use the land," he said.

I guessed this white-haired guy was the advisor.

"Would you like some tea?" I asked, but Leonard said he needed to check on his brother and he'd be back at noon to pick up the professor.

"Leonard, I have a question for you." I walked over to his truck and faced away from the professor. "Do you know this guy, John Jesperson?"

Leonard wrinkled his nose. "Yeah, I know of him. He's been pushing those trap line agreements, hasn't he?"

"Yeah."

"Well Katie, I know how you feel about your trap line. You know that the company is probably offering him a big bonus if he can get you to sign off."

"How big a bonus?" I asked.

"Probably over $500,000."

"Really?"

"Yeah, it's pretty important to them. If they don't get a trapper's agreement it will postpone their mining schedule."

"Oh …. Okay … Well … How's Mike doing?" I asked.

"We just sent him to the Mayo Clinic. He's so strong; I think he can beat this."

"Good. Leonard, I know it's tough, I will pray for him."

Leonard waved and got back in his truck. I said a quiet prayer for Mike and then stood there wondering again how my signature was worth so much.

After I made him tea, the professor didn't waste any time coming to the point.

"You know, the provincial government views this land as theirs because of the wording of the treaty," he began.

"But they say our interpretation of the treaty is important too, isn't it?" I asked.

He nodded weakly. "But they will make you prove it every step of the way."

He mentioned that Leonard had told him about Auntie's experience. I figured that story would be a good introduction, but I needed to tell him our full history.

"After all, our rights are based on our history—being the first people here," I said, half expecting him to contradict me.

"That's true," he replied.

"Despite the treaty, this is our land," I started. "We have lived on it for thousands of years. We never gave it up in the treaty. Our elders told us we only agreed to share it."

"Even though your chiefs couldn't read and likely didn't understand the treaty's written words, the commissioners wrote land transfer language into it. So the province politicians have chosen to believe that they own the land, and quite frankly that is what the written portion of the treaty seems to say."

"Even before the treaty, the government was trying to break our spirit. They even told us that they wouldn't help us when we were starving in the 1890's because we hadn't signed the treaty yet. Imagine! 'We can't feed you because you haven't given up your land.' For over 150 years they have expected us to live off the land and we have been ignored and wounded from their neglect. But we are starting to fight back now."

"Which tribe were *your* ancestors?" he asked.

"My Auntie and I are Dené, but we have some Cree blood too. Also, one of my great grandfathers was a French trapper; a courier du bois, and my other great-grandfather was a Cree who fought in the Riel Rebellion. My earlier ancestors were caribou hunters from the barren lands, the Canadian Shield. My first language was Dené."

"Weren't these Cree lands?" the professor asked. "The lake is named Athabasca. Isn't that a Cree word?" A flash of anger came over me. It annoyed me that so many of the names were in Cree.

"Athabasca is a Cree word meaning 'the tall reeds growing in the Delta!' I wondered how much this so-called professor really knew. "The Cree were relatively new to this part of the country. They came with the fur trade a few hundred years ago. I never learned much Cree, but many Cree words are used because the white explorers used Cree guides and the white traders made those names stick, but they aren't the only names." You do know about the fur trade? I wanted to add.

"My ancestors were called Chipewyan by the Cree because they wore skin shirts with sort of a tail of pointed skin at the back. The Cree word Chipewyan means 'pointed skin' and the Slave River is named after the Slavies because the Cree called the Deh Cho people slaves. These lands were originally Dené lands, before the fur trade. We have been changing the names back to the Dené language when we have the chance. Have you ever studied these cultures before?" I asked.

"Well I haven't studied them in much depth. Did the Cree defeat the Dené?" he asked with a sinister smile.

"No!" I snapped back. "We fought for hundreds of years, but there was much more bloodshed during the fur trade. The Cree did not defeat us, and we did not defeat them. It was smallpox that wiped them out of this country and the Dené only survived because they went back out into the bush away from everybody." The professor seemed embarrassed, but engaged at the same time.

He asked me more about my language and the other Dené tribes. I told him, "I can understand the Deh Cho people when they speak Dené, but not people further north." I explained how my Dené ancestors were called the *Etthen Eldehi*, caribou eaters, and they still travel up to the barrens to hunt caribou.

After some lengthy explanation about our history, Professor Thomas asked me, "Do you dislike the Cree?"

I glanced at him quickly. I didn't expect that question. "No," was my first answer. "I'm part Cree," was my second. "But sometimes I think they are arrogant. Some of them think they are better than the Dené. They think of the poor northern peoples as rough and unsophisticated."

"Oh, I see," he said hesitantly.

I knew I would have to teach this guy about our culture and values before he could help us.

"Are you familiar with aboriginal values?"

"What do you mean by that?"

"Aboriginal values. Do you know what I mean when I say aboriginal values?"

"No, I can't say that I do."

"Well we have different values, different ways of looking at the world than most guys like you; guys that came from Europe. Do you understand what I mean?"

"Yes, that is a major topic in academic literature. There has been a lot written about that," he said good-naturedly.

"Shit!" I almost shouted. "Academic literature?"

"I understand that there is a lot of writing comparing us to monkeys and even birds. We are not lab rats! Academic literature's not going to help you here. You need to listen and learn because you need to know about our values before you will be able to help us. You need to know more about the way we look at the world." Was I the professor now? "For example, our idea of a clean environment is different than yours. We don't value it the same."

He stared at me. "Very good," he said. "Thank you, Katie. I will help you record those values in a way that can be communicated to us European idiots!" He laughed.

I was surprised at his reaction. He was agreeable, too agreeable. I wasn't sure I could trust him. Was he patronizing me?

He was strange. Most guys like Franklin are attracted to me – I mean they really like me, sometimes too much. I usually have to beat them off with a stick, like John Jesperson. But Franklin didn't even ask me if I was married. He seemed to like to talk to me, but he didn't flirt or anything. Was it professionalism or had I just lost my flair?

Shortly before noon, Leonard came back to the cabin to pick Dr. Franklin up.

"We have a lunch in town," Leonard announced. "You want to come, Katie?"

"I'll take a rain check," I said. "I'll see you soon." I went out to the truck to say goodbye and watched the dust settle on the driveway once again. I was doubtful that this guy would deliver what we needed and the community might not accept him. We needed to at least find someone native, maybe a Mohawk from Oka.

Savage Schools; Barbaric Country

Chapter 7

There was a lot I didn't explain to Professor Thomas—my experiences at residential school, my farm life in central Alberta. I couldn't. But somehow he needed to learn about the horrible prison-schools that tried to suppress our Dené and Cree identity.

At nine years old my sister and I were taken away in an old black Chevrolet. We were kidnapped in full view of my parents. We were stuffed in the deep backseat and told to be quiet by a man wearing a thin black tie. I wanted to jump out, but I had to protect my younger sister, who was wailing blue murder. We didn't know we were going to the residential school in Hobbema, Alberta, on a Cree Reserve.

When the agent coldly announced we were to be taken, he scowled at my mother as if she were an ignorant animal. My mother sank to her knees in agony as my father held her. We cried all the way during the six-hour drive. Mother said she never stopped crying. For the next eight years I was not permitted to speak my language or visit home, nor was I allowed to talk to my brother, even though he was in the same school. At least I escaped sexual molestation from the priests, but it seems instead they punished me more, more than other students because I was "too proud." My closest friend, Mary, wasn't so lucky.

At night she would come into my bed, get on top of me and move her hips like the priest had on her. I told her to stop. She was shy to begin with and the priest made it worse. Later, when we got older, she accused me, "He didn't touch you because you are so pretty; it was obvious you were protected."

We were all lonely, lost children longing for the loving embrace of our parents, especially us Dené children. Family has always been so important.

It was in residential school that I first was exposed to the strange ways of the white people. At Easter there was a bunny who gave out eggs. Rabbits are important to our people. We used them for meat and fur and some years they were an important staple. Even the very young children knew that rabbits did not have eggs. That was just plain weird. Birds have eggs, rabbits don't.

Everything in the white man's world seemed upside down. At the church, the rich people were the most popular. They dressed up in expensive clothes and sat in the front to listen to the priest, but they worshiped a man who wore rags. The priest told them they were sinners that they could not get into their heaven without giving up their riches. They all bowed and looked solemn. But they didn't give up their riches. If someone who looked like Christ, dressed in ragged clothes, came to their church, they scorned him and sometimes asked him to leave.

Also, the priests could not marry; they were to be celibate. But look what they did to the children in the school.

Even though mooneow is a Cree word, it is a good description of them. I began to hate church bells because they forced us to go to their upside down church. I hated the school for the punishment, the cold nuns, and the perverted priests.

I had to stay eight years at these schools and when I thought I had escaped, moving to a foster home taught me what hell really was. As I grew and developed, boys were more attracted to me. It got so they were always after me. It was like they knew I was alone-exposed, vulnerable, not protected by my family. It was in the foster home that I was raped.

Shortly after I graduated, after I was free of their clutches, I attended a junior college in Edmonton. It's easy to fall in love at twenty. I met Mark, a good looking Scottish farmer from Leduc. He told me I was the most beautiful thing he ever saw and took me home to meet his parents. I got married in a United Church in central Alberta and his family farm became my new home.

Mark was a farmer's son who didn't want to stay in school. His real love was his farm and I appreciated this. His parents pushed him to get an agriculture degree, but he claimed he learned more each day on the farm than he ever would at some sanitized school. His humility made him easy to love. His walk was a calm and determined gait with knees bent and feet splayed, and even at church I always imagined him carrying two heavy pails of feed or milk. His soul was consumed by his land and its fruits.

But in the starched rural climate of this British-based farming community, I had to struggle to maintain memories of my language and culture. At first, it was like I was on display. I was exotic, but Mark wanted me to be normal, which meant like the other stiff Scottish brides. He was really not too interested in my culture, which gave us plenty to fight about. The neighbours didn't even know what Dené was and the community's experience was with drunk Indians asking for spare change or trying to thumb a ride back to the reserve. The best image they had was when they feathered and leathered up for the rodeo and rode painted ponies in the annual parade. I kept my distance from the Cree People around Hobbema who had a plains heritage; but I was impressed by much of their formal dress which was ornate and full of the images of their culture.

When I told my neighbour, Jane, that I came from the north, she said, "Are you Eskimo?"

I tried to explain. "Eskimo is a Cree word meaning 'raw meat eater'— it's disrespectful to the Inuit People."

Jane was about thirty and had been born into this community. She married her childhood sweetheart from the farm down the road. When I moved in, she seemed happy and even excited to have a woman neighbour.

"I am Dené," I explained, "but we were called Chipewyan by the Cree. It was a Cree word which means 'pointed skins'."

"So, Dené, Cree, and Inuit are all different tribes?" she asked. She was a gentle person and I felt she would be a good friend. One day, she asked me, "Is squaw a bad word? The McMillans called you a squaw."

Squaw was one of those anglicized words that sounded like several similar words in different Algonkian languages. *Iskwew*, which is the basic word in Cree, means pretty intimate things. I was thankful she told me.

"No, squaw is not a good word," I assured her.

"Well, Katie, I think it's neat you are Dené."

Even though the other farm wives knew I was native, they seemed to be too embarrassed to ask for details. I think some of the congregation at the United Church thought or even hoped I might be from the Philippines or China. I overheard some of them talking about "lazy, drunken Indians" and I thought it might not be so bad for them to think that I was Chinese. It helped that I liked to colour my hair with a little red henna and my small amount of white heritage gave me a lighter complexion.

At first, Mark thought it was a novelty that I was native. Then, when he began to notice some of the darker attitudes, he became embarrassed, first of my mother and father, and then of my entire heritage. I tried to stay out of certain people's way and raise the kids the best I could. Sometimes it was difficult because I didn't know what normal family life was supposed to be.

When the kids got older, Mark began to be openly hostile towards me. The first time he called me a slut was after he came home drunk from the bar. Apparently, one of the other farmers got drunk and said he'd like to "fuck Mark's squaw." He said I "was probably a whore like the rest of them squaws." It drove Mark crazy. He tried to fight, but lost badly and came home hurt and angry.

One night at the local woman's bridge club, Anne White commented that the best way to deal with the "Indian problem" was to abolish the reserves and make those "lazy Indians" work for a living. The irony was that the she complained self-righteously about the treatment of blacks in South Africa or in the southern states.

I asked Anne, "How would you feel if you were not allowed to leave a reserve because you were different? How would you feel if your farmers were forced to farm on poor land and then given a subsistence allowance to survive when your crops failed?"

"We would have made it work," she replied. "We would have struggled to succeed as our homesteader grandparents did."

"So, no hardship could stop you from success, could it, Anne?" How wealth had insulated her! But I didn't go too far. If I continued, they wouldn't invite me to the bridge club anymore, so I tried to remain polite. But underneath, the damage had been done; I was a trouble maker.

After I was sharp with her, all she could say was, "I believe that our Indians are the cause of their own misfortune."

These same farm wives loved to buy the stylish parkas that I made of wool felt trimmed with wild furs. I decided not to tell them that I learned how to sew on a trap line. I just quietly sold them the coats. For some reason, during this time the kids were okay at school. There wasn't the same kind of racism. Because of Mark, our kids were half white, but it wasn't the same for me. I felt as though I had served my purpose. Now that the kids were getting older, I wasn't important.

It was after the episode at the bar that Mark started to drink heavily. I was heartbroken to see such a kind man become jealous. Maybe if he'd been big enough to beat up that bastard at the bar, it would have been different. I became an embarrassment. He wouldn't let me off the farm. I think he started to believe there was some truth to what was said about me. I tried to stay with Mark as long as I could, mostly for the kids. Eventually, Mark's drunken talk got really ugly, making fun of my cousins and parents. In the residential school they tried to tell us my culture was evil, but now I had experienced real evil, not-so-subtle racism.

After the kids got older, I enrolled at the University of Alberta, but Mark's jealousy started to interfere with my studies. He wouldn't let me take the car, and with his drinking it became too much to bear.

But until they passed Bill C 31, I couldn't go home. They wouldn't let me back on the reserve; they wouldn't let me live with my family. Because I had married Mark, the government took me off the treaty list. I lost band membership. I was no longer considered a First Nation member and was restricted from my family. The loss of the land and the way of life made orphans of the First Peoples of North America. We experienced government abuse all of our lives, but this re-enforced how important it is to belong and the importance of the land. I had to reconcile my heritage.

In my Aboriginal Law class, I studied the case of Ms. Lovelace, a native from Ontario, who had challenged the government on removing her from the treaty list because she married a white man. But it wasn't the Canadian courts that helped her. She had to take her case to the United Nations and she won. Only then did the Canadian government finally pass Bill C 31.

Because the government passed that bill, I could get back in to the band, but it took some time. What really angered me was that my male cousins who had married white women retained their status and got Indian status for their wives and children. These white women lived in our houses and voted for our councils while I had no rights.

In my course I learned the *Indian Act* was based on assimilation;

its goal was to erase the aboriginal language and culture. The government thought our culture was the basis of poverty and problems. But our poverty came from segregation on restricted lands. And even though hunting and fishing will never completely sustain us again, it's the only way I know that can make us proud again of our heritage.

And so they forced me to fight, even to go home.

Back Home?
Chapter 8

As soon as I became a member of the band again, Chief Charles gave me a job in the First Nation office. I was charged with protecting the band's traditions and negotiating with the companies. My first job was reviewing a new tar mine application which proposed to destroy my family's trap line.

One of the biggest problems was that I had to find my own funding. That was how I first met John Jesperson, the acting community liaison officer. At first, Jesperson was willing to provide a certain amount of funding. He funded my study on the effects of Royal Oil's mine on the trap lines, but I soon found out he was more interested in the payoff to get me to sign the trap line agreement. I had met men like him before, but never one as greedy and selfish.

I was most upset at how much trapping had changed since I was young. It had been quite some time since any family had been able to trap profitably. The spring muskrat hunt had ended after the hydroelectric dam dried out the delta. Then the decline in fur prices, combined with the effects of tar sands mines, forced most people off the lands. After Father's traps had washed away in the last flood, no one in my family trapped enough to replace them. Besides, trapping was even more expensive because everyone traveled by snow machine instead of dog sled. Fewer people went out on the land. Even hunting had declined and our traditional diet was cut in half. With the high cost of fresh foods in the stores, diabetes was now at epidemic levels.

The addictions of some of my friends and relatives were obvious. Some, however, were able to hide it for a while. Then they started showing up late or missing work often. I understood their brokenness, but it depressed me just the same. I think it was hardest for the men. They were once the proud breadwinners, hunters and trappers, but now they could no longer bring home their livelihood. The collapse of the trapping economy may have hit them the hardest, but the women were not spared either. They were hidden away on reserves where there were no jobs.

My goal was to reverse this process. I figured that if I helped preserve the old traditions our people would retain their self-respect and still participate in the modern job market. I had to protect and help everyone adapt, an almost impossible task with few resources. I hoped Professor Thomas would be an important resource.

Rekindling pride in our culture and language must start with the youth. I encouraged the elders to hold youth trips out to the cabins. I wanted Jesperson and Royal Oil to fund it. But now the situation with Jesperson was all screwed up.

Shortly after I took the job with the band I went out to the family cabin to plan the project. When I first got back to the cabin, there was no fire wood, and dirty dishes, garbage, and half-full cups of coffee everywhere. The cabin door had been left open and who knows which animals had been in and out looking for food or shelter. The new forestry and mining roads had brought vandalism from the outside. Normally, the trapper's code allows visitors to use the cabins, especially if it's really cold out. But they must replace the firewood and leave the cabin in as good or better shape than when they arrived.

The vandalism made me feel loneliness and fear like never before. But then I thought of the Grandfathers and how they had given special signs to Willie about me. They want me to be brave. I thought of how the Creator could help me, and soon after I started to fix the cabin up. Even though I was alone, with the help of my spiritual guides I wouldn't let this get the better of me. I filled the holes between the logs with cement, which made the cabin quite warm, even in the winter. I spruced up the inside and brought some curtains and soft bedding. I even brought my father's old 306 rifle which I had never fired. It took me several days to clean up the cabin, and then I began to gather resources for the youth program. I started to feel like it was gaining momentum when Mary called me to chat.

"How's the chief?" she asked slyly.

"He's such a playboy." I shook my head.

"You know, you *are* still sort of sexy for an old broad. Has he come on to you?"

"Mary, we're related!"

"He's your second cousin, that's far enough away," she joked. "But, if he's not good enough for you, what about the pilot? Oooh, the pilot!" Mary said.

"I went out with him the other night, you know," I bragged. "But I think I blew it."

"Oh?"

"Yeah, I took out my pills during dinner and he asked what they were. I told him it was anti-inflammatory for my arthritis. Now he thinks of me as old. I know he does."

"Nah, he probably takes them too. Don't think like that," Mary reassured me. "But he'll probably get fired from the oil company if they find out he's datin' you. Or maybe he's a spy?"

"Yeah, they probably have me on the terrorist list or something," I joked. "A terrorist youth camp, too."

"Did you hear about Phyllis's daughter, Jessie?"

"No, what now?" I grimaced.

"She's still on the street in McMurray. It's one crack house to another. If we don't do something, I don't think she'll make it."

"We can't let her freeze on the street like Jimmy's niece."

"Don't remind me," Mary interrupted.

"Well, we can't force her. What do you have in mind?"

"Maybe if we had a safe house or somethin'?" Mary suggested.

"How many youth from the village and from Chip are on the street in McMurray anyway?" I asked.

"One is too many, but there are quite a few."

"You know, Mary, Royal Oil is offering me a lot of money for that consulting contract. We could afford to set up our own safe house. Maybe we could start a healing lodge, like the one at T'suu Tina? They use Dené spiritual practices to help rekindle self-esteem."

"Just one person rescued at a time," Mary said.

"I met with Dr. Thomas, and I'm trying to get funding for the youth camp," I said.

"Listen, Katie! We need to do somethin' that'll get the government's attention. We need somethin' bigger; every time we turn around there is another problem.

"You might be right. Professor Thomas said that if we accept their money, they'll use it at the hearings to say we've been paid. An' once they're approved the money dries up."

"It's the old divide and conquer," Mary said. "They get the trap line holders to agree to a payment, then they claim you've agreed and they go runnin' to the Conservation Board sayin', 'Look what *we've* done, *we* have consulted, *we* have gotten all the trap line holders to agree. Now approve our project!' Meanwhile the rest of the First Nation loses out. If they get approved the government won't feel the need to help us either. The project approval is our only leverage."

"You're right," I agreed. I knew that Mary could sense I was getting overwhelmed.

Dressed for Battle
Chapter 9

It wasn't too long before Royal Oil invited me to a cultural sensitivity workshop. Vice President Milton James said if I did a good job they would fund more projects.

Their objective was to learn about the culture of the First Nation so that they could consult more effectively. Why did they need to learn about our culture? Just to destroy it? If they want to be sensitive, allow us to maintain it.

The day of the seminar was special. I dressed for battle in one of my best creations. It was sky blue and had a lower neckline that showed off my attributes. I did my hair up and wore a business jacket which I embroidered with my favorite eagle motif neatly above the left pocket. I was going to stand up in front of the engineers, lawyers, geologists, and MBAs and tell them I knew we were being used.

I was sure that Milt James had prepared the description of me on the workshop program. It read:

"Katie Cardinal has her Grade 12 diploma, a certificate in Cultural Studies, and a certificate in Communications from Keyano College. She speaks the Dené language and because of her qualifications, she has been selected by the elders of the community as a cultural researcher. She loves her position and is a tireless advocate of the band's interests."

"Ladies and Gentlemen, I would like to introduce Katie Cardinal, representative of the Denesulene First Nation," Milton James introduced me.

"Thank you for inviting me. I know you have come here to talk about aspects of my culture. But I have to ask you: why do you want to know about our culture? Do you honestly want to know more about us and to help us, or will holding these workshops make it easier to take our culture and livelihood from us, or to assimilate us into your society? You all know that if you continue with this mine, you will destroy our ability to continue our traditional livelihood. I want you to understand our culture to preserve it. I can't help you understand our culture if you will only destroy it."

Milt James turned from the cool, soft-spoken senior executive to a red-faced beacon. He looked like a Baptist minister whose pants had fallen down in front of the congregation.

"But Ms. Cardinal," he interrupted, "What we are doing here is holding a seminar on your people to understand you better. We are not scheduled to talk about the effects or impacts today and these are not the people that you should be talking to about these issues. This is just the beginning of consultation."

"No, Milt," I said. "All of your staff needs to know what you are doing to us. If you want cultural sensitivity, then you should understand how we feel. We have been pushed around each time you want our resources and this is just the latest instance. Why do you want to know about our culture? It won't matter how much you know about us or how sensitive you are if we have no culture and no language left. I am not interested in telling you about our culture if you are just going to destroy it. I want to discuss how we are going to preserve it."

I continued, "Tell me what your plans are for preserving our culture and language after you have destroyed our lands. Our elders will only accept your honorariums for so long. Once they find out that you will destroy the entire area, then who knows what they will do."

Milt took on a more familiar tone. "Katie, we are not prepared to discuss these issues right now. Today we have brought an anthropologist from the university to help us discuss the characteristics of the Dené and Cree peoples in this region and we thought you might be interested in assisting our group. Certainly, if we understand better, we should be able to relate to your situation. Don't you agree with that, Katie?"

"Don't patronize me, Mr. James. You have no right to deprive us of our ability to continue our culture and livelihood. And what about the pollution and disease? The courts say that consultation is more than talking. You have to change your plans to accommodate our culture, protect us from the pollution, and pay us compensation for what you destroy."

At this point, James had had enough. "Ms. Cardinal…" He motioned towards the door. "I would like to talk to you in private." This was obviously what he did when he was going to fire somebody. I stood in front of them looking into their eyes, looking for some feeling, some response to what I just said. Some looked at me as a threat to their jobs, some were sympathetic but frightened to show it, yet others probably thought I was extorting from the company. The one thing they all knew was the natives would have to move.

Outside the door, James tried to change the subject. "The chief agreed to set up some meetings with the elders and said you were the one who set them up and we have agreed to pay them three hundred dollars each as an honorarium."

"No," I said. "No. We need to have a meeting to discuss what you are going to do to preserve our way of life. If that is not what we will be discussing, then I will not participate and neither will my elders. You will not get your check mark for a three hundred dollar honorarium."

"Katie, your chief knows of this meeting and recommended that you come and we offered to pay your daily rate. Is this the correct rate?" He handed me a note with two thousand four hundred dollars written on it. Eight hundred dollars per day for three days. I just stared at him.

He finally said, "Thank you for coming. I think we should talk about this later."

I shook my head. "And now you are trying to buy me off."

"Well, John Jesperson warned me about you, that you were like this. Maybe I should have listened to him. By the way, we let Jesperson go, so you won't have to worry about him anymore." He closed the door to the meeting room and left me staring at the bare oak panels.

I stood there trying to understand what had just happened. I wondered if I had blown it. I thought about the Mohawk people who seemed to have gotten attention in Quebec by roadblocks and guns. One of the youth in town said he wanted to start a warrior society like the Blackfoot people. He said they were very spiritual. Like Mary said, it might be time for something that will get their attention. I had stood up to them but what would it lead to?

Road Block

Chapter 10

A week later, I heard a big diesel truck thumping up the logging road. I got a glimpse of the red Royal Oil logo as it passed by. The brakes hissed as it came to a lurching halt at the metal entrance gate. Last year, when they started logging, the dust from the trucks coated the dry meat that I had out over a smudge at the side of the cabin. When I complained, the logging company put up the metal gate, agreed to water the road and notify me when they were using it. But no one had given me any notices lately.

I peeked out the front door. There was a bridge or a small drilling machine on the back of the truck.

I called my son. "There's this big truck-it's right in front of my cabin."

"A loggin' truck?"

"No, it's Royal Oil. It has some equipment on the back. Looks like a bridge, or something."

"Oil company – minin'?" he asked.

"Looks like it," I said. "Now get down here as soon as possible!"

I hung up and called Mary.

"Mary, there's a mining truck in my driveway!"

"What? Already?"

"Yes." I told her.

"Shit, they haven't even finished consultin,'" Mary said.

"Maybe Royal Oil thinks they can get away with it?"

Just then, a small pickup appeared and pulled up behind the truck.

"I have to stop these trucks," I said to Mary. "I'll call you back."

I remembered that I had an old chain and lock in the shed behind the cabin that the forestry people gave to me. I lugged it out of the shed, wound the chain around the steel bars, and locked the padlock.

"That should slow them down a bit," I mumbled to myself. Then I told the dust-covered spruce tree beside the post, "Hang in there! You have the front row seat for an interesting show."

I went back to the cabin and called Mary back. "We need to demonstrate," I said. She said she'd call some people.

Two men got out of the trucks and walked around the big lowboy. One of them shouted as he reached the front, "I thought so. She locked the gate!"

"What the hell?"

"Have you got cutters?"

"Nope."

"We could ram it."

"No. Get someone to bring over some cutters."

Cutters? I thought.

My heart was thumping fast. I knew this could get ugly.

I tried to think of people I could call. Even if the chief agreed to participate, he would be the first one arrested and he knew it. I called Eleanor, then my son again, and even Leonard. It wasn't too long before everyone began to show up.

We parked around the lowboy truck so it couldn't move forward. Then David sat on the metal gate holding a long wooden staff. He shouted, "Who wants to film me knocking them out with my stake?"

Mary looked at me in a panic. "Katie, gimme your phone."

I yelled back to David, "You just stand there and don't move. We don't want to hurt anyone."

I had about ten friends and relatives milling around the gate. The drivers sat tight in the truck frantically calling for help. Soon, another Royal Oil pickup arrived. At first it was beetling up the road quickly kicking up plenty of dust, but then slowed to a crawl.

Both workmen got out of the truck. They strolled nervously up to David.

"Hey," one of them offered.

"Hello," David responded.

"What's up?" The driver asked.

"You can't take that equipment on to Katie's trap line," David replied.

The driver looked around again at the trucks, cars and our group and glanced towards me. David and Eleanor were standing in front of the gate glaring at him. Everyone else circled around them.

"We have the right to enter that lease," he said.

"No you don't," said Mary. "Your company must consult with our First Nation and you haven't. You haven't even consulted with the trap line owner."

The driver looked at the other and shook his head. They whispered something.

"I guess we'll see about that. I guess we are gonna have to call the cops," said the driver. "And you're blockin' us in. Vehicles are pulled up so close, we can't move."

"We want to talk to Milt James," said Mary.

They stared at her, surprised she knew the name of their vice president and scurried back to their truck, pulling out their cell phones.

Illegal Acts
Chapter 11

"We must report illegal acts like this to the board of directors," Royal Oil's Operations VP, Jed Westerlund, whined as he and Milt James looked out at the Rocky Mountains from their 25th floor office in Calgary.

"It's not a big deal; they are only blocking a few bore holes. It's hardly gonna postpone our development schedule," James argued.

"I'm calling the chairman; the board is meeting today." Westerlund's engineering background reinforced his desire to follow the rules. He waited, tapping his fingers on the desk while the receptionist connected him to the boardroom.

"Jed, you there?" drawled the Oklahoma chairman. "We're havin' a break. Just me an' Guss Frame here."

"Yeah, I'm here with Milt and we have a small problem. One of the native groups set up a roadblock to our new lease."

"Oh, the authorities'll break it up?"

"Well no, we haven't called them yet. We don't want it to escalate into an all-out turf war. They say we haven't consulted enough."

"Those Goddam terrorists," interjected Guss, a new board member representing an investment group out of Texas.

"We don't want to involve the police just yet." James explained. "I'm sure we can negotiate with the chief and provide some kind of program that will satisfy them. We have been negotiating with them for some time, but just recently one of their members has been asking for more consultation."

"Just one of 'em?" asked Guss.

"Well she represents a larger group, but she has some new ideas."

They could overhear Gus talking to the Chairman. "It's simple. Ya just get rid of thar leader and the rest of 'em will fold. Remember what happened to them Democrats fer years after the Kennedys were shot – they was lost in the wilderness. We did it in Africa too. Just get rid of thar leader."

They heard the Chairman whispering, "No, Guss, James is okay. He'll fix this." He raised his voice, "Okay. Jed and Milt, thanks for informing us. Go ahead and do what you have to do."

Victory
Chapter 12

Early next morning, we were outside the cabin talking about the guys who had been camped out in their truck.

"They said they'd call the cops," said Eleanor.

"Yeah, where's the cops?" David asked.

"I guess we sent a message," I said.

"You think this might help us make some progress?" asked Mary.

"I hope so. But what good is it, really? They talk to us, maybe give us some money, and then destroy the entire countryside."

We all looked down the driveway at an SUV pulling up to the cabin. "Maybe that's the VP?" David said sarcastically.

It parked beside my truck. A short fellow with blond hair jumped out holding a notebook.

"It's the newspaper," Mary said with relief.

The reporter politely introduced himself. We explained everything. He took a picture and hung around by the campfire for a while. As we were talking, I got a call from Jesperson.

"What's going on?"

"What do you want? You've been fired."

"No thanks to you," he scoffed. "I'm thinking maybe if I help the company with this, they will take me back," he added.

"I don't care what you do, but I should talk to the Vice President myself."

"Okay, okay," he said. "I'll set up a meeting this afternoon or tomorrow, whenever you like."

"But I'm not meeting with you, Jesperson. We need to meet with the vice president, Milt James."

"I'll try," he replied, "But there may be no need." He told me that he'd heard that the company had already decided to shut down that lease operation until we had talked with them. Royal Oil was going to make an announcement.

"The roadblock worked!" I said, holding my hand over the phone. "So that's how it works. Maybe we just have to assert ourselves."

I called the head office of Royal Oil, but I couldn't get through. Just then, the reporter came to the door. "Have you heard?" he asked.

"Heard what?"

"On the radio. The company has announced that they'll be shutting down all operations on the new leases until they've finished consultation with you," he said triumphantly.

I smiled and went outside. David stood up and cheered, "We won!" he said. "Sometimes road blocks can be fun."

They all got in their cars and trucks and left smiling. I was relieved but I knew this was just the beginning.

Protecting the Treaty
Chapter 13

"As long as the sun shines and the river flows ..." Chief Charles began to grumble, "Where are we going to get that kind of money?"

"Charles!" I glared at my second cousin. "The elders want us to protect our way of life." I probably should have been more sensitive; our people needed jobs and a new economy.

Not everyone could compete in this new world. But I remembered how his grandmother made fun of him for playing golf with the company presidents. So maybe it was best that I was short with him.

"Call me when you have a good lawyer," I told him. "I'm going to my cabin this weekend." With that, I walked out the door of the band office and got into my truck.

Charles was a good man, but he was convinced the oil sands plants were inevitable. He had fought the battle and decided it was time to get some money for his people.

At the Royal Oil offices in Fort McMurray, after flying up in their corporate jet from Calgary that morning, the executives were waiting for Chief Charles to arrive.

Jed Westerlund was responsible for implementing the contracts with the native communities. He had been working as a project engineer for major oil companies for his entire career and had worked his way up the corporate ladder. He had a reputation for getting the job done, but now in his fifties, he looked like a candidate for a heart attack. His fellow VP, Milton James, was a smaller man, a lawyer with dark hair. He looked much younger in his well-pressed suit.

Jed Westerlund was on the phone with Guss Frame. Frame had spent the last ten years building his energy security investment fund in Texas. His investors were Americans intent on protecting the US oil supply from unstable oil rich OPEC nations. They had made a big leap of faith in investing such a large portion of their capital in the oil sands, but he felt their other options were limited. He was sure the Canadian oil sands represented the main source of long term energy security for the US. He felt that the only major threat was global warming nonsense, and there was nothing dirty about this oil; it just cost more to produce.

Westerlund was getting a lecture. "Yes, the oil sands are the most secure source of oil for the US market. I know … no Iraq, no jihad … it just gets a little cold up here. No … these Indians … er … natives are not terrorists! The government requires us to consult with them before we get our operations permit. We didn't want to escalate the conflict by involving the police … No."

James overheard the voice on the other end of the phone shouting, "We put two billion dollas inta your company, and I don't care if those fuckin' Indians are terrorists or not. We ain't gonna let some half-hippies threaten the energy security of the United States of America. Christ, we got the Vice President of the United States comin' up thar next week! It's your responsibility to fix this problem, mista. Ya know what I'm sayin?"

"We'll handle it Sir … yes … it'll be okay. Thanks … will speak to you soon. Bye."

"Whew!" Westerlund said as he hung up the phone. "That guy is scary."

"This situation could get out of hand," James added. "We have to deal with the natives ourselves, because if that group gets involved, all hell will break loose. How did they elect that guy to the board anyway?"

"It's an American energy security fund. A group from the southern states and this Texan has been hired to run it."

"Well, what are we gonna do about the project delays, then?"

"It's just a matter of how much we are willing to give, right Milt? But we could make it uncomfortable for them, too. We just have to watch out for another violent situation," Westerlund brooded.

"It's blackmail," James complained. "The natives threaten us to get what they want and consultation isn't even the company's responsibility. The government should be dealing with this. It is *their* responsibility to consult to deal with these people."

"Fat chance we'll get any support from those government marshmallows. We have to do what it takes. If the government wants us to consult, then we're going to have to consult. The question is how far do we have to go?" He added, "But maybe we need to enforce *our* rights. A little violence would be better than an endless standoff. Just call the cops and get it over with." He smiled insincerely.

"That is what that new director from Texas wants us to do?" asked James.

"Yeah, it reminds me of the eighties," Westerlund continued, "when the apartheid strategy paper was leaked. What a mess that was. You talk about violence; the whole world was stoking the flames; they were really out for blood. The company decided to go on the offensive and try to support the South African government."

"I remember reading about it," James said. "The company attacked the clergy's position and funded pro-apartheid newspapers."

"Yeah, something like that. What a mistake that turned out to be. We were lucky someone wasn't killed. In South Africa, it was the international pressure that was mounting and companies were withdrawing like mad. We can't let environmental paranoia take a hold of us, or we're finished." warned Westerlund.

"And this dirty oil talk could get out of hand with the US and European environmentalists. This oil may take a bit more fuel to produce but we can always get rid of excess CO_2 by pumping it into old gas wells. We need to make sure everyone knows about the half a billion the Alberta government just gave to industry for that type of carbon sequestration. We've got to get the media back on track." James said.

"It reminds me of how the South Africa boycott began and now especially with the Gulf spill. Well, it could get nasty—a media circus." Westerlund shook his head.

"All we need is for this to blow. And now with Frame on our board, we have to be careful. No, we've got to deal with this quietly; we have to consult, but there is a limit."

Westerlund squinted at James, "Have you ever heard a Baptist swear like that before?"

Chief Charles arrived thirty minutes late. The secretary announced his arrival.

Westerlund ignored the fact that he was so late.

"Chief," began Westerlund. "What are we going to do about Katie? She could cause a lot of trouble, you know."

The chief looked surprised at Westerlund's boldness. He had come to talk about the business contracts, not Katie's trap line.

"Well, she has the faith of the elders and she is right. She hasn't been consulted and neither has the First Nation."

"You don't consider those contracts enough consultation, Charles?" replied Westerlund.

Charles knew Katie was making these guys sweat. He needed to keep his band companies alive, and Westerlund knew it.

"Aren't those contracts we promised you enough?" echoed James.

"Well, we need to do some environmental studies and include traditional knowledge in your mine planning. Katie is serious and the only way you're going to make headway is to provide her with what she needs. She has a lot of community support." Charles didn't feel like he was convincing.

"I'm not so sure that more studies will do it, Charles. She was pretty direct in the cultural sensitivity meeting we had, and now the road block on the lease. That was a good one! She says the land use study we proposed isn't enough. She's asking that we include a full effects assessment, but a study that big would delay the plant for a year or more. It's the government's responsibility to do that anyway. It involves all of the other companies, and there are at least ten others. And if the effects assessment shows that there must be compensation, we could be delayed indefinitely. That could mean our jobs and more layoffs. What if the government just won't compensate? Then where are we? This way you get lucrative contracts and we get our operations approved. It's better than both of us going under, don't you think?"

"Well, I'll talk to her, but I don't know how successful I'll be," responded the chief. "I can't control her and the elders support her. I really don't see a solution to this except to do the studies as quickly as possible."

"What about if we were to arrange for her to have a business with a very lucrative contract; then with the money she could support whatever charity she wanted? We'll make her another offer," Westerlund proposed.

The chief looked disgusted. "I don't think she'd go for that." He knew that was the way they thought. "If you're thinking you can buy her off, it won't work. She already feels compromised."

Westerlund got more serious. "You know, if this project is delayed, it will cost us about five million per day. So, if she causes a delay of three and a half months, just the interest alone amounts to about 15 million dollars. A delay of one year would be 60 million dollars, assuming costs don't skyrocket again. It might take us a year to do the assessment. Milt said Katie sounded more like she wanted to stop the project indefinitely. We can't afford a delay, much less cancellation."

Westerlund paused. "You know what that means for us and you know what we can do for you and your businesses. But until we can find a solution to this, we can't give you these contracts. How much money have you spent on support equipment so far? You can't afford to lose these contracts, chief. Let's set up a meeting for next week? Okay? And then we will have a solution."

The chief just stared at him.

Then Milton James started. "Contracts for 100 million dollars over 5 years; contracts for camps and road maintenance. Isn't that worth something to your band? Isn't that enough?" He stood up from the board room table and looked back at Chief Charles.

Before, they just dreamed about contracts, businesses and royalties. Now they had the opportunity. He shouldn't let it be spoiled by stubbornness. The chief had a sick feeling. He wasn't sure about anything anymore.

What Should I do?
Chapter 14

Shortly after the meeting, the chief gave me a call. "Katie, you have to make a deal." He sounded desperate.

Just what I don't need, I thought. My spirit was tired.

The chief continued his appeal. "What can I do? You have really started something. It's not like before when we had nothing to lose. Now we have invested all of that money in equipment. The band needs economic development too."

"I don't know, Charles. All I can say is that you know these projects will kill us if we don't fight back. The treaty says, *"As long as the sun shines and the rivers flow."* I don't want to sound like a broken record, but it *is* a broken promise, another broken promise."

"What do you want me to do Katie?" he asked.

"Okay, I'll tell you what. Go to the press and the government. Mary says the government is the one ultimately responsible for consultation."

"I can call the minister again and I will ask for consultation and money. But I know he will give me the same run around as before. When they say no, then what do I say? Do I threaten them? What if the companies really take away our contracts? Our businesses will go broke. Then what do we do?"

"We need to hire a lawyer." I really didn't know if it would work, but it sounded good.

I had come home just in time to fight the same forces that took me to residential school, the same forces that were threatening my language and culture, my family, and my health. Now I was on the front line. Elder Grandlegs had been right. No wonder it is difficult to get people to stand up and fight. I could roll over and accept the contracts, take the money and let my people be dragged through the oil pits and gutters of Fort McMurray. On the other hand, I could fight back.

Personal Strength

Chapter 15

As I entered Mother's cozy kitchen, I smelled the moose meat on the stove. The house was much like it had been when I was young, and it was so comforting to come home to that aroma. "Mmm, that meat smells good!" I whispered as I leaned over the pan. Mother put her arm around my shoulders.

"*Jamison was out hunting and he brought us some,*" she said in Dené. Elder Jamison always shared his hunts with the elders.

"*It's good you have come back to your people, Katie,*" she said after I got settled at the table. "*No one else can give Charles backbone. I am proud of you.*"

This was so good to hear.

"*They think of people like you as trouble makers, but you are just telling the truth,*" she assured me. "*Just remember, when these oil companies are gone, we will still be here. We have been here for thousands of years without them and will be here for thousands more.*"

She smiled and her eyes danced. "*Katie, you are our Than-ad-el-thur. Remember her strength, remember her courage. You were kidnapped like her and you have come back to help us.*"

I answered in Dené.

"*Mom, I think I need to rest. I have been taking these new pills. And this week has been quite emotional. They have been trying everything to get me to change the demands. I'm really not standing up to the pressure and I don't feel like I know what I'm doing. They claim that they do not have to do what we are asking. They claim it is the government's duty, not theirs. They say proper consultation will delay their plant. I don't know what to do."*

"*Keep going Katie. You are doing the right thing,*" Mother reassured me.

"*I am going up to the cabin over the weekend. Would you like to come?*" I really wanted the company.

"*Sorry, I can't come this weekend. I have to tend to Auntie Mable. But I am glad you're taking some time for yourself. We will come over on Monday, in two days, okay?*"

"*This new stuff,* Troxin; *the doctor gave it to me. I have been taking it for a while and I get heartburn from it.*"

"*I have better medicine for you,*" she said. "*When we come to the cabin, we will prepare some medicine from the land. White man's medicines are not natural. Your Auntie Mable will come too, she knows what to fix.*"

That evening, looking out the window, I saw the metal gate still with the padlock on.

"Mary, is that you?"

"Yes." Mary was cooking and held the phone on her shoulder.

"Mary, I am looking at the gate."

"Katie! I thought you were gonna take a break."

"How can I, when the moment I get back to the cabin I see the lock on the gate? What's going to happen?"

Mary agreed that the chief wouldn't support me once the companies cut the contracts.

"Well, what more can I do? We need to bring this to a head; we can't have the First Nation businesses go broke. Can't we go to court and stop them from doing anything until they have consulted."

"I'll need to ask that lawyer, Jake Maurice. I think there might be a way."

"Good, this mess needs to be sorted out. I have heartburn and I can't sleep. Even when I drink milk, I can't get rid of it. I woke up last night 'cause I thought I heard another truck." I paused before changing the subject. "Can't we get the government to do *something?*"

"It is not really clear who is doin' what. Havin' the companies do the consultation is like askin' the fox to watch the chickens," Mary added.

Mary didn't hold up much hope. Suddenly her voice softened.

"Katie, I'm so glad you are back. It's about time someone stood up to those companies. They've had their way with us for so long."

"Thank you, Mary." I said. "It is nice to be appreciated for doing what I have to do."

I heard a truck outside.

"I'll call you back. I think I hear something outside."

The next day, Katie's mother called Mary. "Mary? I call Katie but she don't answer," she said in English. "You talk to her? No? Somethin'srong."

Mary called Chief Charles.

"Mary! Yes it's horrible. Leonard found her at her cabin. They think it was a heart attack," he said softly.

"Is she alive?" Mary screamed.

"No."

"Oh God, no!" Mary shrieked, "No, it was just heartburn. She just lay down for a rest. Why... Katie, of all people? It isn't right."

Mary fell silent. Then she said, "She said she heard a truck. Who visited her last night?"

The chief continued to explain, "The doctor said that this anti-inflammatory has caused heart attacks before, but they didn't take it off the market."

"What?"

"They didn't take it off the market?" repeated the chief.

"You mean it was poison? They let Katie take it!" Mary shouted through the phone at the chief.

Then she remembered.

"She said she got free samples. Free!" Mary couldn't believe it.

"Yup, that's what I heard too," the chief confirmed.

"That's murder," Mary clenched her fists.

"I don't think she got the free stuff from the doctor. I bet it was the drug company."

"Dr. Smyth plays golf with Milt James." Then she recoiled. "Don't you play golf with them too?"

"Mary, you are always thinking the worst. These guys aren't murderers." The chief sheepishly shook his head.

She didn't stop. "Katie told me she heard a truck pull up to her cabin last night. Where were you?"

"Come on Mary. This is ridiculous."

"The companies told you they would lose up to one billion dollars if the project was delayed for a year, didn't they? Don't you think it's convenient? Who else is here in the First Nation who can defend our rights like Katie? We need to find out who visited her last night," she said.

"They should do an autopsy," the chief half-heartedly suggested.

"Katie's mother will not allow that. She will not use white man's methods. "

"I really don't think someone murdered Katie," the chief tried to counter. "Maybe someone's job or career was on the line, but those guys wouldn't go as far as murder," he said. "Mary, I will call you back later." He hung up and hoped that she would calm down a bit over the next few hours.

Who Can Help?

Chapter 16

Mary called him back the next morning.

"Well, Charlie, I guess we will never know whether it was murder or natural causes, but now there is no one left to defend us," Mary started. "I feel so bad, not only for Katie, but for our entire region. Since you are so involved with the companies, we will have to find someone else who can help us. So watch out, Mr. Businessman."

"Okay, Mary," the chief still didn't know what to say when confronted with Mary's feelings.

Mary continued, "We can work up a consultation case against the companies. But don't get in the way, Charlie. You'll get your business, but we need to protect our rights. Wasn't Katie working with that Thomas guy?"

"Yeah, I met Thomas when he was up here talking to her. He is a good man," Chief Charles said.

"She trusted him," Mary agreed. "I will call him."

A few hours later after talking to almost everyone in the community about Katie's passing, Mary was on the phone to Edmonton.

"Hello, is Dr. Thomas there?"

"Yes, it's me."

"This is Mary Cardinal, I have some bad news."

"About Katie?" he guessed. "Willie called me."

"Oh, the moccasin telegraph. Yes, it is a tragedy. She was such a benefit to the community and her family is devastated, especially her mother"

"I am so sorry."

"Yes, everyone is upset. Dr. Thomas, are you coming up to the funeral?"

"Yes, I am. When is it?"

"I'm not sure but … well, when you come up … well, … we were wonderin' under the circumstances if you would think about helpin' us again."

"Certainly I would consider helping but I don't have much time these days."

"Yes, I know it took a lot of time. Wasn't Katie recording traditional hunting? And don't we need to record the information for the lawyers?"

"You know, one of my students is quite interested in doing the type of work that Katie was talking about."

"A student?"

"Yes, she is quite motivated. She can record the data and she can learn about your community as she goes. She was to go up to Fort Chipewyan but she'll help you too-help you record the data for the lawyers."

Mary was unconvinced. "Don't ya have someone more experienced? You say she's still in school and has only worked for First Nations in the summers."

"Well, I could supervise her, but I don't have time to come up to help."

"Thank you, Dr. Thomas. We'll talk when you get up here." She hung up.

Mary shook her head. "We get a young student girl? And the companies have the top lawyers, engineers and business managers on their payroll. We're getting' a young student who knows nothin'."

Then she started to feel guilty. "It is too early after Katie's passin' for us to even be talkin' about this anyway!" she said to herself in frustration.

Mary called Jake Maurice, an aboriginal lawyer out of Manitoba. She had been looking for an opportunity to get him working for them, and now maybe the chief would listen.

"You will have to teach her," Jake told Mary after she explained what she wanted to do. "She will work up in Fort Chip and we'll teach her. I will talk to Chief Mercredi about it today."

Mary was doubtful. "It won't work without Katie. Maybe if Professor Thomas would change his mind and come up and support this thing."

Mary began to think again about her best friend, her cousin, and death. She started to wonder if Katie had been murdered and if even she herself was in danger. If she took over some of Katie's responsibilities, would they come after her? And what would this new inexperienced student bring to the communities? Would they go after her too?

The Wake
Chapter 17

I am a professor in the field, but Katie had challenged and changed my understanding of what culture really was. I owed a great debt to her courage. I made plans to go to the wake and funeral as soon as I heard the news. University profs can't always get away, but Cormack agreed to take my classes while I flew up to the wake. It was hard to believe that she was gone.

I took a window seat on a small jet from Edmonton to the bustling Fort McMurray. I had always been in awe of the millions of spruce, jackpine, and aspen in the expanse of northern Canada's forests. Through the porthole window, my sunglasses took the glare off the painted barns of tidy farms and pioneer houses.

As we flew north, the farms became fewer and gradually there were no houses, no farms, no roads. But this land was not untouched. Evenly spaced rectangular strips of fresh green growth appeared where the trees had been cut for oil exploration seismic lines.

Finally, once the seismic lines stopped, we passed over a few miles of original dark green boreal trees. Groups of dark blue lakes broke the dense forest terrain. For a moment, I allowed myself to think that this might be what a land without man would be like, but then I remembered what Katie said. "This land was never *terra nullius*! That was just a legal excuse to claim sovereignty from the people who lived in the forest. Don't think like your European ancestors, Frank." She would say, "The early explorers didn't see the moose, woodland caribou, and black bears, either."

Further north, perfectly straight exploration cut-lines appeared again, showing another likely place for oil. These industrial intrusions into the land reminded me why I was asked to come up here.

Katie was my age; too young to die. At fifty-five she was the youngest elder in her First Nation. I didn't even suspect she had a heart condition; she never mentioned it. She was slim and pretty and she appeared to be in shape. Her death was such a tragedy, and just when she started to make a difference. Because of her work, some people were not sad to see her go. That got me thinking. I needed to find out what had been going on since I left three months ago. Something didn't fit.

As we approached Fort McMurray, I saw the Athabasca River, and a newly paved portion of highway with a long cleared area beside it, an oil pipeline right of way. Then I saw the glacially-etched and unusually deep Clearwater Valley that stretched, as I well knew, out of Alberta and into Saskatchewan. I saw Fort McMurray, a cluster of buildings and houses crowding the junction of the Clearwater, Athabasca, and Hangingstone Rivers (in Cree, *Nistawyou*, 'Where Three Rivers Meet.'

As the jet circled to land, we flew north of McMurray over a landscape that looked like the surface of the moon. In the middle of huge, dirty dark pits, there was a city of silver refinery towers covered with lights. There was a tall stack flaring natural gas and large tanks, which must be full of oil.

The first time I came here, I came because of Katie. She had known the aboriginal names of the rivers and lakes. She had known the old trails. She had been dedicated to her people and their use of the land. But now it was too late to ask Katie the names of the rivers or lakes. She had been silenced. Katie would be sorely missed.

Jeanne Phillips, a community liaison worker with Royal Oil, had been asked to pick me up at the airport. She worked for the oil sands mining company that financed Katie's land use project. I trained Katie for that project. Trained her? Sometimes I think it was she who trained me.

"Professor Thomas?" A tall slim woman wearing sneakers, blue jeans, and a Royal Oil black jacket called my name. We had agreed to meet at the car rental stand at the airport.

"It's nice to meet you. I'm Jeanne Phillips."

I grinned back, "Nice to meet you too."

We shook hands. Jeanne seemed nervous. She guided me out the automatic airport doors to a small, light blue car, which was dwarfed by the muddy pickup trucks and courtesy vans parked around it.

"Such a small car," I commented.

"Yes, it was all I could get today," she apologized.

"Well, I guess it'll have to do. But it isn't paved all the way out!" I said.

"Yeah? This is my first time driving up there, I thought it was paved." Jeanne sounded nervous. I tried to hide my alarm, but I shuddered at the thought of driving on back roads in this little tin can with an inexperienced driver. Reluctantly, I threw my luggage into the hatchback and settled into the passenger seat.

As we drove through the city of Fort McMurray, I let my mind drift off and thought about Katie's family, her work, her goals, and dreams of protecting the environment against oil development. I thought of her mother's house in the village. After a few minutes, my attention was dragged back to Jeanne, who was driving slowly, right on the centre line. Cars were whizzing past, close enough to kiss the side of the car.

"Did you know Katie well?" I asked, willing myself not to think of Jeanne's driving.

"Actually, not well at all," she replied. "I had just been reassigned to her project. I only met her once."

"Oh!" I was surprised. "Have you ever been to a wake before?"

"Ya know, this will be my first time." She started to look uncomfortable again.

"They usually have an open coffin," I said, clutching the plastic handle above my right shoulder.

"Really?" she said. "Christ! I could do without that. Dead bodies give me the creeps."

Just then, she turned into a sharp curve in the highway. As she looked over at me to ask another question, I saw a large truck, heaped with long, rough-cut logs coming right at us. It was going too fast. I could see it was having trouble making the turn and the truck's load was leaning far into our lane. I reached over and pulled the steering wheel firmly, jerking the car to the side of the road. A blast from the truck's horn rang in our ears and fell in pitch as the truck barreled past at high speed.

"That was close!" I gasped. I saw the panic in Jeanne's eyes and added a little humour: "We could have been crushed like a Japanese aluminum beer can."

We stopped for a few minutes. She was white as a sheet and was happy when I asked if I could drive. I took over the wheel.

"So, why exactly are you going to the wake?" I asked. "I'm sure it would be enough to just attend the funeral."

"My former boss, ya know, John Jesperson? He got fired, but the company has to be represented, so I got the file. I'm working in the human relations department, ya know, so they figure I know something about native people, but Jesperson was the one who was dealing with them. He said he knew Katie well.

"Ya know, honestly, I'd like it if you'd drop me off at that gas station over there. I could just go to the funeral. I'm sure you're right about that. You could pick me up in a couple of hours when you're on your way back. I'll be just fine here and I'll have something to eat while I'm waiting." I stopped the car and she got out, waving as she walked away.

It wasn't long before I got to the WaPaSu village and drove down the main road following the river, looking for Katie's mother's house. I had been there before and it was easy to spot. The small reserve houses were spread out with dirt or gravel driveways. There were no address numbers, but each house had a view and access to the river. The village had one store and gas station beside the band office.

There was Katie's old blue and white house. At least it had been blue when it was painted twenty years ago. There were cars and trucks all around the house. I stopped by the side of the crudely paved road and started to walk towards their house through the overgrown weeds and tall grass. As I approached, I recognized Mary Cardinal standing in the side yard talking to two men. She noticed me coming up, broke off her conversation and walked towards me.

"Professor Thomas. It is good of you to come. Katie's mother and family will appreciate it very much," she assured me.

"Hello Mary, thank you. I needed to come. It was so shocking. I thought a lot of Katie and this is so tragic."

Mary asked me to come in to the small living room where the body was displayed. It was dark and full of local people, all sitting around on old wooden chairs or on the old green couch and arm chair. Some were sitting on the floor around the coffee table and some were standing in the entrance to the kitchen.

I have heard that some wakes are celebrations and some are drunken parties for drowning grief, but this wake was neither of these. It was a solemn gathering filled with respect for the family and for life and death. But there was an uncomfortable feeling of familiarity with the occasion. How many times had these same people attended a funeral for a friend or family member?

I slid in just far enough to offer my condolences to Katie's mother, who was sitting in the middle of the couch, embraced by what looked like her three sisters. She nodded to me and mustered a smile. Her leathered skin barely moved as her mouth formed the mild expression. She looked at me as if to say, "I am old and wrinkled. Look at me. I should have died before my daughter."

Even with the weight of emotion, she remembered me. She had cooked a moose steak for Katie and me about a year earlier, the last time I had been here.

After speaking to a few familiar people, I walked through the room and back out the door, passing by the grey lifeless body, face covered in makeup. It looked vaguely like Katie, but her beauty was dulled-no longer a vibrant vivacious figure, no more electrifying spirit, only a shell, an empty vessel. It was finality, verification. Her strong spirit was gone. I felt an unusual sensation of anxiety, almost wanting to cry, but I did not have enough emotional permission to do so. I thought of all she had been through and I wondered what would happen to the causes she had worked for. I felt empty.

Fresh air helped to cleanse me of death's presence. I noticed Mary standing by a fire out in the yard beside a fellow with long braided hair and a plaid jacket. He was telling Mary something in a raised and passionate voice. I went closer.

"I tell ya, Mary, those dams are full of it," he said. "I saw 'em dump the stuff in an' cover it up, just like that, just like they were emptyin' the garbage. Only this stuff was toxic. It was all the used oil drums filled with who knows what. An' my boss said it'd make good ballast for the dyke."

Mary's eyes opened wide. "When did this happen?" She asked.

"About ten years ago, when I first got a job with the mine. They were buildin' those dykes then, before people were so worried about the environment."

As I walked up, I just nodded to Mary. I did not want to interrupt because I was interested in what he was saying, too. I looked at

Mary to see how she was reacting. Was this guy a credible witness? I didn't know him, but I respected Mary's opinion.

"Well," Mary looked deep in thought. "Those PCBs will eventually seep into the water table too, like the other 10,000 liters of sludge escaping from the tar ponds." She shook her head.

"Yeah," said the man, whose weathered and wrinkled face belied his age. "If I was a gamblin' man, I'd bet Katie was murdered."

Mary's face dropped and she turned and walked away into the back yard.

I introduced myself. "Hello, I'm Frank Thomas." I held out my hand. The man held his hand out slowly and touched my hand with the tips of his fingers.

"I heard you talking about the dumping of toxic waste in a dyke. Where was that?"

"Hello, Mr. Thomas, I'm Willie. Willie Grandlegs. It was here. They dumped it to make that dyke on the other side of that mine pit, between the river and the tailin's pond. Back then they didn't think of cancer and the environment."

"You saw them?" I asked.

"Yup." He looked up directly into my eyes. "I helped 'em do it. It was my job. I was a worker. I told Katie about it too and she said she would do somethin' about it. But I guess it's too late now, God bless her soul."

"Do you know what was in the barrels?"

"Yup, PCB and old oil. Anythin', chemicals they had left over that they didn't want."

"Well did Katie have a file on it?" I asked.

"Yup" He looked me straight in the eye again. "An' I told her about it an' she wrote it down."

"We can't let this go; we will have to follow up."

"You think that'll happen?" He leaned over closer to me and whispered. "No sir, I think it's too late. People would rather live somewheres else than suffocate in bad chemicals. No, there's two types; the ones that stay and fight and the other ones, the ones that are gonna stay alive."

He exhaled and looked around.

"But there's another way." He continued. "I heard that some of the young people talkin' to the Blackfoot, askin' them about that Old Man River dam gunfight. But that's a young man's battle." He stood up straight.

"Anyways, it's time for me to go." And with that he walked slowly towards the road. After a few steps he turned back for a moment and said. "Good-bye, Mister, it was nice t' meet you."

"Mr. Grandlegs?" I ran after him. "You said you thought Katie was murdered."

He turned and paused. "Yes. I do."

"How so?" I asked.

"A *Whi-ti-koh*," he whispered.

I didn't understand what he had said. He paused and looked and squinted at me.

"She was takin' drugs for her arthritis. They say the drugs were bad, they caused heart problems. I think that Jesperson had some-thin' to do with it. He is a *Whi-ti-koh*." Without hesitation, he turned and walked towards a 4X4 truck.

Jesperson? Jeanne's boss, the one that was fired. I remembered that Jeanne had wondered about him too.

I followed him to his truck. "You think they would murder her because she knew about a toxic dump?" I asked.

"No, she would have changed things and they knew it. They killed her because of their greed. The greed of the *Whi-ti-koh*. I know this. I have been told about Katie's power."

"Told?"

"Yes, told."

"Who told you?"

"I've heard about you too. They talk about a northern man with white hair."

"What-who is they?" I was confused.

"The Grandfathers. You seem like a good man; Katie spoke well of you. You must come to a ceremony. Katie didn't come to the ceremony and look what happened to her."

He closed the truck door, started it and drove off.

I had heard about their ancestor worship; the grandfathers and the spirits in the northern lights. She was murdered by a *Whi-ti-koh*? I thought about all what he had said, about the toxic waste, murder and drugs. I was sure there were many secrets in a major project like this. But no one would murder her just because she knew about a toxic dump, would they? Yes, she was causing trouble with the mine approvals, but there had to be a better motive.

I wished the elder had not left. I wanted to ask him more about the Old Man River gunfight he mentioned and what the Blackfoot youth were up to. That could be dangerous. I remembered meeting the guy who organized it, just about a year ago at the Calgary Stampede. And I remembered reading something in the papers about a demonstration on the Old Man River dam. Somebody got shot or he fired a rifle?

Mary came back to warm herself in front of the fire.

"Elder Grandlegs said that Katie was taking drugs." I turned my head slightly sideways.

"Drugs, no. Prescription, yeah," she said, as tears welled up in her eyes and she put her hands over her face.

I felt awkward, but I held out my arms anyway. She put her head on my shoulder.

"She was the one," Mary cried. "She was our hope."

"Yes." I agreed.

"I can't do it without her." Mary looked at me with black makeup running down her cheeks. "What are we going to do?"

"Mary … Katie was special. I can't deny that, but others can take up where she left off."

"But she had respect. Yeah, I know stuff, but I don't have the respect she had. I loved her so much. She was my best…" She started to sob so much she could not speak. I pulled her to my shoulder again.

"You have survived difficult times before, Mary, and you will come out of this too."

"Katie was strong and beautiful," Mary sobbed.

I tried to console her. "Yes, Katie used all of her powers to protect her people. But you have strengths she did not have, like a law degree. I can get someone else from the university to help you."

Mary looked up at me again and smiled through her wet eyes. "I know you'll try and help. But those drugs that Willie mentioned—her doctor wouldn't prescribe bad drugs."

She shook her head, turned and walked away again; back towards the woods behind the house. I said nothing and watched her disappear behind the tree trunks.

After standing by the fire alone for a while, I decided to go back to see how Jeanne liked the greasy spoon restaurant. I would see everyone again at the funeral tomorrow. I felt strangely guilty. Maybe I should have made more time for Katie instead of leaving her to do her job alone. But now Katie is gone, I have another chance. They have asked me to help them again.

Meeting at the Stampede
Chapter 18

It was just over one year before Katie's death that Miss Miriam Robinson accompanied Dr. Franklin Thomas to her first professional meeting in Calgary.

I guess it's because I grew up in Calgary that I don't like the city during Stampede. But, as a good student, I had to stay to accompany Dr. Thomas to his meeting with Edwin Horsetalker, a counselor from the Piikani First Nation of southern Alberta. Driving down Macleod Trail in the middle of the Calgary Stampede required determination and patience. If the traffic didn't drive you nuts, it was impossible to get around the long lines of hungover office workers dressed as cowboys, waiting for their free pancake breakfasts.

Every business in town would fire up a grill on the street just outside of their office and serve buttermilk pancakes, bacon, and cheap syrup to anyone who happened to come along. For ten days a year, this unfriendly city turns on a country charm.

The Stampede was started by both cowboys and "Indians," but now what was still called the "Indian Village" had been delegated to a small corner of the fairgrounds, and otherwise there wasn't much obvious native participation, except during the parade. During Stampede, every hotel, trailer park, and teepee is full. People flood into this growing oil-rich cow town to celebrate the "greatest outdoor show on earth".

So when we got to the Chuckwagon Hotel, the cafe was filled with vacationing grey-haired couples. It looked like breakfast for an Airstream trailer tour, except there were a couple of native guys sitting at a table at the back.

"Is that the guy who wants the traditional hunting study?" I asked, looking at the only couple without colorful Hawaiian shirts, Bermuda shorts, and reading glasses hanging on strings.

"Yes, that's them, but let me do the talking, at least at first," Dr. Thomas instructed.

As we dodged between the café tables, Dr. Thomas held up his hand, "Edwin!"

Edwin noticed him and stood up. As we maneuvered between the tables, I felt like everyone in the café was staring at us, thinking, "*They are meeting with those Indians.*"

Dr. Thomas shook Edwin's hand.

"Edwin, it is good to see you. How are you doing?" The prof smiled.

"Jus' fine, Frankie."

"This is Marvin. He is an environmentalist from the Nation." Edwin's friend nodded and turned his head towards the professor. Both men had sharp angled facial features and brown weathered skin.

"Nice to meet you, Marvin. This is Miriam from the Anthropology Department."

"Yes. Miriam," I repeated, as I held out my hand to Edwin and then glanced shyly at Marvin.

He nodded his head uncomfortably while looking down. I

couldn't get behind the table to sit down, so I just pulled helplessly at the heavy metal chair. In a surprising change of mood, Marvin jumped to attention, towering over Edwin and Dr. Thomas, who was at least six feet tall himself, and pulled back the large table as if it were made of balsa wood.

"Please sit, Miriam," he said, trying to be polite, as Edwin's obviously strong arm pushed the chair out for me. Marvin's stature projected an imposing image, which did not go unnoticed by the rest of the café patrons. His dark roughly-sewn leather jacket and long black hair pulled into a single braid softened his otherwise intimidating strength. But after he regained his seat, he continued his humble stoop looking down at the table.

Edwin smiled at Dr. Thomas.

"It has been a while." Dr. Thomas turned his coffee cup over.

"Yeah, Frankie, when're ya comin' on the next red ochre ride?" Edwin asked. "I got the same horse as last year ready for ya."

"Thanks, Edwin. But maybe not this time, my legs still hurt from last year," he joked as he looked at Marvin. Each year, the Piikani elders ride up their sacred mountains to the location where they obtained the ceremonial red ochre. Last year, Franklin had the honour of accompanying them on this pilgrimage.

Then, when Professor Thomas looked up at me, he looked uncomfortable. His face changed colour and he glanced at Marvin again. He was clearly uncomfortable.

"So, how are things?" he asked Edwin, now more nervously than before.

"Not too bad," Edwin started. "We're still dealin' with the settlement agreement 'n' the effects o' the dam on the Old Man River. That's why I brought Marvin. I'd like ta do some work on the effects a' the dam on our traditional ways."

"Uh-hmm," mumbled Professor Thomas.

"The dam's had bad effects on our land," Marvin said. "I'd like t' do a study t' give t' the government. It's caused lotsa problems."

Edwin explained, "The agreement has money t' study the effects a' the dam on our Nation an' I think Marvin's the guy who should do it."

Professor Thomas looked up at Marvin, who towered over him, even sitting down. "Have I met you before?" he asked.

Edwin interjected, "Ya remember the Lonefighters?"

"Oh yeah," Professor Thomas replied. "You are ..."

"Yup," replied Marvin.

"You know, I always wanted to know what really happened" said Professor Thomas.

"Well, it was hard to get the truth out. Been so many lies. But I'd like to tell *you* the truth. Y' know, I came back from Oka that summer. I was talkin' to the Mohawk people about the way they defended their lands. Y' know, it's the same wherever in Canada you go, the way they have taken our lands."

"Uh-hmm," responded Professor Thomas again.

"Y' know they had quite a gunfight in Oka," he said and waited for another response.

"Yeah, I heard it on the news," responded Thomas.

"One cop was killed. Shot 'n the mouth."

"I heard," said the professor.

"As soon as we try an' defend our rights, they go off t' court. Those judges're just as racist as the rest. The only ones who listen're the Supreme Court, an' it takes ten years an' a million dollars to get there. Meanwhile, they take our lands, dam our rivers, an' destroy our way a' life."

"Uh-hmm," said Thomas again.

"Anyway, the Mohawks know how t' get the government's attention, but they still got injunctions, y' know, from low-life judges. I c'n see what's goin' on. If they're gonna' take our lands illegally, breakin' more promises, some v'us will have t' go down fightin' too."

"Is that what happened at the Old Man River?" asked Thomas.

"Y' know, a few warnin' shots were fired, an' y' should've seen 'em run," Marvin

smiled. "They finally figur'd we was serious. But then, the bullshit. Instead of talkin' about the dam and our lands, the media wants blood. If they can't get a dead cop, they want a *bad Indian* gettin' arrested. They want action for the couch potato public. Even though they built the dam illegally, no proof o' need, no environmental study or consultin', I was the one who went to jail, not them, the real lawbreakers."

"And now you want to do an environmental study?" asked Professor Thomas.

Edwin explained, "Well, they've put up money, blood money. The government put up the money after Marvin went ta jail n' after the courts ruled that the dam was illegal, so we need ta study how ta protect n' use the lands. But it's hard t' get anythin' done now, with everyone fightin' over the money. Been two years now an' it's the worst thing they could've done."

Marvin added. "Instead of defendin' our rights and educatin' our youth, the chief and councilors, except Edwin, are fightin' over money. Not fer the nation, to get it fer themselves." He shook his head. "The money needs ta be spent properly, ta defend our people."

Edwin chimed in., "Yeah Frankie, we need ta do a study like that, don't ya think?"

"It is a better way to spend some of that agreement money, I agree."

Marvin glared at the professor, "The Old Man River dam project isn't like the tar sands. I got some friends up there n' they've a new project every year. Every year they c'n block a road or somethin'. We'd one project n' they just went ahead n' built it n' stole our river then paid us the blood money after. That's how governments break laws. So what do ya do when the government breaks the law? You fight 'em."

Edwin frowned and looked at Marvin, "The vultures started t' circle right after we got the cash. Sixty-Four million, 'nough ta get the real crooks out. We're gettin' calls from every hustler in New York, got a call from a suspended broker from Wall Street. Other counselors've been tryin' ta get two million t' do a project. It's all bullshit; two million for theirs and the crooks' pockets. The government gave us the money an' now we fight over it."

"We need some help, Frankie," Edwin looked at him with his head cocked to the side.

"Well I don't know what I can help you with, except Miriam here could help you do a traditional environmental knowledge study." Professor Thomas looked at me.

I dared to say "Yeah."

Edwin looked at me and paused. It appeared as though he was wondering how I could help them. Dr. Thomas suggested that I could do something, but it looked like he wasn't so sure.

Then Edwin said, "My name's Edwin Horsetalker. D'ya know why I have that last name, Miriam?"

"No," I smiled, a little embarrassed. I did want to ask him, but I was afraid of being rude.

"Because my grandfather was really good at stealin' horses from the Cree an' Crow. It's an honourable name, Horsetalker. He spoke t' the horses an' they'd come with him."

Edwin smiled at me and said, "Maybe I'm a good talker too, except I c'n talk to white people."

I wasn't entirely sure, but I think he was flirting with me. Professor Thomas smiled too. "And so that means you would be on the advisory committee?" The professor asked Edwin.

"Yeah, but Marvin'd help with the interviews n' stuff."

Professor Thomas tried to mask his discomfort. It was clear that he did not like the idea. He knew it would be impossible to hire Marvin, even though it may have produced the best study.

Dr. Thomas didn't want to actually tell Marvin that he could not use him. It just wasn't the way things were done. He needed to find a way to ease the tension without creating a scene. He held up his cell phone. "I have a call. … Yes, okay, I'll come right away." He closed his phone and said to me. "We gotta' go. Right now. Cindy needs us right away."

Edwin looked a little surprised. I think he suspected what was going on. He said, "Was nice t' meet ya, Miriam, and we'll be in touch with ya, Frankie." And with that we plunked down forty dollars on the table and slipped out of the café.

As we hurried back to the car, Professor Thomas smiled at me. "Are you hungry? I had to pay for their breakfast anyway, we might as well have something ourselves."

"No, I'm okay, but what was that all about?" I asked.

"Well, Miriam, if you really knew about all they have been through, you might not be proud to be Canadian. If I were Blackfoot, I would be standing right beside Marvin—maybe even in jail or dead. Could I stand to watch my relatives feud, my children fail and did you know that a councilor just committed suicide?"

"No. I didn't".

"Yeah, two weeks ago. I don't know what it was about. It seems that death is all around and without some structure for economic development, they have become prey for every con artist around. The problem is, how do we help? We may be able to get some money to do a study, but they won't give us the money with Marvin involved. I will have to talk to Edwin. If this doesn't work out, I am now working with a woman elder from up north. She may need an assistant. Her name is Katie Cardinal. She has started to record her nation's land use activities."

Wow, I thought, there seemed to be quite a bit of work in this field.

So ended my first meeting with Edwin Horsetalker, but it wasn't the last. That summer and fall we did some good interviews with the Piikani Blackfeet, but it all ended when the councilors took all of the project's money. It was my first experience with band politics. I really wonder if we did any good. I suppose recording the land use information is worthwhile, but the idea was to make a real difference. Once the government transfers the money to the band and a crooked chief or councilor wants the money, watch out. Despite the pathetic outcome, I was fascinated with my first opportunity to work with native people.

Northern Lights
Chapter 19

"Miss Miriam Robinson." It was comforting to see my name written in Dad's handwriting. He sent me school money by mail from Calgary to Edmonton. I picked up the cheque just before walking over to the health food restaurant to meet Fred, my boyfriend.

Northern Alberta can get pretty frosty. The frigid air feels like a hundred pin pricks pushing into your exposed cheeks. You can't walk a block without covering your face with your mitts. After only a few days of spine chilling cold, one starts to pray for a little global warming. Then, after a week of thirty to forty below, 32 degrees Fahrenheit feels like a heat wave.

I walked down an ice covered street, and even though it was still below freezing, the change in temperature made it feel like spring. It was a relief to get back to Edmonton after skiing in the mountains and any food would taste good after the four-hour trip back from Jasper's Marmot Basin. When I got to the restaurant, I ordered their vegetarian stir-fry.

In the mountains the reflection of the sun and a cold wind had burnt my face, so we decided to spend Sunday at the Columbia Ice Fields. To get there, we had to drive further up into the Rocky Mountains, following the Athabasca River and the retreat of the glaciers up to the Continental Divide. The Ice Fields are huge sheets of glacial ice cradled between eleven of the Canadian Rockies' highest mountain peaks extending across Alberta and British Columbia. The glaciers slowly flow down the sides of the jagged mountains and melt into the source waters of three rivers, each flowing into a different ocean. It was such a magical place. The fresh spruce aroma filled our city lungs.

Fred and I had both been taken there as young children. It was a standard trip for an Albertan family. My father, the geologist, told us it was the last glacier of the ice age which ended over 10,000 years ago. We wanted to see how much the ice had melted since our youth and we were amazed. The glacier had receded from the highway, leaving a naked expanse of mud and gravel. The ice had shrunk so much it made one wonder why they built the lodge so far back. Gravel made the top of the ice look dirty, but looking down in the crevices of the deep glacier, one could see layers of solid clear turquoise ice representing thousands of years. Blue water filled with grey glacial silt flowed out from under the thick virginal ice. *The source of life,* I thought. It is the source of the Athabasca River, which flows through the town of Jasper and through northern Alberta towards the Arctic Ocean. Fred said that the glacier might not be here in a few years; it seems to have receded so much.

The stir-fry was good, and I was disappointed but not surprised that Fred did not show up. He probably fell asleep in his dorm. After my lonely dinner, I started slowly walking back. The night sky was so clear I could see the Milky Way-even with the light pollution, hundreds of thousands of stars. The university area is generally quiet, a few frat houses and students sharing rooms, some professor's homes and recently constructed row housing. It was a pleasant community with a lawn bowling club, a tennis club which became a skating rink in the winter and a United Church down the street. I felt safe walking alone, although I did need to look down to carefully to cross the street so I didn't slip on the ice ruts in the frozen road.

Suddenly, he appeared in front of me as if he had been hiding behind a snowy spruce tree in one of the front yards.

"'Scuse me," he slurred. He opened his mouth and I saw half dried saliva stretching between his lips. The side of his face had dried blood matted into his hair. He pushed back his dark green parka hood to show his face and I could see his black braids.

"'Scuse me, miss," he said again. "C'n ya give me some money? I need t' eat."

This request made me feel a little culpable because of the great meal I just enjoyed. But my guilt turned into fear as I couldn't tell what this drunk would do. He had a harsh tone in his voice that gave me the chills. He was so skinny, like he had been ravaged by alcohol. I could not tell his age because he probably looked older than he really was, but I noticed he had nice bead work on his shirt collar. It told me that he might have had better days.

He didn't look like some of the street people I'd seen; he looked more together despite his wound and matted hair. He tried to stand up straight and look respectable long enough to receive whatever I might give him, but as he straightened up he slipped on the ice and almost fell in the middle of the road.

I wanted to just keep walking and ignore him. He started to follow me and it frightened me. Why wasn't Fred here to protect me?

The drunk said, "Where you goin', lady? I need t' talk t' ya."

I quickened my pace and looked around to see if there was anyone else on the street. With a little panic, I thought of running up to one of the houses and knocking on the door.

He ran past me on the sidewalk to get in front of me. Then he climbed up on top of the snow bank between the sidewalk and the road. He was far enough away that I realized he wasn't trying to grab me. But now I was afraid he was going to hurt himself falling down from the snow drift on to the ice. I stopped walking. He raised his hand as if he were about to sing and started to recite:

"I was hungry an' ya gave me somethin' t' eat, I was thirsty an' ya gave me somethin' t' drink, I was a stranger an' ya invited me in, I needed clothes an' ya clothed me, I was sick an' ya looked after me, I was in prison an' ya came t' visit me." Then he turned to look the other way as if playing another character.

"When did we see ya hungry and feed ya, or thirsty and give ya something to drink?"

He looked me straight in my eyes and said, "I tell ya the truth, whatever ya did for one o' the least o' these brothers a' mine, ya did for me." Then he repeated it and started to whimper. I thought it was put on.

I looked back at him, right in the eyes for the first time. "That was very good," I said. "How is it that you have memorized this scripture?"

"I learned it in residential school," he replied. "Ya look like a Christian lady. C'd ya spare some money so I can get somethin' t' eat?"

"How do I know you won't just drink it?" I said, feeling a little braver.

"I'm hungry," he said, "haven't been meself lately." Then he stopped talking for a moment and looked at me closely. His expression changed and he started smiling, "Y'll be like Moses, sister. Ya've been among 'em, and now ya c'n give somethin' back t' your people."

"What?" I asked, "What do you mean?" I looked blankly at him.

Then he stated to cry again. "Someone should've been there. I should've been there for her." He cried, "She was only seventeen."

"Who was only 17?" I asked.

"My niece," He said. "She was at a crack house. I should've been there. She passed out an' it was too cold. I lost my daughter, an' now my niece."

I pulled out a five dollar bill from my wallet and held it out to him. But as I opened my purse, he grabbed at the billfold and managed to get a twenty next to the five, which was all the cash I had. He turned and ran.

"Thanks. Someday y'll understand." He ran much faster than I thought he could in his condition. When he grabbed the bill, he had pushed me backwards into the snow bank and my purse and credit cards fell in the snow. My first impulse was to chase him, but I was distracted by the brightness of the northern lights dancing across the sky. It seemed like they were touching the ground and he was running into them. My wallet's contents were scattered and getting wet but I was gazing into the green and yellow ribbons of borealis light. For an instant I lay back in the snow looking and then I sat up straight feeling foolish for allowing him to trick me.

As I was picking myself up and brushing the snow off, Simon, an acquaintance from my sociology class, came running up.

"Meereeam," he said in his African lilt. "Is everything alright? Deed that man hurt you?"

"No, I was trying to give him some money so he could eat, but he grabbed an extra twenty and ran."

"I will chase him and get it back," Simon volunteered.

"No, Simon, leave him, it is not too much and in his state he has nothing to lose. I think he is in mourning. You on your way back to the dorm?" I asked.

"Yes." He looked relieved that he didn't have to chase the guy. "Deed you know him? Who was he?" he asked.

"Oh, a drunk looking for some spare change," I said. "It's okay. He was hungry and I gave him a bit of money."

"He will just drink it up," Simon said.

"Maybe he will," I said. "But somehow I don't think so, tonight."

"He has come to the city, off a reserve," Simon stated almost like a question.

"That would be my guess."

"There's not much for him in the city," Simon concluded.

"The main thing is that I am safe. No real harm done." I changed the subject. "The stars are beautiful tonight. Did ya see the northern lights?"

"It's not too cold tonight; you can take time to enjoy it," he replied. "Have you finished your assignment for tomorrow?" he asked.

I didn't answer. I was still reeling over how the drunk grabbed my money and dumped me in the snow. How did the guy end up panhandling in Garneau anyway? Where is his home and how did his niece die? It was sort of unreal how he suddenly appeared, quoted the Bible and appeared to walk into the northern lights. He was different.

As we walked north towards the campus, I noticed the Northern Lights were still performing. It seemed that they were getting brighter.

"Y'see the Northern Lights? Boy, are they beautiful tonight. They go right across the sky!"

"Simon looked up. "What?" he asked.

"The Northern Lights," I said.

"Oh, the lights-from the city?"

"No Simon. Look up. See the green light shimmering. Sometimes it's red and yellow. They pulse in waves and flutter like ribbons as the energy from the sun hits the atmosphere. It's not city lights."

"I see, it ees a reflection of the light from the downtown," Simon said stubbornly.

"No, Simon they are called the Northern Lights, the *Aurora Borealis*. Don't you know about it? It's caused by energy from the sun reflecting off the ionosphere. They're from sun spot activity and we're lucky they are so bright tonight."

Simon looked embarrassed that he didn't know. But the Northern Lights were incredible. I stood still for a moment. It felt as if I could actually feel the force coming from the light and I was being given power of some sort.

Soon the ribbons of light faded and flickered away. I smiled at

Simon and told him that the Japanese believe that conceiving under Northern Lights is lucky and that the North American natives believe the lights are the spirits of their ancestors.

"These kinds of ideas are holding my people back." He said. "I try not to think too much about spirits."

I thanked Simon for walking me to the dorm and as I walked up the stairs, I looked through the stairway windows at the short metal light posts sticking above the snow banks lighting the campus walkways. I looked up to see if the Northern Lights had come back.

When I got up to the room my roommate Kimiko, was at her desk studying.

"Oooh, your face is so red." She wrinkled the brow of her smooth face. Kimiko had grown up in Lethbridge. Her grandparents had been forced to move there from the west coast during the Second World War. She was so Canadian and yet so Japanese.

"I bought some aloe for it," I told her.

"I will help you put it on. Yes," she insisted, "you must take care. I thought you took some sunscreen with you?" she looked at me with a firm but curious gaze. "You need to take better care."

"You won't believe what happened. I sort of got mugged earlier tonight," I admitted, "by a drunken guy. At least he appeared to be drunk at first, anyway."

"Oh, Miriam, where was Fred?" she asked with a little bit of "*I told you so*" in her voice.

"He didn't make it to the restaurant." I said.

She rolled her eyes and asked, "Are you okay? What happened?"

"It was okay. He just grabbed an extra twenty and ran. Nothing too bad."

"Oh how horrible. Are you still frightened? You look a little frightened."

"No, Kimi, thank you. I'm not scared, to tell you the truth. I am thinking about the native guy. He said some strange things and he looked like he wasn't really a drunk. He said his daughter or niece had just frozen to death. He said something about Moses and he quoted the Bible. I think he thought I was a Christian worker or something."

"Oh, Miriam, it must have been frightening. Maybe he could sense that you are a good person. He sensed your spirituality."

"What?"

"You are a spiritual person. Did you see the Northern Lights tonight?"

"Yes."

"Good time to make love." She smiled.

"You are Japanese!" I said.

"How did they make you feel?" She asked.

"Elated."

"Native people are spiritual too," she said. But I figured she just wanted to reassure me.

"Your Dad was calling, he said he would call back," Kimiko reminded herself to tell me.

"What happens to people?" I wondered.

"Maybe they lose their jobs," she said, "or maybe he didn't know what he wanted and just drifted."

"We know what we want, right?" I smiled at her. "You want to get married?" Kimiko was traditional in a modern way.

"Oh yes, but I can't find anyone. I will probably end up marrying a Caucasian-looking guy, not Japanese, and I don't know what my parents will say."

"Kimi! You should marry who you fall in love with. If he is white or Japanese, it shouldn't matter. We are not in your parent's generation. All the Japanese guys that come here are creepy, anyway."

"I know, I know, but I can't change how my parents feel. I'll just have to live with it." Kimi didn't mention that some white boys just wouldn't go out with her because she was Japanese.

I admitted to Kimi. "I don't know anyone who I would want to marry either. Certainly not Fred! He just drags me down. I don't need to get married now but it does feel strange going home to my parent's house in Calgary after each term."

We talked for a while longer and then she went back to her studies. I lay on the bed and closed my eyes. I was about to drift off when the phone rang.

It was my Dad. "Miriam? I got your note about working up north and I thought I'd phone you tonight to talk about it right now."

I told my parents that Professor Thomas had asked me to go up north to McMurray and work on an ethnographic study for the native community. I had a feeling that they wouldn't approve. Now Dad was calling just after I got mugged. I couldn't tell him or he would freak.

"I hear that you are entertaining the idea of going up north to work around Fort McMurray next year," he said in an official non-approving way.

"Yup, my professor has offered me a job starting in October—next fall," I said apprehensively, wondering what his response would be.

"Well I'd like to talk to you about it. You know, I've been working up there for quite a while now and I'm not sure it is a healthy environment for a young girl like you."

"I have heard you mention Fort McMurray a few times, but I'm supposed to work in Fort Chipewyan." I had heard his stories and opinions about the McMurray oil sands since it was an important part of his business.

"Well, that might be slightly different, but there are several things I am concerned about. The first is that you're interrupting your schooling, and second, you'll be working for the other side—for the natives. You would be working against me. And third, it is pretty rough up there—too rough for a young girl like you."

I expected him to say something like that, but it still made my heart sink when I heard it. I hadn't really admitted it to myself but I knew Dad would not approve of this job. I really hoped Dad would not be worried about me working for a native group. After all, this was the type of service and support that he had taught me growing up.

I began to think of Professor Braid's definition of racism: "*Segregation keeps the poor, poor. Neglecting the cycle of poverty created by racist policies is a continuation of racism.*"

"Dad, you know if we neglect them, we are racist."

"So you are saying if I don't want you to go, I'm a racist!"

"No."

"I have good reasons," he said.

"Well why, if I'm working for natives does it have to be against you? I thought your company supported First Nations," I reasoned.

"We do support them, but we also negotiate with them. Many of them want to stop all development and sometimes they threaten even the company's existence or our profitability. There has been talk of trying to shut down any further expansion and that means my new project. I know how you feel about the company, but it has clothed and fed you and practically brought you up."

"Dad, this is the best offer I've ever had and opportunities in my field don't come along that often."

"If you work for them, it would be like I raised my own opposition." Dad's voice was getting higher as it did when he got angry.

I wasn't sure if going up north was the right thing for me to do, but I wanted him to see my point of view. "I need to take this opportunity."

Dad didn't stop. "I might be able to get you a job with the company doing similar things. But you need to finish your degree. You only have a few courses left."

"Dad, I really don't want to work for 'the company". You know I don't trust them." I knew I shouldn't have said it as soon as it came out. I could feel him grimacing over the phone.

"Now you mean to say you don't trust me?"

I tried to backtrack. "Of course I know you have had your career with CanOil, but well, even according to former Premier Peter Lougheed, the rate of development in the oil sands is completely out of control."

Dad was the vice president for CanOil, which had major holdings in the oil sands. He was heading up the approval process for the next phase of development. It wasn't the biggest oil company in the world, but they were producing hundreds of thousands of barrels of oil per day. He worked hard to get to that position, but I'm not sure he liked it.

I could tell he was frustrated and hurt. "Miriam, you need to come home so we can talk about this more."

"Okay, we'll have lots of time to talk about it over Christmas."

Dad has always been so protective. I was tired and glad to finally close my eyes that night. I hoped my dreams would not wake me.

Maybe I would dream about Moses. I had looked up Moses on the Internet. Moses means 'taken from the reeds' or 'found in the reeds.'

Christmas in North Carolina
Chapter 20

Mom liked to go south at Christmas, not only because it was cold in Calgary, but because she loved to visit her family in her home state. Dad said it would be the last family Christmas trip. "After Miriam graduates," he said, "she will probably get a job or get married, and then she will visit her husband's parents."

Dad's sense of inevitability makes me uncomfortable. Yes, Christmas may not be the same again, but Dad made it sound terminal.

Mom was more positive. "Married or not, Miriam and her husband will come with us when we go somewhere warm."

Husband?

So this Christmas we visited Grandma and Grandpa in Charlotte. Visits to North Carolina had become less comfortable. Cousin Billy upset me during my last visit when he said he wanted some 'freedom fries'. I told him I didn't support the invasion of Iraq and that his government was lying to him. He didn't like that. He said I was acting un-American. I reminded him I was Canadian. I realized that despite the fact we were family we had irreconcilable world views. I mean this whole 9/11 thing was terrible but the warmongers lied even to Colin Powell. The US news media told them about the UN investigations but the American public still went along with the invasion. I was part American but I didn't feel comfortable about what the country was doing.

Charlotte is a big hospitable southern city, but it only took me three days in the rainy suburbs and malls before I needed to get out. Normally, Christmas was magical. I was excited Christmas morning, but it was more the memory that excited me. Maybe I shouldn't have come on this trip. Even Christa, my cousin of the same age, was already married and spent her Christmas alone with her husband and new baby.

Christa said she and her husband were taking over her parent's gas station and convenience store. "Don't need no college degree to run nat store. Ah been doin' it since ah was a young'un'," she said. I guess it is an advantage to be able to accept your lot in life but running a store is not for me. I want to have a career, make my own way, or at least be able to support myself and accomplish something significant.

But in the meantime, there were the Christmas visits of the vaguely familiar relatives who all knew my childhood embarrassments. And then there were Grandma's friends, a constant stream of perfumed grey-haired visitors who would forget their own names, but remembered how mischievous *I* had been in *my* childhood.

In quiet times I looked out the window into the backyard. I loved my grandparents' cozy southern style brick home in the summers, especially the large garden with tall straight pines, perennially green live oaks, holly trees, sweet gardenias and mom's favorite, the stately magnolias. I was a regular tomboy in my childhood and I learned how to walk in the woods and stay safe and how to pick mistletoe. My parents would ask me to climb one of the oaks and get some to put over the doorjamb for New Year's. I'm still a good tree climber today and know about sharp thorns and prickly vines.

There was always a welcoming aroma of Carolina pine as we got off the plane, especially for hot weather visits. In the summer, the needles smell dusty and dry; in the winter they smell sweet, of damp composting pine. Grandma's shaded garden had such a sweet fragrance and it was so deliciously hot. The warm weather in the south brings out the scents, both inviting and repugnant. The magnolia smells like heaven but the smell of the garbage will knock you down.

At Christmas it was a bit too cold to sit outside in the yard. This time of year, the pyracantha was covered with animated birds, feasting on the red berries. Even a cardinal was showing off. How different, yet the same North Carolina and Calgary were. No snakes and dangerous bugs in Calgary. Not this time of year here, either. The grass in the yard still had a greenish tinge and the pines and live oaks were still green. Other trees had lost their leaves and you could see into the underbrush, tangled brown and grey vines climbing up the bigger trees.

I saw a rabbit trying to hide under a leafless bush. It is easy to love the flora and fauna of the Carolinas but Alberta is so fresh and clean. There is nothing quite the same as the pristine pure water of the Lake Louise tea house and the smell of poplar pollen in the northern springtime.

Grandpa saw me gazing out the back window. "It doesn't really freeze much anymore," he said. "We used to take big chunks of ice from the Catawba River, now Lake Norman, and put them in the ice storage cellars to keep things cool in the summer, but now the lake won't freeze. Things er' changin'."

Grandpa also talked about how North Carolina had lost the chestnut trees. "The Cherokee practically lived off those nuts. Now you can't find one, and we're losing our dogwoods, especially the pink ones, due to some kind a' blight."

"Yup, things er' changin'," Grandpa continued. "We can't swim at the cottage by the Neuse River anymore. The fertilizers from the hog farms are causin' dead zones in the sound and when the last hurricane emptied pig waste into the river, it got really bad. Kids are getting rashes on their skin and even lesions from the river water. The kudzu down by the lake was imported from China to help with ground cover along the highways, but now it has taken over.

"And you can't walk in a pasture without steppin' in a fire ant hill. They weren't here when I was young. They got a free ride to North Carolina in Mississippi sod. Those ants are bad news. Times er' changin'," he repeated, as he opened another Carolina boiled peanut and smiled a carefree smile of a man who is comfortable with his world, even if his environment was altered.

Dad had come in and was listening to Grandpa too. He said, "Yeah, there's no free ride. We think air and water are free but they are not. There's always a price to pay. It costs to use them." Dad was an environmentalist at heart, an apparent contradiction with his current job.

Dad liked Grandpa's back yard and pointed to a section of fence. "When we were first married, your grandfather got me to do quite a bit of garden work out there. Visits to this house were always full of projects.

"But speaking of projects, I guess it is time that we spoke more about your proposed job. I have wanted to tell you about the Fort McMurray oil sands for some time now, but I never thought you'd be interested." He sounded conciliatory.

"Yeah, I'd like to talk about it now too," I replied. "I know you care about the environment. I just don't understand why you don't want me to take that job."

"Well, it really has nothing to do with the environment. We can mine the oil sands without creating major problems and the economic benefits are incredible. I'm just worried about you. It's dangerous for a young girl up there."

"Dad, I appreciate your concern but I'm all grown up. I need to take responsibility for myself and I'm not so sure you can mine up there without pretty big impacts."

"Like what? Have you been studying it?"

"The pace of development in McMurray is destroying the health of the Athabasca River, and the aboriginal peoples. You just were complaining about pollution here in North Carolina and there is no huge mine here."

"Miriam, it is not as bad as you think. These projects can really alleviate poverty. We can provide so much for the native people. Like when we went up to Inuvik in the 1960's. The people couldn't believe the modernity we brought them. Now in Fort McMurray we can protect the environment and create employment. It's the government that isn't living up to its consultation responsibilities, not industry."

"So why can't I go up there and help?"

"It is not time for you to do that."

"Well, I'm going anyway."

He started to get angry. Something was wrong. I wasn't getting the whole story. He was angrier than I'd ever seen him, even when I smashed the car, even when I came home drunk. I was glad we were in North Carolina—it was neutral ground. He stomped into the kitchen and I heard him say something to Mom about a car.

"Did you tell Mom I had to give up my car?" I fumed as I followed him.

I had a feeling it was going to be difficult to resolve this one.

Dad continued, "What does Fred think of this job?"

"Fred and I have split up!"

"Oh." Dad really didn't like Fred, but his family was well-off and his father played tennis in the same league at the Glencoe Club in Calgary. I knew Mother had been listening to our conversation when we were in the den and she always knew how her husband felt.

"Mom! Dad is still trying to stop me from going up to work."

"Miriam," Mom looked resigned. "It's more complicated than you imagine. It's not just about politics or oil."

"Miriam, we should go back to the living room." Dad said. I looked at Mom and she nodded.

"This is something we have been planning to discuss with you for a long time." He paused nervously. "Just after we married, we found out that we were unable to have children. But twenty years ago, we were given the most important gift anyone can ever receive. We were given a wonderful baby girl."

"You're telling me that I am adopted?" I gasped.

"Yes, Miriam. We were not told who your biological parents were and the prevailing wisdom was not even to tell you that you were adopted. Since then of course, attitudes have changed about open adoptions and we considered telling you earlier, but since your records were sealed, we thought it would be best to wait until you became an adult."

I was in shock. Was this really happening?

"We were told about your parent's ethnic background. Your parents were native ... from Manitoba."

Mom interrupted, "Half-native, we think. Your father was native and your mother part native. They gave you up for adoption as soon as you were born."

"We will help you try and locate your biological parents if you want."

"But how? How can it be, people say that I look like you, Mom?"

"It's uncanny how much you do."

I just sat, stunned. I was not who I thought I was. I was not Scottish. So, my real family was from Manitoba. I couldn't believe it. I asked my parents again if it were really true.

"How long were you going to keep this from me? What about my genetics? Don't you have to tell doctors and stuff? Why didn't you tell me a long time ago?"

"Well honey, it was a closed adoption and we didn't have information either. Times have changed. It's not the same as it was then. We were going to tell you a couple of times, but it just didn't work out. You were concentrating on school or you were worried about something else, so we didn't want to distract you," Mom tried to explain, but I didn't think there was any excuse for failing to tell me.

"I can't believe it." I was exasperated. I needed some time to think. I thought about my grandparents who weren't my real grandparents. They knew I was adopted all this time and didn't tell me. How could they do that? I thought they were my blood family; do they *really* love me? Do they really love me? Or is it just their duty?

Dad said, "Miriam, you don't know who your blood relatives are. You wouldn't even know who you're related to. You need to do some more research before you go up there."

Was that what Dad was so worried about? What were the chances of me getting involved with my relatives?

Then Dad said, "I was so shocked when you accused me of being racist,"

"So, just because you adopted a native girl you're not racist? Is that what you're saying?" I accused him. I was angry and not careful of what I said, but I needed to clear the air.

"The racism that my professor, Dr. Baird, was talking about was inside the culture; like the Uncle Tom Syndrome, or Uncle Tomahawk. Even though you adopted me knowing I was aboriginal, it doesn't mean you don't harbour racist feelings towards the aboriginal community."

"But Miriam ..."

"Leave her, Phil." Mom softly put her hand on Dad's arm. "She needs some time to calm down."

Mom was right. It was time to get out of the house—call Cousin Billy. I thought about how he wasn't a blood relative of mine either. I needed some time to think about how I was going to deal with this. I thought it was world oil politics that was causing my Dad to be so weird. Now I knew where his emotions were really coming from.

I asked them who knew about my adoption. At least Billy didn't know. They said my uncle and aunt were sworn to secrecy and they didn't know the details. My parents said I might tell Billy if I wanted, but I should let it sink in for a while. I called Billy and he agreed to pick me up first thing next morning. I decided I would act like nothing had changed, and after all, I suppose, nothing really had changed.

Billy and I went for a drive in his redneck ride. He asked me what I wanted to do and I told him just drive. Billy loved automobiles and since Charlotte is the NASCAR centre, he had plenty of local encouragement. His little red truck was a bit overdone for my taste. Plenty of shiny chrome, the suspension raised, and custom-lined leather bucket seats and polished tires. I liked the lighted mirror behind the sun shade.

"Well, Richard Petty," I said to Billy, "let's get the hell out of here." So, off we went in Billy's custom ride.

"How has my "bleedin' heart liberal" bin keepin?" he asked.

"Just fine," I replied. "After all, Canadian medicare keeps my bleeding heart healthy."

"Here comes the commercial," he groaned.

Because we were the same age, Cousin Billy had been a regular companion for my childhood visits to North Carolina. I came from thousands of miles away, but he had hardly ever ventured more than one state away from home. He even bragged about his trip to Philadelphia:

"They's lots ah history in Philly," he said. "But North Carolina is a southern state, part of the confederacy. It's a stock-car racin', tobacca growin', good preachin', basketball state, an' my license plate reads *"First in Freedom"* to commemorate the Mecklenburg County Declaration of 1775."

Billy liked history, wanted to go into law, and shared the passion for the automobile with the rest of his local countrymen. I may not share his politics but we were good friends just the same.

"Billy..." I paused.

"Yeah," he replied.

"I was told something incredible yesterday."

"Oh, what was that?" he asked.

"I'm adopted." I said hesitantly.

"You adopted?" he repeated. "Naw, you look too much like y' ma and dad. You are puttin' me on."

"No, it's true. I'm not your blood relative."

"Oh, so ya think ya can marry me now," Billy joked.

"Yuk! You are bad. You're worse than bad. Not only that, you wouldn't marry a native girl, would ya?"

"Native? You have blond hair and blue eyes." That was all he said. I was still Miriam, his favorite cousin, and he made as much fun of me as before, which was my measure of how much he cared.

I changed the subject. "How's school?"

"My history courses ah great, actually, we ah studyin' something y' know about, the Trail ah Tears."

"Where's that Cherokee reservation anyway? Isn't it around here somewhere?"

"Yeah, it's not too far down I-40 from here."

"That story is typical, you know. Native people all over got that kind of treatment," I said. "But unlike the natives down here, many of the natives in northern Canada are still able to live off the land—at least some of them can."

"Yeah," he said, but I don't think he was listening.

"Where was that Cherokee Reserve?" I asked again.

"Not too far south o' where we ah now."

"Have you even visited the Cherokee Reservation?" I asked.

"No." He looked down at his gearshift.

"Come on, let's go take a look."

"Besides that ya just found out you were native, how come y' were so interested in Indians?"

"You like hunting, don't you Billy?"

"Yeah" he looked at me curiously. "Just don't send me huntin' with our trigger happy vice president."

"You're funny! You know, many of the natives still hunt for their living—almost like they did years ago and there are a lot of guys from North Carolina that go up there to hunt. They say that the 'Indian' guides are the best."

A smile crept across Billy's face.

"But the oil sands industry is pushing the natives off their lands; similar to the Trail of Tears mess."

"Come on." Billy didn't believe that. "There's so much wilderness up there."

"That's what my job is. Getting them to tell me how they can or cannot use the land. You know, because of the oil sands developments."

"Hmm. Could be interestin'. Do ya go huntin' too?"

"I don't like hunting. I'm interested how *they* use the land. In anthropology we're also studying the effects of Christianity on native culture and we're learning a bit about their religions."

"Y' mean, like *bad medicine*?" he asked. It was clear he thought it might be a good story.

"Yeah, some natives call it medicine. An' there's good medicine too, you just watch too much TV."

"Yeah, cool." That captured his attention.

"Each group has different beliefs, but many are similar. Some of them even had flood stories, like the Bible. It makes me think how similar they are to the Jewish people wandering around Mesopotamia 3,000 years ago. Anyway, our stories are much the same and I wonder, is spirituality the same regardless of which religion we have?"

"Y' think they are the lost tribe of Israel?" Billy asked. "Isn't that what the Mormons think?"

"No, I don't think they're the lost tribe, but I know they have their own spiritualism."

Billy had heard my ideas before. We agreed that we shouldn't talk about religion.

"What I am most ashamed of is the racist Eurocentrism."

He looked sideways at me.

"When the Europeans first came, they could shoot an "Indian" if they were not Christian," I explained. "Then, after we stopped shooting, we sent their kids to Bible school. The priests and pastors of the residential schools destroyed their language and crushed their spirit. They were some toxic culture killers."

"They were spreadin' the Gospel, Miriam; that's what they were supposed to do. Even ah church is sendin' missionaries to Africa now. One group just left before Christmas."

"Billy!" I said, trying to appeal to his sense of equality. "The native youth were taken away from their families by the priests and prohibited from speaking their language. Some of them were sexually abused, and most were physically abused in some way. Now they're trying to heal themselves from those 'Gospel spreaders'. They were branded heathens, they were considered inferior, not completely human. Even your modern missionaries have no idea what they're doing to the cultures they encounter; they really don't know how to help the African people."

"Miriam!" Billy said. "They're helpin' people with AIDS and bringin' health services. Ya don't think that's helpin? The're supposed t' go out and spread the Word and build houses and churches. Is there somethin' wrong with that?"

"Who is to say that "*The Word*," our word, is better than their spiritual words? Do they need our churches? Why should we force natives to accept the Christian story of the flood? Why shouldn't we accept their flood stories? The native people have plenty to offer. They have wisdom about the environment; something we have been neglecting. Maybe we should be forced to learn their language and learn their ceremonies instead of them learning ours?"

Billy thought for a moment. I figured that he was going to say *"because we are smarter, or because our story is right."*

But Billy said nothing. He just stared at the road. But after a while when I thought we might have to change the topic of conversation, he said, "Because of Jesus Christ." His voice cracked.

Billy had a way of cutting to the quick. It is because of his balanced judgment that we are still friends. I thought about what he said and realized how he was right.

"Preacher," I said. I thought about how there must be some way of taking the best parts of wisdom from different cultures and religions.

"Doubtin' Thomas," he joked back.

"I am a Doubting Thomas, Billy."

"Yeah, y'are."

"By the way, did I tell you that I got mugged before Christmas in Edmonton?"

"No! Did ya really get robbed?"

"Yeah, but the thing that was so weird was the mugger called me Moses as he left. Do you have any idea what he might have meant?" Billy was good at the Bible.

"Ah don' know what exactly he meant ba that, but Moses argued with the Phara', who thought a' him as his son, until he convinced his adoptive father t' let the Jews leave Egypt. But Moses nevva made it t' the Promised Land. Was this guy a Biblical schola?"

"I don't know. But he quoted the Bible."

"Ah think he sees you as a leada, Miriam. An'for what it's worth, so do ah."

"Thanks Billy … I think?"

"Ya know your name—Miriam is Moses's older sister's name?

"Really. Wow."

As I wondered about the coincidence, Billy pulled up to a gas pump beside a small building with a steep roof. The sign out front said 'General Store'.

"Can ya contribute a twenty?" he asked. "Gas's so expensive these days."

"Here." I gave him my twenty. I was surprised but happy because North Carolina boys are too proud to let you pay. "Gas prices might even go higher," I agreed.

"This here gas station's on the Cherokee reservation an' ah thought ya might like t' stop here. They've plenty a' native stuff in there."

I was thrilled. How thoughtful Billy was. As I walked into the gas store, a bell attached to the top of a brown wooden door chimed and an older woman with long grey hair came through a curtain at the back of the store. "Hey there," she said. "Can I help y'all?"

"Well, I'm looking." I was immediately curious about her. "Do you have any books on the Cherokee?"

"Oh yeah, we do. What kind of book are y'all lookin' fuh?"

"Something about the culture, I guess."

"Where you from?" she asked.

"Canada," I replied.

"Oh well, then I have something interestin'. Have ya heard of the Cree Tribe?" she asked.

"Yes," I said, "in fact, I just found out I have some Cree blood in me, actually."

"Really?" She gave me a big smile. "Well, we in the Cherokee Nation have a Cree prophesy which I think you'll like. It's bin shared between the Cherokee, Hopi, Sioux, and Cree for many years. It's an important connection between our peoples."

She handed me a pamphlet.

"Thank you," I said looking more closely at her wrinkled face.

"This story of the Warriors of the Rainbow is my reason for protecting the culture, heritage, and knowledge of my ancestors. I know that the day Eyes of Fire spoke of will come! I want my children and grandchildren to be prepared to accept this task, the task of being one of the Warriors of the Rainbow. She smiled at me. "Perhaps you understand what I am talking about?"

I quickly read the pamphlet while she continued to sweep the floor. When I finished I found her restacking some jars of local honey. "This was not by chance, my coming here. It is truly an important connection," I told her as I held my arms up to embrace her.

Losing a Child
Chapter 21

I was adopted. I felt betrayed, not only by Mom and Dad for not telling me, but also by my birth mom and dad. Why did they give me up?

Mom gave me the letter they got when they adopted me with my allergy and family illness history. It was written in neat handwriting in black fountain pen ink. My birth mother wrote it, I thought. I wish she would have written something more, something like "I'm sorry we had to give you up for adoption."

There was a return address crossed out with a black felt pen but I could just read the last portion of it. Min- dosa, Manitoba. The letter was very short but it did give some ethnic background-Metis, Ojibwa, Cree. I tried to shine a light through the envelope to see the surname. Tan- . I quickly looked up Minnedosa. It means *"flowing water"* in Sioux. The original name of the town was Tanner's Crossing. There were a couple of reserves west of Minnedosa, on Gambler's or Silver Creek.

Mom said the best way to find out information was to send a letter with my age and description to the Metis associations and the First Nations in the area and ask them to circulate it. But what would happen if they don't want to see me? Maybe they don't want to be found? Why did they give me up?

I read stories about native adoptions on the Internet. They called it the "Sixties Scoop" where thousands of native children were scooped up by the government and placed in white families. They said it saved the government $100,000 per adoption, keeping them out of foster homes or residential schools. The Internet was full of native adoption horror stories from the sixties and seventies. I asked Mom about it.

"Well, I don't know much." she started. "We applied to the government and they put us through interviews and tests to make sure we were gonna be qualified parents. We really wanted you, Miriam. We did all of the tests and more."

"But were there a lot of native children?" I asked. "Were they in poverty?"

"I don't know. They asked us if we would accept a native child or a child of a different race and we said yes. We didn't know anybody else who was adopting at the time. But there was lots of talk in the media about native adoption. They wanted to shut it all down. It was government controlled and seemed pretty strict and careful to me. We were just glad we got you."

"After Bill C31 in 1986 there were fewer native adoptions. I must have been one of those?"

"Well that would have been after that bill, yeah. I wish I knew more. You were only a few days old when we got you."

"Didn't someone tell you why? Didn't they tell you why I had to be adopted?"

"No, they didn't. But I can tell you for certain that it was hard for your mother to give you up. I can't imagine having to do it. There must have been some difficulties like she was sick or something.

Any mother would have loved you, Miriam."

"Was it because they took me against my mother's will and didn't I have a father?"

"I don't know what the government did. But I do know your father had to sign the papers. The lawyer did say that. The father signed the papers."

I was exhausted from this news but I resolved to do all of the research I could about my heritage and even if they never agreed to meet me. I had to know who I really was. I was sure I was Metis because of my dirty blond hair and blue eyes. I did more research on the Internet and I found the story of John Tanner. Maybe the reason I was so white looking was …well, here is some of the story.

"My name is John Tanner. It happened when I was out hiding from my dad in the back pasture up in my favorite hickory tree. Father knew there were Indians around and didn't want me outside, but I couldn't stand to be inside for another moment. I didn't like my step-mother and the new baby was driving me crazy. The farm house was small, but we had cleared this part of the Ohio wilderness and we had enough land to farm.

My brother and I usually helped my father but that day we had other hands who worked seasonally. I was going to be ten and had been promised a special sweet cake for my birthday dinner. I was daydreaming up the tree at the back when, without making a sound, they grabbed me. They muffled my mouth and drug me towards the river. There were two of them and they were so strong and mean. I was certain they were going to kill me.

When we got to the river, there were three more who were holding the canoes. They were dressed in buckskin and had feathers attached to their heads with leather strings. I had always dreamed of seeing them, but this was a little too close. One of them came up to me with his hatchet but the older one grabbed his hand and said something. He backed off but it did not look good for me.

They treated me rough but it seemed they were taking me somewhere, up the river, against the current. After a while, they let me sit up in the canoe. Then, they ditched the canoes and took me across land. They tried to speak to me, but I didn't understand. One of them knew one or two English words. We traveled over land until we reached another group waiting with other boats. They had planned to cover their tracks. I realized that they had planned to kidnap me. But when Father found I was gone he would follow us.

They threw me some pieces of fish for dinner. It wasn't the sweet cake I would have been eating if I were back home. After several days of paddling, we came to what looked like a camp. There was a woman there who spoke some English and she told me that I was taken because they wanted to replace a son of theirs who was killed. "

The caption said John Tanner had been kidnapped in Ohio and lived in Manitoba as an 'Indian' for years. His descendants still live in Manitoba and are Metis and members of some of the First Nations in the area. I quickly skimmed over much of the story. It told about how badly he was treated until he was "traded to a woman chief." They said that a woman chief was quite unusual in that culture in those days. He eventually forgot how to speak English and he was raised as native. He became a warrior and married a chief's daughter.

He told several stories of his life as a warrior and son:

"Falcon."

"Yes, Mother"

"I don't want you to go with the other warriors. You will leave us and I will have no protection and no man to hunt for me."

"The raid will not be long, Mother."

"But you might not come back."

"It is not far to the open lands and the buffalo are there now. I will bring lots of meat back when I come. The Southern Sioux have been coming into our territory and taking our game. If we are going to protect our livelihood, we have to go and show them we aren't going to let them push us back. My pony is the fastest. Do not worry, Mother. I will come back and with meat for you."

John Tanner was white but became native. It was John Tanner's Metis grandson who started Minnedosa! That could be why I look so white. I wonder what my letters to Manitoba will show.

School

Chapter 22

Back at school after Christmas, my adoption was still an obsession. On some level I had always known that I was different from my adopted parents. I took anthropology and was looking at a job for a native group before I knew I had native blood. Cousin Billy said it was just because I was Christian, that I wanted to do good, but I am not so sure. Knowing my true ethnicity made my motivation even clearer. I think biological heredity has a lot more influence than some people like to believe.

Native studies now became more of a passion. One of the native studies courses I took included listening to a local radio show where I heard two professors from the university being interviewed.

Dave was a well-known radio host who aggressively promoted the right-wing theme of the station.

"Dr. Joap," he began. "Welcome to the network. Thank you for coming to tell us about your new book."

"Well, thank you Dave. It is a pleasure. The book's about how the Constitution has given native people more rights than the rest of Canadians."

"Really?" Dave asked. "How does that work?"

"Status Indians don't have to obey the same laws as the rest of us do; for example, they can hunt all year round outside of legal hunting seasons."

"That doesn't sound fair," pouted Dave.

"I agree, I don't think it's fair either and it goes against our fundamental principles of equality." The Professor added, "Since 1982, when the government included native rights in the Canadian Constitution, they've had more rights than regular Canadians!"

Dave then introduced another professor. "Dr. Meeks, I would like to also welcome you to the network. You were a part of the negotiations for the new Canadian Constitution; do you think it's fair?"

Meeks was like a Thomas Jefferson of Canada, a modern author of our Constitution. In another class, I'd had to read a paper by him.

Meeks began, "Yes, thank you Dave. In 1982 Canada finally became an adult by adopting a strong Bill of Rights and a home-grown Constitutional amending formula and it also was the end of a much longer story for the native peoples of Canada."

Dave interrupted, "We don't have time for a long lecture, Peter."

"Just let me give you the background," he continued. "In the late sixties, Prime Minister Trudeau and Aboriginal Minister, Jean Chretien, proposed assimilation for native people. Ironically they called it a "White Paper." The natives had been second class citizens and were only given the vote in 1961. Since 1927 they had been prohibited from paying lawyers to defend their claims; they were disproportionally represented in jails, riddled with alcoholism, and plagued with other abuses.

The reserve system in Canada was comparable to the apartheid system in South Africa. But Trudeau proposed an equality solution, complete assimilation. The Indian Act and the White Paper were just a continuation of 'An Act of Gradual Civilization,' passed for the Canadian colonies by the British Parliament in 1857. Native people would give up their land, language, culture, and rights in exchange for full British citizenship. If a native man learned to read and signed a pledge to "live as a white man," he would be allowed to vote, own property, and serve on a jury. They didn't just discourage their cultural practices, they actually made them illegal."

"But otherwise they were living in poverty?" interjected Dr. Joap.

"Is that true?" the host asked Dr. Joap. "They needed some kind of help?"

"Yes, Dave, that is historically correct," answered Joap. "But the history tells us we should make them equal, not more than equal."

Meeks continued, "John A. MacDonald made it illegal for them to conduct potlatches or sun dances. In 1876 they made it illegal for 'Indians' to sell or produce anything without the permission of the Indian agent. And one of the most insidious laws was the provision in the Indian Act that took away status from a woman if she married a man without treaty rights."

The talk show host was getting impatient. "So, you think they should have more rights than us?" he asked Meeks in disgust.

Meeks ignored the question. "Harold Cardinal was a young aboriginal man from Alberta, who skillfully responded to Trudeau's White Paper. He was about the age of my first year students when he wrote his book which satirized Prime Minister Trudeau's book *"The Just Society."* He called it *"The Unjust Society."* With this initiative, over the next ten years, not only did Trudeau and the Canadian government make a complete reversal of their policy, but in 1982 they included an unprecedented constitutional amendment and granted the protection of aboriginal common law rights in the Canadian constitution." Meeks audibly sighed.

Dr. Joap then replied, "Now, Canadian aboriginal people have more rights, more rights than you! Do you think that is consistent with the principles of our free society?"

Meeks continued, "Cultural practices, principles and traditions form the original basis of laws and rights. Why do common laws recognize aboriginal rights? Because when the Norman French invaded England in 1066, the Norman rulers governed using the local, common laws, of the Angles and Saxons."

"What does common law have to do with it? That is judge made law, isn't it?" Dave interjected.

"Yes." Meeks kept going, "So, in order to properly govern these local peoples, the Norman rulers had to respect the Anglo-Saxon traditions. These local laws included things like marriage customs and trade rules and even religious practices.

Through recognizing the Anglo-Saxon laws, a new system became the basis of a British common law system and was enforced by the Normans, even though they came from a different culture and spoke a different language. So, when the Europeans invaded North America, the British system naturally accepted the legal importance of local custom, just as their customs were respected by the Norman invaders hundreds of years before. Aboriginal peoples really don't have more rights than other Canadians; they just have their own cultural rights based on their own practices."

"But they don't have to follow our game laws," interjected Dr. Joap.

"Yes," Meeks admitted. "But it is like when you inherit property from your parents."

"Oh, this should be good," host Dave said sarcastically.

"Yes," Meeks continued. "You didn't personally work for it, earn it, but you get it. Inheritance is part of our traditions based on our cultural traditions too. The same system recognizes the traditions of the native peoples of Canada and their inheritances."

"But it is not fair," interjected Dave.

"Perhaps in a just society where we all are truly equal, you would be right. But isn't it also not fair to accept the inheritances of the European peoples wealth, language, technology, education, and customs and deny those of the native peoples?"

After hearing that I knew I had to meet Meeks. I decided to go over to Athabasca Hall the very next day. Meeks's office was in the first building ever built on the University of Alberta campus. This beautiful, old brick structure with majestic white wood columns graced the campus. In contrast to the concrete and curved lines of the Tory Lecture Hall, it looked like it contained the wisdom of the ages.

Meeks's office was filled with boxes overflowing with loose papers and books piled on chairs, filling every available space, like he was getting ready to move. After knocking on the open door, I introduced myself and told him I enjoyed him on the radio.

"I have been offered a job recording native land use," I added.

His eyes twinkled, "That's a very good opportunity, Miss ..."

"Robinson."

"Miss Robinson."

"It might not be the most important job." I added.

"Oh, Miss Robinson," he started, "Land use for the native people of Canada defines the extent of their rights. It is the basis of their power to exert influence on environmental policy, to protect their culture and their way of life. Native land use will influence important decisions like the rate of development of the oil sands. You could not have chosen a more important task."

He then suggested that I read some of the Supreme Court decisions, names like Delgamuukw, Van der Peet, and Sparrow. Of course, what should I have expected? You go to see a prof and he gives you something more to read. I thanked him and turned to go back to my dorm.

"How did you come to be interested in this field?" he quickly asked me.

"Well, I am taking anthropology, but recently I found out I am adopted and, well, I have Cree and Dené blood."

"How exciting."

"I guess so. But I'm a bit confused, especially with all of the politics involved."

"Don't worry. I think it will come naturally once you become more familiar with your heritage. Now you have a chance to learn about your background and get paid for it!"

"Yeah, I suppose that is a real bonus."

"Miss Robinson, find out what your Cree name was, not your French or English name, but the name of your Cree or Dené relatives and find out about the spiritual side of the culture. This will help you understand. Talk with your Grandfathers, find out what a "*Whi-ti-koh*" is and go to a spirit sweat. That will help you understand."

Walking back to the dorm, I wondered. I had already read about the *Whi-ti-koh*, but "talk to my grandfathers?" Didn't he mean ancestors? And how is sweating spiritual? Talking to Meeks was fascinating and reassured me that I was on the right track. But he made it sound so important and made me wonder if I was ready to take it on. And I wonder how I'm going to find my parents or relatives; it's going to be like finding a needle in a haystack.

Danger Pay

Chapter 23

I accelerated my degree over the spring and summer, but I still wasn't finished. I had been able to concentrate better since I split with Fred last winter, and instead of going home I took some more summer classes.

That fall, Father made a last ditch effort.

"You need to stay in school and finish your degree. You may not get another chance."

"I might not get another chance to go up either," I replied. "There are other students who will take this job. Besides, Dr. Thomas has just called and … well, one of the native elders has died of a heart attack and now they really need someone."

"Miriam, I won't support this." He paused for a moment. "Hold on, did Dr. Thomas tell you the name? The name of the elder who died, I mean."

"Yes, her name was Katie Cardinal, I think."

"Really? And they need you to take over her work?" "Yes. Why are you so curious? Did you know her?" One moment he was rabidly opposing my new job, and the next moment he was pensive. It made me nervous, especially if he was not going to back me up.

"Well, I heard her name before, Wasn't she involved in that dirty oil advertising campaign? Anyway," he said, trying to change the subject, "Do they have the money to pay you? You know, they are not very reliable."

I had never heard him talk about natives that way before. He was always so respectful.

But honestly, I didn't want to hear what he was saying about the pay because he was probably right, maybe I would have trouble getting paid.

"Miriam, I know you want to change the world. We all did when we were your age, but…"

"But what?" I broke in with another surge of sudden confidence. "That's why I want to go, because they are in prison, because they are having trouble. You're the one who used to say, it is not because they choose to, it's because they have been put down so much that they have ended up like that."

"Honey, I can't have my daughter in the company of the wrong people. Some of them treat women differently, you know. You aren't ready and you don't know your heritage. We should research and find that out first before you go up there."

I started to feel tightness in my chest. I wanted support. I wasn't confident, but I felt I should take the job. Suddenly, I thought of a way that might convince him.

"Didn't Jesus hang out with the lepers?"

"It's different, Honey, he didn't get sick. He healed them."

"That's why I should go," I reasoned. "I'm supposed to help them and it's not every day they agree to hire a woman. And I want to know more about my aboriginal heritage."

Before Dad could respond to this, the phone rang and Grandma, who was visiting from North Carolina, answered. She had been politely quiet during our argument until now.

"Hello." She paused, smiled, and looked directly at me.

"Yes, he is a doctor, but not the kind that helps people," she replied.

Dad had a Ph.D. in Geology, but his mother-in-law was not particularly impressed with titles.

"Who is it?" demanded Dad indignantly.

"Yes, Miriam is his daughter and she is right here," Grandma continued, ignoring Dad's disrespectful tone.

I always loved the way my grandmother could put things in perspective, especially when it came to life-changing decisions.

"It's for you, Miriam. I think it's your new employer."

With that comment, Dad marched into the kitchen.

"Hello, this is William. Is that Miriam Robinson?"

"Hello, yes. William, this is Miriam. I'm happy you called." I was relieved to finally get in touch with someone from up there. I knew from last summer working with natives that there are other priorities in their lives than telephones.

"Sorry about not bein' around," William explained, "There's no phones in the bush. I've been tryin' t' get a moose. It's a good year, but tough t' travel on the land 'til it freezes up. It was only two years ago that a couple a young boys fell through the ice and I'm too old for that. That's bad fer anyone"

"Were they okay?"

"One fella made it. The other one was never found. They're sure he slid under the ice."

"My gosh! Did you know them well?"

"Yes. They was my buddy's sons."

I knew that getting a moose was important, even if it was danger-ous. I had been reading about the Chipewyan people in a northern community called Łutselk'e in the Northwest Territories. I knew that William would need to be able to feed his family and share the meat with others in his community. I thought what a tragedy it would be to lose an important hunter like him. I hadn't thought of hunters falling through the ice.

"Do you *have to* go out again. Didn't you get a moose yet?"

"No moose this month, yet," replied William.

"Well, I was thinking of coming up to Chip this week and I was wondering if that would be okay."

William continued, "It's a good time t' come up, lots a' people around. But it's November. Ya can't drive up because the winter road's not frozen deep yet, so if you're going t' take the road, you'll have t' wait a couple a' weeks at least. The road crosses the delta. It has t'be frozen solid."

Even though Dr. Thomas told me that there was no all-weather road to Fort Chipewyan, I didn't realize it was an ice road.

I studied the Fort Chipewyan history; it was the oldest permanent settlement in Alberta and *the* major fur trade location in the late 18th century. But it remained a small settlement since the trad-ers and explorers, Peter Pond and Rodrick McKenzie, built forts there around 1778. In those days, the rivers were highways and the traders used canoes and York boats. They say that this delta had produced the best muskrat pelts in the world for two hundred years. Then, in 1970, the hydroelectric dam stopped the seasonal flooding and dried up the perched basins. Not long after that, the anti-fur movement depressed fur prices.

Needless to say, I had never driven an ice road. I didn't even own a four-wheel drive. But I had seen ice roads on TV and heard stories about truckers falling through the ice, semi and all. The only other way was to fly, and I didn't like flying. Every time I fly, I realize how far up I am and pray the plane does not do a nose dive, and when there is turbulence, it really frightens me. However, I had to get to Fort Chip somehow. What airline flies to such a small town with only a thousand people?

William told me without me asking, "You can take WaPaSu Air," he said. "There's two flights a day from McMurray."

"What's that name again?" I asked,

"WaPaSu Air; it means 'swan' in Cree. They are in the book. Peter Wells, the band manager, is in McMurray and he'll be coming up tomorrow too, and you can come up with him. Call him in McMurray."

I've never worked in an isolated community. In the summer, I did work with the Piikani and the Shuswap People in British Columbia. It was easy to drive to those places.

While at school, I remembered the film *"Destruction of a Delta."* The film showed how thirty years ago or so, Peace River Electric had built a dam on the Peace River and leveled the flow of the river, stopping the floods that kept the delta alive.

The film had an interview with William, a Cree band elder, who was born in about 1930 up the Birch River, an isolated trade settlement on the delta. I was sure it was the same guy I spoke to on the telephone. He explained the effects of the dam. He told the government many times that the dam stopped the flooding that revitalized the delta year after year. The perched basins became dry and the plants and animals had no more water. He said the government never listened. So, after two hundred years of commercial trapping, most of the Cree and Dené in the area were forced to stop trapping, especially on the delta.

Originally, the band asked the university to help because they didn't know where else to turn. Few people understood the plight of the trappers, so they needed someone to document the way they were pushed off their lands.

Companies who want to develop hire anthropologists like me to help consult with the native land use claims. I figured that after my association with the bands, I would never be hired by Peace River Electric or oil companies. Like Dad said, I was now working for the enemy.

While I was on the phone with William I overheard Grandma talking to Dad. She reminded Dad of what it was like to be young and when he was pushing for environmental change.

After I got off the phone Dad reluctantly agreed to let me take my car up north. "Eventually," he said with a smile, "we might meet across the negotiation table." I thought that was really cool.

I decided that I should drive to McMurray and then fly to Chip. It was only a one hour flight from McMurray. I packed my bags, GPS and tape recorder in the VW Rabbit. Mom said a short prayer and I started my long drive from Calgary to McMurray.

Getting to Edmonton was easy. After Edmonton, I drove for the first two hours on clear dry roads, but when I turned onto Highway 63, the weather and the vegetation started to change.

They say that Highway 63 runs right along the Athabasca River all the way to Fort McMurray. The land immediately north of Edmonton is flat. It was an old sea bottom years ago, flat except for the Swan Hills to the northwest and the Birch Mountains to the north east.

The highway was clear, but an inch of snow covered short brown grasses in the pastures and carpeted the grain-stubble fields. There were manure-splashed, reddish-brown and black cattle wallowing in muddy paddocks covered with steaming piles of manure straw.

How unhealthy the cattle looked, and how could I think of eating beef produced in such dirty squalor? As I drove further north, there was one pasture where there was a small group of enormous buffalo standing close to an even bigger bull. They were so big they dwarfed the double wire fences intended to keep them confined. Such a heavy animal could just lean on the fence and break it.

The buffalo didn't seem as dirty as the cattle. There was something special about them, something appropriate, like they belonged in this country. I felt a new connection to this big ugly beast.

The freezing wind had blown the snow off the spruce boughs and finally stripped the last dead yellow and brown leaves from the aspen and poplar branches. The ponds in the fields were frozen with a thin sheet of clean new ice, but some of the cattle had trampled the thin ice around the black muddy edges.

Further north, spruce and aspen trees replaced the fields of brown grass. The towns were small, only grain elevators and gas stations.

Still further north, some of the spruce trees began to look stunted and crooked like the dwarf spruce on top of the mountains in Jasper and Banff and some of the lower areas along the road were marshy, like muskeg.

I was excited when I saw three deer behind a large rock just outside of the tree line, so I slowed down to take a look. They didn't move and seemed oblivious. But before I came to a stop, a pickup truck barreled past me, blowing a cloud of dry snow and dust, obscuring my view of the road. When the whiteout cleared, the deer were gone.

That whiteout bothered me. Without a cloud of snow, I could see there were no more farm houses and a sign that said no gas for one hundred kilometers. Was this my point of no return? I was entering into a beautiful wilderness.

The radio station got so weak, I had to change channels to get a fuzzy CBC. I heard a newscast about an accident involving four people from around Bonneville. It was a head-on collision and the four were killed. Drugs and or alcohol were suspected, yet no charges had been laid. After my recent stop, it sent shivers up my spine. The family was from the Mirror Lake reserve just east of this highway. We all have heard gruesome stories of highway accidents, but this no longer felt like someone else's problem.

The CBC got so faint I had to turn it off. For a moment I savored the silence. Then the pavement stopped. There was too much loose gravel. Out of reflex, I futilely tightened my leg muscles as if I could steer with my legs, like on a sleigh.

A truck passed me going the other way and again, his wake blew up so much dry snow that I couldn't see a thing. I slowed down to a crawl and lost track of the road. Every truck I passed created a cyclone of snow and caused a temporary whiteout.

This highway was busy for a gravel road. After passing several cars and small trucks going the other way, I saw up ahead a larger plume of snow coming. It was a large truck and it was going fast. I looked behind me and there was another car following. I slowed down so the car could pass. The gravel whipped my windshield. Then, for a moment I could see nothing. I couldn't tell where the road was and another big truck was coming towards me. I panicked. Was I in its path? I felt a pulse in my neck and I steered to the side where I thought the shoulder was.

The car started to shake and a cushion of air from the truck's momentum pushed against the windshield, followed by the sound of rocks hitting my car. I was still moving and as the snow finally blew away, I was on the edge of the shoulder. I pulled a little further over, stopped the car and took a deep breath, praying no one else was coming up fast behind me. I quickly looked over my shoulder to check. No more trucks. Thank God. There were three new star-shaped cracks in the windshield.

"How many more miles to McMurray?" I muttered. "Why isn't this road wider?" I asked out loud.

Just down the road, I saw a trailer camp, construction equipment, and tractors holding big metal loops through which large pipes were slung. Long yellow pipe was laid out along the ditch and big piles of black dirt lined the trench. I thought of how tough it must be to work in that environment.

But even after I passed the pipeline construction, the big trucks continued to come. Then I encountered a huge metal tank on a truck bed supported with wheels from one end to the other. The tank stretched over two long beds, which must have been as long as six regular trucks. The truck bed was surrounded by guide trucks with yellow flashing lights and had pulled over on the side at a wider rest stop.

With all this activity, my illusion of wilderness was dashed. I felt I shouldn't be on the same road with all this traffic. It wouldn't have taken much to make a fatal mistake.

When I got closer to McMurray, the pavement started again. The airport turn off was before the town entrance between two large piles of snow. This place must get more snow, I thought, as I was relieved to finally turn off that perilous road onto the airport drive.

I was exhausted from squinting through the dust and snow and ready to finally extract myself from my little car. I was starving and couldn't wait to wash and eat, but like everything in this region, there were too many people and vehicles around the tiny airport facilities. I had to drive out to a field that had been cleared of snow for overflow parking. The unpaved temporary parking lot was filled with muddy potholes and I tried to find a place that would not swallow my tiny car. I had to drag my bags back to the terminal building while taxis sped by, picking up the throngs of fresh workers for the new tar sands plants.

When I entered the small terminal, despite the crowd around the baggage claim, I immediately saw a tall fellow standing beside the WaPaSu desk.

As I approached him he smiled and said, "Hello, you must be Miriam Robinson." The tall, blond, middle-aged man tried to be polite and formal in this rugged scene.

I was so relieved to hear my name after the insecurity of that drive. "Peter Wells?" I asked as I gazed up into his clear blue eyes. If I had known him at all, I would have hugged him. Instead, I had to settle for a firm handshake.

School Buddies

Chapter 24

"Franklin Thomas speaking."

"Dr. Thomas? This is Phillip Robinson calling. I'm Miriam Robinson's father."

"Oh, yes?

"I am calling because I am curious about Miriam's work in Fort McMurray. "

"Well, actually she will mostly be working in Fort Chipewyan." Thomas replied.

"Okay. I wanted to let you know that I work with CanOil and, as you may know, we have a project up in Fort McMurray."

"Oh, yes."

"Well, as a parent, you might imagine that I wouldn't want my daughter exposed to what goes on up there."

"Well, Mr. Robinson, I really don't know what to say to you about that. First, I understand what you must be thinking, but the First Nation people she will be working with are good people; they have families of their own.

However, from another perspective, it is rather ironic that an executive of an oil company would be calling a consultant for the First Nations to ask about safety. You do realize that in our regular submissions to the ERCB we complain vigorously about the social conditions your projects are creating in Fort McMurray. I suppose

I should be asking *you* to do something about the social conditions up there."

"Well, I'm not asking you for any inappropriate or competitive information, but I do want to ensure she has a safe and healthy working environment."

"Well, I can assure you of that, *Dr.* Robinson."

"Thank you, *Dr.* Thomas. Sorry, titles do sound sort of pompous, don't they?"

"But eight years is a long time to go to school. That makes me think-did you attend the University of Alberta in the late sixties, early seventies?" Thomas asked.

"Yeah." Robinson agreed.

"Were you that student union representative?"

"Guilty as charged." Robinson smiled.

"Well, you of all people should know what it was like." Thomas jabbed.

"Yes, that is precisely why I am worried!"

"I still remember your hair and the placards: *"Students for a democratic university!"* I supported your campaign. And whatever happened to that girl you hung out with?" Thomas asked.

"Ellen? I lost touch with her thirty years ago."

"She was such a looker. So how in the heck did you ever end up as VP of an oil company?"

"It's just what geologists do. Economic geology was a new double major and after the revolution didn't happen, we all had to get jobs. I tried to do my best, under the circumstances. What did you take?" Robinson asked Thomas.

"You don't remember me at the back of micro-economics? It was a big class. I took my undergrad in economic anthropology."

"Oh, sorry. I don't … ah?" Robinson stumbled.

"Well, I now know where Miriam gets so much of her zest for social justice. You know it's not too late. You may be able to make a contribution to what is going on up there. Could we get together and talk sometime. Maybe for lunch?" Asked Thomas.

"Sure, I'd like that."

Fear of Flying

Chapter 25

Peter recognized it was Miriam as soon as she walked into the terminal. Her bright blue eyes twinkled as she scanned the room and her blond hair brushed over her ample breasts. She had a natural beauty and she walked with a swagger like an accomplished athlete.

"Peter Wells?" Miriam asked.

"Yes, that's me. Welcome to Fort McMoney." Peter was in McMurray to finish up his divorce papers. Ten years ago he married a girl from Calgary money. She came up to Fort Chip with him to teach and lasted barely a year. "There's no hope for these people," she said and escaped back to Calgary to teach in an urban school. After being separated for years, she finally asked for the divorce. Peter was happy to comply. He had had enough of prissy oil-patch queens.

And this Miriam Robinson looked almost like a typical oil princess but with a bit of tomboy worked in. She better not be a princess, he thought; the band needs someone who can relate to the elders and not look down on them, someone who understands.

Peter had lived in Fort Chip for quite some time. When he arrived, the trapping economy was good; a trapper might net as much as $50,000 per year. Then he saw the unemployment, alcoholism, and devastation that took over the community after the dam was built. As a teacher, he had to console the neglected children, and as a consultant, he tried to work with the chief and council to get employment or cultural retention projects going. Recently, he was feeling alone and overwhelmed with all the problems.

He told the government, "These unemployment problems are impossible, even with unlimited resources."

But he maintained a strong respect for the traditional talents of his native colleagues and he knew they deserved better. He wanted to publicize the havoc created by the dam and now oil sands projects, but after an initial media splash, the public lost interest. Maybe Miriam and the university would document what happened, maybe even support a court challenge.

I admired Peter's chiseled face. His height and stature would humble most men, but he had the quiet manner of a well-educated person.

"Well Miriam, it looks like we'll have four on the plane to Chip—you, me, Mary Cardinal and William Short. They are waiting for us over there. Have you had anything for dinner?"

"No," I sighed. "I'm starving."

"Okay, there's a hamburger place over there." Peter pointed me to the bar.

The older fellow with Peter looked familiar. I recognized him. He was the same guy they interviewed for that movie on the dam I saw at school. It was Elder William Short.

After I struggled through a portion of a greasy hamburger, I looked across the crowded terminal and saw them surrounded by cardboard boxes and suitcases. They were pushing an overloaded cart out the door towards the small plane. The Caravan seemed tiny compared to the jets I had flown on before.

As they held the door open, a cloud of snow drifted in and the native woman quickly fastened the hood of her fur-trimmed felt parka over her long dark hair. William had a shiny brown fur hat and shoe rubbers without boots underneath, just moccasins. I wondered how he could be comfortable in such small moccasins. His long grey hair was neatly braided and he looked comfortable in his jeans and layered jackets.

The young pilot was wearing a new leather flight jacket and ear muffs. He packed the bags and groceries in small compartments under the plane's cabin. As I pulled my bags over to the door, I heard Peter asking the moccasin man, "Good shopping trip?" He looked up at Peter, and pointing with his lips, he said, "I wish the road was open, the prices at the Northern in Chip will break ya."

As we loaded the plane, I noticed Elder William was wearing a knife holster with the knife still in it. So we didn't have to go through security! It gave me an odd feeling and I didn't know whether to feel relieved or frightened.

Peter grabbed another cardboard grocery box. "It won't be long now before the road freezes; the weather is so cold."

It was already dark at dinner time and bad weather looked like it was closing in. The pilot seemed to want to get going, which made me feel a bit nervous, but I knew I had to get control of my fear. After all, flying was safer than my road trip. Peter quickly introduced me to William and Mary and we all took our seats and buckled up.

The engines whined, thrusting the flimsy plane down the runway.

I used the ear plugs in the seat pocket. It was probably my irrational feelings, but at first the plane seemed to take forever to clear the ground. Then, all at once I felt the air sucking the small plane into the sky.

When we got up, we saw the street lights of McMurray and in the distance the bright lights of the Syncrude plant. For a moment I relaxed and looked in awe at the huge industrial projects which had grown out of an otherwise pristine area. The plant looked like a big city building with no windows and tall chimneys spewing out smoke and steam. The sliver towers appeared as artificial tinseled Christmas trees. Beyond a battery of huge round metal tanks, there were dark clearings and black gravel ponds.

I had read about these so called ponds: "*Billions of Barrels of Sludge*". These toxic ponds were right beside the river. The only lights beyond the plant were the headlights of huge trucks that from our height looked like Tinkertoys in a back yard sand box. They were driving up and down the black hills around the ponds. It was a twenty-four hour operation.

Once we flew past the tar sands plants, the windows of the plane went dark and everything was quiet for a while. I felt a sense of togetherness with the other passengers—isolated from civilization. We knew we were going to a much quieter place. I noticed Peter and Mary sitting beside each other silently holding hands across the aisle of the plane.

The buzz of the engine allowed everyone their own space.

Mary was thinking of her mother, who had just gotten out of the hospital. Until she moved up a few years ago, she had not been back to Chip since the days of the residential school. She knew her story was the same as many other women who had married non-treaty men, but that didn't make it easier. Many had lost their treaty status and had to beg to get back in to their band. It put an extra strain on the family. She resented the racism and sexism the white man had foisted upon her people.

Peter was thinking of getting back to work now that the divorce nonsense was over. The Chip band needed some more programs in partnership with the oil sands companies. He was hoping the chief would exert their rights to get a better deal. He had to get the chief thinking about rights instead of money. There was a rush to get rich in Fort McMurray. Everyone, natives and whites alike, was scrambling to get contracts, a business, or some advantage. Personal greed was the greatest impediment to native recovery. Peter knew what greed had done in his family; his brothers and sister had fought tooth and nail over inheritance.

I was quietly excited. This was an adventure. I just met one of the elders, William, whom I would be working with, and I started to feel more relaxed about flying. I hoped I could make a difference for these people by recording their land use. I thought of my father's attitude before I left and his poker buddy who was president of Royal Oil. What would they think now about what I was doing?

The snow in the lights of the plane was blowing horizontally. The snowflakes looked like white lines appearing and disappearing into the darkness. This was the first big winter storm of the year. Nothing to worry about, I thought. Planes fly in snow.

I noticed Peter nodding off about half an hour into the otherwise quiet flight when the engine started to sputter. We heard the pilot whisper "Shit!" under his breath.

Peter had mentioned that before they took off, the pilot said they had had trouble with frozen fuel lines. Mary started to whisper something in her language and Peter asked the pilot what was happening. The pilot raised one ear of his headphones and promised it would clear up, but just as he finished the engine choked and stopped completely. The lights on the cockpit instruments went dark. The pilot's voice strained as he told us he would have to ditch the plane. We could feel the pilot's fear. William did up his coat.

In a cracking voice, the pilot blurted, "Everyone make sure your seat belts are tight and put your arms on the seat in front of you. Brace yourselves."

He did not want to set down in the trees, but he couldn't really see much. He could try and find the winter road or maybe he could make it to the sand dunes.

He knew the dunes were somewhere close. We all prayed in silent fear as the plane got closer and closer to the ground, and without the sound of the engine, it was eerily quiet. "There's the dunes," the pilot announced with some relief. "Hold on everybody."

The sand dunes were like a wide beach in the middle of the boreal forest. At least there were no trees to run into. We were jarred when the plane hit the dunes and skidded on the snow-covered sand. At first we slid on the snow, but then the nose caught a mound and we were yanked over. We slid on the collapsed roof for what seemed an eternity. As we flipped, I was slung into the arm rest of the seat beside me. A lightning bolt of pain pierced my chest.

Through the pain I felt us come to a clanging halt, backwards and upside down and hanging from our seatbelts. The metal roof had collapsed around us. Peter, who seemed to be unreasonably calm, said we were lucky it did not hit our heads. Sand and snow filled the cabin below us.

After the plane stopped, Peter asked if I was alright. I was crying and moaned that my side really hurt. Peter and William both asked Mary if she were alright. She was quick to respond that she was okay, but she was not so sure about the pilot.

Peter unbuckled his seat belt and fell upside-down onto the broken ceiling of the plane. He then helped me out. I grimaced in pain as I fell into his arms. I did not realize that my rib was broken. Then he helped Mary down. Peter looked up in the cockpit and quickly looked away. "What's wrong?" asked Mary.

Peter replied, "The pilot looks bad; there's a lot of blood on his head and I think his neck is broken." He moved closer. "He's not breathing. We'd better get him out of the plane."

Peter and William had to push the heavy door up and hold it while we crawled out below the broken steps. As I stood up, more pain shot through my chest. Peter went back and checked on the pilot. He did not seem to be breathing and his body was twisted backwards in the seat. Instead of hanging in his seatbelt, his head was caught under the plane's controls. The front windshield was broken and he was covered in chards of glass.

Peter had not known this boy and he paused for a moment. He wondered why this had happened. Why can't anything go right these days? That pilot, just a kid! But first, he needed to make sure everyone else was safe and kept warm until help arrived.

As soon as William got out of the plane, he began to look around for a shelter. "Who knows how long we'll be in this storm." He walked carefully over to the trees on the side of the dunes under a little bluff. The wind was still blowing, so William found the protected area behind the bluff. He called us and started to cut branches with his knife. Mary helped me walk towards William.

Peter thought about getting the pilot down from his harness. There did not seem to be any life in the boy. He felt for a pulse, then tried to see if he was breathing. Dan had blood covering his head from a gash above his hairline. It looked bad. Peter thought the worst. Maybe he should get supplies from the plane first and then ask William if he knew what to do. He got some of the suitcases for more clothes and he got the emergency medical kit and some of the groceries that William was bringing back to Chip. There was a small saw and tarp under the emergency kit and he took it all over to William.

William told Mary to help me sit under the trees he had selected. He had cut some boughs and tied up the tarp that Peter brought him. There was already a wall of snow behind the trees and he placed the spruce boughs against that snow. Then, with the tarp he extended the wall into a roof and sides. He told Pete to gather some wood and continued to cut spruce boughs for us to sit on. Peter had brought the suitcases; we got more clothes out and put the food boxes on the side. Mary arranged the wood and started a fire. It was just big enough for the four of us to sit.

Then William went to the plane to get Pilot Dan out. He knew that if he were still alive and he moved him, he might damage his spine, but he was more likely to die in the plane if he didn't get him down. Peter was waiting to help him. They released the hooks and slowly lowered Dan onto the broken ceiling of the cockpit and tried to carry the limp body out of the door on to the sandy snow.

"He's not breathing," said William. "He didn't make it." William and Peter looked at each other with a sense of horror. They both felt it could have been them lying there. William said a few words in his language as Peter bowed his head. He didn't understand what William said except for "Amen" at the end, but it made him feel better anyway. They wrapped him in an extra down-filled parka they found in the cockpit and respectfully laid him a safe distance from the plane.

During the flight, Peter had heard Dan radioing McMurray, which meant that the airport personnel knew where they were when they lost power. Peter suggested to William that they would come up looking for us immediately. But William commented that they may wait until the storm made it possible for the rescuers to fly. Then he looked at me, the other injured passenger.

"Pete, I think Miriam is okay and at least everyone else is out of danger."

After about fifteen to twenty minutes, the four of us had settled in and were all huddling behind the tarp in front of the fire in a daze of disbelief. The wind was blowing much harder now and we started to talk about what would happen next. William melted snow in a small pot he found somewhere and made some tea out of herbs from under one of the trees close by. I was amazed how he was able to make comfort out of this wilderness.

Then this big solid and stoic guy, Peter, seemed to be hurting. It was just a little sob. He looked away to hide his face from everyone and Mary put her arm around him. The crash was sinking in; probably the pilot's fate was bothering him. So far he had reacted so coolly, probably without thinking too much about what had happened. Mary comforted him, "We are all right. Everything is okay."

I chimed in, "I want to cry, but my side would hurt too much."

Peter mustered a smile and Mary laughed a bit.

"Stop! Laughing hurts more!" I pleaded.

Looking into the fire again, Peter blurted out, "He was just a kid."

After a minute or so, William started to speak, "Sometimes the Creator puts us to the test," he said. "That boy's soul is free now to be with the Grandfathers."

He paused and looked at Mary. Mary asked William, "Do you think Dan was taught well enough?"

William shrugged his shoulders. "He was Métis," William said, "From Saskatchewan- French."

"The airline hired him as a token brown face," Mary sneered. "Those airline guys from Peace River don't care, they just serve McMurray for the money,"

William had taken a different approach. "Out on the land it don't take many mistakes before this type a' thing happens. When I used t' go out on the land wi' your father, Mary, in the winter we took everything we needed and what we don't take, we get from the land. Young people need t' be taught how ta survive, how to live like that. Years ago, I was taught by my father how ta survive.

My dad used to trap with Snowbird—ya know him, Pete. This was a good country, lots a game an' clean water. My father told me we need t' protect this land; in the treaty they promised that we could use it as long as the rivers flowed. Father was there at the treaty an' he told me what they said."

William stopped talking and turned to me. I cringed as I tried to change positions. "This wasn't what I meant by needing excitement," I joked and then seriously asked William, "What if I am badly injured?" A wave of worry came over me as I thought about my father and mother. I I wondered if the crash would be reported in Calgary.

Then William spoke to me directly, "Your parents aren't worried about you; they don't even know ya've had an accident. S'only a broken rib. No one dies v' a broken rib. You'll be okay, an' you'd better be okay, 'cause we need you to help us with our study."

I opened my eyes wide: How did he know I was thinking about my parents?

William looked at Mary and Peter, "We'll be here for a while an' everything'll be fine. This dune's just south a' my wife's family's winter traplines. There's a cabin not too far from here that we can go ta, but in this storm it's better to stay by the fire. When it stops snowing it'll get colder."

Now Mary had tears in her eyes and looked up at William, "William, you remind me of my father."

"Your father was a damn good man," he replied.

Mary reminisced, "I remember being out on the land with my dad. He took my brothers and me up in the Birch Mountains to a cabin one winter. Even my Mosom and Kohkom were there. I don't remember it well because I was only six or so. My Mosom taught me how to tend the fire in the cabin. It was in an old stove and she taught me how to cook things on it too. Dad wouldn't let me go out with the boys; he said I was too young. I remember they would bring in the furs and we stretched them and hung them over the stove to dry. My mom and Mosom made it so comfy by filling the cabin with furs and blankets."

"Your dad was one a the best trappers 'round. I remember when he went out on the land one fall. He only took a rifle, three bullets an' an axe, but in the spring he came back in a new made canoe filled to the top with furs and he was smilin' at all of the women." William smiled at Mary but Mary had heard that story somewhere before.

William continued. "Me an' him were close like brothers, he taught me many things."

Mary said, "But I didn't know you knew him so well. What happened?"

"Everyone knew each other back then. When the residential school took you and your brothers, he didn't know what t' do. Your mother blamed him for lettin' them take ya. She wouldn't forgive 'im. He left an' went t' the mountains. Some say he died in them mountains. Some say he was killed by the *Whi-ti-koh*. But a friend a' mine down in Calgary told me he saw him drunk on the street. A T'suu Tina member spoke Dené t' him – he understood. Your father didn't speak English too well, only Dené, Cree an' French. No one knows where he went or what happened, but he hasn't been in Chip fer years. Your mother lost a lot. She's happy t' see ya again even though your brothers have been good to her."

Mary remembered the school, "At the residential school they didn't use our names. They chopped our hair off and gave us a number; mine was eighty-nine. We couldn't speak our language and my brothers were separated from me. Sometimes I would see my brothers in the halls and they would whisper to me in Cree. I lost most of my mother's language and I didn't even know my father spoke so many. He only spoke Cree to me."

"Ya, your father was true Dené, but he spoke Cree good too. After he left, no one talked about him much. Ya know, his great-grandfather was the Mr. Mercredi who translated the treaty. Father said that Mercredi told them the queen's people lied about Treaty Eight. He told the government men the same an' they threatened him. Ya come from good people, Mary," William assured her.

Mary was proud of her heritage, but she seemed troubled by her challenges; now that Katie was gone she felt like she had the weight of the world on her shoulders.

"I have not seen my father since I was taken to residential school!" William said. "I was happy when they tore down that school building."

Peter chimed in, "It was like a ceremony, a solemn occasion. After tearing it down and burning the scraps, people symbolically left through the front gate like they were leaving their pain behind."

Watching William and listening to the stories I realized that I was already working. I was already learning, but the pain in my side was sharp. I tried not to interrupt, but I gasped when it became sharper.

William noticed my squint. Reaching inside his coat, he pulled out a flask and handed it to me. "Drink some of this."

Peter gave William a double take because he thought William had not taken a drink of whisky for years. He was shocked, "William, why are you carrying that flask?"

William said, "I always carry it with me."

"But you... you..."

"Pete, it's not what you think. I picked this up in Saskatchewan when I visited my family and medicine man. This will ease her pain a bit."

I took the flask, thinking that it was scotch or whiskey and was grateful. But when it touched my lips it tasted like tar and spruce gum, like a repugnant cough medicine. I looked at Peter as if to ask should I drink it. Peter nodded. I took a swig and gave it back to William. "Thank you," I said dutifully.

Peter noticed the fire was getting low. The snow and wind had picked up and it felt like a full blizzard. There would be no rescue flights tonight, he thought. Luckily there was plenty of deadfall around and it was barely covered with snow. Peter was lucky *he* wasn't hurt and was feeling strong and alive, unlike the poor boy still out beside the plane. He looked over, but he couldn't see very well because of the blinding snow.

He was putting a branch on the fire when he heard a sound coming from the direction of the plane. He made his way towards the plane anyway and as he got closer, he caught a glimpse of a dark shadow moving quickly behind the plane. It looked like a dog, a wolf. His throat tightened like he was choking and he felt his blood flowing through his arms and chest. Were the wolves after the body? He ran towards the plane as he called for William. It looked like the wolves had pulled at Dan's parka. He grabbed the hood and started to drag him towards the fire.

William saw Pete and told him to stop, "Don't worry about them wolves; you scared them an' they won't be back." Peter had faith in William's knowledge. William took out a pouch with a handful of herbs and seemed to be getting ready to do another prayer when they heard another sound, but this time it was coming from the parka. He was alive? They opened up the zippered parka and sure enough Dan was moving his head. He was alive.

They carried him carefully over to the shelter by the fire and called to the women, "Dan is alive!" They made room for him by the fire and loosened the parka and tried to make him comfortable. Could they sit him up?

"What happened?" He appeared to be coming to and started to speak. He asked "Where's the plane?" He then closed his eyes again. It looked like he was drifting in and out. Then he opened his eyes again and tried to sit up. "I tried to land on the sand dune," he said. "Where are we?"

"We are beside the dunes Dan. We made it, we are all okay. We made a shelter and a fire and we are waiting to be rescued," explained Peter. Peter thought that they had better get Dan some medical help fast. Head injuries are unpredictable.

Mary got the first aid kit and started to clean the dried blood off of Dan's head.

I was still feeling my side, but it was okay as long as I didn't move.

The worst had passed. The plane went down and no one was killed.

It was half an hour since Peter had tried the radio. We huddled around the fire and no one said much. William had fallen asleep and Peter was still putting logs on the fire. Mary thought of how warm her parka was and how grateful she was to Katie for making it especially for her. The wind picked up and the rest of them crouched in closer under the shelter and around the fire.

Mary was dreaming of when she went out with her family to the cabin on the trap line. Her dad never let her go out with him and her brothers, but she was always excited when they returned to the cabin. She remembered the approaching hum of the Ski-Doo engines when they would return. A faint buzz of the engine would get louder as they approached; that familiar sound. But what? She was not dreaming; someone was out there, close by, on a snowmobile. She turned to Pete, "It's a snowmobile!"

Pete raised his head and listened. "You're right! There's two of them! Maybe even three!"

Peter grabbed a big spruce bough and lit it with the fire. Holding it over his head, he ran up on to the Dunes waving it frantically towards the sounds and the flashing of headlights. These guys must be from Chip, he thought, they are the only guys who could get here so fast. The first machine came right up to Peter and stopped beside him. It was the Marcel boys. There were three of them with Ski-Doos and sleds towed behind. As William said, this area was in the Marcel trapline. If anyone knew how to find them, it was these boys.

"Hey! Are you alright? Is everyone okay? What happened to the plane?" asked the first Marcel.

A wave of relief came over Pete. He was so glad to see Joe Marcel, he could have hugged him. Joe was the older brother and was a well-known hunter and guide in the area. Peter suspected that he would be the first one to find us. "Joe! Thank God you are here!" He gestured towards the fire, "We have one seriously injured; I think we need to get him in as soon as possible." He pointed to me. "Another woman has a cracked rib, painful but not an emergency."

"The cracked rib should ride on the back of my Ski-Doo," replied Joe. "The serious one, we can put him on the toboggan and we will drive real careful. Do we need to take anything else?" he asked.

Pete doused the fire with snow and everyone put on extra jackets, snow pants, hats and mitts brought by the rescuers.

Quickly, the four of us got our belongings from the shelter. We only took things already out of the plane. We all knew we needed to get out of the cold, so we quickly threw the baggage into the sleds and carefully strapped Dan on George's toboggan. William agreed to ride in the other, while Pete, Mary, and I rode on the back of Keith's Ski-Doo.

"The wind chill on a Ski-Doo can be very harsh. Cover your face with the hood and scarves. Your skin can freeze quickly," Joe instructed me.

In a few minutes, we were on their way to Chip. The sand hills were bumpy and we had to maneuver our way around trees and over clumps. We had to go more slowly so as not to cause further injuries. It was not easy at the beginning, but soon we saw the flat plain that was Jackfish Lake. "It's frozen; it's okay, we'll go straight across," Joe said.

"We could stop at the Jackfish Village and stay at a cabin 'til morning," Joe suggested. Joe explained that Jackfish village was a group of cabins in the delta used by the families mostly in the summer months.

"What's the river like?" asked Peter. He was referring to the Athabasca River, which had to be frozen before the winter road could open.

"It was okay where we crossed, but the lake's still open in some places. We have to be careful." I assumed Joe was referring to Lake Athabasca. "The rest of us can stay at Jackfish, but someone needs to take Dan into the medical station in Chip and Miriam should probably go as well." After the comment that the lake was open in some places and remembering what William said, I got worried, but I had to trust our rescuers.

We stopped briefly at the Jackfish cabins and Dan and I continued on to Fort Chip. I rode on Joe's Ski-Doo and George took Dan.

"It's better to take two Ski-Doos in case something goes wrong," Joe explained. "They're not like a dog sled. Dogs are safe; more reliable. When a snow machine goes down in the bush, you're stranded, but dogs, well, they don't break down and if you have to stop, they can keep you warm."

It was not too long before we reached the river. I could only see what was lit by the headlights, but I could tell the delta was flat. They only slowed down for the banks of the rivers.

When we started down the big river bank, I saw that the river was open, full of water. I panicked and screamed, "Stop! Stop! – the river's open." Joe stopped the machine, not understanding why I was upset.

"You aren't going to try and go over an open river in this thing, are you?" I said

From one snow bank on one side, one hundred meters across, to the other side, the river was completely open. No ice. I was sure we would have died if I had not alerted him. What kind of a rescue was this?

Joe removed the frost covered scarf he had over his mouth and slowly turned around to talk to me.

Joe said, "Miriam, right? Your name is Miriam?"

"Yes."

"Miriam, every winter we have to flood the river at the crossings. Do you see the truck on the other side? That's Brian. He's flooding the crossing so that it'll freeze thick here so that big trucks can cross. It's just four inches of water on top of solid ice. He's pumping the water from a hole in the ice he made further up the river. We can cross without any problem. Really, you don't have to worry and Dan will be okay too."

I thought for a moment. "But it looks like the river's open." I twisted to look up and down and my side started to hurt again. In a flash of pain, I decided that I had to trust him. After all, he did know how to find us in the middle of this wilderness.

Down the bank we went into the water. I tightened my jaw and winced as we entered. Sure enough, we did not sink and we motored across on the ice, hydroplaning on four inches of water. I sighed. In just one day I have confronted my worst fears of death and

survived. It is these people who are protecting and helping me when I thought I was going to help protect them—what an irony. And the wondrous part was, as the lights of Fort Chipewyan came into sight, I knew that this was just the beginning.

Injury, Cancer, and Accidents

Chapter 26

I was lucky; this was the day the doctor was in town. I called my parents and told them I was in Fort Chipewyan, safe and sound. I didn't tell them about the plane or my broken rib. I said I had lots to do and I would call them back later.

"Now, this isn't the type of injury that'd keep you from your work," Doctor O'Malley assured me.

"So, I can stay in Fort Chip until I recover and then finish the contract?" I asked.

"There's no reason that I can see for you to leave," he assured me again.

I thought it was odd that since there were no fatalities our crash was treated casually. That was the rugged frontier spirit.

I told the Doctor, "If my parents find out about this crash, they'll demand that I quit, I know they will. My Dad didn't want me to come up in the first place. They would both probably really freak out if they knew what happened."

"Since the accident wasn't reported outside of McMurray, they won't find out unless you tell them," he said. "And since you are the age of majority, all your medical records are private."

O'Malley said the only cure for a slightly cracked rib was to rest and to let it heal. If the pain was too bad, I could take codeine. He came to town once a week and prescribed pills as needed. At least now during my recovery, I would get a chance to get a feel for the town and to meet some of the people. This experience would come in handy for the interviews.

Peter suggested that I stay in the band's trailer in the middle of town. From there, if it wasn't too painful, I could walk to the Northern Store or the restaurant and bar, he said. In five minutes I could walk to the post office and the band office too. Peter had told me that when consultants worked for the band, they would stay at the trailer and I would have company every once in a while. He said that if I got lonely, I was welcome to come to his place.

It wasn't two weeks after the plane went down that the news of another crash on the winter road stunned the community. A van full of teenagers was hit by a supply truck as they rounded a turn. A young boy and his sister were killed. It was all over the newspapers. It was a major blow. I am not used to death. No one had died in my family; even my grandparents are still alive.

I began to understand how everyone in the town was connected, if not by blood or marriage, by spirit. I decided to attend the funerals. I watched as the community dealt with the tragedy. They knew there was something more important than life. Perhaps it was living so close to nature, so close to God.

It took a while for the community to get back to normal. The offices and meetings were all shut down for a couple of days, sometimes longer. The families had wakes, another tradition I was not familiar with. I didn't go to any; I really didn't know the families and I didn't want to view the bodies.

It was a few days before anyone asked or suggested that I start the interviews. I did call my parents and spoke about the car crash with the expected cautions about how dangerous it was in such an isolated community. My Dad said he would like to come up and see me, but I asked him to wait until I was settled. I didn't say until I was healed. After I hung up, the pain started to throb. It was usually not bad, except at night. After only a week, I was out of painkillers.

I went back to O'Malley for more and dropped in on Peter on the way back.

"So I hear we're all going to get cancer," Peter said as I walked in.

I frowned. "No, Sean just said there were more rare cancers here."

Peter jerked his head forward and opened his eyes wide at me. "So it's Sean to you already?" I could feel my face flush.

"Anyway, it's all over the media. Dr. O'Malley found that there were more rare cancers in Fort Chipewyan than normal and asked for an inquiry. He thinks that it was caused by the oil sands. He knows all about the Sydney Tar Pits in Nova Scotia. People in that town had very high rates of cancer because of the poly... er... polycyclic ..."

"Polycyclic aromatic hydrocarbons." Mary finished Peter's attempt as she came down the stairs.

"Yeah, that's it." Peter repeated it, "Polycyclic aromatic hydrocarbons."

Mary continued, "But what about polychlorinated byphenals, or PCBs?"

"Yeah, PCBs," echoed Peter. "So, we're all going to die of weird cancers."

Peter stopped his sarcasm. "But the studies don't include the people who have moved out of the community and we need to trace all of the people who have moved away and who have been exposed to the chemicals up here. It could be much worse."

"Sean told me he received a letter from the government. They're denying that there's any problem with cancer here, and they accused him of causing alarm." I added.

Mary looked angry. "The government is willin' to sacrifice our health to generate more revenue. Anythin' that's negative about the tar sands, they deny. It's so bad that even the tar sands companies are embarrassed by their callousness."

"The worst part of it is they have refused the community monitoring," Peter interjected. "Dr. Schneider has shown that the monitoring for cancer-causing heavy metals is inadequate. But all the oil company reports say is everything is okay. Meanwhile, instead of trying to solve the problem they are attacking Fort Chip's best doctor ever. I'm going for a smoke."

Peter left the office and Mary went back to her paperwork. I was left standing in the front office looking at the pictures of the elders on the wall, just visible over the stacks of oil company proposal boxes. I probably should help Mary go through the 20 binders on her desk. How could this First Nation defend itself against the world's greed and lust for oil? Dr. Thomas wanted me to help but what could I do? If they were attacking Dr. O'Malley, and they say someone murdered Katie Cardinal, what would they do to me?

When Peter came back in, he announced, "It's court day." He put on his jacket.

"Court day?" I asked.

"Court day in Fort Chip," John answered. "It might be quite interesting for you to see since we are going to support a friend of ours. It will give you a better understanding of the community."

Inside, beside the old band office building, there was a court room. It lay behind two birch doors which looked out of place in the old hallway. There were about ten rows of oak benches on each side of an aisle and the sheet rock walls were also trimmed in oak.

At the front was a large elevated desk for the judge with a door behind it. In front of the desk there were two tables, all in the same blond oak. There were two guys behind the left table, dressed in courtroom robes. Both had neatly combed ponytails. Behind the right table sat a plump woman with painfully short hair, dressed in a black suit that was too small for her. There was a secretary of sorts sitting at a side table with a computer.

The pews were half full of anxious people. They were clustered in groups, what one might find at a church with no one in the first row. They looked solemn, apprehensive or angry, and some were holding hands. Peter guided me to a middle row behind a young couple. He explained that the judge and lawyers flew up on a special plane on court day. They would come in once a month and conduct these sessions for a day or two.

One of the lawyers, Jake Maurice, was a friend of his and he was defending William's son, Bill, Jr., who had been arrested for possession of marijuana with the intent to traffic. He was a truck driver at the Suncor Mine, which was a really good job. He was not a habitual user and not a pusher. For some reason the cops wanted to get him. Peter explained that they thought he was supplying the town, but he wasn't. The Royal Canadian Mounted Police could not stop the drugs from entering the town, especially in the winter when the road was open. They were getting frustrated and they figured they had caught a real perpetrator.

Bill, Jr. would be fired if he was convicted of such a crime and he had been such a good example for the community. There were only a few young people making that kind of money up here. Maurice would try and get the charges reduced at least.

In the first case, a man was charged with cruelty to animals. They claimed he was letting his sled dogs starve. A tall, skinny dark-haired man wearing a dirty green down vest stood up and told the judge that it was a month or two ago, that he had no money, and he was away working. He wasn't able to feed them for a few days, but he made sure they had water. He said when he got back he fed them and they are all right. The judge listened carefully. The judge asked the prosecutor if they had agreed to a term of supervision. She quickly responded that they had.

The bush fellow looked relieved and thanked the judge as he left the courtroom.

There were several other cases before Bill, Jr.'s. I was impressed by the sensitivity of the judge. He seemed to know when to be tough and when to be lenient.

"I hope he'll be able to understand Bill, Jr.," Peter said. "This judge is reasonable if you plead guilty and you are humble and respectful, but he doesn't deal the same way if you are too proud."

After Junior's charges were read, Jake got up and quickly explained that Junior had a good job in McMurray and came back to visit his family in Fort Chip when he had some time off. He was a well-respected member of this community and he was not a habitual user of drugs. He had to go through regular drug testing for his job. He said that the charges were too harsh for the circumstances and he would plead not guilty.

The plump woman prosecutor described the character of Bill, Jr. differently. She said that he had been arrested distributing marijuana to several people in the community, that it was clear that he was a trafficker and that this was an insidious problem.

Peter said, "What a bitch" under his breath. "She doesn't understand this community at all. It's only because the cops here are getting frustrated; that's what this is all about. They have the wrong guy. And these officers are useless. They switch them out of the community too often."

The judge asked for a recess and signaled for the two lawyers to come back through the oak door behind his desk. It was a good time to go out and have a coffee. I went to the bathroom.

As I was coming back, I noticed Jake Maurice coming out of the men's room. He looked very handsome in his black courtroom robe. He smiled and paused as if he wanted to say something and then looked down at his watch and pushed through the door.

Peter told me that Jake would be a good person for me to talk to about rights. He was very aware of aboriginal rights and I might enjoy picking his brain. He was going to run in a Manitoba by-election next month, for Parliament. He might win because there are so many aboriginal voters in northern Manitoba. Peter said he wanted to ask Jake to help us out with the presentations to the

Energy Resources Conservation Board and Courts.

William was there asking Peter what he thought about Junior's case. Junior was a big man, but he was humbled by the situation. He walked behind his dad with his head lowered. He was normally respected in the community, but now it was clear he had made a big mistake. Jake appeared and took him aside for a moment.

The clerk called everyone back into the court room. After everyone was seated, the prosecutor announced that the charges had been reduced to simple possession. The judge asked Junior to stand. Jake then stated that Junior would plead guilty. The Judge sentenced him to a suspended six months and some reporting requirements. Junior looked relieved. He could keep his job.

Things had been happening so fast. Ever since I started driving north of Edmonton, it had been as if I was transported into a different world. I was continuously witnessing the edge of catastrophe, only being rescued by good fortune or grace. I had expected it would be different in the real world, away from home and out of the ivory towers of school, but this was more fantastic than I imagined. How could things be so different only four hundred kilometers north of Edmonton? This is the stuff movies are made of.

After Junior's case, Peter said he wanted to go up to the bar after and have a drink, relax, and talk. He said he wanted to introduce me to Nicole McDonald, the Industry Relations Company Director who had been sitting beside us in the courtroom. She had been there as a character witness for Junior if he needed it. Peter said she had a degree in biology and that I would be working with her a lot.

I met them outside and we drove the two blocks to the bar. Nicole was pretty with fine brown hair. She was gentle, but looked as if she was strong in her beliefs. I liked her immediately. I thought she might be a kindred spirit. She looked maybe three or so years older than me.

"So nice to meet you," she said. "I'm really looking forward to getting some of the work on the traditional land use done. We really appreciate you coming here to help us."

I thought it would be nice to work with such a person. "Thank you, Nicole, I'm very excited about getting started myself. Do you want to talk about the scope of the project before we get going?"

But Nicole said she was tired. She told us that she would see us tomorrow and we could talk about the interviews then. In the courtroom, I noticed how she gazed at Jake the lawyer. It was clear she liked him and he even took a few masked peeks at her.

The rest of us met up at the lodge bar. It was a cedar sided hotel on a granite hill overlooking Lake Athabasca. There was a small bar upstairs with a metal door which clearly had been kicked in several times and metal chairs with plywood tables. The ambiance was bare necessity. The bar was well used, but not well maintained. Mary came in with Peter.

I generally don't drink much, but as the day wore on I needed something more to ease the pain in my side. It looked to me as if Peter and Mary were drinkers and after a few drinks the discussion started to get interesting.

"I think I gotta get involved in law again," she said. "We need people in law we can trust. We need to protect ourselves; it's our only choice. Look at what they did to Junior today, and he's a successful guy. We need to protect ourselves," she said again as if she was trying to convince herself. "The Constitution has changed and there are more decisions that can protect our people. We have the right to keep huntin' and trappin' and gatherin' and with the dam and now the oil sands, they're destroyin' the rest of our lands. Miriam, thank you for comin' here, but after you finish we're gonna have ta take these guys to court – they won't stop unless we force 'em."

I really appreciated Mary thanking me. It made me feel important.

"The problem is these downtown lawyers we got don't do anythin'," Mary continued. "They talk a lot and they take our money. Some of the lawyers want to get money for the First Nation. That won't solve our problem. Look at what happened in Alaska and Hobbema with oil money. It went on pickup trucks and vacations and then there are the suicides. They say that after a settlement and a distribution of cash, the suicide rates and deaths from alcohol and drugs goes way up. An' the lawyers try and get a percentage of that money for themselves."

Pete agreed. "The fuckin' lawyers, like that guy who's doin' the residential school claims; doesn't he get a big cut? It's Indian and Northern Affairs' fault, I know, I used ta work with 'em." Peter was already starting to slur his words.

"What about the studies I am helping with?" I asked. "Won't that support the land use rights?"

"Well they will be important. But then again, the studies might just end up in museums." Mary mused.

Peter looked quite serious. "You know that Nicole has cancer, don't you?"

"No. I didn't." I said.

"Well, I don't know if it is one of the so-called rare cancers, but there sure seems to be a lot of people getting cancer here. Have you met Leonard Berube? He's bin makin' lots a money workin' for the companies. You haven't? His son has cancer too, ya know."

Mary was visibly upset. "The filth white men produce causes cancer. It's like a genocide of neglect." Peter clumsily put his arm around Mary, "We're not all fuckin' assholes, Mary."

The mood was solemn and I felt uncomfortable and guilty, as if my white ancestors were responsible for all this.

Mary leaned on Peter with affection and continued, "The treaties took the land, but they wanted us to survive on the land so they wouldn't have to pay us welfare so they left us with extra rights to use the land. And we used it, until the dam took our furs. Then they wanted to assimilate us without compensation for loss of the use of the land. But we didn't want to be assimilated so they started the "do nothing" program. The "let them muddle through" strategy. Their strategy now is to give a bit of welfare and then say, "Get lost." No compensation just cancer and diabetes."

Peter slurred, "Then came the fuckin' lawyers. To *help*? Get lands back? Sue for damages? They sue so they can make money off of ya! They call it the *Indian business*."

Mary took another long drink. "That's why we need new leaders. Where are our leaders?" Peter was gazing at Mary and after she finished her rant, he clumsily kissed her.

Mary's cousin, David, had come in and sat beside me. He was tall and dark with high cheekbones and dark black hair tied back in a ponytail. He was one of the Fort Chip success stories too. He had graduated from university. I first met him at the funerals and felt comfortable around him. I smiled at him when Peter kissed Mary, feeling a little left out.

Suddenly Peter stood up and braced himself on the table as he lost his balance a bit. "Jake!" He exclaimed, "Where've ya been?"

Jake sauntered into the bar. "I couldn't get out, the plane was full." He looked different in street clothes.

Jake looked around the table at the empty glasses. "I'll need to catch up."

"Yup, but yer not gonna catch up to me," Peter concluded.

"Well, give me a chance. I'll join you for a while."

"Jake's a fuckin' lawyer!" Peter said as he looked at Mary.

Jake smiled at Mary, "How are ya doin'?"

"Just fine. It's good to see you," Mary replied dutifully.

"Oh – sorry – this is Miriam, Miriam um – Robinson." Peter apologized. "An' ya know David."

"Yes, hi David." Jake looked at me. "Hello Miriam, what are you doing in this part of the world?" He smiled confidently.

He made me nervous for some reason. I started to stutter a bit and then, "I am working on the dam study."

"Oh, which *damn* study is that?" He smiled at me.

"On the hydro-electric dam that cut off the water to the delta." I bit.

"That was so long ago now. How are we gonna use a study on the dam?" He looked at Peter.

"Jake." Peter changed the topic. "Mary was just sayin' that the lawyers are stealin' our money and the bands have no leaders. Then she says she wants to go back into law again."

"Well, she's right! We need more good men and women to run our First Nations. I was our chief for a while, but I couldn't do what needed to be done. Indian Affairs made it impossible. The Indian Act has set up a competition; one family against another to get the only jobs on the reserve. That's why I decided to run for Parliament, to change the act, because governments can make the changes if they know what to do."

"Jake, you shit. I've heard that so many times before. You're gonna be the big MP. You're in the money. I can't stand this shit." Mary waved her arm so abruptly that I thought she would sweep all of the empty glasses on to the floor. But I was happy that Jake was recoiling from Mary's wrath. As a lawyer, shouldn't he know how useful a study on losses from the dam would be?

"So what do you suggest I do, Miss Mary quite contrary?" Jake blustered.

"Help us with a rights based claim." Mary said without missing a beat.

"Rights, eh?" Jake glanced at me and glared at Mary. "You know rights are the base of almost all of our claims but we need economic development and if you are trying to lead a back-to-the-land movement, well, it's a dead end." Jake leaned back on two legs of his bar chair and took a sip of beer. I noticed how tall he was as his long legs stretched under the table. He wore a dark leather jacket, clean jeans and cowboy boots.

He turned to me, "Will your study demand that they restore the trapping economy?" He leaned forward and pounded his beer down on the table spilling some. "Because the trapping economy is a dead end. It's over! There is no way we can earn a living trapping anymore and no one under 50 years old is willing to even try."

Mary leaned towards him across the table. "We have to defend our culture. We can't let them push us around. We've got to stand up to them and say no more bullshit!"

Mary sank back in her chair as if she were tired. "I know we aren't gonna trap for a living but we have to modernize our rights, force them to live up to the treaties and use our rights to defend our people. We can use the loss of our rights to get economic development. But we need legal support."

Jake leaned forward towards Mary again. "Mary, legal challenges cost millions." He stared at her. Despite his disdain for my work I found him exotic and charismatic with his longish black hair tied in a short ponytail.

I added. "Dr. Thomas says that we need to do a loss assessment for the Conservation Board, losses of opportunity to hunt, fish and trap, to support the legal rights and demand economic development funding."

Jake took another drink of beer and turned to look at me. "Who the fuck is Dr Thomas?" He looked at Mary. "An' where did this little white girl come from? Is she here to civilize us savages?" I figured he was feeling the beer.

"Jake! We hired her to continue Katie's work." Mary snapped. "Do you think Katie's work was not worth it?"

Peter raised his drunken head from the table for a moment and cried. "I loved Katie." His head fell back on the beer soaked terry cloth table top.

"Katie Cardinal?" Jake paused, "with the road block and then she mysteriously died?"

"Ya!"

"See, that's where road blocks will get ya!" Jake looked at me again. "So you do elder interviews?"

"Yeah?" I replied. At that point I realized that I also had too much to drink and worried about what I might say. "I should be going home." I put my hand on the table to steady myself as I stood.

Jake asked Mary. "She can't take it?"

"No, I'm just tired." I retorted.

"Just when we bring up something real you're gonna leave?" He jabbed.

"Yeah, mister big time lawyer, I am so carried away with your charms, I don't trust myself." I jabbed back but it was the most honest thing I said all night.

"Ooh ... white girl like noble savage?" He mocked.

"Maybe if you were an MP I'd like you better." I said.

"Yeah," Mary chimed in. "You'd get more sex as an MP. Ha!"

I cocked my head and smiled. "Maybe Uncle Tomahawk is moving too fast. Maybe he's leaving the rest of his people behind as he climbs the ladder of success?"

"Okay, okay! So what do you women want me to do?"

Peter sat up for an instant and said "Fuck 'em. Fuck the lawyers." And fell back down on the table.

Mary steadied the barely conscious Peter in his chair and repeated, "We need you to help us with our rights case, Jake."

"Well, can you afford to pay me something?" Jake asked.

"Yes, we have some money." Mary responded.

"Okay, I could take a look at what you are doing. Maybe I can help you."

There was something about Jake that was different. He appeared to be living in both worlds and seemed to be able to seamlessly enter each world without misrepresenting the other. Maybe he was a glimpse of the future aboriginal Canadian. I wanted so much to learn about my aboriginal roots.

I needed to go back to the trailer and sleep but when I stood up, I felt dizzy and off balance. I worried about the impression that I was making with Jake, and Mary for that matter. Then I tripped on the chair leg and fell and hit my side on the top of the chair. Suddenly the pain was so bad. Even after those drinks it ran through my body like an electric shock.

I felt strong arms holding me. It was Jake who held me up. I felt I was being carefully transported to safety. He took me down the stairs and into a car. "Don't worry," he said, "I'll drive you to the medical center." I was not worried.

Elder's Meeting
Chapter 27

When I opened my eyes, I heard the clanking of coffee cups and other breakfast sounds. I saw a picture of Mary and Peter on the wall of the bedroom. I was in their house. A short while later, there was a knock on the door.

"Miriam, wakey wakey. Do you feel well enough to go to an elder's meeting this morning?" Mary pushed the door open.

A meeting had been called to discuss what was to be done with the research and to determine the scope of the study. I couldn't really miss it because I was the study coordinator.

I answered Mary, "I feel surprisingly good, but my mouth's really dry."

"Water, you need water," Mary replied.

The chief wanted the community to be properly represented, so he had personally chosen those who were to attend. Mary bragged that Jake Maurice was now coming too. My head ached and my side was still sore, but fortunately I was functional.

The chief said he wanted to see what I had accomplished so far. I was nervous and excited about my first elder's meeting. It would be consistent with the culture and traditions. I found myself wanting to impress Jake and I remembered that he was from Manitoba, where *my* relatives were from.

I figured that the elders would be my toughest critics and I knew the community could be very political.

So I got up and dragged myself to the meeting. But when I got there, barely on time, no one had arrived yet. Then a little later some of the elders started to come in. There were five on the list, three men and two women.

The first to arrive was Elder Daniel. He was born in 1915, which made him the oldest. He was a smaller man with a slight build, shiny black hair and bright eyes. He was a good looking man when he was younger. Next was a middle-aged woman who had been chosen by the council to attend. She didn't think of herself as an elder, but she had been raised on the land and she would be glad to help.

One young man, more like a boy, came in. He had short black hair and a wispy beard which made him look unkempt. He was one of the youth participants.

"Welcome," I said. "Harold?"

"No", he smiled; "Harold won't be comin."

"Oh? You are Al?"

"Yes"

"Where's Harold?"

"Well, he got in a fight a couple of weeks ago and it was court day yesterday. He will be spendin' two weeks in jail, but he says he'll come and help as soon as he gets out."

I was surprised, but thought it made some sense. I thought I had met Harold before at a wake. He was big, but he didn't seem to be the fighting type.

"Where is Tanya?"

"She won't be comin'."

"Why not?"

"Her brother attempted suicide. She's home with her family and I don't know when she'll be able to come back. It was drugs, I think."

Al then told me the whole story. He and Tanya's brother had been working in McMurray and they were laid off. They came home to Chip and I guess some of the McMurray druggy crowd came back with him. Then, a couple of nights ago, he took a bunch of sleeping pills. Maybe he couldn't take the failure of being forced to move back home.

"How about Henry?" I asked, realizing the meeting had to start.

"He's takin' care of his grandfather. One of his parents died and one left, so he's the only one left to care for Granpa. His grandmother passed last summer, so he has to take care of him. But the best part is he's learnin' things from his Granpa. Most kids don't spend time with the grandparents anymore. It's not cool. But Henry has to. I think that's why he wasn't with Tanya's brother the other night, even though he was his best friend. Granpa made him understand some of the old ways of livin' of being whole and in tune with the land. He's becomin' a different guy."

"Will he be coming?"

"Yup, he'll be here."

"Good." I was relieved that there was another youth. It was about half an hour late when the meeting actually started.

Maryanne, another elder, started to talk without being asked, right after the prayer. It was like she had a mission and everyone gave her the floor. She started to talk about having to change businesses after the dam destroyed the harvest in the delta. Her husband, Marcel, had always worked on the river in the summer and hunted and trapped in the winter. It was a good shipping business on the river when they shipped uranium from Fond du Lac down to McMurray. Maryanne's husband had been a pilot because he knew the river so well.

"At that time," she told them, "The tar sands were just beginnin'. There wasn't even a proper road up to McMurray. We could still make part of our livin' by trappin', and the huntin' was good. When we couldn't get a moose we'd live on rabbits. I still like rabbits. Nice fur trim to use around the moccasins, too. Then the oil companies started to develop. They started on our trapline. It wasn't so bad because they were willin' to build us another cabin further north and our neighbours let us go on their line.

"Things were like that then. We shared. As time went on, the river work dried up. And Marcel was gettin' old, so we didn't really mind that he had to stop workin' on the barge. My son got a job with the oil company drivin' a truck and we moved into the village down there. Over the last years, McMurray became a city. There are roads all over the place and there are many oil sand mines now. Every day, we hear of another one. Four of them are runnin' and last summer when I went out to pick berries, well, they were covered with dust. Who knows what's in that dust? The trees have been cut down on land that they will use for mines.

"I don't feel welcome on my lands anymore. They have changed them. Now there is no place to go to hunt or pick berries. There are always people there. No place to get away. I tried to go down below McMurray. You know, down by Richardson Hills. Too many people down there now. There's no place to go."

She paused.

"You've heard about my nephew who attempted suicide and the rest of the youth that are on drugs and the higher rates of rare cancers. The fish are full of mercury; we're worried about the water. It looks and smells bad. Is there arsenic in the moose meat?

"There was an oil spill in the Athabasca and now we have to carry water when we go out on the land. I can't find good places to pick berries unless I go way up the lake, and I can't go up there anymore. No boat, no husband. These lands I've been on for years. I want to know what are you doin' to help us? What's the band doin' to help us?

"Someone in my family dies every four years or so. Do you think that is normal? It's bad, but what is worse, we're used to it. We have gotten used to livin' with this death. It's time to stop this nonsense."

She turned to me. "You're doin' interviews. What good will this white girl do for us? What good will interviews do? How can we fight what's happenin' to us? I thought we were goin' to get Jake Maurice to help us."

She sat down.

I was very interested in what Maryanne had to say, but she put me in the line of fire. I was just hired to do the interviews. The IRC director was in the hospital. The chief had not given me instructions. What could I say to this woman?

It seemed to me that they had become so frustrated that when they saw somebody, anybody who looked white from the outside, it was an opportunity to take out some of their frustration and stress. I didn't take it personally, but it was clear that the level of frustration in the community was building up.

I knew Nicole, the IRC Director, had cancer, but I was supposed to give her my results so that they could be used in the hearings. But now I would have no one to give the document to.

I decided not to respond to Maryanne's criticism, but to ask the meeting what was needed.

I asked, "Do we need information on Mr. Snowbird's traditional lands?" I was surprised when the elders giggled at me and I quickly realized that Snowbird was his nickname, not his surname

"There were many people he trapped with." Maryanne said. "William knows who we can interview."

Earlier, a couple of men had come in and sat at the back of the room. One fellow looked familiar for some reason. After I spoke, the shorter one stood up and started to talk.

"This girl who's gonna do the interviews has a good heart. I can feel she has a good heart, but it's not charity we need, we need ta defend our lands. We need ta be able to fight for ourselves. The white man has lied ta us from the beginnin'. He took our lands, then he forced us into his schools and his churches. The time has come for us ta stop these tar sands plants, to claim our lands, and find our respect. This girl can help us and by the way, she's not white; she's native."

What was he saying? How did he know my ethnic background?

Maryanne stood up again. "Jimmy, you're right. I'm happy you've come to this meetin'. I'm sorry about your niece, she was *my* niece too. But I don't want you ruinin' our negotiations. You can get arrested if you like, but we have to do this the legal way."

I whispered to Peter, "What about his niece?"

Peter said, "His niece froze to death in McMurray last winter."

I didn't know what to say. But it was him. Here he is defending me now in a community meeting after robbing me in Edmonton. Now I knew which band he was a member of. My face flushed with anger and gratitude all at once.

I whispered to Peter. "I think that Jimmy is the guy that stole my twenty five dollars in Edmonton! He mugged me!"

Peter mumbled, "What?"

"The guy, Jimmy, he mugged me in Edmonton about a year ago."

"He mugged you? Really? He was the one you told me about? Yeah? Well, we'll talk to him," Peter said knowingly.

Peter signaled to me to come out of the building after the meeting. We were waiting for Jimmy as he left.

Peter said, "Jimmy! Come over here."

Jimmy, who looked tiny compared to Peter, looked over his shoulder, looked at me looking at him, and then realizing that Peter knew something too, he started to run. Peter just stuck out his foot and tripped him, grabbed him by his embroidered collar and stood him up.

"Do you know this woman?" Peter asked.

"Yeah, I think so." Jimmy said. "She's a very special girl, like Moses."

"Twenty five dollars," he said to Jimmy.

Jimmy was glaring at Peter, but strangely staring at me again.

"Yes, she's a very special girl," he said again.

"Twenty five bucks. Now!" Peter said again.

"Woman, you are truly aboriginal. Can't you help a man when he's down on his luck?"

Peter looked at me. "She's not aboriginal," he said. "She's from Calgary, from North Carolina even."

"No, man, I can see it in her eyes. She's a spittin' image of a woman I knew in Manitoba."

Peter put Jimmy down.

Jimmy reached into his pocket and pulled out a wad of bills and peeled off two twenties. "Here you are, my girl," he said. "After all, I owe you much more."

"Where did you get all that cash?" Maryanne asked.

"I sold one of my paintin's," Jimmy said.

"Don't listen to him, he's crazy," she said. "We need your help, Miriam, and we're grateful that you've come here."

Peter then said to Jimmy, "Now, you do *anything* to harm this young lady again, and I'll have your balls for breakfast. Understand?"

Jimmy looked frightened, but still annoyed. "I think I know her native relatives," he mumbled.

"What?" Peter asked, as we all stood staring at him with his mouth open.

"Well, apparently I have some native blood," I admitted.

"How did Jimmy know?" Peter asked.

"I don't know. He could tell even when I didn't know about it myself." I looked over at Jimmy again. "Why did you call me Moses woman then?" I asked.

"Because you're gonna help us out of our slavery; because you're native and you've been brought up by the white man's kings."

"Pete, I really have no idea. This guy makes me feel really weird."

Peter said reassuringly, "Don't worry about it. He's just a crazy artist."

I hadn't noticed Jake was standing behind us. After everything had calmed down he asked me to go for a walk along the lake with him. Based on the meeting's results I figured he wanted to talk to me about the structure of my studies to make sure that they fit in with the needs of the potential hearing presentations.

After we got closer to the beach, Jake said, "Of course, I didn't know your story."

"What do you mean?" I asked.

"I didn't know that you were given up for adoption by native parents." He seemed to understand more than I had told him.

"Yes." I said.

"I'm sorry I called you those things last night."

"Well, I'm older than you think." I claimed.

"There were many cases like that in those days," he said with a sensitive voice, not like a lawyer at all. "I mean adoptions from native communities. My mother said she had to give up my half-sister," he said. "She might have been your age."

I looked up thinking he was about to tell me...

Jake jutted out his chin. "Oh, no, don't think that – no, you're not my sister, I know where my sister is; we stay in touch now. That's not what I wanted to say. I wanted to talk about how you were sort of saved, but you have not been raised within your own culture. The good part is that you are coming back, coming back to offer your skills and find your roots."

I was listening, relieved not to be his sister. He looked at me again. "I respect that about you, and you're pretty too." As he said that, he put his arm around me and gave me a one-armed hug and I one-arm hugged him back.

We continued to walk.

Jake paused. "How much do you know about our spiritualism?"

"You mean, native religion?" I asked.

"Yeah, sort of." He looked at me as if he wanted to know more about what I was thinking.

"I also have an admission to make to you," he said. "And now I know more about you, it all makes sense."

"What? An admission?" I couldn't believe what this guy was saying.

"I had a crazy dream last night."

"Yeah?"

"A guy was picking someone who looked like you out of the reeds of the Athabasca Delta, out of one of those muskrat perched basins. The guy was an older white man dressed in a suit. It's sort of spooky, don't you think?" he said, and smiled.

"You mean, like Moses?"

"Yeah, and I had no idea about you and Jimmy."

My mind was reeling. We walked a bit further down the lakeshore and he asked me not to repeat his dream to anyone.

"You know, Miriam, the Cree were well known for their medicine.

Good medicine and bad. Some of the Blackfoot elders told me that the Cree had used bad medicine against them. My Cree spiritual teachers do not practice bad medicine, but they are aware of it."

"Does medicine include herbs?" I asked.

"Yes, my teachers tell me we're all connected through the spirit; connected with animals and plants too. That's one reason why we have to give thanks for the use of our food and medicines. Our attitudes and relationships must be maintained in order to remain healthy. In your work, for example, harvesting medicines must be done not only in a clean environment, but a spiritually pure environment or the medicines will not work."

"You mean that if berries have dust on them?"

"Yeah, but more; they have to be harvested with a good heart from a pure place. Thanks must be given and the natural relationships must be healthy."

"So it's a higher standard of purity than the government or industry environmentalists understand."

"Exactly. And that is an idea we have to get across in our presentations."

"Okay."

"We need to talk about your interviews and the information that you will bring to the hearings. Have you got all the files from Katie Cardinal?

"Katie?" I felt odd whenever her name was mentioned.

"Yeah, she passed away before she could finish them."

"Well I don't have any of her materials."

"You need to contact Dr. Thomas and get them."

"Of course!"

"Okay. Ask him for Katie's interviews on the mine impacts. We will need them for the hearings and I will need to go over your questions after you read them. Can we do that soon?"

I was amazed that Dr. Thomas had not given me Katie's files already. He didn't talk much about her; he just told me she had a heart attack but people still say she was murdered. That gives me the creeps. It's like my dad trying to protect me to keep me from getting alarmed. I'll ask Thomas about that tomorrow.

At least I think I've found a real friend in Jake.

Breakfast Clubs and Sesame Street

Chapter 28

A few days later, after Dr. Thomas sent me Katie's interviews, I had to review them with the elders. I went over to the Breakfast Club at the lodge where I was sure someone would help me. I was getting pretty familiar with the community and I was looking forward to seeing the guys.

When I walked in William was telling about his experience last night. He said he had to go over to the police station to pick up some information about the park and when he walked in, the new receptionist looked really busy. He asked for the information and she told him that she didn't know where it was. She was obviously a new recruit. He said she looked about my age and she took her job seriously. He said it was clear she needed some time to get acquainted with the town and she was nervous about it. William could tell she was in for an education.

After a short time rustling around in the file room, she came back to her desk with a file in her hand for him but before she could give it to him she had to quickly answer the phone. She lunged and just before it stopped ringing she was able to hit the speaker button, so now he could hear both sides of the conversation.

"Hello. Fort Chipewyan RCMP, how can I help you?" He could hear a hiss of a poor connection from the other end of the line.

"Is this the cops?" asked the gruff voice.

"Yes," she replied and rolled her eyes.

"Well, you gotta come over here quick, right away!" the voice said quickly.

"Okay, what's the problem?" she asked.

"Buck's beatin' on Boo Boo, you gotta stop him."

"Pardon me?" she said, not quite understanding.

"I said Buck's beatin' Boo Boo," the voice said impatiently.

"Okay," she looked puzzled but asked, "Where are you?"

"Sesame Street," came the reply.

She looked a bit annoyed and incredulous as she grabbed a pen. William was sure she thought it was a prank call.

"Who is speaking?" she asked.

"Killer," came the response. "This is Killer callin'." he repeated.

She was completely convinced it was just a prank. She rolled her eyes.

"So, let me get this straight," she said mockingly. "You are Killer on Sesame Street and Buck is beating on Boo Boo and we need to come over there right away?"

"Yes, hurry!" he shouted.

The sergeant came running through the front office. "Tell Killer, tell him that Robo Cop will be there right away and tell Buck that too!"

She smiled and giggled. "Okay."

"He says to tell you that Robo Cop is on his way and to tell Buck."

"Okay, good," Killer said seriously. "Tell him to hurry."

After the sergeant left she looked at William in amazement.

"Well," William explained, "Killer is a nickname for one of the best hunters in town. Buck and Boo Boo are also nicknames. It was a real domestic dispute and it is good that Robo Cop heard you."

"Robo Cop? The sergeant?" she asked.

"Yes, that's his nickname. Welcome to Fort Chip" William replied.

After William told the story and everyone stopped laughing I was able to get them to tell me about Katie's interviews. They helped me identify the elders and their trap line locations. It really is a close knit community.

When I reviewed Katie's interviews I could tell that the land users opened up so much more to her during the interviews. Not only that, she knew what follow-up questions to ask. I got so much information from her interviews. I wished I could have met her, worked with her.

Ice Road

My side didn't hurt quite so much after another week of healing. I had time to finish a couple more elder interviews and was able to integrate Katie's work with mine. I was discovering what they did to survive in this wild country especially in the winter. The balance between eking out a livelihood and the health of the environment was clear and important. They couldn't survive even if the land was exposed to relatively small ecological impacts. The oil sands and dam had pushed their livelihoods over the edge and no one survived solely on the land anymore.

I was preparing for another interview when Dad called. He was in McMurray checking on his project planning.

"How are you, honey?"

"Good," I replied, thinking about my secret broken rib.

"I'm so close. It would be a shame not to come up. I'll drive up on the winter road if that's okay with you." He asked my permission, which was a level of respect I wasn't used to. Nevertheless, I tried to think of a way to postpone his trip. If he came up now, I probably couldn't hide the pain.

"How are things going with your work?"

"Not bad. We had a special meeting a few days ago and last week I went to court day. That was very interesting."

"Court day?" asked Dad.

"Yeah, that's when the judge comes to town and hears all of the cases. You know, an itinerant hearing?"

"Yes, of course," he said, but I could tell he really didn't know much about it.

"Well, I'll be finished tomorrow and I'll drive up then," he announced. "Is that okay with you?"

"Sure," I said, completely unable to think of an adequate excuse why not.

"At least you won't be working during the weekend will you? I don't want to interrupt your work."

"Well, I can interview anytime. But come on up. You won't bother my schedule."

I thought for a minute. Maybe he could help us?

"Have you heard about Dr. Sean O'Malley?"

"Yeah, isn't he that doctor who was charged with creating

undue alarm?"

"Yes, but it's a smear campaign! Everything he said is true. The cancer, I mean. My supervisor up here has cancer and there are reports on poor monitoring. Have you heard?"

"You mean Schneider's reports or Simmons'?"

"Both."

"Well, those guys are being criticized by the government."

"Daaad?!" I needed him to believe me.

"What?"

"You *need* to come up here."

Dr. Robinson didn't know how to react to his daughter's new emphasis, but he wasn't about to question it. After he finished his work in McMurray, Robinson went out to his new TJ Jeep, which his wife had named *Second Childhood,* and cleaned two inches of fresh powdery snow off the snub-nosed hood. As he closed the door to his new toy, the window rattled against the rubber and cloth top. The roughness and raw strength of the Jeep invigorated him. He sat thinking about Miriam as the rigid seat thawed and the warm air began to clear the frosted front windshield.

In preparation for the trip he had packed emergency supplies: a candle, some canned food, a hatchet, a knife, extra blankets and matches. Of course he had a first aid kit. Although he had grown up on gravel roads, he was a little nervous. His Jeep was pretty reliable and new, but he had never driven on an ice road before.

He started out early in the morning from McMurray. The three hundred kilometers to Chip might take a few hours longer, so he wanted to leave plenty of time.

After he left the pavement north of McMurray, the road was still okay. The surface was covered with sand and ice, but fairly smooth. The tops of the pine and spruce formed a straight cut-line tunnel along the road allowance and the morning sun illuminated the tree tops. It was easy to see if another vehicle was coming down the narrow road.

"Just don't go too fast," his field manager told him. The trip seemed quite pleasant until he got into the sand hills.

South of Fort Chipewyan there are sand hills left from the last Ice Age; the residual effects of glacial Lake Agassiz. The hills are covered with pine and spruce, and are interspersed with occasional poplar and birch.

When he reached the top of each hill, he could see miles out across the pristine boreal forest. But in the valleys he often couldn't see over the snow drifts and snow plow mounds. He was miles from anyone and only one vehicle had passed him since he left McMurray. He passed a lake nestled in a valley which was flat snow-covered clearing where the winds had formed motionless waves of snow.

On the way up the next particularly steep slope he couldn't get traction and the back end of the TJ started to weave. He tried turning into the skid, but the ice was too slick. On the steepest part of the hill, just when he thought he was getting control, the road curved sharply and he lost control of the steering.

The Jeep spun until he came to a stop facing down on the wrong side of the road. He prayed that no one was coming. He jammed it into reverse and quickly turned around and stopped on the shoulder of the road overlooking the windswept lake. He caught his breath.

"Okay," he said to himself. "No more speeding. I've got all day to get there."

After carefully navigating the next hills, he came up on a steep embankment where he could see out over a large prairie. "The delta," he said. Miles of flat ice covered with brown grasses and bare ice and snowdrifts on the lakes. Shrubs lined the edge of the lake shores, and meanders or channels serpentined between the basin lakes.

"What a view." In the distance he could see the round tops of the granite islands of Lake Athabasca which stretched hundreds of miles into Saskatchewan and the Northwest Territories. The delta is one of the largest of its kind in the world. It lays its silt and clay on the pre-Cambrian granite; a perfect study in depositional geology.

"I'm almost to Chip," he muttered, as he triumphantly glided down the last sandy slope.

"Finally, flat ground again," he sighed.

But his relief was short lived. There was no more sand, only marsh grasses, the tops of which were visible above sheer ice. The grass provided a bit of traction, but not much. He figured it would be okay if he were careful. Anyway, it was so cold there was no issue of falling through.

This ice road was straight and even though there was almost no traction, he felt like he could go a little bit faster. But when he realized he was going a hundred kilometers per hour, he immediately took his foot off the gas. But it was too late. The road was now curving to the right and he'd not noticed the row of bushes which bordered a meander.

As soon as his foot touched the brake, the wheels locked and the front of the Jeep began to drift. He had a helpless feeling as the Jeep spun sideways down the curving road. It was clear he was going over the edge of the bank and there was nothing he could do. He clenched his teeth, hoping that he would not be too badly injured. The Jeep flew off the edge of the bank, turning as it flew over the solid river.

Phillip looked down at the surface of the ice about six feet below. The Jeep was still turning, spinning. The two back tires hit the icy slope and then the Jeep began sliding up the opposite bank. The seat gave way as bolts snapped under his weight, jamming the consol into his side. The Jeep slid all the way up the bank and came to a halt right on the side of the road as if he'd pulled over to park. But one side of the Jeep was firmly planted in the drift and the popped tires were wedged well into the ice.

He felt a sharp pain in his side as he opened the door, expecting the door to fall off the vehicle, but it smoothly pushed the top inch of the snow bank. He realized that he was not badly hurt, but he was at least forty kilometers from Fort Chip and he hadn't seen anyone on the road for some time.

After checking the Jeep for more damage, he got his hatchet out and with one hand holding his side he started to dig the back tires out of the frozen pile of dirty snow. It was filled with chunks of ice. He figured if he changed one tire, he could take the other one into Chip to get fixed and if no one came along, he could start a fire and sleep in the Jeep.

He was under the Jeep chipping away when a vehicle drew close. Whoever was in the car couldn't see him, so he jumped out as quickly as he could to let them know he needed help.

A two-door Chevrolet rolled past and a lone woman leaned over to look out of her passenger window. Suddenly, she straightened up and stepped on her accelerator. She quickly glided down the steep bank, losing no time on the river, and scraped her bumper, taking the steep incline on the other bank. He watched in puzzlement as she sailed over the next lake without looking back.

Standing there hurt and confused, he realized that he probably waved to her with the hatchet and didn't notice that his hunting knife was easily visible in his other hand.

Next time he'd be more careful about how he tried to flag someone down. He painfully retreated back under the Jeep to dig.

It was more than two hours after his scheduled arrival at Fort Chip that Mary and Miriam arrived. After he was over an hour late, Mary figured they should drive out to see what had happened. As she pulled her big truck up beside him, she had a big smile on her face.

"You okay?" she asked.

He nodded.

"Daddy!" Miriam was relieved. He looked fine.

"I'm okay, but I've got two popped tires and only one spare. It's sure good to see you. I was wondering what I was going to do," he said, relieved and hiding the pain in his side.

"Yeah, I thought something must be wrong when you didn't show up. What happened?" Mary had a big smile, gloating over this oil man stranded on the delta.

"You may not believe this, but the Jeep completely cleared the river sailing from one bank to the other."

"Oh my God!" Mary gasped.

"Thanks for coming out." He smiled. "It was getting lonely out here."

He threw one of the tires in the back of Mary's truck. "We can bring this tire back and drive in later," Dad suggested.

We had a late lunch at the Fort Chip Lodge. Mary, Peter, Dad and I began to discuss how industrial developments were affecting the First Nations in Fort Chip. I was able to disguise my occasional grimace of pain and unbeknownst to me, Dad was doing the same.

Mary was suspicious of Dad, this oil company vice president, but he was now comfortably human, humbled by his unscheduled flight over the river. Mary jokingly asked him if he would like some wings installed on his Jeep for the trip home. She was being polite to the man who was proposing yet another tar sands project on her lands.

We discussed Dr. O'Malley. We spoke about Schneider's recent studies. Mary spoke about diabetes and cancers. I told Dad about Nicole and her bravery.

"Miriam?" Dad asked as they finished their dinner, "There is something I am worried about. How did you hurt your side? I've noticed you're in pain."

"Oh … yeah?" A short flash of panic ran through me as she remembered the story I concocted.

"I fell off a Ski-Doo," I lied.

"Are you okay? A skier like you should be used to that type of fall."

"Yeah, Dad, I'm okay. It's almost better now."

Then after we finished Dad had to use two hands to push himself up and even then he grimaced.

"What's wrong with you, Dad?" I asked.

"Oh, I … "

"You hurt yourself in that crash, didn't you!"

"Well, maybe a little. But it's not too bad, nothing that can't wait until I get home."

Dad visited the band office and the court room that I had described. We took him to the museum and the medical facility.

Mary showed him where the old mission and residential school had been and told him about how they were forced to move in off the land to keep their families together. She mentioned that the Dené had been the most nomadic of any aboriginal group. They used to take a mate from the next band, which could have been 100 miles away, so they could share information about the caribou migration paths.

"So moving on to one cabin or staying in one town was difficult." She explained. Dad was impressed with her knowledge and the details of their losses. He took that opportunity to ask her how his company should consult.

"After this trip, Ms. Cardinal, I'm going to need some time to think. It appears that more consultation is required than what we originally thought. I need to thank you for taking this time with me."

He sounded officious and Mary's hackles started to rise.

I didn't know what to do. "If you let us off at the lodge … I'm sure Dad's tired and needs a good rest before his trip home tomorrow morning. Is that okay, Mary?"

Mary harrumphed, but realized I was right. Maybe we had made good progress today and we would go again tomorrow.

After a relaxing dinner overlooking the tranquil Lake Athabasca, Dad told me how impressed and pleased he was with my new knowledge. After all, I had only had been away a month or so. He told me that he wasn't worried now that he saw where I was working. "It seems like a nice town," he said.

As we left the dining room we heard drumming. Dad joked, "Are they on the war path?"

"Dad!" I chastised him. "They are having a drummer's seminar this weekend and there are some dancers there too. Would you like to take a look?"

"Yeah!" Dad had seen them at the stampede but he had always felt that it was contrived.

"They have competitions all over North America and they practice with many different Alberta bands. I saw some Piikani drummers here yesterday. I met them when I worked for the Piikani band. They are a part of the Blackfoot Spiritual Societies. When they travel around Alberta practicing they really find out what's going on all over the province."

They poked their heads into the banquet room and saw a young dancer with hundreds of bells coating her colorful dress and two feathers in her hair. Her dress chimed in unison with the drummers' beat. There were about 8 drummers grouped around a couple of large drums and two men with smaller hand-held drums standing in front.

A few other dancers, both women and men dressed ornately, were waiting their turn. Dad looked like he felt the energy and seemed to get a different feeling about their culture from the intensity of their performance. "They are really not taken seriously at the Stampede anymore," he commented as he returned to his room.

The next morning Dr. Robinson drove much more slowly on his return to McMurray with the pain in his side as a constant reminder. He thought about how to reconcile the new environmental studies and his project. It really wouldn't be too difficult to consult with the First Nation on health effects of the river. *We just have to do a few more studies*, he thought.

The big problem was getting the government to move on cumulative effects. If the natives were not compensated for their losses, it would expose every application to the threat of refusal. Yet the government allows our company to spend hundreds of millions of dollars in preparation for these projects, assuming that they will be approved. What happens if one is turned down because of lack of consultation?

He began to think about how the Royal Oil project might· be in jeopardy. They would be a good test case before he and his company stuck out their neck, he figured. With Professor Thomas's help and now with Miriam, they might just have enough evidence to make a good case. Miriam is right, even to protect the company's interest, we should be encouraging the government to make an accommodation deal with the natives.

Doctors and Interviews

Chapter 29

I heard Peter slam the phone down. He immediately came into Mary's office, brushing past me.

"I have some bad news."

"Okay. What now?" Mary lowered the paper.

"Nicole's in the hospital again."

"Not again," Mary said.

"She can't continue to work like this," Peter continued.

Mary looked dejected. "We need her."

"She won't be able to work much longer, if at all," Peter added.

Mary stood up and leaned her head against the wall. "Damn! So much work and trainin', and now this."

"But she's so young!"

"Can't be cured," Peter said.

"Didn't she grow up in Fort Chip? Have they completed that health study for Chip yet?" I asked.

"Nope," Mary and Peter said together.

Peter said, "The government has already published a report that says there's no unusual rates of cancer."

"What did O'Malley say about that?" I asked.

"Well, we had trouble gettin' in touch with him. Ya know, he went to New Brunswick just to get away from the craziness," Mary piped in.

"What?"

"Well, after he announced all this stuff about the cancers, the government accused him of improper billin', causin' undue alarm, and every other thing you could imagine. It's been all over the papers."

"Yeah, it's even in this issue." Peter took on a pedantic voice as he read the newspaper:

"*The Alberta College of Physicians and Surgeons (ACPS) was to hear the claim that he caused undue alarm in the community.*"

"Just for statin' the facts," Mary added. "But that isn't enough. They really tried to do a number on him. Here, listen:

"*He had been accused by Health Canada of engendering mistrust, blocking access to files, billing irregularities, and raising undue alarm in the community—serious charges which could've resulted in his license being temporarily suspended or possibly permanently withdrawn.*"

"He was makin' trouble alright, trouble for industry and those who want to destroy our environment." Peter said, "Take a look at the Slave River Journal. Listen to this:

"*If, as evidence suggests, the charge of "Causing undue alarm" against Dr. Sean O'Malley is unfounded, the federal and Alberta governments appear to be so in favour of development at any cost, they are willing to do anything, including sacrificing the health of Canadian citizens to encourage it. That is unbelievable, and quite frightening. It also appears the Alberta College of Physicians and Surgeons willingly undermined the reputation of one of their members by laying charges and leaving them unresolved, and in the process abdicated their primary role of protecting public safety."*

"O'Malley said that there was an unusually high incidence of bile duct cancer. He noticed several cases and the normal number of these cancers is one out of a hundred thousand. He also saw too many people with lupus and colon cancers, and these numbers didn't seem right to him. As you know, the physician's organization, the College, I think they call it, were investigating him. They put so much pressure on him he had to move out of the province. He's working in New Brunswick . I really liked O'Malley ..."

Pete paused for a moment, smiled and then continued, "That guy had such a sense of humor. I remember when I broke my foot. As he manipulated my leg, he kept asking me, 'Does that hurt?' Then he would twist it again. 'Does that hurt?' Yes! 'Does that hurt?' Yes! I shouted. Then he said, 'Good – you're still alive!'"

"I liked O'Malley too," I chimed in.

Peter looked at me. "You know his history here?"

"Not really."

"Well, O'Malley has been the itinerant doctor in the community for many years. He is well liked. He's helped lots of people. It makes me frightened if the government is prepared to go that far against such a good guy, what else might they do?"

Mary pitched in, "They're draggin' their feet on the health study, too."

Peter continued, "O'Malley told us the government numbers were wrong. So, we hired Simmons to do some work, and his report supports O'Malley's suspicions. Simmons' report said that there could have been exposure to arsenic for many years. He also said that the levels of mercury were too high. He provided a scientific report that showed problems with water quality and implored the authorities to do a proper study, several proper studies. And the scariest part is the exposure to polycyclic aromatic hydrocarbons that come from the oil sands."

Peter then added, "It is the people who are supposed to protect us who are persecuting our local doctor for telling the truth. Maybe they murdered Katie!"

"The government?" I asked.

A hush fell over the room.

"Who in the government would do that?" I said.

Mary added, "Last week, Dr. Don Schneider released two additional reports. This new one says that the river's more polluted than reported in the hearin's. He's done work on both hydrocarbons and heavy metals and they haven't tried to discredit him. Peace River Electric and the tar sands plants have spent millions of dollars on their studies showin' there's no effect on the environment, but it keeps backfirin' on them."

"Yeah, he's untouchable for some reason." Peter said. "I don't think it's the government that murdered Katie. It was Royal Oil. They are scared their new project won't get approved and it's right on Kati's trapline. Now her kids have signed the trapper's agreement. How convenient!"

I was overwhelmed. Here I was trying to do a study and my boss is dying of a cancer. Her predecessor died of a suspicious heart attack. Berube's son has cancer. More than half the elders have diabetes. I was afraid to drink any water or eat any of the fish. I had no idea things were this bad when I accepted this position.

"Peter." I couldn't stand it any longer. "Do you feel that everyone is dying around you? Katie … now Nicole, and the accident on the ice road … and Jimmy's sister … Leonard's son … and I've only been here a month!"

"I know what you're saying and it's almost like people are getting used to all of this."

Peter told me to prepare the interview schedule and that he would get David to accompany me to the first few interviews since Nicole could not do it. He said that we should adjourn to the bar again that afternoon to discuss the whole situation. I knew I shouldn't go. Last time, a few nights ago, it was too much. I protested, but Peter said I had to participate in the discussion at least. "You don't have to drink," he said.

Everyone was there again and we regurgitated everything that had gone on that day. I shouldn't have had the first drink, but it soothed my pain and the emotional turmoil.

When I woke up I heard music and people talking in the next room. I wasn't in the medical center and I wasn't at Mary's house. I felt someone lying next to me. I panicked. Somehow, I had left the bar. There was a guy lying next to me with his arms around me. I moved away from his embrace. I was in someone's bedroom. It looked like a girl's room, fairly small with a plain white dresser and table. There was a dream catcher poster hanging on the wall. I was still hurting, but it was not as sharp like before. I dared not try and sit up—not yet. I wanted to get away from this guy. David came in to the room.

"So you're awake," he said.

"Yeah, what happened?" I replied.

"You just drank too much, so we put you in here to sleep it off," he answered.

"Who is this guy?" I asked with a little exasperation.

"He's my brother. Don't worry about him."

"Get him off of me," I demanded.

David grabbed his brother abruptly and pushed him onto the floor. He seemed to get up without opening his eyes and slithered out of the bedroom.

"I think I hurt my rib again," I admitted.

He looked at me and tilted his head like a dog trying to understand. "Your broken rib?"

"Yeah, I think that's why I passed out, the pain."

"Hmm … he paused. Does it still hurt?"

"I don't think so," I said as I tried to sit up.

"Oh, God," I fell back on the bed in pain.

"Do you have any more pills?" he asked.

"Ran out yesterday," I said.

David looked at me for a moment, "I think I may have something for you if the pain is still really bad."

I could see through the open door and it was quite smoky in the other room. There was muffled laughter.

David left and came back with something white in his hands. "If you try this, it will take away your pain."

 "What is it?"

"It's a pain killer. You can control it, it's not the same as other drugs," he said confidently.

That didn't sound right to me. But, I had some trust for David. I took the white substance and swallowed it.

I could still feel my side, but somehow it didn't matter. I was able to get up and walk into the other room.

People were sitting in a circle, cross legged. One of them sucked on what looked like a thin glass bottle and lay back. David and I sat down in the circle and he told me that it was just like marijuana which I was familiar with. Just try one hit he said. After one or two hits, it was so good not to feel that pain.

David winked at me and I smiled.

David took my hand. I told him not to squeeze my side and we danced, slowly. It was a long time since I had felt this free. It was ironic that I had to injure myself to find some new friends.

After only a few minutes, the pain returned. I felt tired, sick, and I needed to get back and sleep. I tried to pull away from him, but David held on tight. He started to push me into the bedroom and I realized I did not have the strength to stop him. I just went limp, not knowing what to do. The helplessness and fear became overwhelming and I started to cry. When he got me to the bed, he started to pull at my jeans. I felt helpless panic. Just then, I heard a familiar voice "Miriam! Miriam!"

Mary had entered the kitchen. "Miriam!" She called again. "Here!" I yelled. David stopped. Mary's house was just next door and she had come just in time. She glared at David and picked me up.

"You're comin' to our house," she said.

Mary ushered me to the door. Jake was outside the door waiting to talk to me after the meeting. The fresh air woke me up a bit as they both walked me over to her house.

When we got to her kitchen table she started to scold me.

"Miriam! You can't afford to carry on like that."

"I'm sorry," I said. "It got out of control."

"You're not kiddin'."

"I really don't do things like that. I mean, I have tried marijuana, but this is different."

Jake sat down with us but was very quiet except to say, "If you get too stoned in the north country the *Whi-ti-koh* can sense it and he'll come for you."

I felt embarrassed and totally humiliated.

Mary continued, "Miriam, some people here are in bad shape. And you can't always tell. They can appear normal and then at a party, well it's like Dr. Jekyll and Mr. Hyde. Sometimes it's alcohol, and sometimes it's drugs. Some are quiet and some can get violent. It's not something you want to get involved with."

"Well, I'm really sorry. Close call".

Residential School
Chapter 30

Mary poured me a cup of coffee. "I've no idea what you took, but your pupils are dilated. We can talk and drink some coffee for a while. Ya know, young girls are very vulnerable here. Have you ever heard of the sex slave trade? " she asked, as if I were a little dumb. "Well, some of our women have been kidnapped like that. You have to be careful. I like you, Miriam. But sometimes I wonder why you've come up to this community. I think you need to know more about what some of us have been through. You've heard about the residential schools, haven't you?"

"I've heard some of the stories and in classes we discussed it and I heard about that class action lawyer in the newspapers," I said.

"Well, they probably didn't tell you the whole story. You need to know how it has affected us. We were separated from our families and put with people who didn't understand children, normalcy, how to raise children, nor anythin' about sex. Some of the things that happened are unforgivable. I was taken from my family when I was about eight. The first thing they did was cut all my hair off. I couldn't see my brothers and we were treated like animals. It got worse over time. I was asked to go to one of the supervisor's houses to clean and babysit. They were friends of the head Sister and she arranged for me to go and take care of the three children.

"One night, after I had gotten the baby to sleep, a relative of the family came and knocked at the door. He was drunk and I tried to lock the door, but he pushed his way in. He grabbed me and pushed me into the bedroom. I fought him and screamed. He tried to kiss me. He held me down and tried to pull his pants down. But as he moved up I kicked him right in the groin. I ran upstairs and locked the bathroom door.

"It was about an hour before Mrs. Mainard returned with her husband. I ran downstairs and hid behind her and told her what had happened. She looked shocked, but instead of saying she would protect me and it would never happen again, she said, "Stop making up stories. Bernard would never try anything like that. Are you trying to cause trouble or something?" Then she looked at her husband and said something under her breath. I realized they'd been drinkin' too.

"I didn't know what to do. I had to stay the night there before I went back to the school on Sunday. When I got back, I tried to tell Sister Remy about what had happened. She also told me not to make up stories and accused me of tryin' to cause problems. She said I couldn't get out of workin' that easily. I was very frightened. More than anythin', I needed my Dad and Mom.

"I tried to run away, I missed the bus, I hid in the attic. Sister Remy started to call me a troublemaker. I was forced to go back there, up until I was only fourteen or fifteen years old.

"We're goin' through the claims processes for this abuse and the claims processes themselves are abusive. You know, those rapes made it impossible for me to love my husband the way I should have. Many of the people here have gone through situations."

I said to Mary, "I had no idea. I am sorry that you had to go through this."

"Yes, you didn't know about it. How could you? Not only do we have to deal with the psychological stresses, we have to deal with the Canadian legal system."

She looked at the TV and said, "In the residential school when we watched movies with cowboys and Indians, we cheered when the Indians were shot. We hoped for the cowboy on the white horse who saved the damsel from the bad guys, the Indians who were attackin'. How's that for a self-image?" She laughed.

"When I got out of the school I was eighteen. I came home for a week before I went to another school. I could hardly speak my language anymore and I shook my Mother's hand when I saw her. Imagine! I had to struggle to re-learn some Cree but how do you learn to love again?"

Mary suggested we move into her TV room and Jake, who was sitting reading a newspaper by the wood stove, didn't look up.

"So," continued Mary, "Tonight I want you to go up into the upstairs guest room. None of your friends at that drug party are brave enough to break my doors, even if they come in after I've gone to bed."

Jake continued to read the paper, "That's twice now. Do you think we need to send her to an addiction program?" he said to Mary.

"Jake!" I protested.

"Well it doesn't look too good does it?" Mary responded.

Then Jake stood up and looked deep into my eyes, "We're going to be seeing a lot of each other, Miriam." I became excited and a little confused. Then he said, "We can't afford to have someone who can't hold her liquor or get in trouble."

"Okay, I understand." I was embarrassed and frustrated.

I got drunk and stoned and he was looking at me and thinking I was so foolish and young. I knew I didn't have a problem and at the same time I found myself wondering if he had a girlfriend in Manitoba. I was relieved to sleep in Mary's private guest room.

The next day, I got a call from home. "Everything's good," I reassured Dad. "Really, no problems."

"You sound tired. You're not homesick now, are you?" he asked, probing to see what I was really feeling.

"Not really." I tried to sound confident.

"Are you taking care of yourself? Remember what I said while I was there. Here's your Mom."

"Miriam, are you okay? Have you been staying up late?"

"Mom, I'm an adult, you know, I can stay up if I want."

"We miss you."

"Look, everything's fine. I'm doing interviews and I think I can really make a difference here."

"Tell her that the latest report from the company is that there is a lot of crime in McMurray. Watch for the theft. Watch your purse."

"I can hear you, Dad."

"Miriam, you know you can come home anytime," said Mom, "Just keep that in mind … Love you."

Love you, Mom … and Dad."

"Bye."

Than-ad-el-thur

Chapter 31

Peter had organized my next formal interview. It was with David's great grandmother. I would have to go with David to her house, since he would be the interpreter. When he picked me up in his truck he apologized for his behavior of the night before.

"When you're stoned you do things that you wouldn't do other times," he said.

There was not much I could say, since the community is small. I had to accept his apology.

"David, don't you ever touch me again, ever. And that means that I won't be going anywhere with you except to this interview. I obviously can't trust you."

"I understand," he said and we went to work.

"The next elder I have to interview is a hundred-year-old woman," I told Professor Thomas. "She is a Dené elder named Madeline Tripderoche."

Dr. Thomas assured me. "Just go with the flow," he said.

Some people said she was over one hundred, but no one knew how old she really was. When she was born there was no reason to keep track. The only way we could estimate her age was to date the stories she told. She told David that she wanted to speak now about her life, that it was time.

I am sure Madeline Tripderoch had been interviewed several

times before, and I had no idea what more she needed to tell, and why to me? I was hired to do research on the dam. David said that she would talk about that too, but you don't tell elders what they should talk about, they tell you.

Before the interview I looked up the name Tripderoch. It was lichen that grew on the rocks in the north. The natives harvested it and made it into a stew. It was a strong Dené name.

It must have been the coldest day of the month that David took me to her home in his warm pickup. The house was not in the town, but down a well-graveled road that had been cleared of the four inches of snow that had fallen the night before. We curved around tall spruce and pine trees before arriving at a clearing close to frozen Lake Athabasca.

As we drove up, I saw snow-covered packages of insulation and roofing tile stacked beside the driveway. It looked like the house had just been renovated. As we kicked the crisp snow off the newly painted wooden steps, I could see the lake and the rock islands that make a bit of a bay or harbour for the town.

David opened the door without knocking and signaled our arrival as we stood on the wool carpet in the doorway. The house looked new inside with wood paneling and clean shiny floors. I leaned on the metal railing to the basement and David started to take his boots off. I followed suit.

"Grandma, we are here with the land use reporter," David announced.

"What you say?" she replied.

"*The woman who will record you,*" he explained in Dené. It

sounded like no other language I had ever heard. It was not like Cree;, it sounded like the language came from the throat without moving the lips.

The doorway opened into a larger room containing a hot wood-burning stove with a steaming black kettle on top. The room had a large picture window overlooking the lake and a high ceiling with an electric fan. An upholstered couch and chair with crocheted blankets covering them were positioned around a wooden coffee table with strips of fur and moose hide draped across it. Half-finished beadwork slippers were sitting in the middle of the table. On the walls there were photographs of young people holding degrees and posing in academic gowns, paintings of a loon on a glassy lake and one with wolves in a winter landscape.

I respectfully edged my way into her living room. At first I thought she was a child coming out of the adjoining kitchen. But under the bright red knitted shawl, it was clearly a small older woman's curved back, a brown leathered face framed with salt and pepper hair and piercing bright blue eyes.

"Hired by the band?" she said with a crack in her voice and a slight accent that I could not place. Then she said something in her native language. David responded with ease and clearly had been a good choice of interpreter. He was a slim dark-haired student in one of her photographs holding a Bachelor of Science degree. I thought he was only a few years older than me and I suddenly felt that maybe I was too young and too inexperienced to be recording these elders. Yes, I wanted this responsibility, but originally I thought they would speak English and now he says she might not talk about the dam. What will Professor Thomas say about my methods?

"Welcome," she said. "My name is Madeline."

"Thank you," I said. "I am Miriam."

David then explained that it would be best if I were to ask a question in English, he would translate both ways and we would record the interview. He further explained that she would be able to express herself much more comfortably in Dené, although she does speak French and Cree as well. I agreed.

The awkwardness between David and me began to melt away. I figured that I might as well make the best of it. Madeline has agreed to be interviewed and who knows when or if it might happen in the future. I will get what I will get. I can ask about the dam, and if she doesn't want to talk, then it won't be my fault.

As I was getting ready, another woman entered the room. She looked much like Madeline, but younger. She said something to Madeline in Dené and Madeline asked me if I would like some tea. The woman apologized and said that she was Alice, Madeline's daughter.

I set up the recorder. David and I sat on the couch and Madeline sat in a rocking chair covered in a colorful patchwork blanket. She picked up a sweater she was knitting and started to rock slowly.

I really was not able to ask many questions during the interview. Madeline had decided what she wanted to say before we even arrived. I only tried to keep up and understand the stories as David translated each section. Madeline did not give me a chance to ask about the dam, but she did say that she was happy that I was so young, which made me feel better in a strange sort of way. She wanted a young woman who was open-minded enough to understand the Dené point of view, and the story I was about to hear would explain why.

She told me that her maiden name was Platcoute and that I should record that for future reference.

She started out by telling us how it might be hard to believe that this isolated community was the first permanent settlement in Alberta, established in 1778. In 1800, when Calgary, (I told her I was from Calgary) which now has over one million people, was nothing but a river crossing, Fort Chipewyan was the fur trade center of western Canada. Now, Fort Chip still has maybe a thousand people and you can't drive here in the summer. Some of the first inhabitants of this area were her ancestors.

Her ancestors had lived here since the time of the melting head of the Giant. As the Giant melted, the water brought riches to her people. The Dené people lived along the backbone of the Giant, up and down the great rivers created by the melt. She mentioned giant beavers and sacred falls. But she said that she was not here to tell all the history of her people. She wanted to explain how her people were here and how the Cree came to this lake and river. She wanted to tell about a young Dené woman who brought peace to her people. She said that *Than-ad-el-thur* was the Joan of Arc of the Dené and that few people knew her story.

She explained that over three hundred years ago the Kristinaux (the Cree who lived northwest of Hudson's Bay) traveled outside their original homeland in the search of more furs. They travelled outside the lands draining into the Hudson's Bay to trade with guns, powder, and shot, as well as blankets, knives, kettles, and twine. They had cloth which they liked better than hides for clothes, and shiny beads and jewelry, including metal buttons.

The Cree traveled inland, well into the lands inhabited by their enemies, the Dené people. They had obtained guns and ammunition and the inland tribes had little defense against their raids. She said that even before the Cree got guns, the Dené would call them enemy and their name in the Dené language is enna.

"Did you know that the word Cree comes from French, not from a native language? Cree is from Kristenaux or Christian. The fur traders called them Kris after they converted. Many names came from the fur trade like that. It started with the early French traders who only gave guns to their Christian allies, so they called these familiar natives the C-h-r-i or Cree.

"But after the Cree got guns they didn't use them to capture their own furs. No. It was easier to come to our lands, looking for our furs. They traveled far beyond the Hudson Bay rivers, across the portages and up the Athabasca River to where my ancestors made their stone tools beside a crescent lake full of fish. My people, the Dené, had used this lake forever. It had been a good trading place since the time of our oldest legends.

"But the Cree did not come to trade. They showed no respect for our traditions, swooping down the steep river bank, down upon the Dené camp, massacring without conscience, shooting, taking the Dené's furs and goods. It was horrific. With a crack of thunder the strongest Dené warrior was murdered—obliterated. It was now so

easy to kill and they were merciless.

The few surviving Dené escaped into the bush, but after some days the survivors saw a glow from a huge fire by the lake. They crept up to see what it was. When they got close enough, they saw the same Cree warriors jumping into the fire, crying and screaming. They didn't understand. It looked like they were committing suicide from the guilt for what they had done to the Dené. From that time on they called it Cree Burn Lake."

Then she said that she would tell a story about a beautiful young Dené woman named *Than-ad-el-thur* and that perhaps I would understand the Dené experience through her young eyes. David smiled at me when he translated, "And you are beautiful, like she was, too." I blushed at that point.

"The melting glacier provided clean water and made the grass green. The Dené had been here since the valleys were carved by the giant rivers and were dammed by giant beavers."

I thought of my recent trip to the Columbia Ice fields, the source of the same river.

Madeline then started to talk about a young Dené woman, who was even younger than me:

"All Than-ad-el-thur could think about was how to escape, but how could she? She was sitting on furs in the wet canoe during the long days and she had to stay beside this huge smelly man at night. They had been paddling for twenty days camping under the canoes each night and each day they went further from her country, further from the lands of her grandfathers. Than-ad-el-thur's family made small canoes out of caribou hides, not birch bark, and they generally did

not travel down the rivers, they crossed them. She sat in the middle of stacks of beaver and muskrat furs, some of which were stolen from her family.

Her captor, Big Owl, steered the canoe with powerful strokes of his paddle. As she looked back at him, he smiled at her. His blood-stained moose-skin shirt was trimmed in muskrat and his moose-hide leggings were torn. The sun was shining on his muscular bare arms as his detached shirt sleeves were stuffed under his knees for padding. His knife case was decorated not with porcupine quills that she would have recognized, but colorful tiny stones. His Cree woman must have worked hard to make that, she thought.

He kept his thunder stick tied to the furs stacked between Than-ad-el-thur and him. Big Owl had an eagle feather close to his side on the edge of the canoe.

Than-ad-el-thur knew that the eagle feather was used by the Cree as a symbol of strength. But she thought that a strong man would not kill children and women. She thought he might need the feather to support his weak spirit which was now driven by greed.

Her father was a gentle man and did not need crutches. His spirit was strong. It came because he was a part of these lands, a reflection of the lands that created him. Her family took only what they needed and used all of what they took. They treated the land like their Mother and she treated them like her children. The murderous Cree had wasted lives and food just to take caribou and buffalo hides and other furs that they did not need.

Big Owl was a strong and proud man, but she had seen his aggression and his smile did not comfort her as it may have in other circumstances. The memory of the murder of her mother and father was fresh. She had been taken like the Dené women in the stories her grandmother told. But unlike her grandmother's story, her captor's kindness would never erase the memory of his savagery against her family. Big Owl was old, older than the man she was to marry.

She still was in shock. It was like a bad dream.

Than-ad-el-thur's family were the people and the enemy had come to kill and steal from them. They were part of the land and they had been there since the time of the head of the Giant and the melting of the glaciers. They came to this land after crossing a land with lakes and snow and there were no other people or enemies in this land. They had come with the first animals."

Madeline knew that modern biologists called the land that *Than-ad-el-thur's* family was camped in the Taiga. She explained how they stayed below the barren lands because it was much easier to camp. In the barren lands it is so cold and harsh that trees do not grow.

Madeline told me how sometimes her ancestors traveled south into the dense boreal forest, but they camped in the transition zone because the caribou herds passed by them during their migration south.

Elder Madeline said that *Than-ad-el-thur's* family were her ancestors and that she had descended from *Than-ad-el-thur's* brother.

She continued:

"Than-ad-el-thur began to think how the times before they were attacked had been good. The caribou had come near the camp and they had plenty of meat. It was also a good year for smaller animals

in the nearby woods. The animals had been kind to them this year and they were grateful. They had thanked the caribou and each and every animal they took. They had to give back to the land that was providing for them.

It was part of the cycle of life, part of the relationship, part of respect and responsibility. Than-ad-el-thur loved the smell of the spruce trees. They were good cover for her special animal, the marten. The lodge pole pine, tall spruce, and aspen were common in that area. But the dwarf spruce looked like they had been stunted by cold weather—prevented from growing to their proper height.

She thought the trees were being punished perhaps for some mis-behavior. Her family stayed along the tree line south of the barren lands until late spring, and then they would travel north to their lazy summer lake where they fished, hunted birds, and prepared for the next caribou migration. They had a happy life.

That fateful morning, some of the men in her family group were out hunting for birds because the geese and ducks had come back from their southern migration. Than-ad-el-thur was preparing some caribou meat and her Father was stoking the camp fire, getting the stones ready for cooking. Than-ad-el-thur had prepared the hide, which was placed around a hole in the soft ground, just big enough to make a good soup. She had poured the cut meat, herbs and water inside and was ready for her father to place the red hot stones in to boil the meat. She loved the broth it made.

Her father had taught her many things and since she was the old-est, she had taken on more responsibilities. He had taught her things he would have reserved for an oldest son. She was taught how their lives were one with the land and animals around them. Even the stones had spirits. He had begun to talk about the weather and the spirit of their relatives. He told her about the man she should marry and how his family was very successful and in tune with the caribou.

Suddenly, with a clap of thunder, her father fell forward into the fire. Her mother instinctively ran out of the shelter to pull him out when a Cree warrior jumped from behind and stabbed her through the back. The camp was in shock. How was the enemy using thunder? What spirit or magic did they have now? A big enemy warrior held a staff up to his shoulder and 'crack,' thunder erupted from the end. Her uncle fell backwards, blood spurting from his chest.

Before she could react, Than-ad-el-thur was tackled by the same large warrior and held to the ground. There were too many enemies and the camp quickly grew silent except for her protests. Somehow she could understand their language. Her grandmother had taught her some words and she understood through words and actions that the big enemy had claimed her and was protecting her from the other enemy braves.

She heard him say that both of these women were very pretty and they should keep them. She thought she should stab him with the knife she had hidden under her skirt but she didn't. She paused, remembering grandmother's stories; this is how she would survive- she would be his slave. She saw another warrior claim her cousin. Together they were dragged away from the carnage to a temporary camp and tied to a tree.

She was spared and her younger brothers, frightened by the thunder, managed to escape into the thin forest of the Taiga. Thank the

Creator that her brothers made it without being slaughtered. At least they knew this country. They probably ran out over by the snares they had just set and hid under a bluff behind some remaining snow. She hoped that the Cree were satisfied with their spoils and not chase after them.

It was the next day that she was thrown into a birch bark canoe at the edge of the large lake. The Cree called the lake Athabascow after the reeds in the southern delta of the lake. The Dené called it Tu Nethe. They were on the northern shore of the east end of the lake and they headed east where the lake became clearer, narrower and deep. The trees were bigger and crowed the lake shore. The birch, aspen, spruce, and pine made camping much easier-easier than on the barren lands where there was no shelter or wood to burn.

In the summer and fall there were many berries in this region: cranberry, blueberry, mooseberry. And mint, rat root, and Labrador tea were among the many herbs her parents and grandparents had taught her to find. She knew this lake. The caribou crossed it when it was frozen in the winter and would come for lichens and grazing in the sand hills and the boreal forest south of the lake. The east lake was clear blue and fresh and full of big trout.

It was not long before they left the lake and they started paddling upstream against a strong current. At night, she was forced to sleep close to him under his canoe and her cousin with the smaller man who was her captor. All they did was grunt and point, but as they traveled, she listened carefully to their conversations and began to learn more of their language.

Her family had told her of this enemy, the Cree. She had been taught to fear and hate them from childhood and now she was experiencing why. Over the last month, her captors had taken her far out of familiar lands and each night she would long to get back home. She thought about her people and hoped he would leave her alone that night.

Her cousin was not as lucky. Her captor hit her. He was impatient because she did not speak Cree and Than-ad-el-thur thought he might kill her in his rage. She knew she had to be the strong one and she needed to plan an escape. Being strong seemed to have been her lot in life since she was young. Perhaps if her father had had a son first, it would have been different.

Her people were used to traveling long distances, but never on a river and they had been traveling upstream, so she had to paddle. They struggled for almost a week working against the current. They were all relieved to finally get to the portage where their canoes could flow with the river's power.

Now their captors became more relaxed; they were in lands more familiar to the Cree. The first night they camped at a large clear and blue lake where the edges of the water were warmed from the day's sun. The mornings were warmer now and they started down a new river with the current behind them. The melting snow had made a faster current and raised the level of the water above the stones along the bank.

She heard the Cree warriors talking about going down this river to bigger water to trade. She had heard her father talk of water so wide there was no end. His relatives had lived closer to the big water and he told her stories of large water animals that were not fish. He told *her that he had not traveled to the water because the Cree would try to kill him if he went, and about massacres of the people by the enemy using guns.*

Before the attack on her family, Than-ad-el-thur had been looking forward to meeting the Dené man she was to marry. It was time for her to become the wife of Naghaye, from the family by the mountain river. This family had always been able to find good caribou herds and her family hoped to prosper by establishing this bond.

She had heard that Naghaye was very strong and kind like her father, but now she was a slave of the Cree. Now Naghaye would not accept her, and what was left of her family? She was sure that her brothers and those out hunting would regroup and re-establish their band without her; but how would she get back to them?

As days passed, they glided down the river and as it began to get wider, the warriors started to talk about their families and friends. They made jokes about their women and jeered at Than-ad-el-thur and her cousin. They were jealous of Big Owl and his co-captain, who kept these women during the long trip. They too wished to get back to their families.

All the camp could hear him grunting on top of her at night. And every time Than-ad-el-thur thought of stabbing him with her knife, but she did not know this country. She did not think she could hide from the others afterwards. The time was not right. She would have to wait, submit to these filthy Cree and wait for her chance.

Big Owl was a bit older than the other braves, like a leader. He wore tight leggings, reaching nearly to his hip, and a strip of deer skin between his legs and under a belt around his waist. Than-ad-el-thur had seen this type of clothing before, but her family wore leggings with moccasins attached. He had shiny stones or shells sewn on his shirt and when he cut the meat his knife was shiny and bright like his stones.

She was impressed with the tools. They were so easy to use but not as sharp as a freshly cut stone. The Cree cooked in containers that were not made of hide. The pots seemed to be made of a very light stone since they put them on the fire and they did not burn. Big Owl had to teach her to cook with them.

And these things called guns. Her father had spoken of them but she had never seen one until he was shot. He spoke of the English traders on the salt water. He did not want to trade with men who had no limits to their greed. He said this trade turned good men into monsters.

After several more days of traveling, the river turned into a large lake. She could smell the fish and rotting wood as the weather turned warmer. Across the lake she could see a larger settlement in a bay created by a small creek emptying into the lake. They heard camp noises from the lakeshore.

It was a large Cree camp framed by tall spruce and aspen. There were some thick birch in the middle of the camp and wafts of smoke billowing from the fires. There were many huts and tee pees using wood and soil instead of hides as shelter. And so many people, all enemies.

Once they made it to the beach, the women and children of the camp rushed down to the shore. Some ran up to the braves and hugged them and some came over to finger the furs piled up in the *canoes. They looked at Than-ad-el-thur with spite and one tried to slap her as she looked in the canoe.*

Big Owl just cleared his throat and told them she was his property, his slave, and if they harmed her, they would be harming him. They backed off reluctantly. Than-ad-el-thur pretended to be dumb, but she had learned a lot of the Cree language and was able to understand most of what they were saying.

The Cree camp was different. Their shelters had so many logs lined up they hardly needed skins. They used bark as covers and some were sunk into the ground and covered in soil. The earth huts had moss floors and Big Owl called them "astchiiugamikw". She thought it must have been a seasonal gathering because there were so many people, from many shelters.

Tied between the huts were hides full of plants, more kinds than the Dené berries. Their clothes were different too. Some were wearing a different, lighter caribou hide and some were wearing very colorful hides that she did not recognize at all.

Than-ad-el-thur's shirt had a pointed tail in the front and back. Like a classic Denesuline, they called her Chipewyan and laughed. Her leggings were attached to her moccasins because of the cold weather. The dress of the Cree women came down to their knees, being fastened over the shoulders with cords and at the waist with a belt, and having a flap at the shoulders; the arms were covered to the wrist with detachable sleeves. They were wearing shiny rings on their arms like the Dené Yellowknives but these were white shiny, not yellow, and they had the same shiny rocks like those on Big Owl's knife case.

There were guns and containers and silver knives. They had birch bark containers and many tools not of bone.

Big Owl took her to a tee pee where there was another woman who looked a little older than her and two small boys. He pointed to Than-ad-el-thur and said something to the woman that Than-ad-el-thur could not understand.

To her relief, the woman looked at her with kindness and beckoned to her to come. This woman was a part of his family, but she did not know if she were his sister or wife. She wanted her to come inside the tee pee. The woman said "rabbit" and pointed to her nose. She then held out some different clothes. Than-ad-el-thur could understand: "No Chipewyan shirt; now you are Cree."

Than-ad-el-thur wanted to change out of the clothes she had had on for weeks, but she would never be Cree. She was a slave, even if this woman was kind. She was forced to be here and she would escape at the first opportunity, but until then she would survive.

Rabbit had an ability to talk slowly and with her hands. She said, "The Big Owl is right, you are very beautiful. What is your name?"

At that point, Big Owl entered the tee pee and put his arms around Rabbit like a man would touch his wife. Than-ad-el-thur was confused. Did Rabbit not know what Big Owl had been doing to her? How could she welcome me into her tee pee without jealousy?

There were many things that Than-ad-el-thur would learn while in this Cree camp. It didn't take her long to get used to living in the settlement. She learned about the lands in the area. She had figured out which river they had taken to get there and which river lead to the salt water and how the Cree travelled and gained their living. She learned to cook with the new pots and to sew beads and buttons. She watched the Cree medicine men and learned something about their traditions and spirits.

Big Owl's Cree woman, Rabbit, showed Than-ad-el-thur much about cloth and what the mooneow traders at the Bay had given them. She showed her very thin material, not warm or thick like a hide but flexible and easy to wear, especially in the warmer seasons. She liked the bright colours of the cloth. Rabbit let her wear one of her nice red shawls. She showed her blankets and beads, metal knives, and buttons. She learned about all of the trade goods. She loved the red cloth especially.

After a while, Big Owl left to go to the Salt Water Fort to trade the furs. He would be away for many days. This was her chance to escape. She planned to go by land upriver until the portage, and then she could quickly make a small canoe and go down river back into her family's territory. She longed to get home and try and put what was left of her family life back together.

But it was not to happen yet. Just as Big Owl left and she had more freedom, her cousin told her that she did not feel well. As she spoke with her, she found that not only was she sick, but she was pregnant from her captor. If she left now, she would leave alone. She decided she could not leave; her cousin needed care and could not travel with her. She resigned herself to caring for her cousin.

She thought about the Cree and how much they were different and how much they were the same. In her culture, she had heard of the men fighting for the women, but having a slave and a wife she had not seen. She was familiar with the abundance of animals in the forest and she was surprised that this Cree camp stayed in one place for such a long time. It was not like when the people found thousands of caribou. They seemed to be able to find more meat than possible.

However, even though she had only been there since spring, she noticed that many Cree families would leave on seasonal hunts. But the warriors would keep returning from raids with furs, goods, and meats. Their summer clothes were different, but she was able to show them how to make better fringes on the leathers. She realized that many of the new tools were not from the Cree culture, but from the traders. She also listened to Rabbit talk about how Big Owl had changed when he started trading and raiding. She used to be proud of her War Chief, but now she was happier when he was away. "He has been infected by the Whi-ti-koh spirit." Rabbit complained. Than-ad-el-thur had experienced his murderous lusts and nodded, skillfully disguising her plans.

It was fall before Than-ad-el-thur finally felt she could risk an escape. She had never lost her desire to return home, even though she was impressed with some of the Cree way of life. She understood what was Cree and what was from the Mooneow. The Cree were able to live differently in the forest than the Dené people. But most of their life-changing possessions came from trade with York Factory. Her people could benefit from those trade goods too, especially the guns. They needed guns to defend themselves from the Cree raiders. Then maybe her people could journey to the Bay for trading too.

It was time for her to go and tell her people what she knew. She could help her people get guns and kettles. She could do it. She could get back before it got too cold.

She waited until the middle of the night. Her cousin was reluctant to come. She had recovered from her unsuccessful birth, but was still apprehensive about escaping. She knew winter was near, but her hate won over her fears.

The two began traveling north without too much trouble. Big Owl and his friend had gone to the Bay and wouldn't be following them. But it wasn't two days into their journey that it started to snow. It was a big early snowstorm and deep freeze. Some falls were like that in the north.

They tried to snare some rabbits, but they were not dressed properly for the cold. They tried to keep warm, but it was impossible. Finally, they spotted a Mooneow tent. Since they were at the point of no return, even if the mooneow killed them, at least they might die warm. The tent was made of cloth, not furs, not poles, nor bark. They spoke yet another strange language. She had never seen a mooneow, but it was warm in the tent. How different could they be? Than-ad-el-thur spoke to them in Cree.

The Mooneow men took them back to the Salt Water Post. It was a stone house, a "Kihci-wâskâhikan" in Cree. They saw a fire inside holes in the walls and the doors were made of smooth wood. They were to be taken to the chief inside the house. Up until then, they had been treated very well, not molested or hit. Even though the Mooneow did not speak Cree well, they seemed to understand what was needed.

When they approached the Stone House, they noticed that the trees had been cut all around the house and it stuck out like a lonely rock in the middle of a field. The river beside the house was starting to

*freeze, and in the distance they could hear the roar of the waves of
the shoreline of the large salt water.*

*Than-ad-el-thur still did not have proper clothes for the weather
and wanted nothing more than to get warm. They quickly entered
into what seemed like a cave opening. There was a warm fire inside
and bright colored cloth around the openings. Those inside were sitting on pillows supported by wooden sticks, and underneath was
a shiny wood floor. They all stood up when the mooneow hunters,
Than-ad-el-thur, and her cousin walked in.*

*She was impressed with their respect. Despite her tattered condi-
tion, Factor James Knight seemed attracted to her at first sight. He
had been without the company of women for months and he had
never seen such a native woman. When she walked, her hips moved
like a martin; when she smiled at him, she seemed to communicate
joy. Even after all she had been through, she still seemed to have a
spirit for life.*

*Now, after their journey, her cousin was even sicker than before
and the first order of business was to get them warm and to give them
a hearty soup. "Who are they and how did you find them?" the Factor
asked. He was told that they were Chipewyan women who had been
enslaved by the Cree.*

*At first, James Knight was overjoyed. The Chipewyan have finally
come to trade, he thought. Then he was angry that the reason they
were here was because the Cree were still murdering the Chipewyan
with the guns he had given them.*

*But this was his first real contact with the Chipewyan. Maybe he
would be able to increase the trade now if he could communicate*

with the Chipewyan through these women. What a coup for the Company, he thought. The hunters began to fill them in. They were slaves of the Cree and had escaped.

From the moment that Than-ad-el-thur entered the Stone House, she knew she would be able to bring her people here to trade and to get guns and pots, too. Even if the trade made men crazy, they had to have guns if they were going to protect themselves from the Cree.

"She could now see that she had only learned a small part about the mooneow people. But the moment she saw the Factor, she knew he wanted her. They were men like other men. She could tell when Big Owl wanted her. This power may be her protection here too.

But it was only one day later that the news traveled to Big Owl that she had arrived at the Stone House. It was, of course, here that he had come to trade. He came right to the Factor's quarters and demanded that he return his slave. In Cree, the Factor asked Big Owl who this young woman was. She had said she was Dené or Chipewyan and had been captured in a raid. 'Did you raid the Chipewyan people with the guns I traded to you last year? I told you I would punish any Cree who used these guns for war and not for trapping'. Now, the Factor was angry. Although Big Owl was much bigger and stronger than the Factor, he became quite frightened of the Factor's anger. It was if the Factor had some hidden magic or some unseen power.

Then the Factor pulled out a small stick with shiny buttons on it, not a knife, it looked like a small thunder stick or gun, and waved it at Big Owl, who began to back out of the Stone House door. The Factor followed him with all of his hunters. The Factor told Big Owl in

Cree—'I will not kill you today. But these women are mine now. You take the goods that we have traded yesterday and that is all you get.'

Big Owl protested, "These women are worth much more," he said. The Factor made the stick make its thunder and Big Owl backed away. 'Also, I will not trade any more powder and shot this time. You have not used it well. If I hear you have raided the Chipewyan people again, I will not ask, you will die before you say a word.' Big Owl looked convinced at this point. He respected the small stick that the Factor held.

She was now free of Big Owl and free of the Cree captors. Now she could return to her family. She thought of her cousin. Perhaps she would go back in the spring.

Living at the Stone House, Than-ad-el-thur learned many English words. She was becoming good at different languages now. She told the Factor of the murders and how she was the slave of the Cree. She told the Factor that she wanted to go back to her people and give them guns so that they could defend themselves. The Factor wanted that too, he explained, but he wanted peace between the Chipewyan and the Cree. They could trade and make peace with the Cree instead of fighting.

There was more than a desire to make peace in the Factor's heart. He was completely taken by this feisty Chipewyan beauty. He asked her to come to his room and slowly closed the door behind her. She was not unaware of what he was thinking, but she knew to expect this from men. She was also interested how this man had been so forceful against Big Owl and made him look small.

She opened herself to his advances. He first reached out to her *gently as if to help her remove her shirt. She responded to his lead and lifted her arms. As the shirt came up, her breasts appeared and the Factor carefully kissed them as he dropped the shirt on the floor behind her. She thought his lust was revealing. He then went for her leggings. He untied the strings that held them together and they fell off easily. She stood there naked, her strong slim body standing erect and proud waiting for him.*

It was an important union between the English leader and the Dené woman. They soon were to share a love and were able to communicate honestly. The Factor understood much more about the group he called the Northern Indians because up until then he had rarely seen them. She learned about the power of the Mooneow and from where the many new goods had come. The Factor soon found out that she liked the bright red cloth and she made many clothes from the roll he gave her. When the Factor was happy so was the Factory and the Dené woman had found her stone castle.

She told the Factor about the Yellowknives and he thought maybe she was talking about gold, but she was actually describing copper. She told him about the oil sands, but he really didn't understand what she meant."

Madeline's story was fascinating and her description was as if she were *Than-ad-el-thur* herself. How could she know so much about this experience? I started to think that much of this was her imagination. She noticed my attitude and stopped. She said something to David and he asked me if I would like to see a special document. I said, "Of course," so she called to her daughter and in very short order her daughter brought in an old leather-bound book. She opened it and presented it to me. It was a copy of the Hudson's Bay Journals:

> Wm. Stewart & the Slave woman I gave Considerable so as to make presents to Engage them to come to trade wch I hope will be Completed, before they went I had some Discourse abt the Great River it runs into the Sea on the Back of this Country & they tells us there is a Certain Gum or pitch that runs down the river in Such abdundance that they cannot land but at certain places & that it is very broad & flows as much water as this does here & yt the rocks are of Divers Coulour & by Description full of Mineralls & very warm weather in those parts to what it is here &c. delivered 200 beavrs & 700 Moose Skin here came 10 Canoos from port Nellson of Uplanders sent to the Netts ketcht some fish. I gave Along wth Wm Stewart some Written Orders for his Instruction & Behaviour in this Affair wch are Viz;

I could not believe my eyes. This was the first mention of the oil sands. So *Than-ad-el-thur* was on the Athabasca River. The first time the white man had heard of the oil sands. Madeline nodded her head and went back to the story.

"*The Factor then sent Than-ad-el-thur back with his assistant, named Stuart, with strict instructions that no man was to touch his beloved. He would go himself, but the company would not allow it. But after they left, he dreamt about the future of the trade, about oil, about gold, and about his Indian princess. It was a long journey, but Than-ad-el-thur found her people who had been hiding from the guns of the Cree. She got them to come out and encouraged them to trade. She spoke to the Cree and helped her people and the Cree traders start the long process of reconciliation. She was very brave and determined and it was not easy to reassure her people that they would not be butchered by the Cree.*

From then on, both the Cree and Chipewyan people would be the middlemen of the fur trade but not without some fighting. This pivotal moment in Canadian history was punctuated by this strong and beautiful woman. Such a vibrant woman made peace between the two largest tribes in Canada, and our country has benefited from her efforts ever since.

Another trip had been planned for Than-ad-el-thur, but it was not to be. She succumbed to the same fate of so many of her people. She died with a fever in the Stone House at the Hudson's Bay Post and her grave is there still."

I looked into her deep blue eyes and said, "Thank you so much for telling me this incredible legend. This certainly was never in my Canadian history books. What a heroine—such an important woman. I cherish the opportunity to record this for posterity."

Madeline continued with some of the Dené legends about giants and giant beavers. She told about how her ancestors had used the lands in this area, but they preferred the caribou because they were so plentiful. She said that the caribou didn't come down to Fort Chipewyan anymore. The last time was in the early 1950's. She thought it was because of a forest fire that burnt the caribou's food. Now they had to go further to get caribou, which she preferred over moose anyway.

After our long interview, she served us a savory moose meat stew with bannock. The moose meat was milder than I expected. I liked it even better than beef because it didn't have the same fat. The bannock was fried doughnut, like biscuit. It was delicious and so moist we didn't even need butter. We had sweet wild cranberry jam to add to the bannock and a bowl of preserved blueberries as well.

Just before I left after the last interview, she said, "*Be strong like Than-ad-el-thur, my girl. We need to make peace with the oil sands people. They are killing us like the Cree with their thunder sticks.*"

As I left her front porch, I wondered why she would think I was the one to make peace. After all, I was just the interviewer. I kept thinking about how *Than-ad-el-thur* used her body and her looks to her advantage. It was almost like a currency, her beauty. I couldn't help thinking that a big part of her beauty, her attractiveness for men, was her spirit and her desire for life. I thought how little things have changed. Do women still need to use *all* their resources to protect themselves? What was Elder Tripderoche really saying to me?

Interviews in Chip
Chapter 32

The next morning, after the early flight, I had breakfast at the lodge overlooking Lake Athabasca. From the restaurant, I could see miles out over the bright snow-covered ice. In between the spruce-covered granite hills protruding from the lake like muffins on a silver cookie sheet, we could see Ski-Doos buzzing down the trails from the tree-lined peninsula. The snow on the lake was reflecting the rising sun. We soon had to lower the blinds so we could see without squinting.

Peter had introduced me to one of the elders named Reggie and the other members of the Breakfast Club, which seemed to meet every morning.

He said, "As long as Nicole isn't coming, you might as well talk to these fellows, even interview them. Reggie is Nicole's dad." There was a row of characters at the table closest to the server's counter. I figured they liked that table because it was easier to get coffee refills.

Old Reggie shouted to me over the talk of his table mates as I looked out at the islands. "Mike keeps his sled dogs on that island during the summer. They can't get off. It's a good idea."

I imagined I could see way down the lake where *Than-ad-el-thur* must have traveled. Then I thought of my Ski-Doo ride over the flooded river and lake. Every location around started to have meaning to me.

The club varied from five to ten men, depending on the time of the week. Some were younger, but most were over forty-five. Occasionally, the local RCMP boss would join them decked out in his blue uniform. There were a couple of Métis, too. One wore a red woven Métis sash. Most of these men had chiseled windblown features, looking like they just walked out of years in the bush.

They were discussing the condition of the winter ice road, the world price of oil or gossiping about a recent car accident, divorce or affair, or the pollution in the river.

Albert was a familiar face among them and he welcomed me to the table. I told them I was interested in hearing about the effects of the dam. They all tried to speak at once, but Albert won out. "So you want to know about the dam, eh?" Albert paused and looked at Peter who fit into the group like a native.

"Once you gather up this information, Pete, what are you gonna do with it?

Peter said, "We are gettin' Jake Maurice to take it on."

"Jake Maurice?" Albert repeated. "Isn't he working on that dam case in Manitoba?"

"Yup, but he is the kind of guy that might be able to do something for us," Peter agreed.

"Great, do you think he will join us out at the cabins?" Albert asked.

"Yeah, he likes that. He will want some fish and dry meat too," Reggie added.

"Well, where have you been hiding this great looking woman, Pete?" Albert looked at me again.

I blushed.

"She's been around," Peter said casually. "She'll record these stories and then she'll work with Jake Maurice to take the government and the companies to court to defend our rights."

That was the best explanation of my job anyone had given me thus far. I knew it was important, but I really didn't understand exactly what they wanted until that moment.

Albert turned to me and said, "You want to know about the effects of the dam. Well, there are no more ice jam floods. After the dam they stopped. Since then the perched basins have never really filled up again and muskrat trapping died in this region. The dam lets water out during the winter. Unnatural flows keep the ice high instead of sinking to the low level of a natural winter flow.

"Before the dam, the spring run-off lifted the fallen ice, hurling it downstream, causing ice jams in the river narrows where the frigid water flooded the flats and refreshed the delta lakes and ponds. But now the unnatural winter flows create a channel under the ice, and when spring comes the water flows under the ice leaving it to melt. No ice dams, no floods, no muskrats.

"Before the Peace Dam was built, every March the entire community would move out to their rat camps on the Peace Athabasca Delta. My cabin was at Jackfish where I would build a stage above the flood waters. There were plenty of small lakes on both sides of the river there and we always had a good harvest. Me and my brother would first go out by Ski-Doo and shoot a few with a .22, when the little buggers came out of their pushups. While they were out around the lakes, they would set some traps too, lots of small

muskrat traps. These lakes in the delta were shallow, perfect for muskrats.

"As the weather got warmer, we used canoes to get around. Normally, each trapper would get over a thousand muskrat, in good years even double or triple that number. And at three to four dollars a pelt, that was good money. Mary bragged that she could skin one in less than a minute. Then they had to be stretched and dried over the stove. The cabins would be full.

"By the end of the season, I was sick of eating muskrat; that's the time I wished the ducks and geese would arrive. 'Bring on the warm weather,' I'd say. Muskrats were great food for the dogs, though."

Then Reggie chimed in, "After 1969, there was a lot of unemployment. No more rats. I didn't stop, but a lot of trappers just gave up. Not enough to keep going. Then there was lots of alcohol and problems. We used to have a good living. We were independent and proud. After the dam, we had nothing. Those were bad times. A few guys did trap after the '74 flood, but it really died down after that. It's difficult to talk about the dam here without getting everybody mad."

Reggie then said, "I've got another quickie for you."

"I bet you do!" said Albert.

"No, no … you … that's not what I mean! Anyways, I want to tell you about the Cree chief during the war with the Chipewyan."

"Yeah," I said with a broad smile after Albert's interpretation.

"Well, about a hundred Cree warriors were raiding the lake area. You know, somewhere out there." He pointed to the lake. "And the chief's assistant came in to tell him that they encountered a party of ten Chipewyan warriors. The chief ordered his assistant, "Get me my red shirt." The assistant asked why. The chief answered, "Because if I'm injured in battle, my enemy won't be able to tell and I can fight with advantage." The battle took place and the Chipewyan were easily defeated.

A short while later, the assistant came to the chief again and said, "Chief, we have encountered more Chipewyan, should I bring you your red shirt?"

"Well, how many Chipewyan this time?" asked the chief.

"About a thousand," his assistant said.

"Well then," he said. "Bring me my brown pants."

The table erupted with laughter.

The Breakfast Club adjourned and I got a ride to the band office with Peter. I asked Peter when Jake would be coming back to town and when would we start to work on the presentations. Peter told me that Nicole was supposed to play an important role in that, and now with her being ill we had to improvise. He said Jake would be here soon enough.

"Just keep going, Miriam, you're doing great," he said, as he dropped me off at the trailer, but it wasn't too encouraging. I wasn't sure I could take on all this responsibility.

Buffalo-Wood Buffalo

The next day, I returned to the club at the lodge. How would I find the right people to talk to? Suddenly I saw what looked like a buffalo coming through the door.

"Guillaume!" Reggie shouted, as a broad-shouldered hunter wearing a buffalo coat came striding into the lodge's café. At first I thought Gabriel Dumont himself had just walked in. Guillaume's broad shoulders filled the coat and he was the same height as the prince of the prairie, the historical chief of the Métis buffalo hunt.

"It's late. Where have you been?"

"Oh, I bin helpin' the wife," Guillaume said in his low casual slang.

"Here's the man who can tell you about the park. I mean, we all can tell you, but Guillaume used to work for 'em."

"Guillaume, this is Miriam. She has been hired by the band to record some of our land use. She needs to know about hunting in the park."

"So what're ya up ta, Reggie, what're ya up ta this time?" Guillaume looked at Reggie as if he were about to hit him.

"No, it's true," he said. "She has been hired by the band. She's from the university, not the RCMP."

"Oh, hello Miriam, forgive me, but this rascal's always up ta somethin'. He's jealous 'cause I get more game than he does."

"He doesn't," Reggie snapped back.

"Oh, ya get more?" Guillaume said. "From the park?"

"Sure do, and you know it."

"Did you get that bull a couple of weeks ago?" Guillaume asked.

"Yeah, but not so loud. What are you trying to do?" Reggie frowned.

"I just wanted ta know if what ya said about Miriam was true. I wanted ta know if I could trust her like you obviously do."

"You're a sly one," Reggie said.

"So, what is it ya wanna know, Miriam?"

"Well, I am supposed to research the Peace Dam effects."

"Oh, yeah. The dam, eh? Well, the dam's had a big effect on the park. Our people've used the park for a long time. Just around treaty times there were two Dené settlements at the mouth of the Birch River. D'ya know the Birch River?

"No."

"Well several miles ta the west, here, look out the window. That's Lake Athabasca. Ya see that river? That leads ta Quatre Fouche, where two rivers cross. Keep goin' down there and ya'll come ta Lake Mamwii. Keep goin' past that up the river, past the prairie and ya get ta Lake Claire. The Birch River drains all of the land on the other side of Lake Claire up ta the Birch Mountains. It's deep into the park."

"Wow, that's a good explanation," I said.

"It's a big park. Those rivers were our main transportation corridors until the dam was built. Then the water in Lake Claire was too shallow. Yup, there were hundreds of people in those settlements. They'd horses and cattle. They grew their own vegetables. The river and lake were full of fish and the game was plentiful. Lots of furs, too.

But disease struck those settlements. They say it was around 1920. Now there's no people out there, just graves. Don't know how many people survived. Not many. Survivors moved up ta Peace Point on the Peace River. A little later, the tradin' company built a post up the Birch River and there was a good Cree settlement 'round the post. Ya know Ol' William? He was born there."

"The Hudson Bay Company Post?" I asked.

"Yeah, furs were good up there in the '30s. The Cree'd hunt up in the Birch Mountains and come up and down the creeks there. They'd relatives in the mountains up at Moose Lake.

This was our land. This was our life. Rats were important in the springtime, but Lake Claire was a major place for birds too, ya know, ducks and geese. And the water was our transportation route. It's bad when ya take away water. It affects everythin'."

"What about the buffalo?" I asked.

He looked at me straight in the eyes. "Well, *secret agent* Miriam, I'll tell ya 'bout buffalo."

Everybody laughed, but I still didn't really get the joke.

"In the early fur trade, buffalo meat was a staple. There were plenty of them and they were easy ta track. But the early trappers pretty well wiped the buffalo out of the area by the mid - 1800's. When my great-grandfather came ta Chip, he was the chief factor of the post and he was concerned about the effects of huntin' on the buffalo. The trade had almost wiped out the beaver, so much they had ta put limits on beaver too.

"Then there was other over-harvestin'. The white trapper came inta our area, especially during the Gold Rush and put more competition for all the game. It was ugly in the late 1800's and early 1900's. That's when we started ta demand treaty and government help and then we asked for our own land, like we were promised. I should show ya some of what's called the TARR Interviews. Some of the real old timers are on tape.

"In the '20's the chief of the Dené asked for land for the Cree and Chipewyan both. He asked the feds for the land on the delta and around Lake Claire with enough land around ta support our people. But instead of givin' us land, they created a park.

"At the treaty in 1899, they promised that our people could continue to hunt buffalo so we would always have food. D'ya know how long one buffalo will last for one family?"

"No," I said.

"With other food, it could feed ya for three months. But after we signed the treaty they prohibited us from killin' any of 'em. The hunters would kill 'em anyway and rarely get caught. But when they made the park it got worse."

I stayed all afternoon listening to Guillaume and the others talk about the park. He said that he would be hunting the next day, so I hoped to interview him again after he got back.

People who are comfortable with themselves, you know, self-confident, can make other people feel comfortable around them. Guillaume was like that. It was clear that he was a hunter—a good one, and he knew the park.

This was his land. Even though it was illegal, he would take a bison a few times a year. He knew how many there were and that it was his right to do so even if he didn't know the details of the law. Taking a few was just enough with the moose and other meat available, but it was time to take another one. He said that this winter he would take only one. He would fill up the Ski-Doo when the park rangers were out on the other trails.

His father told him that the area of the park was the same area that the Chipewyan chief asked for as a reserve to support the Chipewyan and Cree peoples. It was not the same as a reserve. He had told me, "They promised us that we would have meat an' then they made it a crime ta kill a buffalo. The park rules were for wardens, not for us."

He frowned. "I don't wanna talk about it too much, but the government brought sick plains buffalo up here. What a lot of problems that's caused."

Hunting buffalo can be dangerous, but not for someone who has hunted all his life. He would butcher the carcass in the field and just bring the meat home in the snow machine trailer.

It was Sunday night when Peter came up to my door.

"I've got some more bad news", Peter said.

"More bad news?" I asked.

"Yes, Guillaume Simpson was killed yesterday out in the park."

"What? How?"

"The police say he was gored by a bull. I can't believe it. He was the best hunter in the park. He knew buffalo like no one else. I can't believe it."

Peter was tired. It was in his voice.

"They say it was just him and the bull. It was dusk and he must have found the bull while he was on his Ski-Doo. Even though it was getting a little dark, it was an opportunity he couldn't pass up. When they checked his gun, they found it had jammed. He got one shot off and hit the bull, but didn't kill it. Judging by the marks in the snow, it was a fight-a noble end to a true buffalo hunter. The bull was lying dead not too far away. It had bled to death."

Peter then started to rant. "Maybe if the park regulations were different ..." he trailed off.

"The way the government handled the buffalo has been a disaster. Guillaume was from a long line of buffalo shepherds. He was the descendent of the first white conservationist and his native wife. They were sent out here to protect the lands from the white trappers. Eventually, his great-grandfather adopted the native way of life and became a member of the band" Peter stopped and turned away. His shoulders dropped as he walked off into the darkness.

The tragedies in this community were getting to me. So much death.

Peace River Electric
Chapter 33

Out of the corner of my eye, I saw Jake peering at me from behind a wall in the lodge. When he realized I saw him he quickly came up to my table, took on a professional tone and told me that I had done enough interviewing and would have to go out and verify the locations to prepare for the court application.

"Unfortunately I have been asked to speak at a political meeting in Ottawa," he said.

"You're still running?" I asked, surprised that he hadn't abandoned that yet.

"Well, I can't rely on what this First Nation is paying and I haven't maintained my law practice since I committed to run," he responded.

"So what will the politician have me do for this study then?" I replied.

He smiled and said, "We need to ensure that the story is complete – consistent. You need to make sure we have elders describing what they have done in the oil sands region and what they can no longer do and you need to make sure the locations are identified."

"So you're sending the *white girl* out on the land are you?"

"Just don't get drunk out there," he quipped.

Shortly thereafter Jake left for the airport and Peter arranged for a boat and equipment to go out on the land. I was looking forward to the boat ride, but the chief contacted Pete and requested that we attend a special meeting with Peace River Electric instead. Ground truthing or confirming locations out on the land would have to wait.

That afternoon seven Peace River Electric representatives flew in on a corporate jet from Vancouver. They came to the town hall to talk about the effects of their dam on the community. All wearing suits and carrying briefcases, they filed into the council room and occupied one side of the big semi-circular oak table. The chief and councilors occupied the other side and a few elders and interested community members sat in the gallery, which consisted of four rows of chairs just inside the main entrance. Peter ushered me in right after the parade of suits entered and we sat beside the last councilor, gazing at the officious looking visitors.

Peter leaned over and whispered to me, "Peace River Electric has to consult with First Nations and honour the law." The chief had asked me to come to the meeting to tell everyone about my interviews, about how the community used the lands.

The leader of the Peace River Electric team started. He introduced the studies that they had recently done on the Peace Athabasca Delta. He spoke about the effects of the dam after it was built and how the water flow was changed.

Then the chief had his opportunity. "Our community has been devastated by the effects from this dam," he started. "It has dried up the perched basins and spoiled the muskrat harvests. Now our people can no longer make a living off the muskrats and other animals of the delta. We can't even travel to the Birch River or into

Richardson Lake anymore because the water is so shallow. How can we get ducks, geese, and fish if we can't even get out there?"

Then William told how the delta was drying, and poplars and grasses were growing in the dried up muskrat lakes. He had worked for the park and he explained in detail how the dam had leveled the water flow, created tunneling under the ice, and stopped the revitalizing ice dam floods.

The chief then said, "After the dam was built, no one had work. With no muskrats we needed other work, but there was nothing here but trapping."

The chief then asked me to tell them about the interviews I had done. I told them that the delta had been the most important part, the core, of their traditional lands and that the drying of the delta had destroyed the precarious economic balance of trapping, not just eliminating a few muskrats, but pushing most of the trappers off the land entirely.

No one from the Peace River Electric team spoke, but several were frantically taking notes. One grey haired fellow was very grim and frowning the whole time. I wondered what this was all about. Then their leader started to speak.

 "We have done extensive studies of the delta from the time of the dam construction to the present date," he announced. "We have spent over one million dollars on these studies."

He then put up a slide.

"The studies show that the dam has had little or no effect on the Peace Athabasca Delta and therefore Peace River Electric is not liable for any of your fur or economic problems."

At this point, the entire council gasped in unison which made many of the Peace River Electric team raise their eyebrows. No one expected the visitors would make such a ridiculous statement.

"This is in total contradiction of the Way of Life Study," Peter whispered angrily. Some of the elders were shaking their heads in disbelief.

Phil, a younger man sitting in the gallery, stood up and shouted, "Screw you assholes! I am not going to stand here and let you tell lies like that."

Another of the guys at the back stood up quickly and grabbed Phil's arm and dragged him out of the door just behind the chairs.

"Fuck you!" he shouted as the door closed.

The leader started to close his book. "If we can't discuss this civilly, we will have to leave."

The chief also stood up. "We can ensure there won't be any more of that. If we have to, we will clear the room of spectators."

"Okay, well, I will describe what our studies have shown, then."

"Fine," said the chief.

The leader continued.

"The studies show that the dam had some effects in lowering the water levels when it was filling up, but after that the effects were minimal. The effects that you have experienced in lower water levels have been caused by global warming."

At this point, Steve, one of the councilors said, "I was helping your men do one of the studies and it showed how the channeling of the water during the winter had prevented ice jams and ice jam flooding. What has happened to that study?"

"I'm sorry. You must be mistaken, ah … Mr?"

"Flett." Steve said.

"Mr. Flett. Yes. The ice jams are now not as frequent because the ice is softer and thinner and there is less water in the river, caused by global warming, not from water channeling. What you heard was just a hypothesis of one scientist and the data does not back it up," replied Sheldon.

"But I saw the study and discussed it with the scientist." Steve maintained.

"The study you refer to is part of the global warming study and as I said, was only a hypothesis."

The chief asked, "So, you are saying that global warming has caused our problems and your dam had no effects on our delta fur trapping?"

"Yes"

"And you are not willing to pay any compensation."

"Well, we do not *owe* you anything, but perhaps we could arrive at a settlement to pay your existing legal expenses."

The chief paused, turning sideways to consult with Steve. They both turned again towards the table. The chief stood up and addressed the Peace River Electric team and the gallery.

"Your position is unacceptable to our First Nation," he started. "I grew up during this time. I was a trapper and hunter, out on the land when the dam was built. I saw with my own eyes the effects of the dam ever since the beginning. No one talked about global warming then, and many respectable scientists and elders, our scientists, have studied this dam. They have told us what we already saw with our own eyes, that the dam stopped the water and changed the patterns, and the result was the devastation of the muskrat population and other animals and plants we use. Now, after you spent a million dollars studying, you have found that the dam really didn't have any effect. Even our experts and the experts from the World Bank say that all dams of this size have significant effects on downstream populations. Instead, you now say that global warming was the only cause."

Chief Mercredi shook his head. "If your face wasn't so serious, I'd think that you were just trying to tell a joke. You must really think we are dumb or so powerless that we'll sit and take your nonsense without standing up for ourselves. If you only want to talk about legal fees, then we have nothing more to talk about. Thank you very much for coming. I hope that your jet does not cause too much more global warming on your way home."

He sat down. I was devastated, amazed and angry. The chief looked over at me, noticed how I was reacting, and he came over to talk.

"Miriam, you haven't been working with us for long and we really appreciate you coming here and doing this work, but you should remember what has happened here isn't new. We've been treated like this for more than one hundred years. We've been told that white is black and up is down. We'll decide how to counter their lies. It's just another lie."

Dan drove a taxi some days. He was retired and had enough money to survive. It wasn't very often the town needed his large van, only from the airport on special occasions. Dan had picked the dam guys up and would drive them to the hall. On the way there, one of the younger suits had commented that he was glad it wasn't too cold today. Then he went on to comment about the poor conditions of some of the houses and the mess in some of the yards. Sheldon told him to be quiet and motioned towards Dan.

Dan was an elder. He was perhaps the only elder who still participated in sweats, in ceremonies. Almost everyone else in his generation had given up on the old ways or had become Catholic.

Once they got to the meeting he didn't have much to do, so he went in for a short time just to see what was going on. He didn't like politics and he didn't like the attitude of the Peace River Electric people anyway, and this was confirmed by what he heard in the meeting. He was content to be just the driver. He went back to the van.

Just as he got back, he saw Phil get thrown out. Phil returned to the bar across the road from the meeting hall. Phil probably shouted at them; he could see it coming. *They will probably be a while*, he thought as he sat back in his comfortable driver's seat and took a short nap.

The Peace River Electric representatives were a bit surprised that the meeting was brought to such an abrupt end, although they seemed to be happy to be leaving. They packed up their computers and equipment and filed out the door of the chambers into the white van they had hired at the airport. They were leaving earlier than expected so they hoped their pilot would still be at the airport and not getting lunch at the local restaurant.

Sheldon, their leader, knocked on the door of the van, "Hey, wake up old man." Dan had locked the doors by accident. They quickly jumped into his van.

Just as they started to wheel out of the parking lot, Phil staggered out of the bar across the street. He saw they were leaving and began to shake his fist. "You motherfuckers! If I only had my rifle!"

Sheldon smirked as he watched Phil weave behind the van shaking his fist. Old Phil stumbled and fell hands first on the road in the wake of the van's dust as it sped away towards the airport. "So much for this town," Sheldon mumbled. The younger lawyer sitting beside Sheldon rolled his upper lip saying, "I hate working with these drunks. They think they can blackmail our company and live off taxpayers' money. All they think they have to do is complain."

As they drove past the lake, the sun was reflecting off the snow waves and the spruce and bare aspen were swaying in the breeze. It seemed like a quaint place if it there wasn't so much junk in the front yards. *What a mess*, he thought. As they rounded the corner just after the turnoff for the airport, a white pickup began to follow the van. Dan squinted as he tried to see who it was. He thought he knew everyone in town, but he didn't recognize the truck.

"He's driving too close," Dan said. "Maybe he's late for a plane." The paved road was wide enough, but the extra speed made everyone uncomfortable. They passed the first curve in the airport road, which put them about a mile out of town just before the turn off for a small lake. At the next road there was an older dark blue van waiting to turn onto the road, and just as the van approached them, he pulled out in front forcing Dan to brake. Dan looked at Sheldon, "People are driving crazy today."

Sheldon shrugged.

The three vehicles moved together as they approached another curve in the road. They had to slow down for the curve, but the blue van in front kept getting slower and slower, forcing everyone to slow down. Dan said, "What's wrong with this guy? I'm gonna pass him." But as Dan started to pull out, the white truck was already beside him. It looked like he was going to hit Dan's van so Dan swerved towards the ditch and came to a stop. The blue van stopped at the side of the road and the white truck pulled up beside. Two men got out of the truck and three men got out of the blue van. They were all wearing masks with camouflage pants and jackets and carrying rifles, high powered hunting rifles. They pointed them directly at the van. "Everybody out of the van! Everybody out of the van!"

Dan shouted "What the hell?"

The Hydro guys got out of the van quickly, holding their hands up. They looked frightened. The younger one who had made the comments tripped and fell as he left the van, which made everyone really nervous. When he got up his pants were covered in dirt and twigs. Dan just sat in the van.

One of the riflemen said, "Ya know, someone could hit that jet fuel tank with a few rounds as it took off. I wonder if it would explode. D'ya think ya can cheat us again? D'ya really think you'll be able to get away with destroyin' our delta, our livelihood, and not pay us for it? Many people have died because of what you've done."

One of the masked men turned towards the woods and fired two shots into a big pine tree. Sheldon could see the bark breaking and falling.

The masked spokesman told them, "Remember how easy this was when you go back to your bosses. Let them know it isn't so easy after all."

The one who shot the tree barked, "Get back in your van."

Dan drove the frightened suits back to their jet. When they got to the small airport the seven ashen-faced company reps slowly crept out of the van, and looking in all directions, they made a bee-line to their aircraft. Sheldon glanced at the fuel tank before he entered.

As we left the municipal hall, I asked the chief what he would do to tackle Peace River Electric. He said, "I guess we'll have to go to court. They told me it will cost about five million dollars and maybe five years or more."

The chief looked down at the ground and said, "What else could we do, attack them?"

The next day I had to pick up Jake at the airport. When I told him the Peace River Electric story, he said that he was sorry that he hadn't been able to be there. I told him about Nicole and he said he had heard. I told him that I had never been in any place where there was so much tragedy.

"I know how you feel, but at least we are here to do something about it," he sympathized. "But we can't get all teary about it. We need to explain to the courts what development has done to the First Nation here. Then they will understand how important the remaining untouched areas are. Eventually the First Nation will have no land left and we have to show the court that."

Out of exasperation, faith, fear and affection we held hands as we walked from the car to the bar. I asked him if he had a girl in Manitoba.

"Why do you ask?" he said, as he stopped and looked at me before we entered the bar.

"Just curious." I said. "Maybe she could comfort you after things go wrong?" I added.

"Well, I had a girlfriend for quite a while, but if you can believe it, she told me she couldn't marry me because I was native. She lives in Toronto now."

"She actually said that?"

"Yup." He shook his head. "It's hard when you think you love someone and she does that to you."

"I was told that some of my relatives come from southern Manitoba," I said. "They were Cree and Chippewa. Where do you come from?"

"Well, I come from the northern Cree, northern Manitoba. We didn't have much contact with the Chippewa;, they were way south. My ancestors were fur traders in the north. We moved along the rivers and settled around the deltas. I think that my ancestors may have been the first to trade with York Factory. I don't think we're related, if that's what you were thinking. In fact, when I first met you, I didn't think you were native at all." I immediately thought of how he may have been related to Big Owl of *Than-ad-el-thur* fame.

"That's amazing. You know, as a child I didn't even know I had native blood."

"Then you can marry me," he joked.

"Yes," I said, without missing a beat.

He chuckled. "You know, the legal definition of aboriginal has to do with life ways, culture, and livelihood more than it has to do with blood."

"Then I'll marry you if you like drymeat," I said. I couldn't get my mind off what he had said.

"No, you have to know how to tee pee crawl to be a true native," he said.

"What?"

"Tee pee crawl. Ask Mary."

It didn't take more than one drink that night until he looked at me with big eyes and leaned over and kissed me. I kissed him back. I felt like I had come home. It was a strong feeling, like I was energized.

We went back to my trailer. This time, he didn't stand at the door. I asked him to come in and he hugged me close. He was so strong and he told me I was beautiful. For the first time in my life I made love, we made love. He was very gentle and I was so happy to have found such a man. But I wondered if he felt the same way. There is a difference between lust and love and after a few drinks it is difficult to separate. Would he get up and leave in the morning? What would happen now? I guess it really didn't matter, except I knew I was in love and this kind of feeling is not good if it only goes one way.

Preparations of Spirit and Health
Chapter 34

"That kangaroo court ruled against us!" Mary cursed.

"Those judges are in the pocket of the oil companies," Peter echoed.

"Which case is this?" I asked.

"We challenged the government's consultation practices for leasing oil lands. They sell the lands before they consult with us. So, we took them to court and the court said we didn't object in time."

"It would have helped if we knew they were leasing in the first place," Peter added. "You have to be an oil guy to know how it works, but they say we should have known.

We weren't even notified."

"If we could afford to take them to the Supreme Court, we would, but we can't. So we will have to rely on the Conservation Board process."

"Well, I've been working on the evidence." I wanted to reassure them. I had finished the interviews and location research, but I was concerned that we didn't have enough.

Everyone had become more irritable. Mary was ranting. "We need to rekindle the pride."

Peter started, "The James Bay settlement was a success for the Cree. But here we can't even get the government to talk to us. Now even the Innu have a hundred and twenty-five million dollar deal with Hydro Quebec and the native peoples in BC have ten percent of the new pipeline. The Gwitch'en, the Inuvialuit, and the Sah Tu got millions of acres, but Alberta denies they have any responsibility to consult."

Mary turned towards the door. "I'm goin' out to the bush. Gerry's been tryin' to get me out for some time now. The Creator knows we need to talk to the Grandfathers."

"But Mary, this hearing is coming up and we have to prepare," Peter pleaded.

"What do you know about it, *white man*?" Mary glared at Peter. "Gerry said he had an eagle feather for me."

Gerry TwoFeathers had worked under an old Cree shaman. He

held ceremonies and spent all of his time working on understanding and healing. He had gained quite a bit of respect in the Cree community.

I stood at her office door as she walked towards me. "How's Jake?" She almost sneered.

"Oh… fine. I guess."

"Yeah, you guess. What did I tell ya? Just don't get too hurt. But from the looks of you, it's too late."

The chief called from his office. "Mary, Jake's on the line."

"Speak of the devil," she said.

Mary went over and grabbed the phone.

"Honour of the Crown? We have to rely upon the Honour of the Crown, Jake. We're screwed."

Mary put him on speaker.

"It's the basis of the cases from BC. It's our argument that the Crown has not lived up to its responsibility to consult. It has not acted honourably."

Mary smiled. "That shouldn't be too hard to prove. It's just that no one cares. What's honorable for them isn't the same for us. You've spent too much time in law school, Jake."

Jake continued, "But we can show that they have infringed on the First Nation rights to hunt. It seems every time we get some momentum something happens and we end up back at square one. We need those interviews to show that they have hurt the ability to hunt and fish, to use the lands."

"So Miriam, have you filed those interviews with the board?" Mary asked.

"Yes and copies have gone out to the oil companies too," I replied.

"Good. Now they know we're gonna challenge them, and you'll need to testify. You'll be one of our key witnesses, right?"

"Right," I said, only half confidently.

I heard a click as Jake hung up. Mary was calmer.

"We are doin' our best, aren't we?" she said looking at Peter for approval. "I'm sorry, Pete." Mary finally relaxed.

"At least Jake's not like those other lawyers." Pete said.

"Other lawyers?" I asked.

"Yeah, the ones who take a big commission. They call it the "aboriginal business." Minin' the aboriginal gold, sort of. The crooked lawyers take a portion of every deal they help with. They get them to sign an agreement giving them a portion of the lands and money. Imagine lawyers getting part of a treaty settlement! And a lawyer out of Saskatchewan, he gets part of every residential school settlement!"

Mary left the office.

Selling Your Right?

Chapter 35

Jake returned from Ottawa with news. He said that the companies had convinced the government to pay off all the First Nations in the region so the oil sands mines could go ahead.

"How much?" I asked.

"Well, one of the chiefs tried to get them up to a billion between the five bands over forty years, and I think they considered it."

As soon as I got home, I told Dad I was helping with the Regional Agreement. Without missing a beat he said, "Boy, I hope the First Nations realize how good that agreement will be for them. I have been encouraging the governments to fulfill their responsibilities and make that agreement. Good luck with it." I felt my Dad finally approved.

The meeting was held in a tower of tall glass and marble downtown Calgary. I took the elevator to the thirtieth floor. When I got off, I had to buzz to get in. *Security and wealth*, I thought.

There was a bronze statue of cowboys roping a calf in the reception room and a large painting of a farm house during a snowstorm behind the reception desk. It looked like they were rented from the local gallery. The walls were a dark mahogany and the door handles were gold.

"Hello, I am Miriam Robinson. I'm here for the Regional Agreement meeting."

The receptionist replied, "Yes, Ms. Robinson, the meeting will begin shortly. It's in the boardroom, through the first door in the hallway."

"Thank you."

I was in awe of the wealth of the law firm. It was much more opulent than my Dad's office.

Some men in suits were already in the room. They stood up as I entered. A shorter ruddy-faced man with cropped hair introduced himself as John Pearson, federal negotiator, and a tall younger man introduced himself as William Slate, provincial negotiator. They told me the company negotiators were out getting copies and Jake had not arrived yet. They introduced me to their smiling assistants.

Everything had a strange air of formality and tension.

Jake arrived last, even after the companies' lawyers came in. He formally greeted everyone and sat down beside me. I was nervous, but they all looked at home around this large polished table.

Jake began, "Gentlemen and lady...." He looked at me. " ... I have a response from the new chief. It is not good news for this table. The First Nations will consider your offer if you are willing to meet their financial expectations but ..."

The industry lawyer looked at Jake smugly as if he knew what Jake was about to say.

" ... the issue of consultation still remains. My clients put a great deal of importance on their rights." He looked around the room at each person. "This agreement offers money, but does not address their environmental concerns, the health concerns, or their rights."

The provincial government rep rolled his eyes.

"Jake, we have worked out a consultation plan," the federal negotiator, John Pearson, said.

"That plan is an excuse. It is an excuse for the government to postpone consultation until after all the damage is done. It gives a pardon for all of the oil sands activities that have gone on without proper consultation, and you are only offering them what you would have to pay them in compensation anyway."

Jake continued, "Consultation on the environment is a matter of respect, respect for the culture and respect for their health and their ability to maintain their historical role. Some of the First Nation councilors described this agreement as a sellout. They will not sell their rights. It is ironic that you accuse them of always asking for handouts and when it comes down to it, when you offer them some money, you find out what they really feel is important. They want their rights to their culture and lands and they intend to force you to live up to your responsibilities. They will enforce their rights even if it means halting development and reducing Canadian economic development."

"They won't get that much," piped in John Ferguson. "Not even close."

"Well, the short story is that they have rejected your offer unless it contains protection for their rights. The consultation process must take place immediately, before the next project is approved." Jake laid down the position.

The provincial lawyer stood up. "Jake, we were hoping that you could convince them that this deal was good for them. I mean, we are talking over a hundred million dollars for every band in the area. For a band of five hundred people, that is close to half a million dollars each. And you just lost that legal challenge; how can you ask for more after that?"

"Jake, we can't introduce a full consultation process that fast," the plump ruddy-faced Morton complained.

"You can build the largest industrial project in the world and spend billions of dollars exporting oil to the US, but you can't fulfill your legal obligation to the First Nations of this area and ask them how they are being affected?" Jake squinted at the other negotiators.

"Your proposal for postponing the consultation process is another affront, another putdown. Money is important and must be part of a proper package. As I have said before, the consultation process will tell you about the problems in the communities and how we can start to solve them. There may be changes in the plans in the way you do business that might help. We have to look at the cancer rates, the death rate, the employment rates, the number of businesses, the continued use of the land maintenance, the language and more.

"Just giving them money and telling them to wait is a death sentence for many more people. The chiefs know this. They would really like to be able to take the money and try and use it to change things. They know it is a lot of money, but they also know it is a matter of respect. It is respect for their rights that can really save them. Money without respect is like prostitution.

"They are asking you to commit to a proper consultation process with commitments, money, and deadlines. Then you might be able to get a deal. Respect their rights in the spirit defined by the Supreme Court of Canada and you will solve this problem. Ignore it and it will come back to bite you, hard."

"Well, Jake, I will have to take this back to my clients for a response. But if you want my guess, these negotiations are over. I don't expect the answer to be favorable." John Ferguson stared at Jake as if what he said might change things.

"Yes, Jake," the provincial guy chimed in, "I will do the same, but don't hold your breath. We'll probably see you at the hearing or in court. You know, if you lose at the hearing, it'll be really hard to stop an oil sands plant that has already been built. There is little incentive to make a deal like this."

With that response, Jake said, "Thank you gentlemen," gathered up his papers and nodded towards the door. We left.

On the way out, Jake was exasperated, "Mary was right. They all think it is just a money grab, a scam. They really don't understand. What would they feel if the moccasin were on the other foot?" He smiled. "How can we make them understand?"

I had no answer.

War and Peace

Chapter 36

Jake returned to McMurray knowing that the future of the First Nation's success would come down to the evidence we could bring to the hearing. Mary, Peter, and I had started to rearrange the boxes of evidence. We had worked for three months putting the materials together. We had evidence on the seepage from the tailings ponds into the river and a German scientist to speak on it. We had some elders who would talk about how difficult it was to use the lands, and we had a water specialist to talk about critical low water times, like the fall and winter. We had a fish specialist to talk about the fish populations. And we had our report on how the people got much of their livelihood from fish, berries, and hunting moose.

We were ready, but the first issue that we wanted to deal with was the report of the rare cancers. We wanted Dr. Sean O'Malley to tell the board what he had observed.

On the first day of the hearing, I set up in the Sawridge Hotel in Fort McMurray. It was just a large convention room, but they would try and make it as much like a courtroom as possible. There were tables for the company proposing the oil sands mine, and there were tables for interveners like us, all set up in front of three board members. Each table was covered with a white tablecloth, and microphone cords were strung everywhere.

When the three board members came in to sit at the head table, one of them tripped over a cord and almost knocked the entire speaker system down. They retained their decorum. After all, they would make the decisions, like a judge.

The Chairman, Jim Pearce, had worked for the board for twenty years. He had worked his way up through the oil department and he was very conscious of the environmental record of the oil industry. The board was responsible for conservation policies. Not too many years ago, he was personally responsible for setting up the abandonment and reclamation policy of the board and he prided himself in making the regulations strict and environmentally sound. The conventional industry had a good environmental record, he thought, and it was partially due to his efforts.

Jim Pierce was an engineer, while the other members of the board panel included an economist and a lawyer. He was the only one who understood the technical details and he wanted to learn more about the way that the natives used the land. The scale of these developments was unprecedented.

The lawyer for the board asked that everyone take their seats and someone closed the back doors. The room was full of various interested parties. I noticed the all-terrain vehicles club and several other First Nation representatives with their straight-laced lawyers sitting beside them. The chief and some of the councilors were attending. I noticed environmental organizations like Eco Peace were in the back with some reporters, and it looked like street people were sitting there too. Or maybe they were just in off the land.

The chairman of the board started to speak. He welcomed everyone and described the proposed agenda for the entire hearing.

He expected that it would take several weeks. The proposal from the Royal Oil Company to build a new plant and mine would be heard first and then we would present.

The oil company took four days to tell the board that there were no major environmental effects of their new huge mine and plant, even though it would completely destroy fifty square miles of land. They said that it would have no major impact on hunting and trapping and that it would be reclaimed over the next sixty years to a level that could be used again for hunting.

Mary whispered, "And I'll still be alive in sixty years?"

I could hardly believe that they were able to keep saying it without bursting into sarcastic laughter.

The Royal Oil representatives bragged that it would produce two hundred thousand barrels of oil per day and that it would generate billions of dollars of profits, taxes for the government and employment. They would generate more electricity and they were working on new technologies for treating the sludge tailings ponds. They claimed the project was in the public interest and environmentally benign.

Then came our turn.

I worried if I had recorded the land use adequately to prove the importance of the use of the lands.

It was Jake's strategy to plead our case to the Energy Conservation Board and test the capability of the board to deal with the infringement of rights by the massive oil sands developments. He said it was time to rely upon the aboriginal rights promised by the treaty.

We asked the board if the first testimony could come from Dr.

O'Malley.

The Chairman nodded, "Would Dr. O'Malley please come up to the head table?"

Bonnie, one of the employees of a southern band came running in. She looked distressed. "Dr. O'Malley will not be testifying," she announced.

The chairman looked at Bonnie, who did not have status to address the board at that time, but he still asked, "Why not? Why won't he be testifying?" The chairman caught himself and addressed the legal representatives.

"He has been instructed by his lawyer not to testify," answered Bonnie.

The chairman was looking for advice from the board's lawyer. The flustered lawyer nonsensically announced that the information presented by the messenger was inadmissible as evidence.

"Do you have confirmation that Doctor O'Malley cannot attend, Mr. Maurice? Immediately every lawyer in the room was on his or her feet shouting that this was irregular, that this was not proper evidence or that process was not being followed.

The chairman shouted, "Order! Order!"

Bonnie then came up to Jake and whispered to him, "His lawyer told him not to testify until after his license hearing."

Jake whispered back, "Slimy bastards."

The Chairman looked at Jake. "Mr. Maurice, is your witness ready?"

Jake stood up. "No sir. I have been informed that he is no longer available to testify."

"Okay, move on to the next one." The Chairman looked disappointed.

"Mr. Chairman, honorable members of the –"

Suddenly from the back of the room, the door swung open. It looked like someone was trying to hold him back, but Dr. O'Malley managed to escape her grasp and pushed through the door.

"I'm gonna testify even if they take away my license," said O'Malley. His face was red, which matched his hair, and there was fire in his eyes. He was charming even when he was angry, and right now he was a ball of fire.

The room was completely silent.

O'Malley turned around to face the audience, noticed the silence and cleared his throat.

The chairman said, "Dr. O'Malley?"

Jake came over to O'Malley, greeted him and started to whisper in his ear, "Under the circumstances, Doctor, it might be better if you did not testify. The board may have difficulty with the evidence while these issues or charges have not been cleared up. It may even hurt whatever other testimony we will present. It challenges the validity of your testimony and the board will probably make its decision before you can get all of this cleared up."

O'Malley frowned at Maurice. "The evidence I have is damning for them and they know it. Don't worry; it won't affect your other evidence. The board wants and needs to hear the truth. Look at how receptive the chairman is. And they won't forget it, not a chance, even if they try to strike it from the record later."

"Okay, okay" said Maurice. "But stick to the facts."

Jake turned and approached the board table. "Mister Chairman, the proposed testimony of Dr. O'Malley is very important in determining the potential extent of the effects of oil sands mining on the health of the people of the Fort Chipewyan community and to demonstrate the sensitivity of the potential environmental problems. There have been no comprehensive health studies in the community and Dr. O'Malley has been the physician in the community for five years now."

"Thank you, Mr. Maurice," the chairman said. "We would like to hear what he has to say."

"Yes, Mr. Chairman. Dr. O'Malley, could you describe for the panel the anomalies that you have discovered in your Fort Chipewyan practice?"

"Yes, over the last two years I have encountered several cases of rare cancers, higher levels which would not normally be found in such a small population."

"Dr. O'Malley, sir, how many cases of the rare cancer did you find?"

"Three."

"Three? That does not sound like too many out of a population of twelve hundred people."

"Well, if it were all cancers combined, it may not be. But this is a rare cancer called cholangiocarcinoma, and it's linked to exposure to specific carcinogens. My father passed from this illness. It occurs at a frequency of approximately one in one hundred thousand."

"One in one hundred thousand?"

"Yes. It's a very aggressive, nasty cancer, difficult to diagnose, and often by the time it is diagnosed, it's too late."

"So, what carcinogens are associated with this rare cancer?"

"The findings of Dr. Nelson indicate that there is cause for concern in that there are contaminants in the food supply that are associated with the types of cancer observed in the community. I defer to Dr. Nelson because I am not a toxicologist."

"Thank you, Dr. O'Malley."

After his testimony, Mary took Dr. O'Malley out of the hearing room and asked him what happened.

"They're trying to revoke my license. I haven't violated anything, the confidence of a patient, nor have I made a gross error in practice. I've just stated what I've seen. I'm not creating a disturbance. I'm telling them what I know and I am being attacked by those who don't like what I'm saying. They don't want to believe it." He was exasperated.

Back in the hearing Jake was questioning Dr. Nelson.

"You performed a study of the chemicals in the river?" he asked.

"Yes. It was a study done over several winters now."

"And what did you find?"

"Well, we found higher levels of heavy metals and also increased levels of polycyclic aromatic hydrocarbons. It is more difficult to determine the sources of the heavy metals, and we will need to do more work further up the river, but it appears that there are few sources of the hydrocarbons other than the oil sands activities."

"Are these substances which you found in higher than ambient levels known to be linked to higher rates of cancer?"

"The simple answer is yes," responded Dr. Nelson.

Hearing Blues

Chapter 37

The next day Jake cross-examined the water specialist. One of the important points we needed to make was that there was seepage from the large tailings ponds which were full of toxic chemicals. Our expert was explaining how the process was likely to happen and how the monitoring was inadequate. Our scientist was a big white-haired German with a heavy accent named Dr. Schultz. He was so animated when he spoke, his cheeks would shake. Even though one could not understand every word he was saying, you definitely knew what he was feeling.

He showed how the aquifers were connected and how the ponds could be leaking toxic chemicals into the river, which then flowed through the Fort Chip community.

In the rebuttal, a Royal Oil scientist carefully created a contradictory story. The slick academic claimed the German scientist had made an error; the seepage was not occurring because the clay was preventing the water from flowing through. Then the lawyer asked our scientist how he could make such a foolish error and started to question his qualifications.

Our scientist's thick German accent started to get in the way of communications. He began to get red and loosened his tie. He tried to protest, to describe what we knew to be his very good qualifications, but the panel didn't seem to listen. The lawyer for

Royal Oil said. "I have finished my questions, thank you Mr. Shultz. That will be all."

The chairman said, "Thank you Dr. Shultz, you are excused."

Jake stood up. "Mr. Chairman, we would like to have Dr. Shultz return with his undertakings tomorrow."

"Mr. Maurice, there were no undertakings required." The chairman said.

The chief was becoming angry. He had been watching how the presentations were being manipulated. He stood up, and from where he was positioned the panel could not ignore him.

He said, "You can't ... um ... You shouldn't ..." Then he looked down, turned, and walked towards the door out of the room. Several other band members were visibly upset and the legal counsels of the other interveners were shaking their heads. A mumble filled the board room.

"Order! Order!"

The hearing went on.

After the cross examination of other witnesses, our elders spoke with such honesty and conviction. We were able to show the area that had been used and showed how the new oil sands plant took up another fifty square miles of their lands. There were hundreds of square miles already destroyed.

Then we had to have William testify about the lands which were destroyed. It was his hunting area. But I hadn't seen William since the hearing started, and I was getting nervous. If we could prove that these lands were integral to our use, the company and governments would have to finally listen to us.

I went out to find Mary and ask if he had made it to the hotel.

Mary was in his room. "It's almost like they planned it this way," she said.

"What are you talking about?" I asked.

"William's sick."

"Sick?" I repeated.

"Sick," She confirmed.

"How sick?" I asked.

"In the hospital," she said. "with severe stomach problems. De-hydrated. Can't testify either. I think he was poisoned."

"Aren't there any other men who can testify who used that land?"

"I asked William and he said he'd try and get his wife to contact someone, but you know how that goes." Mary was ill with despair. This was just another failure.

I told Jake that William was in the hospital and he said he couldn't make the board wait for this witness. This would really hurt the case. We needed to prove that the land use in that area had been historical as well as current. If we had known, we could have gotten someone else, but so many of them have already passed on or would not be able to testify.

While Mary frantically racked her brain for another elder, Jake put the fish expert on the stand. This scientist explained how fish habitat was threatened and that not enough study had been done to protect appropriate spawning opportunities. Our next scientist questioned their reclamation policies and told the board that the plant would irreversibly affect the future of the First Nation lands.

But Jake knew it wasn't enough. William was supposed to confirm that the lands used by our people were the lands destroyed by the tar sands.

After waiting for as long as he could, Jake decided that he would sum up and hope for the best. He started to talk about the effects and the importance of protecting the aboriginal right to use these same lands.

"The Crown has a duty to consult even if there is only the claim that a project will impact aboriginal rights. The greater the impact, the greater the consultation required. And, if the First Nation is affected so much that their livelihood is threatened, then the court has the responsibility to stop the project."

He paused and looked at the panel.

"We have shown that these people are affected and insufficient consultation has occurred"

Mary knew we were missing the final piece of evidence and couldn't stand it. We needed William's testimony that he could no longer live on the land. She walked to the sidewalk outside of the center. There were some others smoking outside beside her, but she wasn't in the mood to talk. She was staring out across the parking lot thinking about what they would have to do after they lost this case when someone tapped her on the shoulder. She thought, *I don't have a light! I don't even smoke anymore.* "What do you want?" She turned around angrily.

"*Pipisu?*" A handsome old man said. He was dressed in a plaid long-sleeved shirt with a down vest and jeans. She could tell he used to be taller, but age made him stoop a bit. He still towered over Mary. "*How are you?*" he said in Cree.

There was only one person who called Mary *Pipisu*, and he was supposed to be dead.

"*Daddy?*" she said in disbelief. "*Daddy? Is that really you?*" She began thinking of the last time she had seen him, when she left for residential school and how her father had been so sad.

She threw her arms around him feeling the years that were lost without him.

He smiled and hugged her close. "*Yes, Pipisu it is me. It has been so long. I didn't know you had returned to this country.*" He looked her in her teary eyes. "*I would have come to see you if I'd known. It was William's wife who asked me to come here and talk to the lawyer. She didn't say you had come back. She told me that William needed me to tell the judges our hunting stories and how our lands had changed. You know about Snowbird, William and me. Oh, we used to have good times out on the land.*"

"But where have you been?" she asked. "I was told you were dead."

"*I was dead to your mother I guess. And maybe my spirit died but my body is still alive,*" he admitted. "*I have been living up way north of here, up in the barrens. When they started building those oil plants I couldn't live in the bush around here anymore. I wanted to be close, but a few years ago I said goodbye to your mother and moved up north. She said she didn't care where I went.*"

"You said goodbye to Mother."

"*Oh yes.*"

"She didn't tell *me*."

"*Well, she never forgave me and I still can't figure out what exactly I did wrong. I couldn't stop the government from taking you children.*

She thought we should have moved to town, but the only way I could make a living was to trap out on the land. But this time I thought by testifying maybe I could help make things better. When I visited William in the hospital he told me you were here and he said it would help if I spoke up."

"Yes Daddy, it will help. Follow me." Mary marched through the doors with a new spring in her step.

She was still teary eyed as she entered the hearing room and introduced her father to Jake. I wasn't sure if it was because she had finally found her father, or because she had the best witness in the bush, but they were happy tears.

Jake immediately asked for a recess to brief his new witness.

When the hearing resumed, Jake introduced Mr. Mercredi, a band elder and senior hunter.

"Mr. Mercredi. You are a member of the band and you have knowledge about the lands used by your First Nation in this area."

"Yes. Yes, all my life." His words were immediately translated from Cree.

"Can you tell us about what you know about your First Nation's members using this land?"

The translator nodded as he listened to Mary's father explain and then spoke, "We lived in small groups, around the time that the park was created. My father and mother would travel with other families throughout the area where these big pits are now. Sometimes we didn't even know what band we were members of because there was the Chip Band and the Cree Band and we were both Cree and Dené. Mother was Dené and Father was Cree. Mother spoke

Cree, Dené and French and so do I."

"Can you tell us about where you hunted and fished?"

Again, the translator spoke immediately after he finished. "We traveled up and down the main river, but we would go up small rivers too. We crossed the land mostly in the winter, trapping. In the fall we had special berry and herb patches and my mother would pick berries when Father went after moose. Father and his buddies would bring back a moose already quartered and they would help pick berries and prepare the meat. My father was a humble man and a hard worker. Mother would take care of the hide and Father would build the fire."

"You stayed with your parents. Where did your family spend the summer?"

"*I need to tell this in Dené because in the summer we mostly lived in the land of my Dené relatives. It must be described in Dené.*"

Jake was able to understand what he had said in Cree. He asked, "Do we have a Dené translator?"

The translator said that he also spoke Dené.

The translator looked towards the chairman. "Mr. Mercredi says that he will let me know if I have not translated properly since he does understand some English."

Jake then asked again, "Where did you spend your summers?"

The translator took a bit more time to start. "Yes, this area just east of the river, up the small creek here. There were three families that used this area in the summer. I think two of them lived in WaPaSu Village. But we didn't trap there; we spent most of our time fishing and hunting. There was a lake close to the river. It was very peaceful."

"Did you use this land in the winter?" Jake pointed to a map.

"We would go through that area, but we did not trap here. We would travel through to get to the area beyond the lakes. Sometimes we would hunt here but if we did, we shared it with Snowbird's brother."

"So how much did you use this land?"

"Every summer, and after I grew up, both winter and summer until I was forced out by the oil men. I used to live in this area all year long."

"Why?"

The translator tried to capture Mr. Mercredi's enthusiasm. "Because it was my home! It was the land I knew and it knew me. It was the land of my ancestors. But then Snowbird's brother didn't trap here anymore, and for a while I was able to trap on my own. Until they cleared the trees and started digging those wells. Until then I was able to stay.'

"Thank you, Mr. Mercredi."

Then the company lawyer rose to ask Mr. Mercredi some questions. "When was the last time you used these lands?" he asked. "Yes, the lands where the pits are."

"I think it was about thirty-five years ago." He looked at Jake for confirmation as they had figured out the dates in their preparation. Jake nodded his head. "And after my children were taken away to residential school, I had to leave for a while."

"So you didn't use the lands for twelve years before the second plant was built, because the plant on your trapline was actually built

23 years ago? So, it would seem that the plant was not the reason that you stopped using the land," the lawyer replied.

"I left because my children were taken away."

The room began to buzz with discussion. "Order, order." Chairman Jim Pearce knew it was time to call it a day. "We will begin again at 9:00 a.m. tomorrow."

"Mr. Chairman—for tomorrow's schedule!" Jake approached the front and proposed to the chairman that the First Nation would bring other witnesses. He knew he needed to show that there were other land users during those times. However, the panel would have to believe Miriam's testimony. If they did, he figured despite the Elder Mercredi's admission, they still could force the postponement of the project until consultation was complete.

The chairman agreed to have additional witnesses and pounded the gavel confirming adjournment for the day.

Relieved, Jake came back to our table. "With Mary's father's testimony" Jake said, "we have a good chance, especially if Miriam testifies about additional land use first thing tomorrow morning. It will be important for you to support Mr. Mercredi's testimony with other elder's experiences. Then I will sum up before the other interveners take over." He smiled at me.

Mary's father said he would meet up with us later. He wanted to visit William in the hospital again. Jake, Peter, Mary and I retired to the bar. As we ordered our drinks, Jake looked a little preoccupied. He knew that tomorrow depended on my testimony. I was frozen with nerves, but at the same time, sitting beside Jake, I was bursting with happiness.

Jake was the first to talk. "After tomorrow, if we can demonstrate that the key lands are being destroyed to such an extent that your people can no longer use it, then the panel will be forced to act. If they don't, we can get the attention of the courts. But Miriam has to summarize the interviews as we discussed and show how many people no longer use the lands. If they don't accept her testimony, well …"

Jake paused for a moment and then looked seriously at each person at the table. "I cannot advise you to do anything which would break the law. Remember, shutting down a road or doing something violent never really works. Look what happened at Oka or at the Old Man River dam. Nothing will have changed after the road is re-opened except some people will be behind bars. We have to make this hearing process work. We are in the center of the most active economy on the planet. Your bands are crippled by the Indian Act and a deaf, dumb, and blind government. We have to rely on the tribunals and courts. Let's go in there tomorrow and finish this process with a bang."

Jake turned and put on his jacket. "Since tomorrow is a big day, I suggest we all get some rest." He got up and walked out. I was shocked and hurt that he didn't wait for me.

"Why didn't he stay? He didn't even wait for me to stand up." I wondered out loud. But Mary and Peter got up too. They said he was probably just preoccupied and encouraged me to get some rest. Mary eagerly said she was going to see her dad again. I watched them head for the elevators in the hotel lobby. I was nervous about tomorrow and still shocked that Jake had left so abruptly. I knew I couldn't sleep; not just yet. I remembered the Peace River Electric meeting and what the chief had said, "What has happened here is not new. We have been treated like this for more than a hundred years. We will decide how to counter their lies. It's just another lie." Maybe tomorrow we can cut through some of the lies, I thought. I started to get up to go but that creepy guy, John Jesperson, appeared again, sauntering up to the bar. He was still the old company man.

"Miriam? How are you?"

"Yes. Good," I said a little reluctantly.

"So how was your day today?" He asked.

"Could have been better," I replied.

"Just a normal day?" He suggested.

"Yeah." I wasn't about to tell him anything about what was happening.

"Can I buy you a drink?"

"I already have the only one I will have tonight," I replied. My one unfinished drink was still on the table in front of me.

"Oh? Looks like the Oilers are losing." He pointed to the TV.

"Yeah? I'm not into hockey," I said as I made a motion to get up and continue my departure.

"Wait!" He quickly moved closer, "After we met, I figured you'd be a good person to ask about cultural retention projects, so I'm glad you're here tonight. Can you tell me what I should do about this situation I'm in?"

"I guess so." I immediately thought it was odd he would ask. I took one last sip of my drink and tried to remember which programs Royal Oil had established. The last time he didn't seem to know what he was talking about either, so I baited him a bit.

"What good are cultural retention programs anyway if there is no vacant land left to use?" I asked.

He pulled up a chair. "Hmm, you remind me of somebody." He snickered. "Tell us what kind of program should we have then?" Even though he was working for the companies, he seemed like he was just acting, there was something else going on. I decided it was time to leave and stood up.

"You're a very good lookin' woman," he said.

What a desperate creep. I started to feel very uncomfortable. "Thank you, but it really is time for me to turn in." I turned in the swivel bar stool so I could get down and go.

"Oh, what are you going to turn in *to*?" He tried to be funny. "Give me your number or I'll give you mine so we can follow up on a program proposal," he suggested.

I figured I would take his number to get rid of him but when I got up I felt dizzy and had to lean against the stool.

"That's funny, I didn't ... I ... didn't drink that much," I slurred.

"Let me help you," he said. "I'll help you to your car or room if you want."

"No! No, that's okay. Well, maybe just to the elevator." I answered.

He helped me the short ten yards to the elevator and pushed the button for me. When the door opened I leaned in and grabbed the rail and pushed my floor number.

"Are you sure you'll be alright?" His hand suddenly reached out and he held the door open. "You know, this town's more dangerous than you think."

"Yeah, I'm fine," I replied.

"I'm worried about you." He came into the elevator and smiled at me. "Drank more than you could handle?" he asked.

"I didn't think so," I said.

"You *are* very attractive," he repeated.

He frightened me, but I was so dizzy I couldn't defend myself. After the elevator doors closed I felt his arm around my waist and he put the other on my breast and started to kiss my neck.

I tried to shout, but it came out as a slur.

"Don't worry honey, everything's gonna be alright."

Miriam's Room

Chapter 38

Later that night Jake knocked on Miriam's hotel room door. He felt bad that he left the bar so abruptly. He was deep in thought about the hearing but now he wanted to go over her testimony. He started to feel more confident that they could win.

When he knocked on the door, it opened slightly. It wasn't properly latched. He thought she must have had too much to drink if she had left her door ajar. He worried that she would be unable to testify properly. He leaned politely into the room. "Miriam?" The bed was still untouched. He looked around for her purse or her jacket to figure out where she might have gone. *She wouldn't try to drive, would she?* She had parked her car in the hotel garage, and if she wasn't in the lobby, he'd check there. He sprinted down the stairs, jumping five stairs at a time. His heart was thumping rapidly as he entered the garage. Her car was gone!

She's driving. Where and with whom could she be going?

He didn't have a car. What could he do? As he ran back up from the garage he thought if he called the cops and she was driving drunk, he would get her in more trouble, but where could she have gone? He wasn't sure he wanted to know the answer.

Back in the lobby, Jake began to sweat more than from just running into the car park. He was really worried. Maybe she met someone new in the bar? What a time for that to happen. "*Shit! This seems like it is always happening with her. I shouldn't have left. She is so young. And I haven't really told her the way I feel about her. Maybe I've given her the wrong impression when I didn't stay at the bar."*

Fly on the Wall

Chapter 39

The next thing I realized, I was in the back seat of my own car. I had no idea where I was. However, I could hear the voice of the creep, Jesperson.

"I just wanted to have some fun with her," he whined.

"You're such a fool," an unfamiliar male voice replied. "We only need to stop her from testifyin, nothing' more. Why would you think you could do somethin' with her anyway? You know it's only safe if their families don't care or have no money."

"But look at her." Jesperson pleaded.

"No! Are you sure no one saw you with her? You know what happens if they start lookin' for her too soon. And as far as foolin' with her, if there was any evidence, you'd be finished – hell, we'd both be finished."

"Look! There's someone at the end of the road!"

"Let's get her out of here."

Jesperson and the stranger lifted me out of my car and up into a truck, I imagined. I was barely conscious.

After throwing her in the small back seat of the Chevy truck, her two assailants jumped in the front and took off towards the southern highway. They didn't realize that the vehicle they noticed was purposely parked behind a bush. The driver watched them turn towards the highway. Jimmy had been in the bar all afternoon, but he was sober enough to notice Jesperson approach Miriam. When he saw she was dizzy he wanted to get up and interfere. He thought he saw Jesperson put something in her drink, but he wasn't sure, so when they left he got up and followed them into the lobby. He saw Jesperson pause at the elevator door and then grab Miriam as the door closed. He had seen enough. He watched to see which floor they went to and took the next elevator up, but when he got up there no one was in the hallway and the door of one room was ajar. He quickly took the elevator down to the parking garage just in time to see a yellow VW leave the lower parking level. He lunged up the stairs the best he could and pushed the hotel's back door open.

His truck was parked in the dirt lot behind the bar. As he neared his truck, the automatic garage door of the underground hotel parking lot opened and out shot a yellow VW Rabbit. There was only one VW Rabbit in McMurray like that—Miriam's. He tried to make out who was driving. All he could see was one head. Then a large black Chevy truck pulled up behind it on the street. They headed towards the river. Jimmy frantically twisted the key in his ignition but the tired battery barely turned the engine over. "Shit, baby. Just give me a little more juice one more time," he pleaded with his truck while he watched the black Chevy turn the corner.

Pop! One of the cylinders fired and the old truck sputtered and choked. He jammed the truck into gear and it lunged forward. As he stepped on the gas he thought about how worthless his life had been. "Everything I touch turns to shit," he muttered. He couldn't paint worth a damn. His wife's death was his fault, he couldn't save his niece, and now my - God damn it! He swore as his back wheels skidded, slamming into the curb. "That crook Jesperson!"

There was no way Miriam could have gotten drunk on one drink. He began to sob as he craned his neck to see where they had gone. He saw red taillights pull down the dirt road by the river. It was only about two blocks from the hotel, but no one else would be down there this time of night. He figured he would see what they were up to before blundering in. He stayed at the entrance of the dead end road and quietly rolled down his window to try and hear what was going on.

The two men were walking around the car but as soon as he turned out his headlights they bolted. They jumped in black Chevy and spun their tires up the icy dirt road right past him. The yellow VW was still down the dead end. He pulled up beside it. The open door allowed him to see that no one was inside.

Why would they take her like this? It wasn't just for sex, he thought. He knew he had to follow them carefully so as not to alert them. It was going be hard to keep up but the roads would be deserted this time of night. He would stay far enough back on the two lane highway so that they wouldn't suspect him. Jimmy kept back about a mile, just far enough back to see if they were turning. It was a clear night and their headlights were easily seen.

After following them for about two hours, suddenly he could no longer see their lights. He squinted to make out any shadow or light. But over on the left side of the road he saw a band of light. It wasn't their headlights. It was the street lights of the Janvier Reserve. And then he saw them—bright northern lights like he'd never seen before, swirling and crackling right over Janvier. He knew where they were. The northern lights were telling him that they stopped for gas in Janvier. "Good." He said. He was running low on gas too but the Janvier station wouldn't be open until 6 a.m. Plenty of time to find them in this tiny community.

He drove into the town. Jimmy had friends in Janvier. There weren't that many streets in such a small village, and sure enough, behind a clump of trees just beyond the closed service station, there was the Chevy.

Jimmy turned and headed for Nokoman's house. He knew him well enough to wake him up in the middle of the night. It wouldn't be the first time Doug had helped him out of some trouble. But this time it was different. This time *he* was protecting someone else. This time he was making a difference.

Doug came to the door in his housecoat, his eyes squinting. When he saw Jimmy he wasn't sure he wanted to open the door.

"What's goin' on, Jimmy – it's too late, ya know." Doug spoke through a crack in the door.

"Doug, ya won't believe it. I think she's been kidnapped."

"Who's been kidnapped? Are you hallucinatin' or somethin', Jimmy?"

"No, Doug. No. It's hard ta explain. Don't ya have a community cop?"

"What do *you* want with him. Ya wanna get arrested? You can stay here to sober up – you don't have to go down there."

"No. Damn it, Doug. Just call him and ask him ta come over here, okay?"

"Shit, Jimmy. Okay, but what's this all about?"

Terrorists?

Chapter 40

At 6 a.m. Peter came into the breakfast room. He saw Jake sitting there and looked around. "Where's Miriam?" he asked. "Shouldn't she be down by now too?" He looked at Jake, who was as white as a sheet, holding the phone up to his ear. "Last night at the bar was the last time I saw her."

"She didn't get drunk?" Peter said.

"Don't know." Jake admitted, thinking about her last drinking escapade in Fort Chipewyan.

"No, Jake I don't think so. She wouldn't have. She knew she was part of an important hearing." Peter shook his head.

"She's been gone since last night. No car, nothing!" Jake grimaced as he slammed the phone down. "I don't know where she went. I expected her back by now."

"Who was that you were callin'?" Peter asked. "Anyway, it's too late now. She should have been back by now. She won't make the hearing."

Mary entered the breakfast room and spotted Peter and Jake. "Where's Miriam?"

"She's gone. She didn't sleep in her bed last night and her car is gone." Jake was frantic.

"Missin'?" Mary wrinkled her brow at Jake as if it was his fault. "Why?"

"Don't know." said Jake.

Mary stared at Jake suspecting what he was thinking. "Well, she didn't get drunk and she didn't get scared. I know she wouldn't. She takes this seriously."

"Why isn't she here then?" Jake responded.

"Something must have happened." Mary began to look through her address book.

 "I'm gonna call her parents and see if she contacted them." She reached for her phone. Miriam's father answered and she immediately asked if Miriam had called home, or if they knew where she was. Even though she knew it might cause them some angst, she thought the situation was serious enough to be painfully direct.

"She just disappeared," Mary told Dr. Robinson. "We don't know where to."

"Last night at the bar, we just had one drink and all the rest of us went to bed; she said she couldn't sleep. Jake checked her room before he went to bed and she was gone, car and all."

"No, the hearing was supposed to be this morning and she was the main witness. You're comin' up now? Company jet?"

Miriam's father was now certain that his worst suspicions about Fort McMurray had been correct. He was going to use everything at his disposal to defend his daughter. He didn't care if the company criticized him for using the jet for personal business.

While Mary was calling Miriam's parents, Jake called the panel chair, Jim Pearce, to ask for a postponement of the hearing. The chairman agreed to a temporary postponement and expressed his concern about Miriam's safety. "We cannot allow such circumstances to appear to affect the board's decision," the chair said. "The results of this process must appear to be completely fair."

Mary mobilized community members by contacting her relatives living in McMurray. They spread the word through the moccasin telegraph and word quickly came back that she had not been seen anywhere.

"What about the bartender?" Mary asked Jake.

"Yeah, he said that a fellow came in and was talking to her before she left but he didn't notice anything unusual." He looked at Mary, squinting. "I asked him if they left together." He lowered his head in disgust, partially at his own stupidity and partially because he thought she may have gone somewhere with this other guy. "But the bartender said he didn't notice."

"It's not what you think," Mary said. "Even if they left together, he was followin' her and if he took her somewhere, he probably drugged her. This is more serious than you think, Jake. She told me how she felt about you. She wasn't about to do somethin' stupid."

"What?"

"She is in love with you, idiot. She wouldn't have picked up anyone else. I hate to say it, but I think she was taken, kidnapped or something."

Mary's suspicions spread quickly through the community. As soon as she said the word that Miriam had been kidnapped, the community was convinced. After what they had been through it sounded like the type of thing that would happen, especially if they had a chance to win. It didn't take long for word to spread through the drummer's conference at the hotel convention center. Shortly thereafter several other community members arrived at the hotel asking questions about the hearings and Miriam.

Jake tried the local police again, trying to convince them of the seriousness of the situation. Jake was still conflicted. He didn't want her to be kidnapped but he didn't want her to be with someone else either. "She's my key witness," he said, wishing that she was beside him instead of anywhere else on the planet.

He realized more than ever that he *was* madly in love with Miriam and he knew his feelings were affecting his judgment.

About four hours after they figured out that she had probably been taken against her will, Peter came into the meeting room where everyone had gathered. Various people had brought in lunches and about 15 people were sitting around the tables.

"Oh, God!" he said. "Turn on the TV."

"Now what?" Jake asked.

"There has been some kind of incident up on the mine road north of McMurray. Not an accident. Somebody is blocking the road. They have called the police. They say the buses cannot get to the mines. Turn on the TV."

Jake grabbed the remote. The first channel showed disguised figures positioned in front of pickup trucks. Their camouflage garb and masks made it impossible to recognize them, but it was clear they were natives. The announcer said he was broadcasting live from just north of Fort McMurray.

After staring at the television for a moment, Peter thought he could tell who the demonstrators were by their gestures. Dan had told him about the Peace River suits car chase to the airport in

Fort Chipewyan and he had suspected some community members since then. There were few people in a small community who were capable of such a confrontation.

Jake remembered the TV images of the Oka crisis in Quebec. Five old pickup trucks were parked across the main road blocking the oil sands plants, completely stopping traffic both ways. It looked like some of the protesters had long staffs, not guns. The shift change buses were lining up waiting to get through, and were already backed up a mile or so. Police cruiser lights flashed as they rushed up the shoulder to the blockade, past the rows of worker-filled buses.

Peter and Jake were guessing who could be part of the blockade.

The TV zeroed in on a protest sign. "THE UNJUSTICE SYSTEM," it read. Another one said, "KIDNAPPED WITNESS." Clearly the word had gotten out, but how did they organize so fast? He had no idea just how organized they were.

"Who organized this?" asked Mary, who also had her suspicions about who had been involved in the Peace River suits hijacking.

The police cars pulled up close to the offending trucks. They jumped out and rushed the protesters without stopping to assess the situation. But before they reached the closest protester a loud pop stopped them in their tracks. One of the cruiser's tires rapidly deflated.

"Was that sniper fire?" shouted the TV commentator as the cops looked around frantically.

Bang! Another tire popped. "We're under fire!" yelled the police sergeant.

The protesters were holding their sticks together like a Roman phalanx. None of them appeared to have guns. Most of the police had pulled out their revolvers and were crouching or ducking behind vehicles.

Then the TV picture zoomed on to the trees up the riverbank. "There is gunfire coming from the hill!" the announcer yelled. "It sounded like a high powered rifle."

They could recognize nothing but blurred trees. Then the camera panned on the hill immediately above the road, sweeping the trees, trying to spot some motion. They could see nothing but the tops of spruce and pine trees.

The camera returned to the police huddled behind their cars. Then another shot rang out from the hill and another tire exploded.

The workers who had gotten out of the buses scrambled back in. Everyone took cover. The media retreated into their vans and tried to film through the windows.

They switched channels. The same scene was even on CNN-US prime time. After repeating mindless commentary and speculating about where the shots had come from and who might be behind this road block, a CNN commentator broke in and announced that the Canadian Forces had been called in. He said that the police confirmed that there were snipers up in the hills above the road and they had called in some jet fighters from the Cold Lake Air Base to flush them out.

Peter said that he thought it was the Warrior Society from the Old Man River dam who had come up to McMurray for the drumming project. It was the only group he knew who could pull off such a coup.

"But it's not their lands. Is that Old Man River rebel, Born-with-a-tooth, with them?" Mary wondered.

As they surrounded the TV trying to figure things out, Willie Grandlegs casually sauntered into the room.

Mary noticed him out of the corner of her eye. "Willie!"

They all turned around. "Hello," Willie replied, a bit shy with everyone looking at him. As he walked over to Mary, he whispered. "Things're gettin' bad."

"Yes ,Willie, have you seen the TV?"

"Don't need ta see it." he whispered with everyone curious and wanting to listen to what he was saying.

"The Piikani Warrior's Society and some Dené hunters heard that Miriam was missing an' decided they'd had enough." Willie announced.

"The Blackfoot Warrior's Society?" Mary asked.

"It's the Rainbow Warriors." Willie explained. They had a ceremony this mornin' an' they were told what ta do. They're blockin' the road."

"Who are they!?" Mary asked.

Willie's voice got louder. "The Rainbow Warriors." He expected Mary would know who he was referring to.

"They went up on the hill this mornin' ta send a message. Now they're gone; no one'll see 'em, an' no one knows who they are."

The TV started to show scenes of the road again. Some of the buses at the back of the long line started to turn around.

Peter said, "These guys in the woods aren't just angry Indians who were fighting for their lands, they're gonna be considered terrorists! The US news will say they are supported by Al-Qaeda. There's gonna be a big backlash. We're screwed."

There was a bomb expert on TV talking about the environmental devastation that would be caused if the dyke holding the toxic tailings pond was breached. Of course, the last thing that native people would do to their lands was blow up the dams holding the tailings ponds. But the international media didn't know that; they were interested in the spectacular. That's what terrorists would do, isn't it? The more fear, the better the ratings.

"How do you know it's the Rainbow Warriors, Willie?" asked Mary.

"I just know," he replied.

Everything appeared quiet on the road. The protestors were still standing; the cops were still behind their cars.

"Is this about our hearin' or somethin' else?" Mary began to wonder. She gazed at Willie.

"It's about us," he stated quite confidently. "About our lands." He sat down in one of the comfortable leather chairs at the side of the meeting room and took out his tobacco.

"It's about Miriam too. The Piikani People know Miriam. She worked for them."

"Yeah, that was on her resume," Peter chimed in.

"I did some research," Willie continued. "With Professor Thomas, that guy that used ta work with Katie." He pulled out his rolling papers and scraped the inside of his tobacco pouch, gathering the right amount of tobacco.

"About the *Whi-ti-koh*," he said almost casually. "Katie didn't go t' the ceremony like I told her. She should've gone. It killed her."

"Katie?" Mary looked incredulously at Willie. "This is Miriam, not Katie!"

"Yeah, Miriam too; we all need ta go t'a ceremony."

"But why are you talkin' about Katie?"

"Because she was murdered by that same *Whi-ti-koh* who has Miriam!" He raised his voice again.

The TV interrupted their conversation as file footage of ominous dark green helicopters armed with guns and rockets came on the screen. The announcer broadcasted, "It looks like Black Hawk helicopters must have been performing training exercises at Cold Lake Base." It was apparent to them that Canadian forces did not have such helicopters. Then the TV showed fighter jets flying down the river valley and buzzing the blockade and row of busses. The Cold Lake Air Base is only a half-hour flight away.

An exasperated Peter sighed. "It isn't enough to have our people die of cancer, but now they are going to get blown up by rockets."

"We gotta burn some sweet grass." Willie said. "I don't like the smell o' fear."

"Willie, what else do you know about Miriam?"

"The *Whi-ti-koh* took her. He wants t' rape her an' maybe get money fer her. He's got too much greed and desire."

"That's what I thought." Mary scoffed.

"Wasn't she kidnapped so she couldn't testify?" Peter asked.

Jake shook his head. "Shit, shit, shit, does it really matter why she was taken!"

"What else do you know?" Jake asked Willie almost accusingly.

"Professor Thomas's on his way up with Miriam's dad, the oil company guy. And they know more. They found out what happened to Katie and now Miriam. Miriam's dad knows the RCMP big shots in Calgary and they're on his jet too."

"Phillip Robinson didn't say anything to me about that. I called him a few hours ago," Mary argued.

Willie looked at Mary. "Professor Thomas was helpin' me after I told him bout Jesperson givin' Katie that free bad medicine. He found out about Jesperson bein' fired from Royal Oil; he was gettin' money from Mr. Frame in the US. When Dr. Robinson called Dr. Thomas askin' bout Miriam's job, he told 'm bout Katie, but he didn't know 'bout the extra money from the US. He called me 'bout that yesterday. He called Dr. Robinson, and they put it together. Then he called his friend, Zak, the Royal Canadian Mounted Police Commissioner. They're all flyin' up here together."

"But if Miriam has been kidnapped, then shouldn't they be checking the airport and roads?"

"That RCMP guy fixed all of that this mornin' before they left Calgary," Willie said. "They're on their way now and I told them to bring some tobacco for the warriors."

Mary was really worried. "Won't those military jets conflict with CanOil's jet?"

* * *

"Fort McMurray Tower, this is Cherokee three-five-niner-romeo-foxtrot. Nine miles south heading to Royal Oil air strip. Chief Commissioner Zakarsky aboard wishes to speak to Canadian Forces Command and Control Supervisor. Over," the pilot barked.

Just as they were approaching McMurray, they were joined by two Canadian fighter jets positioned on either side of their Lear jet.

"Yes, three-five-nine-romeo-foxtrot, understood. Will inform Forces Supervisor."

"This is operations control supervisor. This air space is closed. Please divert to southern facilities."

"Call your flyboys off now. We must land at the site." Commisssioner Zak's face was red.

"This is Chief Commissioner Zakarsky of the Royal Canadian Mounted Police. We have authorization to proceed. Please facilitate safe passage commands as we will be using the Royal Oil air strip."

"Commissioner Zakarsky … Zak?" Clearly the commander had recognized his voice.

"Yes. Who is in command?"

"This is General Kenneth Foster."

"Ken, I have information and an offering that will diffuse this entire situation, but I must talk to the protestors personally."

"We have shut down this airspace Zak. You should turn back."

"Ken, don't you remember Haiti? I wouldn't do this if I didn't know what I was doing! Tell your boys to stand down. We are diffusing this situation. We must land at the Royal Oil air strip."

"Well I suppose if this is important enough for the *Commissioner of the RCMP* to fly up to Fort McMurray for," General Foster joked.

"We have captured the kidnapper and recovered the witness.

The ERCB hearing will be postponed and I'm going to give them tobacco to show our respect and they are going to break up their blockade." Zak explained. "Yes, it is strange. Thanks, Ken… I trust you too."

The corporate pilot softly placed the jet down on the back woods tarmac. Elder Willie's son was waiting by the terminal trailer. Willie's son, Prof. Thomas, Dr. Robinson, and the RCMP Commissioner jumped in the green camouflage Hummer and asked the driver to take them to the blockade. Simultaneously, an officer came out of the trailer and hopped in the front seat. "Do as they say," he ordered.

Zak was on his cell phone with the General again.

"Yes, tobacco … Well, Ken, it's a matter of cultural respect."

"We've managed to rescue the person they are demonstrating about. She's safe and I need to deliver this peace offering. I've been speaking to one of their elders"

"Yes. The demonstrators on the road block were convinced that the oil companies had organized the kidnapping. We caught the kidnapper and he is a local criminal, but I have to get them this tobacco before anyone gets hurt. Now do you understand better what I am talking about?"

"Thank you, Ken." Zak smiled at Phil as he put his phone away.

When Commissioner Zak arrived at the blockade, he approached the masked men in front of the central truck. He held up his hand with the blue plastic tobacco pouch and the masked men lowered their staffs. Shortly thereafter, Zak was shaking hands, smiling and making small talk. Zak turned towards the police cars and waved them off to the side. They made a path for the protestor pickup trucks to return to McMurray.

Putting the Pieces Together
Chapter 41

"Miriam … Miriam. You've had quite a night." It was mom.
Then Dad said, "How are you feeling?"

I was pretty confused. I slowly looked around. Mom and Dad were there and behind them a fellow dressed in what looked like a military uniform.

"Miriam, you are safe now." Dad noticed I was staring. "This is Jim Zakarsky, Chief Commissioner of the RCMP. He's the one that saved you, really."

"It was Jimmy who found me," I said weakly. "It was Elder Jimmy that really saved me." The commissioner agreed, nodding his head with his arm around Dad.

Jake rushed in. "Miriam, are you alright?" He pushed past my mom and dad and the commissioner, not even knowing who they were, and put his arms around me and kissed me.

"Yes, Jake, I'm just fine. Dad, Mom, this is my friend, Jake."

"How do you do, Jake?" Dad said formally locking his gaze onto him. Mom held out her hand. "Jake," she said softly.

"Mr. and Mrs. Robinson, hello." Jake shook their hands, looking embarrassed for butting in front of them.

"What a nightmare this has been for you. I looked all over for you," Jake shook with emotion.

"I don't know, really, what happened." Miriam began.

Then a nurse came in and suggested that they all clear the room. "Miriam needs to rest some more." she said.

In the hallway, Dr. Robinson introduced the commissioner.

"Jake Maurice, Mary Cardinal, and Peter Wells … Commissioner Zakarsky."

"Pleasure to meet you, sir," replied Jake. Mary and Peter echoed the greeting.

The commissioner told them that they managed to capture Jesperson with Miriam on Highway 68. They had tried to get some gas from the Janvier Reserve and a local native RCMP officer identified him from the circular and with the help of an elder named Jimmy Voyageur. Jesperson surrendered easily and the ambulance brought Miriam to the hospital.

Dr. Robinson explained to Jake, Mary, and Peter. "Miriam had told me at first she was hired to take over the work Katie Cardinal started. That was fine untilDr. Thomas and Willie told me that they suspected that Jesperson had something to do with Katie Cardinal's death.

"Then about a week ago, I was told by a Royal Oil executive that Jesperson had been fired because of unprofessional behavior with Katie Cardinal. I started to become concerned. The same executive explained what he thought was inappropriate US Director involvement in the Canadian company which meant there must have been some connection between Jesperson and the US board member, Frame. I looked up the itinerary of Guss Frame and found out he had visited Fort McMurray with the vice president's tour, just before Katie died. Now that we have Jesperson in custody, we should be able to trace his bank accounts and watch for which funds turn up.

"Elder Willie convinced Dr. Thomas and me that Katie Cardinal was murdered by Jesperson with an overdose of those painkillers, and now Miriam was in Katie's shoes! Elder Willie had tried to convince the police by showing them all of the empty pill bottles. But the cops made some racial slur about prescription drugs and no one followed it up. Willie even brought one of the old bottles to my office and told me that a *Whi-ti-koh* had murdered Katie.

"It was my executive friend from Royal Oil who explained that when Jesperson was fired, Frame had asked for Jesperson's contact information. My contact told me that Jesperson even threatened one of the younger Royal Oil vice presidents, claiming that he could get him fired because he was a friend of a US board member. That clinched it for me. He tried to get the lease signing bonus even after Katie died. That's when he was fired. They knew something was very wrong."

Dr. Robinson affectionately put his hand on the Commissioner's shoulder. "So, when Mary called me yesterday, there was only one suspect. I immediately called Zak and told him the story."

The commissioner smiled. "We had been watching Jesperson anyway since Royal Oil fired him and alerted us to his strange behavior, but when Phil told us what he found out about the connection to Frame, we issued an urgent circular to pick Jesperson up for questioning on this matter. Elder Jimmy contacted our unit in Janvier. But Willie is the real hero," the commissioner said as he noticed Willie exiting the elevator in the lobby. "This is the man who explained why the road block was caused by Miriam's kidnapping."

Willie sauntered up and held out his hand in his soft manner to each of them.

"With Prof. Thomas's help, Willie explained to us why there was so much suspicion and mistrust in the community, how they had attacked Doctor O'Malley and then how Elder William got mysteriously sick. If my daughter got a rare cancer like that, I'd be out there on the road block too." Zak looked at Phil. Then Phil Robinson added, "Zak contacted the military command and the local RCMP to tell the demonstrators that Miriam had been rescued." He looked at Willie. "But the road blockers were still unconvinced."

"So, Willie got his son to meet us at the airstrip with a pouch of good tobacco, and when Willie's son, Professor Thomas, and the commissioner showed up with tobacco at the roadblock and told them that the RCMP had arrested the kidnapper and the ERCB had postponed the hearing so Miriam could testify, they believed it."

"I am glad we diffused that situation, but I still must pursue the issue of the dangerous use of firearms," mused the commissioner. "But Willie says I'll have to catch them first." He smiled. "I guess it is the same as in Quebec. It's hard to arrest someone if you don't know who they are."

A couple of hours later, the entire entourage was back in my room. I jokingly commented to Dad, "No wonder you didn't want me to come up here to work." Dad and Mom said they still wanted to take me home. They said that I had had enough frontier challenges to last a lifetime.

Mary then came back in. She was upset. "Dr. Robinson?" she

asked. "How far would a company go to get a project approved? I mean, with Katie Cardinal, for example."

"What do you mean?" he asked."I know it wasn't your company, but would a company go so far as to murder someone to get their project approved?"

"Absolutely not," he said emphatically. "It wasn't the company, it was criminals and zealots. The guys in those executive positions do not deal that way. Sometimes bribery would be considered, but never murder. It isn't worth it to them. But I'm not sure what some might do in the name of national security."

"So, you think it was just Jesperson's greed? He wasn't told to kill her?"

"I think he murdered her by providing her with those deadly drugs, but I bet those who paid him didn't tell him what to do. They just gave him the money and let him know what their interests were. His greed did the rest."I was still sleepy, but I had to let them know what I heard when I was half-conscious in the back seat of Jesperson's car. "I heard Jesperson bragging about giving more painkillers to Katie. After what he did to me, there is no question in my mind he murdered her."

"So, if the Texan was paying him?" Mary looked at Dr. Robinson.

"It's just like Willie was saying all along," Robinson concurred."Whoever paid him, murder intended or not, would be an accomplice. We'll check on how he got paid by tracing his bank accounts," added Zak."But these guys are directors of an oil company. Then isn't the company guilty too? Civilly, I mean," Mary suggested.Willie held up his right hand with his palm open. "This talk won't bring Katie back. We got t' remember how Katie stood up t' the company, even though they was offerin' her big money. She's a hero. She helped me an' Dr. Thomas meet each other. An' Miriam took over Katie's work. Katie was Mary's rock. She was our *Than-ad-el-thur* and her memory gave me the idea to give Commissioner Zak tobacco t' make peace. We must remember why Katie did what she did an' try and honour her memory."

Willie's speech was like a prayer. "We should pray for Katie," he said.

Everyone's head was bowed when Jake returned again from his call to the board where he had asked for a recess and postponement of the hearing. He got the postponement, but there was something else. He respectfully interrupted the silent prayer. "Nicole McDonald's dad was on the elevator. She passed away this morning."

"Nicole!" gasped Mary.

"Well, we knew it was coming," Peter responded.

"We pray for her." Willie motioned for Jake to join their prayer.

"Creator, we struggle t' protect our land an' health an' t' live peacefully with our neighbours. We thank You for returning Miriam t' us; she's been a blessin'. Please take care of Nicole, now she's returnin' t' be with You. She is our child but we did not know how to cure her. Thanks for Katie and for the strength she gave us. Take care of her too."

Mary started to cry. "Amen." Willie put his arm around Mary. Peter looked out the hospital room window.

"The federal government is challenging the provincial monitoring process because of Schneider's new report. You know, the one showing the levels of contaminants are much higher than measured by the companies," Jake announced.

"Why does it always come too late?" mused Mary.

Even though I was still so tired, I wanted to participate in the conversation. "His new reports?" I asked.

"Yeah, they show that the company monitoring was faulty. And we have been fighting them for years to implement community based monitoring, while they have claimed they already had the best system possible. Yet Schneider's group shows the levels of chemicals related to bitumen mining are high and there are heavy metals present in the water—cancer-causing heavy metals."

Mary looked over at Dad. "Dr. Robinson, will you help us now? You saw how they denied and attacked Dr. O'Malley. You've seen the faulty monitoring; you can see we are dying of cancer. Then our witnesses get sick and your daughter, our researcher, gets kidnapped."

"Now you have had a little taste of what we have been through." Peter added.

Dad just shook his head at Mary and looked at me while he held Mom's hand. I remembered they wanted to take me home so I said, "Come to Fort Chipewyan with us! I want you to meet everybody else and see what I have been doing for the last year."

Jake and Mary and Peter all chimed in with the invitation too.

"Okay." Dad held my hand, too. "Okay."

Where Do I Belong?

Chapter 42

The next morning, after being discharged from the hospital, I had a long interview with the police. I told them I would be in Fort Chip if they needed me further.

I wanted Mom to see how the people lived and what we were trying to protect. I wanted both of them to experience more of what I had found in this incredible northern village.

We were able to get the next scheduled plane back to Fort Chip. They say you have to get back on the horse when you get bucked off and I couldn't go through the rest of my professional career being afraid to fly.

Of course, the flight back was uneventful. There were plenty of people around the small airport all waiting for the plane. As I entered the main room Maryanne, the elder from my community meeting, approached me and said, "Have you heard what happened?"

"Happened?" I asked.

"Yes, how David's brother died."

"Oh, no!"

"David's brother, Mark," she repeated. "He fell through the ice."

"What?" I couldn't believe it.

"He was an expert bush man." A tear formed in her eye as she told the story. "He wouldn't have fallen through without somethin' bein' wrong."

"Oh my God!" I repeated.

"He must've been drunk," she finally said.

Mom and Dad were standing behind me. "Who was that guy?" Mom asked.

"His brother helped me with the interviews." I told her. "The death never seems to stop." I looked at Mom. "Every time I turn around, someone else has died."

Maryanne then greeted more of her family coming for the wake. I waved goodbye as we jumped in a cab. As Mom and Dad checked into the bed and breakfast, I had a chance to talk to them a bit.

"You know, it's pretty devastating. There're violent deaths from accidents on the road, or on the land, exposure to drugs and alcohol. Then there is diabetes, other disease and death from old age. I know that's the same everywhere, but add the extra deaths from rare cancer and Katie died of an overdose of painkiller, murdered or not. Every time I turn around, someone has died. I just don't want to get used to this."

Mom responded, "I can see how it makes you feel. It's not all from the oil companies. It looks to me like it is from the system, the way people live here. You have told us so many stories and Phil and I are going to try and help."

It was nice to hear that from my mother but *I* didn't want to 'help' anymore. I wanted to enjoy the clear blue sky and the pine forest. I wanted to go skiing or hiking and just forget all that had been happening.

The next day, once Mom and Dad were settled in, we arranged

for one of the native fishers to take them out on snow machines on the lake and the delta. I knew coming here and meeting the people, listening to the elders, would give Dad all the extra incentive he needed to understand, especially now since Nicole's and Mark's death were having a big impact on the community and there would be two wakes and funerals. They were both so young. All formal meetings would be cancelled. The whole town was in mourning.

Jake wanted an elder to give Dad and Mom a real exposure to the language, culture, and spirituality of the people he was representing. Jake went to Nicole's family and asked permission to have such a meeting at a camp fire. He told them we meant no disrespect. I asked Elder Madeline about her grandson's funeral and wake, if it would be alright if we held a camp fire. In tears she hugged me and told me my work was now more important than ever.

She told me to listen carefully to the elder since he had something very important to tell me, maybe about *Than-ad-el-thur* or Moses.

I couldn't help remembering that *Than-ad-el-thur* died awfully young. I wasn't so sure I wanted the job anymore.

That evening, Jake introduced the storyteller, who would be speaking in Dené. A young girl was there from Fondulac, a community across the lake that had protected their language.

"She will translate," he said.

"The people here have a special relationship with the lands," Jake continued. "This relationship is spiritual and embodies who they are as living spiritual beings. Their concern about the environment flows from this base. The offering of tobacco is a spiritual offering. When you take something from the land, or when the land gives you something, you must give something in return. You must be connected to the nature of the land to survive. Your hosts do not separate these things into categories like politics and religion, science and arts.

"The aboriginal world is holistic. Everything is one. The aboriginal people think of themselves as part of the land and it is part of them. So let me introduce Elder Jimmy Voyageur who will be telling you some of the legends of this proud nation."

I had not seen Jimmy since he brought the RCMP to the truck and arrested those bastards. He was my real hero now.

"Before we start I want to thank Elder Jimmy for his heroic actions." I announced to everyone. "Who knows what would have become of me if he had not followed us? Thank you, Jimmy!"

Elder Jimmy nodded to me and smiled as everyone clapped.

After my speech, Jake came over. "Miriam! Are you coming or not? You need to let the elder talk to your parents alone."

I was a bit surprised, but I could feel Jake's hand on mine and I willingly walked with him towards the lakeshore. Across the lake I could see the aurora borealis flickering like spirits dancing around a camp fire.

Jake turned to face me. "I think your whole story is exceptional."

I looked up at him. "What story?"

"Well, you have had real privileges in your home. I am sad that your biological parents had to give you up, but you certainly were given a good education and it looks like a lot of love."

"Thank you, Jake. But the last year or so has shown me a new world, a world that I am actually a part of and didn't know."

"It is good because it has given you a chance to give back, maybe even give others what your birth parents did not have so that all our families can be complete again." He sounded very philosophical. "I know you may think this is bad and I don't use Biblical examples very often," he said, "But your position sort of reminds me of the way that Moses could negotiate with his adopted family, the Pharaohs."

"What did you say?" This was a bit too much.

"Well I just thought it was similar. I mean, I don't want to take it too far, but you came to help and you happen to be the daughter of one of the senior executives, one of the decision makers."

"Jimmy called me Moses when he first met me."

"Yeah, I heard. You encountered some aboriginal spiritualism."

"What do you mean?"

"All I mean is that some people are given a gift. I think Jimmy is one of those people."

"Yeah, well, I'm not so sure I like all this Moses and *Than-ad-el-thur* stuff. It gives me the creeps actually."

"Well it shouldn't! You should take it as an honour," he stated softly. "Anyway, I was thinking that with your permission I would ask your dad's lawyer if we could have a formal negotiation meeting. It would include the chief, me, their lawyer, and your dad. I'd like to ask them if they would join our cause and push the provincial government into fulfilling their constitutional obligations instead of having to fight every step of the way."

"That sounds fine," I said.

"Oh, good." Jake was noticeably excited. He continued, "If he can help then there will be a much friendlier environment. We can work together to find good projects and employment, and environmental protection for everyone. Would your Dad go for that?"

"Maybe he'll jump at it. I will talk to him, too."

"Can I call the chief and the other side's lawyer?"

"Please."

As we got back to the fire, everyone was standing up, staring at us return.

"Is everything okay?" I asked, wondering why everyone was looking.

Jimmy was standing in front of everyone smiling.

As I approached the fire, he held his hand up in front of him. He said, "I told the good Dr. and Mrs. Robinson that about twenty years ago I moved to southern Manitoba to be with my wife, Gloria, the love of my life. We had a baby together, but my beautiful Gloria died in childbirth. In those days I was challenged by alcohol and I was forced to put our baby in foster care. I wasn't sure when I first met you in Edmonton, but no one could look so much like my Gloria and not be her kin. When I checked out the dates with your parents, they confirmed it. I believe you are my daughter."

"You …" I could hardly talk. "You think you are my father?"

This crazy elder was now claiming he was my father? Worse, my parents looked like they had accepted it.

I looked at my Mom and Dad, "What's going on? What is he talking about? How could he be my father?"

"Well. Miriam, he knew your birth date exactly. He told us the same medical history the adoption agency gave us and everything fit. Then he told about the town you were from and spoke about many of the people who live there, people who are likely your other blood relatives," said Mom.

"I think we have to take this seriously," said Dad.

I looked at Jimmy again, searching his face for familiarity and some indication that I really was related to him.

I guess if this were true, I would be a real member of the band that I was working for and I began to think that it was not a coincidence that I ended up here. If this were true, I now started to wonder who else I was related to in the band. Who are Jimmy's relatives in Fort Chipewyan? And I thought how I would never see my birth mother.

I looked over at Jake and he was smiling from ear to ear. I sat down with Jimmy and asked him about Gloria. I began to rethink my relationship with my new home in Fort Chip. So, Jimmy's niece, the one who froze in the snow, was my cousin. I have relatives all through this community and more in Manitoba. Dad said he was proud of my bravery and determination in coming here to work. "You must have had some intuition about it," he said. "Yeah, now this whole thing makes sense. It makes sense that I came up here to work and studied land use. It makes sense that you and Mom adopted me too."

"Thank you, Miriam. I assume that was a compliment." Mom opened her eyes wide.

"Oh yeah, but do you see how there is a difference between having native blood and being native? It's got nothing to do with blood, it's more to do with understanding. The racism on the street, at the hearing, and in negotiations, is truly based in fear and greed, not ignorance. It isn't that they don't know rights exist, it's that they don't want them to exist. They don't want us to have our rights, our heritage. They don't think we have earned them."

Dad didn't say much, he just looked at me and nodded.

"And I don't want to be the one who has to fight for them anymore." Mom put her arm around me and said, "Oh Honey, there's been a lot to take in, in one day. But I'm so glad we are here together for it." We hugged and kissed goodnight and I felt so sure of what the Creator meant for me to do.

The next morning at breakfast Dad gave an impromptu speech to Mary, Pete, Mom, Jake and me.

"I need to tell you that I used to think I understood aboriginal rights. I didn't really. I didn't really believe they were just, that natives should have extra rights, more rights than other Canadians. Like so many others, I paid homage to rights because I wanted to get my project through.

But I have had some experiences in the last few days I will not easily forget. When the lives of one's family are threatened ... well, now I realize that my daughter is your daughter too and like the Dené on the northern tree line who shared their knowledge of caribou migration, I will share the knowledge about my company with you. I better understand how much we have to learn about each other."

The room was silent.

"I will work as hard as I can to help you defend your rights."

He paused.

"However, I would also like to add that despite the different approach, I think there could be some room for a few healthy environmentally friendly oil projects as well."

Everyone laughed.

Jake shot me a smile and leaned over to kiss me.

CPSIA information can be obtained at www.ICGtesting.com
Printed in the USA
BVOW070851020812

296814BV00007B/1/P